LOVE, REDEMPTION & FELONY THEFT
A NOVEL OF THE FRENCH QUARTER

PELIKAN

DAVID LOZELL MARTIN

SIMON & SCHUSTER

SIMON & SCHUSTER
Rockefeller Center
1230 Avenue of the Americas
New York, NY 10020

SIMON & SCHUSTER and colophon are registered trademarks
of Simon & Schuster, Inc.

Designed by Ruth Lee

Manufactured in the United States of America

1   3   5   7   9   10   8   6   4   2

Library of Congress Cataloging-in-Publication Data
Martin, David Lozell, date.
Pelikan : love, redemption & felony theft : a novel of the
French Quarter / David Lozell Martin.
p.   cm.
I. Title.
PS3563.A72329P4   1999
813'.54--dc21   99-36099
CIP

ISBN 0-684-85348-5

Arabel, anyway, anywhere

Everything in this book complimentary to New Orleans and the French Quarter is true. Inaccuracies regarding geography and history, along with anything unfavorable to New Orleans, the French Quarter, and most especially the Quarter's residents, bar workers, and street artists, are the result of my pandering.

David Lozell Martin
New Orleans

. . . Physiol'ogus tells us that the pelican is very fond of its brood,
but when the young ones begin to grow
they rebel against the male bird and provoke his anger,
so that he kills them; the mother returns to the nest in three days,
sits on the dead birds, pours her blood over them,
revives them, and they feed on the blood.

—*from* The Dictionary of Phrase and Fable,
by E. Cobham Brewer

Pie pellicane, Jesu Domine
(Dutiful pelican, Lord Jesus)

—*from the hymn "Adoro te devote,"*
by Saint Thomas Aquinas

PELIKAN

FELONY THEFT:
THREE JACKS ON THE FLOOR
ON THE FLOOR

1

A ONE-WAY TICKET ON A TRAIN
CALLED THE CRESCENT CITY

"I have something to tell you, Charlie . . ." This is my father talking, he's dying. "When your mother was giving birth to you, she had a bowel movement—"

"What?"

"She didn't mean to, Charlie."

My father and I had seen each other infrequently over the past several years, and now we were supposed to be enacting a solemn deathbed scene, my father having summoned me to a Charlottesville, Virginia, hospice where he was waiting for cancer to complete destiny.

"I wasn't around when your sisters were born," he said. "As I'm sure your mother told you, I never quite mastered the husband-father thing."

That's one way of putting it . . . my mother had put it many other ways over the years, in fact all my life she sang to me the litany of my father's sins: drunkard, gambler, womanizer, felon, heartbreaker. He left our family—my mother, my three older sisters, and me—when I was four years old and didn't reenter my life until almost a decade later when my mother, against her better judgment, allowed me to spend a summer in New Orleans where my father hustled a living with his half brother, James Joseph Pelikan. When I told my mother yesterday that Dad had called from a hospice and wanted me to come visit him before he died, she said it's probably a trick, he's not dying for real, he wants money, don't give him any, don't go see him, don't give him the satisfaction.

That single summer I was supposed to spend with my father in New Orleans stretched into three years, from when I was thirteen until just before I turned sixteen, years that broke my mother's heart and programmed me for life.

"From what I gather," the old man was saying, "a woman usually gets an enema before she goes in to give birth but you came on real quick and there wasn't time—"

I told him I didn't want to hear it.

"I was out in the waiting room when a nurse asked if I wanted to see you get born . . . I figured, what the hell, in for a dime, in for a dollar. I arrived all suited up and masked just as your mother was bearing down to get you out and I guess she squeezed her bowels—"

"*Why* are you telling me this?"

He held up a quaking hand, trying not to laugh. "The nurses are wiping away the shit while your mother is bearing down and shitting even more, which is the moment you choose to arrive, right in the middle of it all . . ." He laughs and loses his breath, then catches it again. "So that's what I wanted to tell you, you were born in shit and blood, it was a mess."

"Thanks, Dad."

"I just wanted to tell you . . . to let you know I was there at the beginning."

"Thanks."

"And also to say, life's tough . . . you're born in shit and—"

When I suggested he leave it at that, the old man fixed me with a dull gaze. "So how's your business?"

"Good, knock on wood."

"Lunch boxes and Barbie dolls?"

"Collectibles, memorabilia . . ." He knew what my business was. For the past three years, since I turned thirty, I've been doing it full time, buying and selling toys that Baby Boomers played with as children, but I also deal in political memorabilia and occasionally rare books, old coins. I started out as a broker, purchasing items only when I knew I had a willing buyer. But I came across so many good deals from sellers desperate to unload collections (often a widow eager to sell her dead husband's "junk") that I leased a warehouse and began buying and storing items for eventual resell . . . this is either going to make a lot of money someday or lead to bankruptcy.

"You don't do PR anymore?" my father asked.

"Not for three years, Dad."

"Schmoozing."

"What?"

"All that stuff you did for that PR company, marketing and media, you told me, it's schmoozing . . . like you learned from me and your uncle James Joseph back when you lived in the Quarters."

"Yeah." My father's dying, I wasn't going to dispute what he should be taking credit for.

"That skinny little black-haired girl, you still shacking with her?"

"No, we broke up last—"

"How many's that since college?"

"Girlfriends?"

"Serious ones you couldn't keep, yeah."

"Couldn't keep?"

"If you can't make it work with women, Charlie, that's just one of the things you got to accept."

Where do parents get their ideas? I told him, "I parted on the best of terms with all my old girlfriends, in fact the ones who've gotten married have invited me to their weddings—"

"You take it as a *compliment* . . . you're so safe that old girlfriends invite you to their weddings? Any of my old girlfriends, they didn't want me in the same *state* when they were getting married."

"All I'm saying, Dad—"

"Is how tame you are . . ."

"Is how I'm not leaving behind a lot of bitterness and anger."

"Meaning what?"

I shook my head.

"Meaning what?"

"I'm not the man you were, Pop."

He stared at me and blinked, then said, "I'm laying here dying and you're *insulting* me?"

"Forget it."

"And what did you mean, the man I *was?*"

I shrugged, but of course he must realize it's true . . . my father was in the past tense now.

"You're more like me than you want to admit," he said. "Marketing, schmoozing, trading, selling, working deals, hustling . . . the apple doesn't fall far from the tree."

Because he abandoned the family when I was four, as a child I had no distinctive memories of him, but when mother wasn't around, my sisters would tell stories of our father . . . how he could talk birds from trees and make everyone laugh, how people at a party waited upon his arrival like they were auditioning for *The Iceman Cometh.* When he was tapped out he'd bust open your piggy bank to steal the last quarter, but when he was flush he gave extravagant gifts all around, and people who knew him but didn't have to depend upon him loved our father dearly for his bonhomie. A thief and con artist, in spite of his moral corruption he was a physically beautiful man, according to my sisters and to photographs they had hidden away like contraband from our mother, who upon finding any lingering evidence of her ex-husband, would burn the item like it carried typhoid.

My father's good looks and high spirits and felonious nature were all still evident when I was a teenager and lived with him in New Orleans, but now, in this hospice room, he is desiccated and traumatized and it seems that the tubes in his arms and at his nose, instead of helping, must be vacuuming life from him. Mother would be pleased.

"I got a deathbed assignment for you," he announced.

Assignment . . . I remember that word from hanging around with my father and James Joseph, how they inclined to the dramatic and instead of asking me to run an errand or do a little job, they'd bring me in close and whisper about an *assignment* they had for me. Usually these assignments were mundane, run get a pack of cigarettes or go tell someone to be at a certain place come midnight . . . but occasionally James Joseph would offer something bizarre. One time he had me running around the French Quarter gathering up things I thought might be soothing to pygmies . . . who supposedly were being imported into this country as jockeys but ended up being so stricken by the crowds and shouts at the track that, between races, they needed to be kept in quiet rooms, surrounded by items they found soothing. Even at the time I knew it was ludicrous . . . but my uncle was such a magical man I would've gone to sea in a paper boat for him.

I guess this pygmy memory made me smile because suddenly my father was demanding what the hell I thought was so goddamn funny.

Funny was me bringing pygmy-soothing items to Pelikan who laid my treasures on the cypress bar of the joint where he worked, a place called Your Mother's, and questioned me carefully why I chose a piece of colored glass or red foil, please explain my pygmy-soothing philosophy. It was because of the close way he listened that I eventually came out of my shy-boy shell and flourished in the French Quarter.

"*What?*" my father was still demanding.

"Deathbed *assignment?* I was just thinking how dramatic you and—"

"I'm dying here!" he shouted. "For me, that's pretty goddamn dramatic!"

"Okay."

"Dramatic?" he grumbled. "Change places with me, see how *dramatic* you feel."

"You're right, I was out of line."

"What, I should just lay here and die *politely,* is that how they do it in the suburbs?"

He thought it was a sign of my milky nature that as a single man in my thirties I was living in a family-oriented suburb rather than downtown in some big city, preferably New Orleans, although New York or Chicago would've sufficed . . . places where a young man can grab the world by the ass and shake it, my father would say. Hoping to avoid his lecture about the soulless suburbs, I asked, What's the assignment?

"I got several, sit down."

I took a chair by his bed wondering if he was going to ask that I hold his hand as he spoke.

He didn't. "Your uncle, James Joseph, might be in trouble . . . over his head. It's this business with the Edessa. At least it started out as business, now it's—"

"The *what*?"

"Edessa. It's famous, two thousand years old, made by Thracian goldsmiths who—"

I laughed. "Thracians, huh?" This had all the marks of another farce, like the pygmy jockeys.

"If you're ignorant, don't be proud of it," he told me, "that's one of my dying philosophies you can have for free. Now I want you to go down to New Orleans and bring your uncle up here to me. If you make it before I croak, I'll be able to see him one last time, great. If I die before you get back, the two of you can go to my funeral together and make sure people pay attention."

"Why don't you just call him and tell him to come see you?"

"You know James Joseph, he won't leave New Orleans unless someone goes down there and gets him. What's he always say about New Orleans being his cradle and grave?"

"I'm not the man for the job."

"What's he always say, is what I asked you."

"He always says New Orleans was his cradle, New Orleans will be his *coffin*. And what *I* say, Dad, is I'm not the person to go down there and get James Joseph—"

"Sure you are . . . in fact you're the *only* man for the job, the only person in the world James Joseph would leave New Orleans for."

"I'm not going to do it . . . ask me something else."

"Why, because he took that girl away from you, you still holding a grudge over that, how many years's it been?"

"He's my uncle, he should've—"

"He couldn't've taken her away from you if she didn't want to be taken . . . he didn't knock her over the head, did he?"

"No, but that's not—"

"He give her drugs, slip her a mickey?"

"No, although he's been known to—"

"Then what'd he do to *take* her away from you . . . . as opposed to you just *lost* her, huh?"

I didn't know the answer . . . maybe James Joseph whispered *New Oy-yuns* in her ear . . . and cried her to sleep with zydeco and woke her up with beignets, I don't know what the hell Pelikan did but I was

in love with Amanda, deeply, dangerously in love with her, and I took
Amanda down to New Orleans for Mardi Gras, but she didn't come
back with me. Amanda stayed with Pelikan. I haven't returned to the
city since then (twelve years ago, when I was twenty-one) and haven't
spoken with or forgiven my uncle.

My father was summarizing this trauma: "You bring a girl down
to Mardi Gras when you're in college, James Joseph takes her to bed,
the rest of your life is ruined . . . that your story?"

"I'm not going to talk about this."

"I never thought you'd grow up to be a sissy."

I looked away.

"When your sisters were visiting me the other day, one of them
was wearing a cute blue dress with white piping and a matching
jacket . . . I think it might fit you."

"Fuck you." Then immediately regretted it.

"Whoa, tough guy, huh . . . I'm laying here with tubes up my
nose, out my dick, and suddenly you're a tough guy, huh?"

I wish. Life would be easier if I was tough like my father and his
half brother, James Joseph, men who never fell in love, whose idea of
romance was getting a blow job without having to pay for it, men
who go hard eyed when a woman cries in their presence . . . meanwhile I regularly fall in love, break my heart, go to pieces. I think New
Orleans did this to me, living there during my formative, puppy-love
years. It tends to skew the rest of your life when at age fourteen or fifteen you're hanging out in French Quarter bars, protected as I was by
the royal status of my uncle, eating dawn breakfasts with weary strippers who wanted me to rub their feet, getting oyster kisses from female bartenders. Then I left the French Quarter just before I was
sixteen, my experiences there becoming personal myth and legend.

"You used to be such a happy kid," my father was saying, "how
come you turned out so sour?"

"I had a root canal yesterday."

"And a smart-ass too. You know, your uncle could arrange for you
to get rich."

"The only thing he's good at arranging is blow jobs for conven-
tioneers." Arranging things is how my father's half brother made his

way through life. When I lived in the French Quarter, Pelikan
arranged the loss of my virginity and then sent women to me on a
regular basis . . . which of course is one large reason I stayed there for
three years, until my mother's almost daily admonishments and pleas
by telephone and letter finally wore me down and I returned to the
leafy suburbs of Connecticut as a jaded kid about to turn sixteen . . . convinced I'd already done and seen everything life had to
offer. Maybe all sixteen-year-olds think that way, but after three years
in the French Quarter with Pelikan, I was closer than most to being
right about it.

"I'm worried about James Joseph," my father said. "People tell me
he's become weird, maybe even mentally ill."

"Yeah, how could anyone tell?"

My father laughed and coughed, then suddenly his eyes went
wide and he grabbed his side and seemed about to scream. "I coughed
loose one of my tubes." I went looking for nurses.

While waiting in the hall as they worked on him, I offered a silent
prayer: *Please God don't ever let me be the author of that statement: I
coughed loose one of my tubes.*

After he was put back together, the nurses said I could have another ten minutes with him, then I should leave.

"When you get down to New Orleans," he said right away, speaking hoarsely and allowing no opportunity for either of us to mention
what had just happened, "look up Three Jacks On The Floor before
you go into the Quarter, he'll tell you what condition your uncle is in,
if it's safe to go see him."

"Safe?"

"Yeah, there's a lot of stuff going on, Three Jacks will fill you in."

"Okay."

"Okay what?"

"Okay, I'll do it."

He stared at me for a long time. "I'm dying, you're lying."

I didn't deny either.

"I can't believe you're not going to do this thing for your dying
father."

I really did have a root canal done the day before . . . and now it's throbbing. "All right, Pop, the nurses said I got to go ... . I'll come see you again tomorrow."

"I'll be added to Pelikan's list soon."

"What list?"

"He keeps a list of all the people he's ever known who've died, he takes it out occasionally and goes through the list, saying each person's name and remembering something good about that person. You never knew he kept a list?"

"No."

"Soon I'll be on his list . . . and I have to tell you, Charlie, it's a comfort knowing that after I'm dead, *someone* will occasionally speak my name and say good things."

"Dad, you're busting my balls here."

He closed his eyes and began fooling around, pawing the air with one hand, speaking like he was already a ghost. "Charles, Charles . . . my dear son, Charles, go to New Orleans, get rich . . . eat a muffuletta for me, drink a Dixie beer, and remember me to Herald Square."

"That's New York."

He opened his eye and tried for a sly grin . . . which came across as death's grimace.

I stood.

"Don't you want to go to New Orleans and get rich, Charlie?"

"What's this about getting rich, how's Pelikan going to do that?"

"Go down there and find out."

"We'll see." Now I was sounding like the parent, putting off a persistent child.

He gave me a dirty look. "One last favor? Go to my funeral and if you catch anyone checking his watch or yawning or talking business or comparing gas mileages or anything that's not about me . . . give 'em dirty looks. Man, I can't stand that. What's a funeral last, an hour or so? For that lousy hour it seems to me you should concentrate on the business at hand and not be making lunch plans. So that's what I'm asking of you, come to my funeral and scowl at the clock-watchers."

"You got it."

"One other thing."

"Yeah?"

He didn't speak for a moment, then shrugged. "A man's dying, he tries to set things right. I talked to your sisters, they forgive me for being a lousy father to them or no father at all, they always have forgiven me. And they all turned out just fine, careers and marriages, great kids. I haven't called your mother because I knew she *wouldn't* forgive me, which is fine too. That leaves you. I don't know how much responsibility I owe for you not being a very happy man at age thirty-three when you should have the world by its ass—"

"I'm fine."

"No, listen to me. I should've taken better care of you when you were living with me, shouldn't have let you run wild, shouldn't have let you spend so much time with James Joseph. But what's done is done, now, if you can find it in your heart, I'd like you to forgive me."

"For what?"

"Everything I just said. Jesus Christ, I'm dying here and you're still not listening to me? For not being a good father, not taking better care of you."

"I forgive you."

He looked at me for a long time, then said, "You're lying again."

I shrugged.

"Like I said before, the apple doesn't fall far from the tree . . . but you know what, Charlie, I'm glad you're tough hearted. It'll hold you in good stead."

"Tough hearted? Dad, you have no idea how soft I am."

This seemed to alarm him and he asked what I meant.

"Nothing, I'll come see you tomorrow."

"Here."

His outstretched hand held an envelope. When I took it, he said, "Don't come back tomorrow."

"No?"

"It really burns me."

"What?"

"People not paying attention at a funeral. A death should *mean* something. I should have you say Kaddish."

"Say what?"

"Not that I expect you to even remember your old man, much less do anything in my honor, every day for eleven months, that's a laugh . . . an hour after I'm dead you'll be drinking cocktails from fancy-stemmed glasses and I'll become some story you tell every few years when you get in your cups after a dinner party."

"I have no idea what you're talking about."

" 'My father, the colorful character from New Orleans.' Go on, get the hell out of here, don't come back."

I hesitated. Was this the last time I'd see him alive?

He made it easy. "I *said* get the hell out of here, Charlie . . . leave me to die, huh?"

I left and didn't stop until I was away from the hospice in a taxi, where I opened the envelope containing $900 and a one-way ticket on a train called the Crescent City.

2

WAXING AND WANING

A deathbed *assignment* is apparently powerful gris-gris because here I am on that train arriving in a city I promised myself I'd never visit again, to see an uncle I swore never to speak to again.

When I lived here as a teenager, James Joseph was so well connected and well known in the bars of the French Quarter, especially those off Bourbon Street, that I was always welcomed even if my underage presence put the bar at legal risk. I spent more time with my uncle than with my father, who was busy with various felonies and misdemeanors. James Joseph told me ghost stories and gave advice on healthy living (most of it having to do with foot maintenance and frequent hand washing) and sent me on those assignments like they were spy missions (Charlie, take this envelope to a tall guy in a red shirt at the end of the bar in Giovanni's . . . tell him the black dog howls at midnight, he'll know what to do). Pelikan lived in a city that offered some of the greatest food in the world but he seldom sat down to a regular meal, and except for beans and rice on Monday, I never saw him eat any of the traditional dishes, mostly he snacked. He was full of quirks, crossing himself frequently and mumbling hoodoo incantations the way you or I might sing an old song under our breath. Although he worked in bars all his life, I never knew him to get drunk. He was surrounded by beautiful women, many of whom adored him, but didn't have girlfriends. (James Joseph said he "received gratuities" for arranging dates but he was virtually a pimp and as such considered himself an expert on women . . . telling me right after he met Amanda on the first day of that Mardi Gras trip that she was playing me for a fool: a prophecy he made come true.)

I got off the train carrying all this history. And wondered: now that I'm thirty-three and run my own business and have adjusted relatively well to a non–New Orleans life, will I finally be able to close the book on this city?

Heading for a cab I lecture myself about keeping mentally healthy, no tunnel trips to the past, no recriminations to Pelikan or demands for explanations, and especially no participation in his strange adventure-assignments. Just give him the message—your brother is dying and wants you to come see him—then go back North with or without my uncle in tow.

When the cabbie drops me off, I think I must have the wrong address because this high-rise looks way too pricey for Three Jacks. I'd called Three Jacks before I left on this trip and although we hadn't seen each other for nearly twenty years, he seemed eager to fill me in on what my uncle was doing. Inside the building I ask a janitor and he says yeah, not only does Karl Gruber (Three Jacks's real name) reside here, he lives in the penthouse.

On the way up I'm trying to figure how Three Jacks On The Floor managed to rent a penthouse because, when I was in New Orleans as a kid, he was a sad-funny character who hung around the edge of the action, ran disability scams, and was famous for being unlucky. He liked me because I was one of the few individuals below him on the pecking order . . . though Three Jacks and I both understood that my low status as a teenager was temporary, his wasn't. He got his name in a high-stakes poker game that took place before I was born. Karl the Grub (as he was known then) apparently was on this winning streak that he couldn't dismount no matter how foolishly he played . . . but winning made him so nervous he got shitfaced on Maker's Mark, becoming sloppy at the table, spilling drinks, knocking over ashtrays, dropping cards. When he told me this story years ago, my father explained that normally the poker players would've kicked Karl out of the game for this sort of behavior, but he had won most of the money by this point and the other players wanted a crack at winning some back. The only other guy who was ahead that night turned out to be a high roller from St. Louis who dressed, my father said, like a riverboat gambler, including big black hat and handlebar mustache heavily waxed. Around dawn, this high roller and Karl were in a final round that tied up just about all the money that had been played that night, a winner-take-everything pot. The game was seven-card stud. Karl called. The high roller from St. Louis turned over a full boat, queens on top of fours. Karl looks at the boat, then at the high roller, then says, "I got dat beat, I got four of a kind." Showing no emotion, the high roller from St. Louis tells Karl, "Let's see 'em." But in his nervous, drunken fiddling, Karl dropped part of his hand on the floor and has to scoot back from the table to look for the missing cards, finally announcing, "Okay, here we go, four of a kind—dat jack of diamonds on the table and dese three jacks on the floor." The high roller from St. Louis goes cold in the eyes. "Three jacks on the floor? Where I come from, 'three jacks on the floor' would get your throat slit." To save blood being shed, the other players decide to give the pot to the high roller and kick Karl out of the game . . . nothing to show for his winning streak except a new nickname.

Up at the penthouse I rang the bell and Three Jacks On The Floor answered wearing a towel, holding a cigar.

"Hey kid," he said brightly. "You grew up!"

I shook the hand that wasn't holding the cigar and told Three Jacks he hadn't changed at all . . . which was almost true, he'd gone from forty to sixty without seeming any older, just a little fatter, a little balder. What hair he had was on his belly and chest, thick black fur all the way up to the line on his neck where he pruned back the thicket so it wouldn't stick up out of his shirt collars.

"Howz ya momma an 'em sistas?" he asked.

"Fine," I said, surprised at this cross-reference between a New Orleans character and my life back home.

"Come on in," Three Jacks said, turning to lead me through his apartment, high ceilinged and overstuffed, everything beige and white, pillows all over the place like the apartment was a pillow ranch where they breed them in all shapes and sizes, some big enough to hug with both arms and dozens of smaller ones lounging around

couches and chairs. You could get falling-down drunk in this apartment and never worry about bumping your head.

"Great place," I said, getting ready to ask how he was paying the
rent . . . but Three Jacks spoke first, telling me I hadn't seen nothing
yet. He pulled apart a pair of ten-foot glass doors that opened onto a
patio with potted plants, swimming pool with waterfall, and a fancy
iron fence around the whole thing to keep you falling fourteen floors
from penthouse luxury all the way down to the Warehouse District.

"Wow," I said softly.

"Check out the view," he said.

I turned to where he was pointing and saw a naked woman standing next to a wheeled table . . . she was mid-twenties and perky looking, the yellow blond hair on her head cut shorter than an army
recruit's. She was also shaved bare between the legs.

"You'll never guess," Three Jacks said, "what she's here to do
to me."

"I don't even want to think about it."

He laughed. "Come on, I'll introduce you."

We went over and Three Jacks said, "This is Maria."

She had a fishhook in her lip.

With considerable effort, Three Jacks climbed up on the gurney
and lay on his back, keeping, thank God, the large towel draped
across his groin.

"I'm waxing his belly," the woman said cheerfully.

I nodded as if this was something I encountered all the time.

"The way it works, Charlie," Three Jacks explained, "she's new to
the hair-removal business and wants to put the word out, and there's
no better person in the world to put the word out than me, so she's
comping me this wax job."

I looked down at his big belly carpeted in curly black hair and
asked the woman, "You've heard of the labors of Hercules?"

"No," she said, opening a tin of wax.

"Hey, Charlie, go over and check out the swimming pool," Three
Jacks told me as he took a puff on the fat cigar, then closed his eyes
like he was ready for a nap.

I went over and looked in . . . the water was green, not algae-dirty green but green as if someone had dyed it. "The water's green," I called to Three Jacks, raising my voice to be heard over the waterfall made of concrete fake rocks three or four feet high to create the splash.

"I dyed it green!" he called back to me.

"How come!"

I thought he said something about the FBI but didn't catch it and returned to the gurney and asked Three Jacks, did he just say something about the FBI.

"Foreign-born Irish," he explained. "I had a bunch of FBI priests here and in their honor I dyed the pool green."

"You're not Irish, how come you had a party for—"

"Bulgar," he said.

"What?"

"I'm Bulgar. It wasn't much of a party anyway, not with Jesuits, they're shock troops, not cocktail drinkers. My sister's a nun, one of God's guards, you didn't know that?"

I said I didn't. I tried to get a lingering look at Maria's body but each time I glanced her way she caught me so I tried being a gentleman by looking her straight in the eyes, which were blue. I was about to ask about the fishhook in her lower lip when I caught a smell on the wind and turned left, toward the Mississippi River a few blocks away. "America's alimentary canal," I said.

"What?" she asked.

"That's how my uncle used to describe the Mississippi," I told her. "He said it was America's alimentary canal, America's gut, getting nastier on the way down, finally dumping its load out in the Gulf of Mexico, a hundred miles from here."

"His uncle is James Joseph Pelikan," Three Jacks said, maintaining his policy of telling everything to anyone.

"You're Charlie Curtis?" she asked with a curious smile.

"Yeah, how'd you know?"

She smiled more.

I didn't press her for an answer, saying instead that I was here to talk to Three Jacks and would appreciate it if she could leave us alone for a few minutes.

"You're here to see *who*?" she asked.

"Three Jacks On The Floor."

He snickered but kept his eyes closed.

"Who's Three Jacks On The Floor?" she asked.

I pointed.

"Him?"

"Yeah," I said, "what do you know him as?"

"The Lion of Judah?"

I searched her eyes for signs of irony, sarcasm, wit . . . but came up dry. Three Jacks offered no comment except to puff on his cigar. Welcome to New Orleans.

As the woman dug a large wooden spatula into the tin of sun-softened wax, I looked more closely at the fishhook through her lower lip. It wasn't a decorative, hypoallergenic, jewelry-type fishhook, it was a regular old tackle box fishhook . . . the shank came out through the skin just under the curl of her pouty lower lip, the fishhook's barb arching out from inside, coming over the top of that lip so it looked as if the hook's sharp point was standing guard there at the entrance to her mouth.

When she caught me staring, I apologized and said I'd never seen anyone who had a fishhook through their lip on purpose.

Three Jacks spoke without opening his eyes, "Tell him what it's for."

I waited. The young woman looked at me with what seemed to be—and obviously I was dreaming here, fantasizing—abiding affection as she kneaded the wax onto Three Jacks's belly flesh, rolling under her touch like hairy dough for a really big loaf of bread . . . but she said nothing.

Three Jacks finally supplied the answer himself: "That fishhook discourages blow jobs."

I have a really stupid laugh so mainly I've taught myself to chuckle or smile, not laugh out loud, but Three Jacks's remark caught me unaware and a laugh belched out of me . . . the young woman raising her eyebrows (were they the only hair she had beside that blond burr cut?) before smiling again and returning to the task of waxing the stomach of Three Jacks On The Floor.

With her attention now riveted on depilation, I took the opportunity to stare . . . Maria was five and a half feet tall, her legs and arms slim (and also hairless, I noticed now that I was staring), her titties nicely chubby and high on her chest and topped with nipples like scoops of plum purple ice cream. I realize it's risky comparing nipples to food products, but her nipples were truly unusual in size and color . . . so much so that I fixated on them for several long seconds before noticing the tattoos.

On the inside of her right breast was a fiery red devil about the size of a quarter, a cartoon devil with pointy tail and pitchfork, looking more mischievous than evil. Then over on her left breast, tucked in the same position and of similar size, was a blue cartoon angel with all the usual angel accoutrements—wings, halo, and a benevolent smile similar to the one on this young woman's face as she asked me without looking away from her waxy task, "You enjoying the view?"

I said nothing and she continued spreading wax as if belly was the main course at tonight's banquet and she was in charge of marinade.

"When she gets done with me," Three Jacks said sleepily, "I'm gonna be slick and sleek like a twelve-year-old boy."

Yeah—if the twelve-year-old boy is bald, weighs three hundred pounds, smokes stogies, and has bags under his eyes like Buster Keaton.

"Maria," I said, "could you leave us alone for just a few minutes?"

She held up both waxy hands. "Sure. I have to make a call anyway." She went over to a chair by the pool and took a towel out of her gym bag. After wiping her hands, Maria removed a cell phone from the bag and flipped it open . . . I couldn't hear what she was saying because of the waterfall.

Three Jacks opened his eyes and struggled to sit up. "She works naked," he said, flashing his bushy brows.

"So I noticed . . . how'd you end up so lucky?"

"I got money coming in."

"From where?"

He lay back and closed his eyes again.

"Three Jacks, I'm down here to convince Pelikan to come back with me and see my father before he dies, but Dad said I should talk to you first because Pelikan apparently has been acting a little weirder than usual."

"You and James Joseph going to break into the Suppository, huh?"

"I don't know what that means."

"A play on words. Suppository, the Louisiana State *Repository* . . . don't you get it?"

I shook my head.

"I thought you went to college. Hey, Charlie, you been in the Quarters yet?"

"No."

"Don't you love this city?"

"What's not to love about New Orleans?" I said, intentionally pronouncing it New Or-*leens.*

Three Jacks laughed. "N'Awlins, Ne-Orlyuns, New Orlans, New Orlins, New Oy-yuns, it prolly doan matta, hawt, long as you end up in Da Franch Kwatas."

He was talking *yat,* what they call working-class whites who used the universal greeting, *Where y'at!* When I lived in New Orleans as a kid, *yat* was a relatively neutral term but over the years it became pejorative, like peckerwood.

I asked Three Jacks when he last saw Pelikan.

"Couple weeks ago. Your dad and Pelikan were kings of the Quarters, warrior kings who—"

"One of the kings is dying."

Three Jacks took the cigar out of his mouth. "Yeah, I know that's how come you're here, I heard your father's got the cancer, sorry . . . he's a good man."

Apparently finished with her phone call, the naked woman, Maria, came over and asked me if I really was Charlie Curtis.

I said I really was . . . then took another journey starting at that fishhook under her lower lip, descending to her titties with their tattoos and fat purple nipples, then on down her hairless little tummy to that equally hairless place between her legs, and back up from there, bumping through it all again. I wondered how utterly stupid I would sound asking her to come into the Quarter with me and have a drink . . . after she got dressed, of course.

"James Joseph Pelikan's nephew?" she asked.

"The one and only . . . why?"

"I just wanted to make sure." She walked back to that metal chair painted enamel green where she had her gym bag.

I asked Three Jacks what that was all about, he said he didn't know. Then I asked him again about Pelikan.

"Well, kid, there's some heavy rain about to fall and ol' Three Jacks might have to lay low for a stretch."

"Tell me something I can understand."

"I've been playing both ends against the middle, Charlie . . . a profitable but dangerous endeavor."

I leaned over and took the cigar from his mouth and stuck it, smoky end up, in his waxy navel, where it stayed, plenty of room in there for a fifty-four-gauge Churchill.

"Hey, why'd you do that?" he whined, squinting in the sun to look at the cigar.

" 'Cause you're not paying attention."

"Oh Charlie," he said, closing his eyes again, leaving the cigar in place.

The woman was walking my way again, smiling like we were in love, holding a towel across her hands. Like an idiot, watching her plump dumpling breasts diddily-bopping like no factory tits ever can, I smiled back and suspected nothing until she pulled her right hand from under that towel and pointed a .38 Special snub-nose revolver at me.

I looked at the gun, then up at her face: sweet countenance, fish-hooked mouth, white teeth, cute smile—like Mary Poppins if you can imagine Mary Poppins completely naked, shaved of all body hair including short curlies, sporting a burr haircut, and aiming a .38 Special right square at your nose.

I nudged Three Jacks, who grunted but kept his eyes closed, oblivious of the drama unfolding right next to the table.

When she was close to that gurney, she lowered the muzzle until it was pointing just below the cigar still sticking out of Three Jacks's navel and then, smiling like flashbulbs flashing, she pulled the trigger and blew a splattering hole in that big hairy waxy watermelon of a belly.

I gasped and Three Jacks yelled, *"YEOWWARGGFUCKET!"* or something to that effect, and right away he was spouting red like a harpooned whale.

NAKED WOMAN IN GREEN WATER

Her gun hand remained steady as Three Jacks strangled on something deep in his throat, struggling to sit up until she placed the muzzle to his temple and pulled the trigger again, making me jump again but at least putting an end to Three Jacks's distress as his body shuddered off the table to land on the patio tile *thump-splat* like a side of beef to the butcher's floor.

In her other hand was the cell phone. The woman punched 911 and said, "There's been a shooting." Then she gave Three Jacks's address.

Stepping over the body, supine with the cigar still waxed in place, still smoking, she looked down at him and said in self-amusement, "Three Jacks On The Floor on the floor." Then pointed the gun at me.

I waited, wondering how much it's going to hurt . . . and how brave will I be about it?

She said, "I'm waiting."

"Waiting?"

"For you to go crazy, run around and howl like a scalded dog."

Now when I looked at her eyes I realized there was an absence behind them, that what I'd taken as some kind of instant affection for me was, instead, drugged-out bliss.

"This whole thing," I told her, "to me it's very strange."

"It's about to get worse."

I didn't ask what she meant, but when Three Jacks's body farted, I said, "It wasn't me." Which made her laugh and gave me hope maybe I wasn't going to get shot after all.

We heard a siren. "There you go," she said, flipping the revolver in the air, catching it by the cylinder and handing it to me grips first, upside down.

I turned the revolver right side up and pointed it at this strange, naked, zonked, nearly hairless woman, close enough now I could smell her, all mint and moss.

"Are you going to shoot me?" she asked mockingly.

"I'm really confused."

She laughed, cranked the voltage on that smile one last time, then swayed over to the pool where she dove in with such splashless grace it seemed a leap into some waterless void.

I went to the pool to watch her swim laps or whatever it was she did after waxing and icing someone, but the woman was under the surface and I couldn't see her because the green water was opaque. I checked the time . . . how long can she stay under, three minutes max? I'll wait and then tell the cops—

Tell them what? Those sirens were closing in when it occurred to me how vulnerable I was here. The cops would come running out onto this patio and see Three Jacks shot dead and see me standing here by the pool with a revolver in my hand and if I was lucky maybe they wouldn't shoot me where I stood, maybe they'd settle for pointing weapons at me and screaming mortal threats.

I threw the revolver in the pool where it sank quickly out of sight under the Irish green surface.

Checking my watch I figured it had to be four minutes now and she can't hold her breath that long, can she? Did she jump in and hit her head on the bottom and drown? The cops are going to think I shot Three Jacks and killed the naked wax lady too.

With sirens winding down I hurried to the railing and saw four cops getting out of two cars parked in front of the building. They'll be up here in a couple minutes, do I wait and explain, or take off?

Checking the pool again, wondering where she was, I stood there *willing* that green water to yield a naked hairless woman . . . maybe I should jump in and try to find her body, she must be dead because it's been six or seven minutes.

I looked over at the ten-foot glass doors, imagining them opening with nervous cops running out onto the patio, seeing a bloody body, then pointing their weapons at me, accusing me of murder.

And what am I going to say in my defense . . . no, Officers, you got it all wrong, it wasn't me, it was a naked woman with tattoos on her titties, no hair between her legs, and a fishhook through her lip, she's the one who killed Three Jacks On The Floor and then drowned herself in that swimming pool full of green water.

Saying something like that, I would deserve to get shot.

Still longing for her to surface, I rushed through the pillowed apartment, out into the hall, opened the door to the stairway, and fled as if surely guilty of *something*.

THE FRENCH KWATAS

Like Br'er Rabbit and the brier patch, I needed to get into the French Quarter. I should walk there because if I use a cab and the driver is later questioned by the police, he'll place me near Three Jacks's building at the time of the killings, but after the third patrol car passed I became convinced the cops were checking me out, so I grabbed a cab and when the driver asked where to, I told him the French Quarter. Where in the French Quarter? I don't care, just get me across Canal Street.

He glanced in the mirror. "You here for a convention?"

"No."

"You want, I could take you for a little tour, I know the city, I'd make the tour real historical . . . we could do it on the meter or work out a flat rate."

"No thanks."

Waiting for the light at Canal, the driver, a young black man wearing a three-color knit cap, said, "Canal Street marks the upriver border of the original city where the French and Spanish Creoles were living when the Americans came to town after President Jefferson bought the Louisiana Purchase from Napoleon." He checked the rearview to see if I was impressed.

"Yeah," I said.

"The Creoles," he continued, "didn't mix well with those newly arriving Americans, river men and land speculators, so many of them from Kentucky that the Creoles took to calling all Americans *Kaintocks.* The Kaintocks settled upriver from the original city and whenever business had to be conducted between them and the Creoles, the two sides would meet here on Canal Street, which became known as the neutral ground. Now in eighteen—"

"The light," I told him.

He looked at the green, then back at me, then took off across Canal, sufficiently displeased that he didn't say another word and would, I was sure, remember me vividly to the police.

I didn't need his history lesson: as a boy I studied this city more fervently than any subject at school . . . in love with New Orleans and especially the heart of New Orleans, the French Quarter, where I lived with my father. The Quarters, as yats call it in the plural, the *Franch Kwatas* . . . the original New Orleans where eight thousand people, half of them slaves, lived when the U.S. took possession, and that's probably close to the population of the French Quarter now, a small neighborhood of fewer than a hundred blocks, the most old-European looking urban plot in the U.S. and also the most Caribbean . . . narrow streets and iron balconies, world-class restaurants and sleazy bars, expensive art galleries and exclusive jewelry stores where you have to be buzzed in, hot dog carts, go-cups you can carry out of serious drinking establishments where the motto is *Laissez les bons temps rouler,* let the good times roll. Although old-line residents of New Orleans will say the French Quarter isn't representative of the city and Bourbon Street isn't representative of the French Quarter, as an adolescent I adored everything about the Quarters, most especially her vulgar vein, Bourbon Street . . . I loved the Quarters' looks and her attitude and the way she smelled, white tea olive blossoms, *Osmanthus fragrans,* jasmine in the spring like thick-sweet airborne sugar, and even the summer stink of stale beer and shellfish remains.

Even with all the trouble I'm in, it still seems as if the whole French Quarter is happy to have me back . . . like joining a party where they've been waiting for you . . . lights bright and doors open and barkers inviting you in.

I tipped the driver a five, got out on Chartres, and went into the first bar I came to, a strip joint: small, narrow, dark, and dirty. The bartender was standard issue for a place like this, in his forties with a lot of upper-body fat, bristling beard, his hair pulled back in a greasy ponytail, ex-biker . . . he asked warily what I wanted (did my despair show that obviously on my face?) and I told him Tanqueray over ice with a splash of tonic. I was a fool for buying a premium call brand in a place like this but I needed Tanqueray's higher-proof serenity, needed to sit and sip and figure out the consequences. One of Pelikan's favorite sayings, a paraphrase of what Ingersoll said about nature, was, *There are no rewards or punishments in the French Quarter, only consequences.*

A stripper came over and asked if I would buy her a drink. I shook my head and she didn't press the issue . . . one advantage to looking desperate, people tend to leave you alone. Of course, my acting nervous will ensure everyone remembers me to the cops.

I should call my dad . . . no, find Pelikan first, he'll be here in the Quarter somewhere.

"You got a phone?" I asked the bartender.

"In the vestibule," he said.

I brayed a laugh and he gave me an acid look. *Vestibule?* . . . no one uses that word anymore, I hadn't heard it since Catholic school here in New Orleans.

In the vestibule I took out my wallet and called the number I had for Your Mother's, known to locals as Mother's, the bar Pelikan managed, and after some shouting back and forth (music too loud on both ends of the line) I explained who I was, where I was, and could Pelikan come up here and meet me. I didn't want to go down to Mother's, where he'd be surrounded by drunks and clowns.

Back at the bar I had another Tanqueray . . . this one arrived with too much tonic so I warned the bartender to get it right next time and he assumed that weary-wary expression bartenders get when they're wondering if you're going to be trouble. Been a long time since I'd drunk gin.

The janitor . . . I just remembered speaking to the janitor at Three Jacks's building, so there's one person who can place me at the scene.

A new stripper mounted the tiny stage, a foot-high plywood platform. The woman's interest in removing her clothes was about the same as mine in watching her do it . . . she was tired and pale and had a little belly roll that might've been cute when she was young and JFK was in the White House.

Newer strip joints are big bright places where guys take dates and the strippers are young and athletic, taking off their clothes with chirpy enthusiasm, like it's an aerobics class. But what I remember from living in the French Quarter as a horny teenager are places like the one I'm in now . . . walls painted black, the floor sticky, the lighting low and red so you always feel like you need eyeglasses. Even the jukebox sounds tired. The stool and the edge of the bar are clammy from too much continuous contact with human skin, the whole place like a bell jar that never gets thoroughly cleaned or aired or shined on by disinfecting sunlight. I didn't want to think about the glass from which I was drinking, and although I was ravenous with the gin and the aftereffects of adrenaline, I dared not ask for a menu.

A redhead came on stage, she'd obviously had breast augmentation but, just as obviously, had accepted the low bid, her nipples out of kilter, the right one pulled low, the left nipple high and outside.

When she winked, I muttered something and turned away. Having caught this, the bartender told me in that false-polite tone that cops use right before employing pepper spray: "If you don't enjoy the show, sir, you might want to try some other place."

Instead of apologizing, I ordered him to bring me another gin . . . then watched that he didn't spit in the glass.

I finished several more of the overpriced drinks without feeling any effect and thought, this is stupid, drinking gin right after witnessing a murder that I'm going to be accused of committing . . . I can't wait for Pelikan, I got to go find him. Picking up my change, I sensed someone behind me just as a hand landed on my left shoulder and something hard pressed the small of my back. "You're under arrest."

I guess I'd been expecting it, turning around with my hands up.

"Chaz!" he exclaimed, laughing as he showed me it was his finger he'd been pressing in my back.

Only one person ever called me Chaz . . . Gene Renfrone, a cop we knew as Mean Gene.

"Gene," I finally said. "I'm surprised you remember me."

"Are you kidding?" He looked hurt. "Your father and uncle used to be my best friends."

Eugene Renfrone, aka Mean Gene, was one of the uniformed patrolmen well enough connected to get part of the French Quarter as his beat. He was grayer now and, like Three Jacks, a lot fatter . . . 250 pounds, maybe more. I remembered Renfrone as a thick-armed slab of a man who might not have the wind to chase you more than a block but if he did catch up he was capable of crippling you. Gene wore a big, triple-X windbreaker, yellow with blue trim, barely covering his belly. I don't think Renfrone is fifty years old yet, but it's hard to tell with fat guys.

Was it coincidence he'd seen me here? Another of Pelikan's sayings: *If it changes your life, it wasn't an accident or coincidence.*

Without being asked, the bartender brought Renfrone's drink and said, "How you making, Detective?"

Renfrone said he was fine, then introduced me. "Charlie here is Pelikan's nephew. Charlie, this is Eddie."

The formerly unfriendly bartender was grinning at me now, wiping his hand before he offered it for me to shake. "Hey, good man, let me bring you a drink on me." While he hurried off to pour a stiff one, I remembered how being my father's son and Pelikan's nephew was like carrying credentials in the French Quarter.

"He called you Detective?" I said to Mean Gene.

"Oh yeah." He raised his drink and we touched glasses. "Not in uniform anymore, Chaz . . . now I work Homicide."

My heart went cold.

"Hey how long you been back in town?" he asked.

Was this the beginning of an interrogation? "Just got in," I said, trying to sound casual.

"How's your momma and them sisters?" he asked.

How do these people know to ask about my mother and sisters? "Fine," I said.

"What've you been up to these past few years?"

"It's been *twelve* years since I saw you."

"Get out of here."

I told him it was true. "Twelve years since I set foot in this town."

"I knew you couldn't stay away . . . ten million visitors a year and each and every one falls in love with this ol' city."

"I hate New Orleans."

Renfrone widens his eyes. "You just kidding, ain't you, Charlie. How can you hate a city's got four seasons—crawfish, shrimp, crab, and King Cake?"

I said I was serious, hated New Orleans, detested the French Quarter. "Living here ruined my life."

"Then why you back?"

"My father's dying and I have to tell Pelikan."

Mean Gene Renfrone nodded . . . but his eyes were working on other agenda.

Go ahead, I thought, take your shot . . . ask me if I was just at Three Jacks's penthouse.

He smiled. "It's good seeing you again, Chaz. I got something to tell you about Pelikan, but we'll have ourselves a few more cocktails first."

The bartender, Eddie, brought another round but wouldn't accept payment, then that redhead with the misplaced nipples came over to give Renfrone a kiss. He introduced us and we nodded at each other without speaking, and she suggested to Renfrone that he should stick around until ten, when she got a break.

I checked my watch, it was a few minutes past nine . . . I'd been in this bar for more than three hours?

"She blew me once," Renfrone said after the redhead left. "Pelikan arranged it."

"I'm not surprised."

"You never did tell me what you been up to since I seen you last."

"Got my own business now."

"Yeah? Doing what?"

"I'm a collector."

"Of what?"

"Old toys, books, buttons and banners from political campaigns."

"I thought only old farts did that kind of thing. You get married?"

"No." Been engaged, though, fallen in love, had engagements bro-

ken, fell out of love, got the blues, got over the blues . . . glancing
down at my hands I thought I saw blood and freaked that it was from
Three Jacks. Standing too quickly, I lurched the way you do when
you've been on a bar stool drinking for a long time without moving,
thinking you're perfectly sober until you stand up and discover you're
not. No blood on my hands, it was just shadows from the bad
lighting.

Renfrone had caught my shoulders to prevent me from falling.
"Whoa there, cowboy."

I checked my hands again to make sure they were clean . . . then
brayed laughter.

"What?" he asked.

I shook my head.

He finished his drink and held up the glass for a refill. "Let me
catch up with you, Chaz, then we can be drunken assholes together."

I toasted that idea, we had another round on the house, and I lectured myself to keep quiet, just sit here and let Renfrone talk about
the good old days . . . which I did, listening without registering until I
heard him say "Three Jacks On The Floor."

"Three Jacks?"

"Yeah, that's where I've been for the past few hours, bizarre,
huh?"

"What's bizarre?"

"The way he was killed, weren't you listening to me?"

"I guess not."

Renfrone explained there'd been a 911 call from Three Jacks's
apartment, uniformed officers found his body, the Homicide Division
was called. Renfrone wasn't assigned the case but he came along as
part of the crime scene team. Three Jacks was found on the patio,
naked, a still-smoking cigar in his belly button, shot once in the stomach, once in the temple, no evidence of a struggle or break-in.

I wanted to ask if the gun had been recovered from the swimming
pool along with a naked woman but was overruled by whatever part
of me was still sober and interested in self-preservation.

Renfrone told me anyway. "No murder weapon recovered."

Look in the swimming pool. "Who would want to kill Three Jacks?"

Renfrone said he had no idea, it was almost like some sort of cult killing, with that cigar in his belly button, and also he had hair removal wax on his stomach, very strange. Renfrone speculated that Three Jacks must've got in over his head on some shady deal. "For example, what the hell was he doing in a penthouse?"

I nodded. "Yeah, I wondered that too."

"What do you mean, you wondered it too?"

"About the penthouse."

"How'd you know he was in a penthouse?"

"You mentioned it before."

He gave me a look. "I did?"

"Yeah."

Gene laughed, let it pass. "Anyway, the swimming pool water was dyed green so we couldn't see if there was anything in the water."

The naked woman who killed him.

"So they're draining the pool but it's going to take a while," he added.

The redhead stripper returned but now instead of giving me the cold shoulder she was all over me with both hands and when I saw her eyes I knew why, she'd been goofballing in the back room. She asked me and Renfrone, didn't we want to go someplace with her during her break and party. Mean Gene was considering it but I said no.

"Hey, honey, don't be so high and mighty," she told me, "I saw you looking at these." With that she gleefully reached into her top and pulled out those breasts with their wayward nipples.

"Jesus," I muttered and pushed her away, shoving harder than I intended, then fleeing out through the vestibule, stumbling into a night of such wet hot air that my lungs double-clutched to suck that first heavy breath.

Half a block away, Renfrone caught up with me, taking my arm and asking what the hell was my problem.

"You see those nipples?" I raised one index finger up, pointed the other down.

"You push a woman because of her nipples?"

When you get that pool drained, you're going to find a naked hairless woman with fat purple nipples.

Gene tightened his grip on me. "Come on, Chaz, I'll buy you something to eat."

We went into a place around the corner where I ordered hot garlic sausage, beans and rice, and a cold Dixie beer in a mug straight from the freezer. Renfrone said he wasn't going to have anything to eat, just a beer.

"You didn't get that belly by passing up *too* many meals," I told him.

He considered me a moment before speaking. "What I remember from when you lived here as a kid, Chaz . . . you were a happy."

"I was fourteen, fifteen years old, you were a cop . . . you shouldn't have allowed me to drink in all those bars, Gene. Even if they were serving it to me in Coke cans, you knew it was beer."

He looked sour. "Let me ax you something, Charlie . . . is this one of those recovered memory things where you go around and accuse all the people from your childhood?"

I waved him off and started eating.

"I don't know how much of your family history you were ever told. Your father was twenty or so years older than Pelikan, different daddies. Your father went to an orphanage as a baby but Pelikan grew up with his mother. I don't say *raised* by her because she was a two-dollar whore with a jones for cheap cognac. That shock you, your grandmother was a whore?"

"I've heard the story."

He continued anyway, "Your grandmother would undergo periodic religious conversions, get off the cognac, stop whoring, and start going to church, get a job flipping burgers at the Krystal, whatever. She and Pelikan would move out of their flophouse into a cold-water flat. To make a little extra cash, his mother would sell those plastic containers you put leftovers in, whatta you call it."

"Tupperware?" I hadn't heard this part of my family history.

"That's it, she's selling Tupperware and Fuller brushes, kitchen gadgets and personal care products, and her little boy, James Joseph, he throws himself into the selling venture with the same effort he put into working the streets, when he was organizing the tap dancers on Bourbon Street or running errands for bartenders . . . he's demonstrating the plastic ware to his mother's friends, hookers and strippers, showing them how to get out the air by burping a lid . . . Pelikan told me this, is how I know . . . and soon he's setting sales records and he and his old lady are doing okay. You want a smoke?"

"I quit."

"Me too," Renfrone said as he reached into his windbreaker for a deck of Marlboros. After lighting up he said, "Pelikan still sells it."

"Sells what?"

"Tupperware."

"This is the urgent news you had to tell me?"

"Pelikan's got a lot of street smarts but there are huge gaps in what he knows, gaps other people can exploit. We were talking once . . . he's never been in a house."

"What do you mean?"

"I mean he's never been in a regular house, a detached house with a yard, never stepped foot in one, and he's also never sat down at a regular table to have a regular dinner in a regular house with regular people. All he's ever known is bars and drunks and hookers."

"My heart bleeds."

Renfrone shook his head . . . and I was mystified too, why I was acting this way. You'd think, considering my predicament, I'd be meek in the presence of a Homicide detective.

"By the time James Joseph was a teenager," Mean Gene continued, "his mother had turned into a real slattern . . . Jesus, I haven't used that word since I said it once in front of my grandmother and she slapped my face." Laughing at the memory, Renfrone hacked on Marlboro smoke, cleared his throat, and spat wetly on the floor between his feet.

"Just tell me what you have to tell me, Gene, this is lasting longer than some of my engagements . . . and I still have to find a room for the night, okay?"

"Back when your uncle was a teenager, he insisted that his mother, your grandmother . . . Pelikan insisted she earn her fair share of their living expenses even if that meant he had to help her put on makeup, had to brush her hair, he even plucked her eyebrows and dressed her in clothes appropriate for a night on her back or down on her knees in the alley, whatever it took. And when she was too drunk or lazy to leave their room, Pelikan went out in the street and hustled up customers, brought them home, collected the fee, and stepped out in the hall while his mother got fucked. You see what I'm telling you, the first whore he ever pimped was his dear old ma . . . your grand-mother." Renfrone lit up another one and hacked again on smoke, then said, "Soon Pelikan had a whole crew working for him, not just regular hookers either. Performers too. James Joseph *arranges* things. Stag shows, fetishes, kinks, whips, chains, donkey, dogs, girls, boys, queers, cross-dressers . . . whatever appetite you got, Pelikan for a price will arrange to feed it."

Finishing the beer, I put the mug down with a bang and stared at Renfrone's fat face, potato nose, and cauliflower ears—a face con-structed from vegetables for a state fair exhibit. "*I know the story.* Pel-ikan was still a pimp when I lived here as a teenager."

"Pelikan isn't his real name, it didn't come from his mother or whoever his father was."

"Yeah, it came from some German biscuit company."

My dismissive attitude was pissing him off, Renfrone's eyes nar-rowing into slits like gun slots in a concrete bunker . . . which con-cerned me enough that I apologized.

He nodded but was still simmering. "I thought your uncle got his name because the brown pelican is the Louisiana state bird, but then I heard otherwise. Did you know the pelican is a symbol for Christ and—"

"Hey Mr. Peli-kan," I said, quoting from some half-remembered ditty, "does your pouch hold more than your belly-can?"

"I wouldn't make fun of his name if I were you," Renfrone warned.

"Pelikan doesn't scare me."

"You don't know how much he's changed since you saw him last."

"I give a fuck?"

"You know about the clowns, how they took care of him when he was a kid and now—"

"*I give a fuck?*"

"He killed a man once by stabbing him in the face with an ice pick."

I didn't have anything smart to say about that.

"He went to prison for it."

I knew James Joseph had done time, but he never talked about it.

"Don't get taken in by Pelikan's supposedly benevolent nature," Renfrone continued, "the way James Joseph always speaks softly these days and makes a point of putting a hand real tenderly on your shoulder or arm. He wants people to think he's Christlike, it's no accident he keeps his hair long and parted in the middle, wears that little beard, always has a sad-gentle look on his face. His followers treat him like he's Jesus Christ come back to earth, but Pelikan ain't no Lamb of God, we think he's mutilated people."

"Mutilated?"

"He's a savage motherfucker without a trace of conscience." Then after a long silence Renfrone murmured a word that I thought was *nuts*. I asked him to repeat it.

He shook his head.

"Did you call me nuts?"

"Nuns," he said quietly, looking around as if it was a secret. "Old-fashioned ones, the penguins, full habit . . . wherever Pelikan is, you see these nuns around."

"Nuns?"

Gene nodded.

"Lots of nuns in New Orleans," I pointed out. "I went to Catholic school here and—" Then out of some dark corner slithered memories of the sexual fantasies I had about nuns . . . when I made the mistake of telling Pelikan about those fantasies, he arranged for a young woman to visit me, she was dressed in full habit and we spent all of one afternoon and evening together, the most powerfully erotic and guilt-ridden hours of my life. At the time I didn't know nun-humping was commonplace as a sexual fantasy, I thought I alone was perverted enough to lust for the brides of Christ . . . convincing myself I would go to hell for what I'd done with that nun-dressed hooker.

"Nuns are keeping an eye on Pelikan," Renfrone was saying. "Watching over him. My father fought the Nazis in Sicily, Charlie, and now Pelikan has these nuns over here."

"What're you talking about?"

He acted as if he wanted to tell me but couldn't.

I stood and he grabbed my arm. "You ever done time?"

"What?"

"If you've been through the system, your prints are on file."

I didn't know what to say, I could feel a confession burbling its way up my throat.

Renfrone grasped my right hand and shook it, smiling, telling me, "Welcome home, Chaz . . . good to have you back."

5

MIDNIGHT, PELIKAN'S TIME

I walked across the plaza between St. Louis Cathedral and Jackson Square where a pod of retro hippies had gathered in the dark, adding their noise to the New Orleans night, a hot and wet burden. The calliope from the river was already giving me a headache. Why had I acted that way with Renfrone, what's wrong with me? I should get a lawyer and return to being what I was yesterday, a *reasonable* man from Connecticut, instead of whatever I've become here in the Quarter, another mumbling, stumbling, crazed drunk.

With the big iron gates to Jackson Square locked for the night, the New Age hippies collected so thick on the plaza I had to wade through. I'm not one of those people who regret missing out on hippies the first time around and I was in no mood to hear it again, Michael still rowing that goddamn boat ashore. *Get outta my way* . . . you affected, pious, hairy, grinning assholes . . . which is the mood I'm in, murderous.

On the periphery of the hippies was a street person sitting on a bench and I did a double take because this guy looks like God, how white Western art would have you think God looks. He's in his sixties, and he has long hair and a big beard that're both yellow like gold . . . and his face is open and serene and wise. Or maybe it's Santa Claus he looks like. Or Buddha. I start toward him but his big blue eyes catch me and he shakes his head, warning me off.

I head for St. Philip Street but instead of turning right toward

Mother's, I made a left and walked to Bourbon Street where I stopped in Lafitte's Blacksmith Shop for a drink to settle my buzzing head. One of the oldest bars in the Quarter, Lafitte's is kept dim and quiet, no bright lights or cool air-conditioning to take the edge off my dark, hot mood. The piano player had gone home for the night and there weren't any tourists in evidence as I found a shadowy corner table and ordered a gin and tonic and then another one, then a gin martini, and then two more of those . . . my lips going numb by the time I gave a twenty to the kid who was sweeping up, paying him to run five blocks where the A&P is open all night to get me a couple packs of Camels—almost three years now since I quit. By the time he got back I'd switched to rum and Cokes, trying to numb other parts of me, the memory of Amanda, for example.

I was a twenty-one-year-old student and she was twenty-eight, teaching an English lit course at college, the most sophisticated, beautiful, exotic woman I'd ever met. We went out . . . drank beers, talked poetry, never slept together. I thought or she led me to believe that she'd been sexually wounded at some point in her life, raped or abused, and had chosen to be celibate. I guess what enraged me about the Mardi Gras trip was my sense, right or wrong, of being played for a fool . . . that after knowing Pelikan just a day or two, Amanda would give him what she'd been denying me the entire time I knew her. It's a male thing.

And now here I am getting stupid all over again, leaving Lafitte's at two in the morning and walking St. Philip back toward the river. I stopped in for more fuel at the Sequel, another funky local bar, surprised to see two guys who were regulars here the last time I was in this place. One of them is called Tender Buttons because he has all sizes and colors of buttons sewn everywhere on his clothing . . . the other, Reverse, got his name by walking backward everywhere he goes, his right arm held diagonally across his chest and his head turned hard around on his thin neck so he can see where he's going, walking backward and reversing himself onto a bar stool, which I guess is the only place where he ever turned around and faced front.

I bought them both a drink but they didn't remember me.

Two senior citizens down from me are very drunk and I overhear the man urging the woman to tell the female bartender what a great lover he is, but the old, drunk, ugly woman is shaking her head and saying in a slow slur that she knows better than to advertise her man.

After a couple shots of Maker's Mark in memorial to Three Jacks, I left the Sequel to walk these dark streets, as dimly lit as they were a hundred years ago, no illumination from shuttered houses even though front walls began right here on broken sidewalks, residents turning their focus toward interior courtyards I couldn't see. Even drunk I noticed how these famous Baroque wrought iron balconies, Castilian ironwork from two hundred years ago, were braced against the effects of age and rot and rain, the Quarter an old prostitute who paints over what is pale and shores up what is sagging, looking best when light is lowest and you've been drinking . . . I wonder whatever became of Amanda, she'd be forty years old by now.

The only others out this time of night were vampires, Anne Rice fans, terribly thin and pale faced, fingernails and lips painted black, dressed in black, looking like tall, starved children, their mesmerizing eyes staring at me with a sobering frankness. I said things to them, rude and aggressive, but here's the kicker: even though they were slightly built and sickly while I was strong and drunk and felonious, they never looked at me with fear in their dark eyes.

I walked to the river and peed off the rocks into water too black at this hour to look muddy, barges playing a requiem on their horns . . . and here by the chemical Mississippi I sensed I was sobering up, alcohol deserting me just when I most needed its reckless abandon.

As I climbed back off the rocks a pair of hopeful muggers came over to sniff at my potential, asking me the time and standing close to check my eyes for vulnerability, seeing something so desperate they decided I wasn't worth the game.

Though there was no moon, I walked the Moon Walk, crossed tracks on which no trains ran, and entered the French Market from its ass end, where maybe I saw a couple nuns in full black habit lurking around the loading docks, but more probably it was my overheated imagination trying to distract me as I finally came to Mother's and hesitated one last time before opening those shuttered doors.

6

ENTERING MOTHER'S

Located downriver from the French Market in a section of the Quarter where out-of-towners don't go of a night because the warehouses and loading docks look sinister to the tourist eye, Mother's is a long, narrow, dim bar rumored never to have closed for even one hour since the end of the Second World War . . . Mother's, where the French Quarter's artists and artistes hang out, where if you go there for a drink at the end of the working day you'll be elbow to ass with clowns and mimes, watercolorists and oil painters, hookers and transvestites, strippers and Elvis impersonators, poets and fortune-tellers, and where if you stay late enough to watch who gets drunk you might see a man made up to look like a cat eating out of a bowl without using his hands, and in the corner gazing into the smoked mirrors that line one wall is Marilyn Monroe crying into her/his beer over the Kennedys.

Mother's was headquarters for James Joseph Pelikan, where he worked and hung out and held court.

When I was a shy thirteen-year-old, he brought me to this bar and introduced me around and I thought it was the single most fascinating location on earth . . . just as I thought my uncle was the most wildly romantic of men, encyclopedic in his knowledge of the night, a performer who used his hands and voice to sculpt a story. I always considered him a wise, older man because he was slow and serious in his manner, a man many times wounded and recovered, but in fact

Pelikan probably wasn't even thirty yet when I came to New Orleans and lived three years with my father on St. Peter Street.

Back then, Dad told me that someday James Joseph would be a millionaire and own half the French Quarter, he was already on his way to acquiring a piece of one of the most profitable bars on Bourbon Street. Because he'd grown up on the streets and had been working in bars since he was a boy—sweeping out, stocking coolers, washing sidewalks, running errands—James Joseph probably knew more about drinking establishments than men twice his age. At twenty-one he was offered a crack at managing a biker bar at the edge of the Quarter, a job that over the years got him shot and knifed and beat with sticks in his effort to expand the bar's clientele from motorcycle gangs to college students. He became a legend in the process, his notoriety based on how he could sweet-talk a raging, psychotic drunk into settling down and having a cup of coffee at the bar, disarm a man of his knife or pistol before the guy was even aware he'd been touched, inspire fanatical loyalty in those who worked for him. James Joseph epitomized an earlier era's celebration of unhurried, unruffled Rat Pack cool—narrow lapeled, lean and slouchy, Continental. My father told me that one Halloween the bar filled with Hell's Angels and LSU football players and after a few skirmishes inside, the two groups faced off in the courtyard, where there was an air of such mayhem that a group of off-duty cops decided it was time to go, maybe they'd return just behind the riot squad but there was no way they were going to step between those two collective pools of testosterone . . . that task was left to James Joseph, who went quietly among the football players and motorcycle gangsters, talking and listening, offering a stick of gum to one, a cigarette to another, a cigar, a mint, not passing the stuff out like trinkets, but making the offers casually to anyone he happened to be talking with as he opened a pack of gum or tapped out a cigarette. "As soon as they accepted something from him," my father explained, "a bond was created . . . that's why peace pipes are passed around, why diplomats sit down together at banquets." Chains and brass knuckles were put away, fists unclenched, the mob dispersed. They weren't suddenly all friends, but at least they took their fight elsewhere.

Because of his talent for management and peacekeeping, James Joseph was approached by the absentee owners of that bar on Bourbon Street: if he could make their bar profitable and if they could have a few years of collecting those profits to recoup their investments, they would then sell the bar to James Joseph on an installment plan. He could have it paid off in five years and be on his way to respectability, property ownership, could buy a house, end up at a destination completely different from the one toward which the trajectory of his early life had aimed him.

After I left New Orleans to return to Connecticut, Pelikan's course changed again. The bar's owners, deciding that he had made the place too profitable for them to sell to him as originally promised, sold out to another group of investors, who brought in their own management team. I'd heard that this betrayal was engineered by one of Pelikan's former friends, with whom he'd had a falling out. After that, his spirit coarsened, and he fed off the pain of others, having a feast with me and Amanda.

In the hospice, my father said James Joseph had changed again, and Detective Renfrone had warned me too. Who was Pelikan now?

All this was on my mind as I opened Mother's doors.

You enter through one of three thin, tall shutters on hinges, the doorways so narrow that if you are broad shouldered you have to turn a little coming in . . . then walk up two wide, worn wooden steps. The long, polished cypress bar is on your right. On your left along an entire wall that's covered floor to ceiling with smoked mirrors is a shelf bar, a foot deep and high enough to stand at and rest your elbows on. The space between the regular bar and the stand-up bar is less than six feet, packed with people.

I was glad for that crowd this particular night, maybe I could slip in and see Pelikan before he saw me . . . but as soon as I walked up those two wooden steps, the nearby patrons stopped their conversations and turned to look at me. Was I that obviously drunk? Something was said at the back of the bar, followed by the crowd's shuffling effort to part like the Red Sea before Moses . . . and through that ragged gap I could see at the far end of the bar, surrounded by clowns, my uncle James Joseph Pelikan.

He looked like Christ or a Celtic warrior with a beard and long blond-brown hair parted in the middle and hanging around his face, eyes of a predator, hawk nosed, lanky, rangy, long arms and big hands, the bearing of royalty, of a man accustomed to being paid homage, deferred to, listened to . . . I understand now what Detective Renfrone meant about Pelikan trying to pass himself off as the Lamb of God . . . James Joseph looking down the length of the bar and, seeing me, he smiled.

He seemed damaged, his eyes with a million miles behind them . . . but one thing hadn't changed, that smile open and warm like a mother's arms. He looked at me as if my presence here had made him profoundly happy.

Now, in *his* presence, I felt a surge toward Pelikan . . . all was forgiven, I wanted to embrace him.

But a clown got in the way.

A fat clown. Oblivious of this impending hallowed uncle-nephew reunion, he stepped in front of me and said something about buying him a drink . . . I think his actual words were, "Hey, buddy, buy a clown a beer?" He must think I'm a tourist. I tried to maneuver around, eager to see Pelikan's holy smile once more, but the clown was persistent, in my face with his blue fright wig and red nose, the little derby hat with a fake daisy growing out of it, white pancake makeup, big floppy shoes. "Come on, pal, buy a clown a beer, why don't you?"

Me: "Fuck off."

Clown: "What did you say?"

Me: "You heard what I said, you fucking clown, get away from me."

Clown: "Hey, buddy, you prejudiced against clowns?"

Me: "That's right, I'm a clown bigot."

When he stuck his tongue out, I snapped, releasing on him the fury of the day, the booze and fear, witnessing a murder, convinced I was about to be shot by that naked woman, thinking I was about to be arrested by Renfrone, the trauma of being back in this city. I snatched off his big red nose and threw it onto the floor in the beer and butts and trash, telling him, "You are a fucking clown."

Like he's ashamed of his real nose, he covers it with both hands.

"Take off that stupid hat too," I said, grabbing the little derby that apparently was connected to his fright wig because they came off together.

Now he's got one hand on his exposed nose, one hand on top of his head, and I'm throwing wig and derby to the floor, stomping on them and hollering, "You fucking clown!" The epithet strikes me as funny and I start laughing like an idiot as I scream, "Back off, you *fucking* clown!" My ass-braying laugh embarrasses me but it's the night for self-hatred and I command the clown again, "Back off, bozo, before I bust your ass!"

He was *trying* to get out of my way but I was standing on his floppy shoes, hollering into his ridiculous face, "And take off those stupid clown shoes . . . you *fucking* clown!" Then with a drunk-lucky punch to the chin I knocked him on his polka-dotted ass.

Somebody grabbed me around the waist as I was trying to take another swing, then someone else had my arms and I was being dragged backward, screaming to James Joseph, "Hey *Peli-kan,* does your Tupperware hold more than your *belly-can,* you fucking hump . . . this is where you deserve to be, to end up and die, in this filthy dive surrounded by these fucking clowns—" Further sacrilege halted when I got punched in the stomach.

Pulled by many arms, shoes bumping on two steps, I was turned sideways to fit out the narrow center door and eighty-sixed into the street.

Of course, once I got to my feet, I immediately attempted reentry, a drunk's prerogative, but a fat, scowling, white-caped Elvis stood in one of the flanking doors, a mime in the other, and in that center doorway a massive Judy Garland with beard, prison teardrops tattooed in the corner of one eye, daring me to try getting past. All around these principals, clown faces were peeking out at me. I told 'em all go fuck yourselves, and as I staggered on down the street, Fat Elvis hollers, "The asshole has left the building," and like Disney mice, all the clowns laugh shrilly at my expense.

7

A HATRED OF CLOWNS

When I lived here as a kid, female bartenders and I allied our-selves against clowns. James Joseph held them as precious be-cause they'd taken care of him while he was growing up in the French Quarter, giving him nickels and dimes, letting him help out with their acts, but those female bartenders and I conspired against Pelikan's clown charity whenever we could.

They adopted me, those bartenders. I was a shy boy who blushed too readily and tended to look at the floor when spoken to, embar-rassed by my own laugh. At one time or the other I was in love with each of them, tough women who thought nothing of leaping one-handed over a bar and beating the living shit out of some trouble-maker. You didn't want one of these women angry with you, she could make your life so hellish it was easier to leave the bar and never come back until she got a job somewhere else. But if these hard-drinking, heavy-smoking, mood-swinging women liked you, you were golden. And for three critical years, I was golden . . . they thought I was cute when I was thirteen, and by the time I reached fifteen and had been pestering them for two years, a few took pity on me.

I remember flirting with one of them and having no idea I was getting through to her with any of my bullshit, holding her hand and touching her cheek and saying that by looking through her eyes I could see into her soul . . . I was fifteen and horny and shameless. When her shift ended she said she was taking me home with her. *You are?* I asked incredulously. *Oh Charlie,* she said with a resigned sigh, *you got me all greasy.* It was, and remains, the most erotically filthy thing any woman ever said to me.

Another of these bartenders, Lauren, had a maniacal laugh even weirder than mine and gave me my first oyster-flavored kiss . . . I didn't know it was a New Orleans tradition, the subject of an old song, I thought she had made it up just for me. We were together one slow afternoon, Lauren and I, eating oysters on the half shell at a bar, when she asked if I'd ever had an oyster-flavored kiss. I said no. She smiled and slithered an oyster into her mouth, then grabbed the back of my head and planted a deep, wet, salty, fishy tongue-and-oyster kiss that confused me about what was oyster, what was Lauren . . . a kiss I can still taste.

These earliest of my loves were strange mixtures of tough and vulnerable, feuding with one another, usually over men, but also bailing one another out of trouble; they were addicts to drugs and love myths; they adored tequila and puppies and longhaired skinny guys with tattoos . . . and almost to a woman, they hated clowns coming in their bars and mooching drinks and playing with string. I became their anticlown hero, their knight against buffoons. One afternoon when a particularly obnoxious clown came into the bar Lauren was working and kept trying to chat her up, I went over and told him he was sitting in a no clown zone and he'd have to leave. I got away with it even even though I was only fifteen because the clown could see I was ready to start banging on him. (I think it was the next day, in fact, when Lauren laid that oyster-flavored kiss on me.)

The female bartenders and I didn't particularly like mimes, either, not even relatively harmless, immobile ones who painted their skin white and draped sheets over their shoulders and tried to pass themselves off as Roman statuary. But whether a living statue or trapped in a glass box or blown by wind you and I can't feel, at least a mime is someone you can walk by without being molested . . . not so the clown. He'll get right in your face, forcing you to deal with him, fresh with his hands and standing too close breathing peanut breath on you as he smiles yellow teeth against greasy whiteface, mouth painted in a monstrous red grin.

Lauren told me many of them are rampant sexual perverts. She knew a woman who had a thing for clowns and dated several of them until their perversions finally just weren't funny anymore. This woman confessed to Lauren that clowns liked to have sex while dressed in their clown suits (the woman didn't mind this part, she found their outfits charming), but then when the woman was on the edge of climax, the clown would squeeze his ooga horn and ruin everything. Also, her clown boyfriends were always trying to talk her into a threesome with another clown . . . or a foursome or a fivesome, whatever she would agree to and the bed would hold. Lauren thought this kink for multiple partners was related to the way clowns are forever crowding into tiny cars . . . for some reason they like squishing themselves in small spaces with others of their kind. Lauren's friend said she slept with one clown who kept trying to get household pets in bed with them, it was a circus.

Drunk, stumbling, and angry on Governor Nicholls Street, I suddenly realize I'm heading toward a place that terrorized me when I was a kid, Lalaurie House, and even now, at thirty-three, I can't bring myself to walk past it again.

Turning back toward Jackson Square, past all-night bars on Decatur Street, the un-air-conditioned ones with their doors open to the sidewalk, I pass two teenage girls holding reptiles, one with a snake draped over her shoulders and the other with an iguana on her head. A derelict black man is leaning against a building weeping loudly, saying he's scared to death about getting mugged, though I wonder what he possesses worth the taking. Two gay guys, hand in hand, stop to talk to him and I hear them reassure the old guy, "Don't worry, nothing but queers around here, and we won't hurt you."

Entering a bar with a crudely lettered sign offering a room for the night, I manage to make myself understood, manage to rent that room in spite of my red, stricken eyes and freakish manner—the bartender asking simply, "You're not going to throw up, are you?" I assured him I wasn't, just needed a place to sleep it off.

Which turned out to be on the third floor, the topmost, hottest floor, no air-conditioning. The room must've been an office once—the

door to the hallway had frosted glass in its upper half. Opposite that
door is a window I can't get open. Suffocating. The furniture is army
surplus, gray metal bed, gray metal cabinet. The light by the bed
didn't work and the bathroom was down on the second floor and my
clean clothes and shaving kit were in a suitcase at the train station, so
I fell in bed fully clothed and shod, the room taking this as its signal
to start spinning like a carnival ride. I sat up, oh shit, not going to
make it to the second floor, grabbing a gray metal trash can and up-
chucking into it in spite of my promise to the innkeeper-bartender. I
can't remember the last time I threw up from drink . . . yes I can, it
was my last time in this damned and evil city, when I got drunk after
the humiliation with Pelikan and Amanda.

Back in bed, I started thinking about the Lalaurie House and
wondering why Pelikan took me there, was it just a prank to scare his
nephew or something more sinister.

During the early 1830s a doctor and his wife lived in that house,
imprisoning slaves in an attic torture chamber where men and women
were experimented upon, mutilated, chained to the walls, tied to operating tables, kept in dog cages. When the attic was opened by firemen in 1834, they found one slave woman strapped to a wooden
table, all her limbs severed, left to exist as a torso with a head whimpering soft epics to pain. Another woman had all her long bones broken and reset at unnatural angles, formed into a creature forced to
scurry belly-down across the floor like a crab. A man's body hung
from one wall, the victim of a bizarre attempt to change his sex by
cutting off his male parts and then "constructing" female organs with
incisions made between his legs, by grafting on breasts that had been
removed from another victim. Other Lalaurie slaves had their faces
mutilated to make them into living monsters.

When I was thirteen, Pelikan arranged to get us in the Lalaurie
attic, above the luxury apartments that then occupied the building,
and there we stayed the night, my uncle telling me the tales of horror
that occured here . . . I'd never before or since been so scared, hearing
muffled screams (though they might've been from someone's television) and pissing my pants in little terrified spurts, but steadfastly refusing to ask Pelikan to take me home to my father: I wanted to be

brave for James Joseph, who frightened me even as I revered him.

Pelikan still scared me, which I suppose was why I overreacted in Mother's . . . *none of this would've happened if I'd stayed away from New Orleans.* Tell this to your children: don't go to New Orleans.

From a deep sleep I am awakened at some indecent hour . . . my shoes were off and there is a figure sitting on the bed, massaging my bare feet.

When I said, "Mom," the apparition growled a low, rumbling thunder.

And when I tried to get away, it grabbed more tightly to one foot and told me to relax because "This isn't the part that's going to hurt."

8

PELIKAN'S FOOT CARE

"You gotta take better care of your trotters, nephew."

I tell him to get his hands off me.

"Shhh."

I kicked my feet, but Pelikan held on, bending the second toe on my right foot until I hollered for him to stop.

He laughed. "If he hollers, make him pay . . ."

"You pervert, leave my feet alone." I felt thirteen again, teased and tormented by my uncle.

James Joseph shook his head, causing his long hair to hula-dance around his face, he had perfectly straight brown-blond hillbilly hair, Jerry Lee Lewis hair, and he wore it now like a shaggy crown. In the dimness I couldn't see if he was angry with me for insulting him in Mother's or pleased with himself that he'd managed to find me in this room and break in, awakening me by massaging my feet.

"Get a haircut," I told him. "You look like a hippie."

"Tone control," he softly cautioned.

Still trying to come fully awake, the first thing on my mind was Three Jacks . . . I wondered how I should tell Pelikan.

"I might not always get a chance to shower each and every day," he began lecturing. "And maybe I don't floss regularly and occasionally forget the daily vitamins, neglect my gums . . . but I always take care of my feet, they're the foundation—"

With his attention diverted to the podiatry lecture, I snatched my subject feet away and quickly shoved them under the sheet.

Pelikan laughed, hands resting on his legs, serene as Buddha. "I always wear two pairs of socks . . . a pair of white cotton socks goes on first, next to my skin, then over them I put on a thicker pair of dark socks, that way you get good sweat absorption and cushioning too."

"I'll keep that in mind."

"Massage your feet every night. And at the end of a long day be sure to put your legs up, your feet above your heart. After washing your feet, which you should also do every night, make sure you dry them thoroughly, especially between the toes. Always cut the nails straight across."

"Yeah—"

"Your feet contain twenty-five percent of all the bones in your body, along with thirty-eight muscles, two hundred and fourteen ligaments, and six arches . . . your feet determine how you stand, how you walk, how your back functions . . . amazing that people are so negligent about their feet, I've always taken very good care of mine and in return they've always served me well. When I massage my feet of an evening, I work in some mild lotion. You should feel my feet, the skin's as soft—"

"No thanks, I don't want to feel your feet . . . get off the bed, how'd you find me here anyway?"

"This is the French Quarter, Charlie . . . trying to hide here is like trying to hide from me in my pocket."

"I wasn't trying to hide—"

"I have perfectly formed feet."

"Good for you."

"They match, it's rare that a person's feet are exactly the same size. You should see my arches, how beautifully they vault, the almost perfect roundness of my heels—"

"I'll take your word for it."

"Never skimp when it comes to shoes."

"Hey, Pelikan, did you hear me—"

"You used to call me James Joseph."

"I used to like you."

He paused a moment, then said, "Sometimes I put a bunch of different items on the floor—a pencil, a marble, a cigarette lighter, a golf ball—then I practice picking them up with my toes, it's great exercise for the feet."

When I started to swing out of bed, he hit me flat-handed in the chest, knocking me back against the metal headboard. He must be close to fifty now, tough and sinewy. I was probably in better shape but he was a trickier infighter who knew where to squeeze and gouge to disable a man. Would it come to that?

But this time Pelikan didn't touch me as I got out of bed and went to sit on the windowsill. Patting my shirt pockets for cigarettes, I asked him if he knew my father, his brother, was dying.

"Nothing's more important to me than family."

"Yeah . . . then how come you stabbed me in the back?"

"I beg your pardon?"

"You know what I'm talking about—*Amanda?*"

He waited a moment before quietly saying, "That was twelve years ago."

"And *that* is not an answer."

"She wasn't family, Charlie . . . she was pussy."

I came off the windowsill and charged him, but Pelikan simply lay back on the bed and brought his foot up, letting me run hard into his heavy shoe.

The breath knocked out of me, I leaned forward and put both hands on my knees.

"I added your father to my list tonight," he said.

As soon as I could breathe, I cursed.

"Do you understand what I'm saying?" Pelikan asked as he reached over and turned on the lamp.

In the light I saw one of his jailhouse tattoos, the one on the inside of his right forearm, the one that warned in blue-black ink like a terrible bruise: *I will fuck anything.* Pelikan's forearms, from his elbows down through his fingers, were covered in tattoos, not pretty college boy ones, but Christ on the Cross and Mother Mary in a shawl and death threats and rising suns, the thick, dark, blue-black tattoos of passionate amateur jailhouse needle artists.

"You touch me again," I warned, "and I'll kill you."

"Noted," Pelikan said, patting the sheet, urging me to come sit with him on the bed.

I muttered additional curses.

"I added your father to my list," he said again.

Then I remembered my father telling me that Pelikan kept a list of all the people he'd known who had died, a list he updated and referred to frequently. "He's dead?"

"Yes . . . your sister Nancy got ahold of me at Mother's, I don't think I've ever talked to Nancy before. By the by, Charlie . . . how *is* your momma and them sisters?"

I knew that asking after someone's mother was a New Orleans tradition but this concern for *my* mother and sisters seemed more like a conspiracy. I asked Pelikan when my fathers's funeral was being held.

"You won't be able to attend, I'm sorry."

"Don't tell me what I'm able to do or not do . . . Dad wanted us both there at his funeral."

"Tell me how it was growing up with three older sisters to take care of you."

I remembered then how maddening Pelikan could be, refusing to give straight answers.

"Come on, Charlie Chan . . ."

That's what one of my sisters used to call me . . . how'd Pelikan know?

"Tell me about your childhood, how you grew up spoiled rotten and pampered by your mother and three older sisters . . . how the girls would run home from school when you were a toddler because the first girl in the house, the first one to find you, would get to hold you on her lap and kiss you and pet you like you were a puppy dog, then she'd hand you off to another sister, who would do the same, then give you to the third sister . . . how you got that treatment every day of your life when you were a little boy before you started school, treated like a pasha . . . princeling, potentate."

I went over and sat on the windowsill. "When did he die?"

"You grew up in a big old two-story wooden house with a wide front porch, a swing hanging on chains, lots of windows, even windows in the attic, the house painted white with green trim, vines growing up one side, a big yard with another swing under the old oak tree."

"Maple."

He smiled, making his angular face beatific. "How do I know these things? Your father told me. How did he know? He kept tabs. Your mother might have banned him from the family, but your sisters stayed in touch with their daddy."

"She banned him from the family because he gambled away every dollar she ever made, she caught him more than once with another woman—"

"Many sins were committed . . . but you still came here to live with him."

"The biggest mistake of my life."

"Let's talk about your perfect childhood."

I remembered what Detective Renfrone told me about Pelikan having never been in a regular house, never having eaten dinner with a regular family . . . my suburban Connecticut childhood, fatherless though it was, must seem to Pelikan like something from television, happy and perfect and unreal.

"How come you never asked about my childhood when I was living here?"

"Other items on the agenda back then, your education."

"You ruined my life."

"How?" he wanted to know. "By introducing you to sex?"

"When I went back to high school in Connecticut, guys were bragging about getting a finger inside the waistband of some girl's panties, touching her bra . . . and here I was coming from the French Quarter where any morning I wanted I could get a blow job at breakfast, the most beautiful women in the world . . . how do you think that made me feel—"

"Happy?"

"Made me a cynic about every place that wasn't the French Quarter, about all my friends . . . no one was as worldly as I was, no place was as cool as the French Quarter . . . I went around the rest of my life being disappointed that nothing lived up—"

"Should've stayed here."

"I couldn't have survived, spiritually or physically . . . this is the only city in the world where when people talk about going on a health kick they mean they're going to switch to Bloody Marys and start eating the celery. It's not funny. If I had stayed here I would've been dead by now."

"Then I would've added you to my list and kept you always in my thoughts. Did you build a tree house in that big old maple?"

"Steinbeck."

"What?"

"*Of Mice and Men,*" I told Pelikan. "And you're Lenny . . . except instead of obsessing on living off the fat of the land and taking care of the frigging rabbits, you're obsessing on this bizarre sitcom image you have of my 'perfect' childhood . . . too strange, too effing strange . . . you got a cigarette?"

He slowly shook his head no. "Steinbeck?"

I remembered that Pelikan had never attended school, remembered what Renfrone said about the gaps in Pelikan's knowledge. "You might be a warrior king of the French Quarter," I told him, "but you're an ignorant man."

"That I am," he said, looking at me softly, as a woman might. "Tonight you insulted me in front of my friends and followers."

"Followers?" I laughed.

Pelikan stood.

"What're you going to do, take an ice pick to my face?"

He seemed surprised to hear this.

"Oh yeah, I heard about you and ice picks . . . that's what got you sent to prison, isn't it?"

"I'd never use an ice pick on you, you're my nephew, we're family."

"*And?*"

When he came to the window, I walked to the bed.

"You don't even want me near you?" he asked in a hurt voice.

"I don't trust you . . . don't particularly like you either. And we both know why."

He ignored my reference to Amanda and asked, "Do we both know why you came all the way here to see me?"

"I've been trying to tell you. My father wants us at his funeral."

"You've come because of the Edessa. We have almost all the

equipment in place, just waiting for the right storm." He smiled and again used both hands to brush back his hair. "This is your dad's legacy to you, Charlie . . . his *share*. I know you miss him."

Miss him? Then why was I waiting to feel loss, grief, sadness, *something*.

Pelikan came over and spoke softly but with a strange, robotic enthusiasm: "Say good-bye to tired feet because from now on every step you take will be on a cushion of pure TheraGel."

"*What?*"

He handed me a pair of thick plastic insoles filled with some kind of blue gel.

"Molds to your feet, massages as you walk," Pelikan said as if quoting from a sales sheet. "How much would you pay to walk all day on a pure TheraGel pillow that cushions every step . . . ten dollars, fifteen . . . is twenty-five dollars too much to pay for rejuvenated feet?"

Was I supposed to answer him?

"How about four ninety-five, that's right . . . I'm going to *give* you these inserts for the ridiculously low price of only four ninety-five."

"You're not going to give me shit."

But Pelikan was already sticking the inserts into my shoes and then, pointing at the floor, he asked, "What's this?"

I looked down and saw three cards he'd apparently just dropped there, jack of clubs, jack of hearts, jack of spades.

"What would you call this?" he asked again.

"A cheap trick . . . you're famous for them."

"What?"

"I get it."

"Get what?" he asked.

"Three jacks on the floor . . . so you know what happened, huh?"

"You were set up, I know that much."

"Who . . . who set me up?"

"A man named Gallier."

"I don't know that name."

"Gallier intends to use you as a bargaining chip."

"What're you talking about?"

"Powerful forces is what I'm talking about."

"Powerful forces as in . . ."

"Good and evil."

"I forgot about all your mumbo jumbo." I had a splitting hang-over headache and a foul-tasting mouth and I wanted to go back to sleep. "Leave me alone, we'll talk in the morning."

"We're going to a party, put your shoes on." Then he lapsed again into that salesman voice. "See if those cushioned insoles don't revo-lutionize the way—"

"I'm not going anywhere with you."

"Sure you are, I've arranged a happening tonight . . . a woman will fill your champagne glass without using her hands . . . won't use a bottle either."

"Little bubbles give me a headache."

He held out his hand as if he wanted to shake . . . so I extended mine too, thinking he was going to leave.

But like a striking snake he grabbed my wrist and threw a power-ful arm across my neck, then took the third finger of my right hand and bent it until something cracked, the pain quick and hard.

"You son of a bitch," I said.

Pelikan released me and stepped back.

I held my hand and tried not to cry like a child . . . to cry from the frustration of being manhandled by him, from the pain of that finger he'd bent back.

He was pouring gold tequila into a glass . . . I didn't know where the bottle or glass came from. "Here," he said.

"Go fuck yourself."

"It'll make your finger stop hurting."

I downed the tequila, which left a strange taste in the back of my mouth, similar to the way a multivitamin tastes, dusty or wheaty.

Now he was putting my shoes on me, insisting we had to hurry or we'd miss the opening act. I wanted to kick free but couldn't seem to make my legs work.

When he finished tying the shoelaces he said, "Stand up and take a few steps, tell me if those inserts don't make you feel like you're walking on cushions."

Pelikan had to help me stand. I was still holding my right hand close to my chest, that third finger sticking out unnaturally. I wondered if he'd broken something.

"Go on, take a few steps."

I couldn't move.

"Come on," he urged.

"I can't walk."

"Yes you can, princeling, you just have to concentrate."

And he was right, by focusing my mind on each aspect of moving one leg forward, then the other, I managed to walk like Frankenstein newly awakened.

He asked me how they feel.

"What?"

"Those miracle inserts."

"What was in that tequila?"

"Four ninety-five," he said.

"What?"

"For the insoles."

I felt distant from reality, as if I could see it from here but was unable to participate.

He held out his hand and wiggled his fingers. "Come on now, you old wascally wabbit, pay up."

9

BIT O' THE BUBBLY

I dreamt I was Sasquatch. But instead of fearing me, men pointed their fingers and laughed. Am I awake now? I must be because my head wouldn't hurt like this in a dream, my mouth wouldn't taste so dirty. I'm in bed but I don't know where, disoriented and confused and not wanting to face this daylight reality . . . like a creature pulled from the depths I beg, *Throw me back.*

But sleep will have nothing more to do with me and, turning in bed, I make a ripe discovery: someone's in here with me. Carefully lifting the white, starched sheet, I see that it is a woman and she's naked. Is this Maria, who killed Three Jacks . . . how did she get out of that swimming pool, how did we end up in bed together? Is she alive?

"Hey." I nudge her.

Her body is warm.

"Hey, baby," I said to the woman whose face I couldn't see but I don't think it's Maria because this woman has cotton candy blond hair like Connie Stevens, if you remember her.

She grumbled sleepily.

"Hey *doll*," I said more sharply.

"Diminishing me," she murmured without opening her eyes or turning over to face me even after I took the sheet completely away from her naked form . . . the woman on her belly with a pillow under her hips, offering up a sweet ass like candy on a cushion and I wondered: Did I have sex with her last night?

"Calling me 'baby' and 'doll,' " she said sleepily. "Those are words men use to categorize and diminish a woman."

I looked at her blankly.

She raised up on her elbows. "Do you understand?" she wanted to know.

"Did we fuck last night?"

She looked startled, then laughed in a manner you could call rueful and collapsed facedown again without removing the pillow from under her hips or trying to cover up with the sheet . . . while I remained distracted by the possibilities, what might have happened last night. I remembered that unaired room where Pelikan bent my finger, then gave me tequila. I looked down at my right hand, the third finger swollen, colored black and blue and yellow.

"Hey . . . adult woman, what happened last night?"

"Which part?"

"How'd we end up in bed, for example?"

She raised her head to look at me, to see if I was serious. "You don't remember carrying me up the staircase?"

I didn't.

"Well, at least to the landing," she continued. "That's where you collapsed. You wanted to sleep there. When I tried to get you back on your feet you said we were climbing the Himalayas in search of someone called Yeti and the landing was our base camp and we needed rest before attempting the final ascent."

"I said all that?"

She assured me I did. "How much do you remember from *before* that . . . from the party, for example?"

"The party?"

The woman laughed again, intrigued enough by my memory loss that she came around to a sitting position, her back against the bedstead, exposing breasts full and low and sticking out to the sides like the nipples are checking both ways for oncoming traffic. "You don't remember drinking the champagne?"

I shook my head.

"You put on quite the performance."

I asked her to explain and she spoke patiently, "We're still in the same house we were last night, on Esplanade . . . we're upstairs in one of the bedrooms."

I looked around and realized that although the bed was freshly made, the room was trashy, the plasterwork on the fifteen-foot ceilings having crumbled in spots, the plaster left to accumulate on the floor, which was wide-plank pine and filthy. The drawn shades were yellow and torn. A big square room, twenty or thirty feet to a side, it might've been elegant at one point but obviously hasn't been cared for in years, decades.

"Abandoned house," I said, speaking more to myself than to the woman as I try to knit together remnants from ragged memory. "Big old mansion, I remember Pelikan bringing me here and at the time I wondered why . . . because obviously no one lives in this house, but then we went inside and there's something going on—"

"A party," she says.

"Right, a party."

"You remember?"

"Not really."

She said it was a James Joseph specialty. "He arranges these things . . . pays off the cops to look the other way for one night, brings in temporary power and air-conditioning, hires the entertainers, finds the clients and collects the fees—"

"You a hooker?"

She gave me a withering look. "I'm one of the entertainers . . . but I'm not the champagne girl, honey . . . she's the one you fell in love with, you remember that?"

I admitted I didn't.

"Bubbles has a very talented twat . . . you sure you don't remember this?"

"I'm positive."

"Big table set up in the dining room downstairs, all the clients around it, Bubbles comes in and does a little strip, but that's just the beginning of her act. She's on the table, see, and she struts her stuff to an opened champagne bottle and she squats over the bottle until the neck is fully inserted into her talented little twat, then like the gymnast she once was, Bubbles sits and rolls onto her back, up on her shoulders, and the bottle, which is still inserted, upends and drains into Bubbles, who does all this without using her hands."

"I can't believe I don't remember—"

"Oh, it gets better . . . or from your point of view I guess I should say it gets worse."

I flinched.

"The bottle comes out of Bubbles but the champagne stays in, not even a drop spills as she does a little dance and finally goes to a client's glass, squats over it, and fills the glass to the rim, again without spilling a drop . . . Bubbles can turn that twat on and off like a spigot."

"So you're going to tell me I drank champagne she peed into my glass?"

"Drinking from a glass that Bubbles filled is what *some* clients do, they consider it a rite of passage . . . but last night when she got to your glass, you pushed her knees so she landed back on her ass, and then you crawled up on the table with her and *you* slurped the champagne straight from the container, so to speak, no glass for you, *doll.*"

Instinctively I wiped my mouth, and Connie Stevens laughed.

I got out of bed, asked about my clothes.

"You took them off during the final ascent."

"What?"

"From the landing to here, you were taking off your clothes as we went."

"Where's Pelikan?"

She held up her hands to indicate she didn't know, didn't care.

As I headed for the door she said, "You gave quite a speech last night."

"Speech?"

"About how you hate New Orleans and especially the French Quarter, hate the food, the people, the nightlife . . . you said you even hated the music, hated how the yuppie, public-radio-listening tourists get googly eyed over the old-fart jazz musicians with names like Blind Willie and Crippled Jack and Diabetic Dave. It was pretty funny . . . your speech and the way you acted."

I continued for the door while my bed partner, watching my bare ass, laughed cruelly.

On the way down the wide staircase I found my things—clothing, wallet, watch—except no shoes or socks. On the first floor, temporary electrical wiring is festooned from room to room along with eight-inch flexible tubing, probably used to bring in cool air, though the air-conditioning is obviously off now, these rooms stifling in spite of their tall ceilings. I walked by what must've been the mansion's dining room, where a huge table-cum-stage has been constructed from sawhorses and plywood—where Bubbles and I must've performed. My finger hurts and in my head there's a monotonous drumbeat of pain, but mainly I suffer from shame.

I followed voices to the back of the mansion, through rooms and hallways full of moisture-swollen cardboard boxes and ratty furniture covered with yellowing cloth, brown-green mold on dirty white walls, and finally I find the kitchen . . . where Pelikan and half a dozen women were watching a television set that's on a table along with various products, gadgets, plastic food containers. He wore a pair of half glasses that made him look studious, dressed in blue jeans and white shirt, wearing brown Doc Martens and presumably two pairs of socks . . . the women in robes or just their underwear, one of them is bare breasted, jeans on but no top, oohing and ahhing at whatever's playing on the TV. When Pelikan saw me enter the room, he stood and smiled like he did at Mother's last night, a warm, welcoming, be-atific smile, and one by one the women turned . . . when they recognized me, they laughed, then started clapping.

After the applause died down, Pelikan said, "You're the first one who ever—"

"Yeah, I know," I quickly interrupted, red with shame. "I need to talk to you in private, right now." I checked the women's faces wondering if one of them was Bubbles.

"She's gone already," Pelikan said with that peculiar talent he had for knowing what I was thinking.

"There's some champagne in the cooler," one of the women told me, getting a laugh from the others.

"It's almost over," Pelikan said, turning from me to watch television.

"Bye-bye, Dipsy," one of the women said.

"Bye-bye, Tinky Winky," said another.

"Did you ever see such a happy sun?" asked a third.

I caught a glimpse of Pelikan, smiling like the sun there on TV, and told him again that I needed to see him alone.

He held up a hand indicating I should shut up until the program was over.

"Jesus Christ, how long does it take them to say good-bye?"

Several of the women shot dirty looks my way.

When the program ended, the women left, giving him kisses and hugs around the neck while I got looks that ranged from pity to contempt. Pelikan packed his merchandise, and I demanded to know what was in that tequila he gave me last night.

"Agave?"

"You small-time, hustling little—"

"Careful, milord."

"Selling plastic bowls, sitting here watching cartoons with a bunch of hookers, strippers, and professional cocksuckers."

"Wake up on the wrong side of the bed?" he asked as he continued packing away his merchandise. "And we weren't watching cartoons . . . those little tykes are real, they live in England."

"You lurid son of a bitch, I wish I'd never met you, a goddamn hustling pimp."

"I'm sorry if my profession offends you."

"*You* offend me."

"Did you know that a blow job can cure hiccups? I handled a case a few years ago, guy from Iowa had suffered hiccups for nearly a year, he'd been to doctors and clinics all over the country. I set him up with Diane O'Rourke, and halfway through the blow job, he stopped hiccuping without even realizing it. If we weren't such a repressed society, there's no limit to what I could accomplish through the promotion of oral sex. I had discussions with a dentist, telling him if he had male patients who were anxious about dental procedures, who were so frightened they wouldn't make an appointment even when their dental health was critical . . . if these patients were administered blow jobs while in the dental chair—"

"I don't want to hear it."

"Why?"

"You're sick."

"What's sick about—"

"You're so contaminated, you don't even—"

"The biggest call I get now is for old women. I don't know, maybe men of a certain age are reliving fantasies about their aunts or school-teachers or grannies . . . but if I could find half a dozen eighty-five-year-old women who'd suck cock, I could retire."

I was too astonished to comment.

He continued, "But when a woman hits her eighties, she no longer has interest in sucking cock . . . not for love nor money. I know, I've tried to recruit several."

I have to leave this town, I really do . . . maybe I can hire a lawyer back in Connecticut and handle everything long distance. "What do you think I should do about Three Jacks?"

Instead of answering me, Pelikan continued packing, at one point holding up a slender stainless steel cylinder about seven inches long, with bulbs or spheres at both ends and one in the middle. "You know what this is?" he asked me.

"Some kind of dildo—"

"It's used to strengthen the pubococcygeus muscle, you ever hear of doing kegels, a form of exercise that enables a woman to squeeze her—"

"I don't care about your product line, I just want to know when—"

"Bubbles uses one of these," he said, holding the cylinder close to my face.

When I knocked his hand away I bumped my swollen finger, which hurt like a bitch . . . forcing me to sit in a chair and hold that pain in my lap. "Where're my shoes, I'm leaving."

"You asked about Three Jacks."

"I changed my mind, I don't want your help."

"You're going to need it, Charlie. Gallier will be contacting you soon."

"Are you going to tell me who he is?"

"Gallier is a toad . . . a toad who inherited an estate that was discovered to be full of contested items."

"Contested?"

"Art objects and antiques, all manner of things that had been looted by the Nazis, then sold and resold until they ended up with Gallier's uncle, who died and left everything to Gallier. But my old friend Gallier can't cash in on his inheritance because it's been sealed by court order until the ownership issues are decided. And guess where his inheritance is being kept?"

I had no idea.

"The Louisiana Repository, right square in the heart of the Quarter. The building takes up a whole block, it's where gold bullion is kept and cash from local businesses and items being disputed in lawsuits when the courts haven't decided yet who the rightful owners are. But here's the kicker, Charlie. The Repository is being renovated and that's why we can move in our equipment with no one the wiser."

"Move in your equipment?"

He looked at me as if I was being dull witted on purpose. "The court cases have been going on for two years and Gallier doesn't want to wait any longer. We're going to remove his inheritance from the repository."

"And do what with it?"

"He wants it back."

"You're going to steal his stuff and return it to him?" I asked.

Pelikan held up a finger. "Ah."

"Ah what?"

"That's where you come in, Gallier is trying to use you to leverage me."

"There's nothing to leverage if I leave town."

"They won't let you."

"We'll see . . . where are my shoes?"

"Nephew, I need to tell you something so you'll know what Gallier is capable of . . . he studied to become a doctor—"

I stood but Pelikan came over to put his hands on my shoulder, staring at me so intensely I had to look away. "Just hear me out," he said, "then I'll get your shoes."

I slumped back to the chair.

"A terrible thing happened to Peter Brent when he visited New Orleans."

"Who?"

"Shhh . . . just listen."

10

PETER BRENT'S KIDNEY

Peter Brent, Pelikan said, visited the French Quarter during Super Bowl week, hoping to hook up with a Super Bowl chick, a mythical creature residing in Peter Brent's overheated, extended-adolescent mind. Thirty years old, chubby, and socially awkward, he suffered extensive problems with body odors, especially his feet, which stank so hideously that even his devoted mother, with whom Peter Brent had a smothering relationship, made him keep his shoes on in her presence. Although lonely and perhaps pathetic, Peter Brent was not an entirely sympathetic character . . . if he hadn't been timid, there are many unpleasant things he would've done. When, for example, he read about a woman who got drunk in a bar and passed out while patrons of the bar took turns raping her on a pinball machine, instead of being ashamed for his gender, Peter Brent wished he'd been in that bar and had a turn.

He worked with a man who went to the Super Bowl in New Orleans years ago and said he slept with three women during that weekend . . . women in the French Quarter for Super Bowl would do anything if you let them stay with you, plus these Super Bowl chicks, a term the coworker used without irony, were showing their tits to anyone who cared to look, right out there on Bourbon Street . . . you could look and feel and take pictures, it was like an orgy. In truth, Peter Brent's coworker had engaged in sex with one woman that weekend, and she charged him $100 . . . but Peter Brent had little

experience in such matters, was a momma's boy, a compulsive mas-
turbator who at age thirty could count on the fingers of one moist
hand the number of times he'd had intercourse, for money or
free . . . and the idea of a Super Bowl weekend with topless women
walking around right out there on the street, offering themselves to
him in exchange for a place to stay, was so powerfully intriguing that
six months in advance and at great expense he rented a room in a hotel on Bourbon Street, telling his mother he was going to a business
conference.

Initially, the French Quarter lived up to Peter Brent's lascivious
expectations . . . he saw beautiful women arriving by limousine at expensive hotels, prostitutes and professional escorts coming from all
over the country to make themselves available to high rollers, and the
occasional intoxicated college girl would lift her shirt to get a cheer
from the assembled on Bourbon Street. But no one, neither pro nor
coed, offered herself to Peter Brent. One night when a girl near him
lifted her blouse and Peter Brent reached over to touch, the girl's
boyfriend pushed him to the ground, getting a laugh from the crowd.

During the game Peter Brent found a bar that wasn't crowded,
he was on a stool feeling sorry for himself when a beautiful young
woman sat next to him and asked, "What did you say?"

"I didn't say anything," he quickly replied, afraid she was going to
berate him the way other women had when he'd tried to talk to them
in bars.

"I thought you asked if you could buy me a drink." She smiled,
showing white teeth.

"No." When she kept smiling he said, "But I *will* buy you a drink
if you want me to."

She said that'd be nice . . . the woman looked young enough to be
in college, she was five and a half feet tall and petite, very short blond
hair and a sweet open face, also she was wearing a top made out of
soft cotton like a T-shirt but with a swooping neckline that kept
falling open, letting Peter Brent look in to see her bare breasts with
big purple nipples like clown noses. She seemed interested in everything he said and laughed at his jokes and took opportunities to
touch his forearm and bump against him . . . Peter Brent becoming

feverish with the realization he had at long last discovered his uni-
corn, the Super Bowl chick.

She's the one who suggested it . . . did he have a room, would he
like to go there and watch the rest of the game in privacy, just the two
of them?

He floated back to his hotel with chick in tow, wishing his bud-
dies were here so he could high-five them. In his room he immediately clicked the game on, but the Super Bowl chick clicked it right
off, and that's when Peter Brent knew for sure he was going to get
laid, relayed, and parlayed . . . which is exactly how he planned to describe it to his friends back home.

The Super Bowl chick took out a small package of powder that
she unfolded on a glass-topped coffee table. Peter Brent told her he
didn't use drugs, but the woman told *him* that when she got a snoot-
ful of this shit she felt like getting naked and sucking cock. Peter
Brent said, well, help yourself *please*. But I don't do it alone, she insisted, it's a train ride we have to take together. Wary but horny, he
agreed, and she unscrewed a ballpoint, filled the pen's outer plastic
tube with powder, and had Peter Brent lie on the bed so she could
blow powder up his left nostril, then the right.

He thought his head was going to explode. Literally. He thought
his skull was actually going to blow apart and splatter brains all over
the room. Peter Brent couldn't speak or move, could only wait for the
pressure in his head to kill him.

But it didn't, he simply remained immobilized on the bed. His
Super Bowl chick let two men into the hotel room. Peter Brent could
hear them speaking but didn't make out everything that was
said . . . one of the men chastising the woman for "getting a fat one"
and then when she took off Peter Brent's shoes and socks, all three of
them made rude remarks about the smell.

He was stripped and rolled onto his side, still paralyzed, but able
to see a metal stand brought to the bed, able to hear metal instru-
ments clicking as they were unrolled from cloth packages, able to feel
coldness and wetness as someone washed the side of his body from
armpit to hip. Then he was given a shot in the spine which hurt like
hell though he was unable to react to the pain. While receiving an in-

jection on the inside of his elbow, Peter Brent looked up at three blurry faces and was lifted suddenly into unconsciousness.

He awoke the next morning. To Peter Brent it could've been a week or lifetime later, he was so terribly disoriented, not even realizing at first what was wrong: he was naked and in the bathtub and he felt numb because he *was* covered to his chest with ice cubes and water, numbed by this freezing slush. In red lipstick someone, presumably his Super Bowl chick, had written on the white tile above the tub's spigots: *CALL 911.* And now he saw that she had also placed a phone right there on the side of the tub. Should he call? And say what? I'm in a tub of ice and have a lot of pain? But when Peter Brent finally moved, intending to sit up, he experienced such an exquisitely gut-ripping sensation that it needed a word bigger than pain . . . pain was what you felt when you hit your thumb with a hammer, but Peter Brent was now host to a suffering like they say hell will provide. He was just able to make the 911 call before passing out.

Next time he awoke he still hurt but this was a more manageable aching, one that had been dulled by legally prescribed drugs . . . Peter Brent in a hospital bed. When a doctor came in to check on him, Peter Brent asked, "What happened?"

"Your kidney was removed."

He demanded to know why, was it diseased, who gave the hospital permission?

"You don't understand, Mr. Brent . . . *we* didn't remove your kidney. It was taken out in that hotel room last night."

11

GOOD QUESTIONS

"A myth," I told Pelikan when he finished. "An urban myth like alligators in the sewers of New York City."

He insisted it was true.

"No, I've read about these myths . . . like the one that was going around a few years ago, a guy is in Los Angeles, gets picked up by a famous actress or supermodel, they go back to his hotel and have incredible sex, and the guy can't believe his good fortune until he wakes up the next morning and she's gone but there's a message scrawled in lipstick on the mirror, *Welcome to the wonderful world of AIDS.*"

"Peter Brent's fate *began* with an urban myth," Pelikan said. "There was a story going around about a person being picked out of the Mardi Gras crowds in the French Quarter, taken to a hotel room, drugged, his kidney removed for sale on the organ transplant black market. When Gallier heard this story, it so intrigued him that he decided to make the myth real by actually doing it."

"Gallier again."

"That's right, princeling."

"Does this guy even exist?"

"What do you mean?"

"I mean, when I was a kid you were always pulling my leg—"

"Pulling your what?"

"Where are my shoes?"

"What's wrong?"

"Wrong?" I said. "Returning here to New Orleans was wrong . . . everything else followed from that. I'm going back for my father's funeral, are you coming with me?"

"Neither one of us are going to that funeral, champ . . . we have a job to do."

"Breaking into the repository?"

"I already have most of the equipment in place. Construction workers have been well paid to get that equipment up there. No one suspects anything because of the renovations, it'll be perfect."

"Where are my shoes?"

"Charlie?"

"I'm not going to be a part of any robbery."

"Burglary. We'll wait for a storm, which will divert the police, prevent helicopters from flying."

"You're crazy."

"You know these summer storms, how they hit so hard that the police are busy with accidents and directing traffic because the power goes out, no traffic lights . . . and even if the storm doesn't knock out power, I got a way to disable the substation."

I laughed.

"What?" Pelikan asked.

"Do you remember when you had me going around collecting underpants that women had worn?"

"Say what?"

"Come on, you remember . . . told me that Japanese men would pay a hundred dollars each if I sealed a woman's well-worn pair of underpants in a Mason jar, maybe more than a hundred if I pasted to the outside of the jar a picture of the woman who'd worn the underpants. I devoted one entire summer to this project, sometimes I sweet-talked one of your female bartenders out of her knickers, sometimes I had to pay for a replacement pair, and sometimes I got my face slapped. But eventually I had a dozen or so jars. Then when I told you I was ready to start selling the product, you said—"

"The bottom had dropped out of the Japanese underwear market . . . I remember now."

"It's funny, all right, ludicrous . . . like importing pygmies to work as jockeys . . . and this repository storm heist is just another one of your jokes, isn't it?"

He was smiling. "Do you still have those jars, I might be able to—"

"You're an asshole."

"Maybe . . . but the repository job is no joke, Charlie. Your father and I have been working on it for more than a year. I've even mapped out how we don't get caught *afterwards,* that's the hard part. You and I wouldn't flash money around or brag about how smart we were, pulling the job . . . but you can't absolutely rely on everyone to keep their mouth shut and not go out and start buying Cadillacs. The great thing about this job? The people we're working with are all leaving the country as soon as the job's over. With them out of the country, there's no one to finger us."

"What exactly is the Odessa?"

"*Edessa.* I got everything all taken care of, trust me."

"And you're ready to go, just waiting for the next big storm to hit?"

"One more compressor to move to the roof, and I'm working on that." He pulled his hair back with both hands. "I got a place for you to stay on St. Peter."

"Where I lived with Pop?"

"No, but close to there." He sat next to me and asked if we were partners.

"Yeah sure," I said to shut him up.

"Let me get your shoes."

He brought them back polished better than new, and Pelikan also had two pairs of socks for me to wear, one white and one black, just as he'd said the night before.

I asked him, "Did this Gallier really remove some guy's kidney in a hotel room?"

"Absolutely."

"It sounds like bullshit to me."

"Gallier's uncle bought artwork from Nazis or Nazi sympathizers. Gallier comes from an old-line Creole family." Pelikan knelt in front of me and unwrapped the socks. "I call him Johnny Crapaud."

"If you ever drug me again like you did last night with that tequila or try to break my fingers or pull anything that's weird, then it's all over between us. I'll go to the law about Three Jacks and take my chances. You understand?"

I expected him to bristle but Pelikan meekly said he understood exactly what I was saying, then took my foot and started to put on one of the socks.

"And leave my feet alone," I said. "That's also a deal breaker."

He looked up at me. "You know what's another good exercise . . . the inchworm. You stand on a towel and use your toes to scrunch the towel inch by inch under your feet, then use your toes to move the towel out again."

"What should I do about witnessing Three Jacks being killed?"

"They drained his swimming pool."

"Good, maybe when the police link that woman to Three Jacks, establish a motive for why she killed him . . . that gets me off the hook."

"They didn't find a woman," he said, watching me pull on the socks.

"What do you mean?"

"Nothing was found in the pool."

"No revolver either?"

He shook his head.

"I saw her jump in, I threw the revolver in, the police were on their way as I was leaving . . . what the hell happened to the woman? Who took the gun?"

Pelikan said those were good questions, then knocked my hand away to retie a shoe he said I had way too tight.

12

NUNS ALONG THE MISSISSIPPI

After picking up my stuff at the train station, I took a cab to the St. Peter Street apartment Pelikan had arranged for me, the owners away during renovations. The address was just a door on the sidewalk . . . you could never tell from the outside what these doors opened to, shitholes or mansions. Using the key Pelikan had given me, I entered a long narrow tall passageway, the walls wet and mossy, that led to a small courtyard of paving stones and wild growth. In the center of this overflowered, viny courtyard sat a little brick two-story cottage out of a fairy tale: outwardly charming but with the aura of a place where something Grimm will occur. I would be staying in slave quarters . . . typical of the old Creole town estates in the French Quarter, which had these small brick buildings out back where slaves lived and where the cooking was done to keep heat and odors out of the main house.

I entered from the side of the cottage where the courtyard wall pressed so close that I could put a hand on the cottage door and still touch the stone wall. Inside, everything was a mess of sawhorses and five-gallon buckets and plastic drop cloths. The first level was basically one large room with a circular brick fireplace in the middle and a kitchen along one wall. In a corner of the large room, a wrought iron circular stairway led to the second level: two bedrooms separated by a small bath. Both bedrooms had outside doors that opened onto a narrow balcony overlooking the courtyard.

I took a long cool shower and slept for two hours, awakening with no memory of dreams. A large heating/air-conditioning vent was positioned over the bed and as I lay there trying to sort out my situation, I heard a furious scratching and scurrying inside the vent. Cockroaches? The renovations had put them on the move, and I made a mental note to drag the bed out from under that vent.

After another shower and putting on clean clothes, a black T-shirt over a pair of jeans, I set off through the Quarter to find a meal in spite of Pelikan's warning I should lie low. The sky was hazy and hot with no sign of the storm Pelikan needed to launch his burglary. I wondered what assignment he planned on giving me . . . and I also wondered, with a small illicit thrill, if I was sufficiently courageous and self-destructive to go along on a felony theft. And stupid enough too, because I still didn't know what was being stolen. Fantasizing about all this, walking along in a dumb daze, I didn't spot Detective Renfrone coming toward me on Dauphine Street until it was too late to duck him . . . so I waved and said hello like we were friends, adding, "Strange how we keep running into each other."

"I've been following you," he admitted without guile. Renfrone was red faced with the heat but still wore that windbreaker. "You want to go get something to eat?" he asked.

"How come you're following me?" If I was a suspect in Three Jacks's killing, I wanted Renfrone to come out and say it.

Which to my surprise he did. "The maintenance man at Three Jacks's building gave a pretty good description . . . you were in the penthouse when Three Jacks was shot, weren't you?"

Should I deny it?

Renfrone let me off the hook by asking if I wanted to eat at Mother's.

"The bar or the restaurant?" I asked.

"The bar, you don't want to eat around a bunch of *tourists,* do you?"

"Whatever is fine by me, Gene . . . you sure you want to chance running into Pelikan?"

"Why would that worry me?"

"You guys used to be friends but now you're on the outs."

Renfrone sneered and rolled his shoulders in a theatrical tough-guy display, saying, "Let him avoid *me*."

On the way to Mother's we passed Fat Elvis (the same one who helped eighty-six me last night?) lumbering along, every bit as fat as the real fat Elvis, who, according to the autopsy, weighed 350 pounds when he died from the strain of a particularly troublesome bowel movement. This French Quarter Fat Elvis wore a cheesy white jump-suit made of material so thin we could see through to his heavy, hairy tits. Probably tailored for someone in the two-hundred-pound cate-gory, which Fat Elvis overflowed, the jumpsuit came with a chintzy cape that spread atop Elvis's fat-humped back like a little cloth on a big table.

"More Elvises in this town than Las Vegas," Renfrone muttered.

"America's first secular saint," I said. "The largest number of calls to the White House came the day Kennedy was killed, the second-highest number came the day Elvis died."

Renfrone said he hated Elvis when the greaser was alive and even more now that he was being imitated all over the place.

"My boy, my boy, my boy," I said.

After we entered Mother's thin doors, I braced myself in antici-pation of someone remembering my performance of the night before and telling me to get the hell out, but of course French Quarter bars are like God in their all-forgiving nature, make a fool of yourself one night and get welcomed back the next.

Renfrone and I sat at the bar, Pelikan wasn't around . . . but another Elvis, this one a Fifties Elvis, was there eating a peanut butter cheese-burger, drinking a glass of milk, wearing a purple velvet shirt and tight black pants, the guy's waist couldn't have been much over thirty inches and he had that trademark greasy black hair and dark kohl eyes, look-ing foolish and innocent and sexually dangerous at once.

"Wonder what that one's going to think," I asked Renfrone, "when he runs into Fat Elvis?"

"What?" He hadn't been listening to me.

"If that Fat Elvis comes in here and meets up with Fifties Elvis, we'll find out what they have to say to each other."

Gene said he didn't care and lit a cigarette.

The female bartender came our way with raised brows and I ordered a shrimp po'boy and iced tea, Renfrone said he'd have the iced tea and a salad.

I asked why he wasn't eating a meal.

"On a diet," he admitted sheepishly.

"How'd you get so fat?"

"Fuck you, Chaz."

"Hey, Gene, what can I say . . . you used to be a beefy guy but you never had that huge gut."

"It was quitting smoking," he said, taking out his Marlboros to look at the pack. "I put on so much weight I had to start smoking again, but I think it's too late." He offered me one.

I declined.

"The detectives who caught the Three Jacks case are looking to haul in the man described by that janitor, they figure this man—which we both know is you—either saw Three Jacks get shot or was the shooter himself . . . which is it?"

"Is this an interrogation?"

"No, Chaz, this is lunch . . . you'll know when I'm interrogating you."

Before the food came I exchanged my iced tea for a double gin on the rocks, splash of tonic.

Mean Gene laughed and said during a *real* interrogation I wouldn't be allowed the comfort of gin . . . then while I was trying to eat he asked again which was it, did I kill Three Jacks or was I just visiting when he got whacked.

"If this is lunch, let me eat . . . if it's not lunch, let me get a lawyer."

"Eat," he said, *"eat."*

But I'd lost my appetite and just picked at the food. Renfrone finally said if I wasn't going to eat then let's go, because he had something to show me. Once outside, he leaned close and with cigarette breath told me that Pelikan was trying to fuck me over.

"How so?"

"He's the one who called me and said you were with Three Jacks when he got killed."

"I thought it was the janitor—"

"The janitor gave a description, Pelikan called me with your *name,* told me you were at that strip joint."

"I don't believe you."

Renfrone shrugged like he didn't care if I believed him or not. "They drained Three Jacks's swimming pool."

"Yeah?"

"Didn't find the murder weapon." He paused. "Nothing in the swimming pool."

Was he setting me up, trying to trap me into mentioning the woman?

In a stalemate of silence, we walked up Decatur, past Jackson Square, then over to the Mississippi River, where calliope music from a docked paddle wheeler tortured us with incessant gaiety all the way to Woldenberg Park, at the upriver edge of the Quarter.

Renfrone stopped and used his chin to indicate I should look.

When I turned toward the fence along the edge of the river I saw Pelikan with five nuns in full black-and-white habits. One foot up on the railing and occasionally gesturing, Pelikan was obviously lecturing the sisters about the river.

Since Pelikan was looking away from us, we were able to approach fairly close. He was dressed in his version of snazzy: black boots we used to call engineer boots, pressed jeans with razor creases, a red T-shirt under a long-sleeved shirt buttoned at the neck but open below that, tails hanging out from his blue jeans. The nuns made up a poker hand: two pairs and an ace. One pair of nuns was short, thin armed, and dark . . . Mexicans? In large contrast, the other pair was masculine and muscular, girth straining their habits . . . like a couple of East German female athletes at the Olympics during the Cold War, before gender testing. The ace of the hand and obviously the nun in charge was tall and plain and reminded me a whole lot of Janet Reno. All five nuns wore the same heavy, black-framed eyeglasses from the Buddy Holly line.

I heard enough to know what speech Pelikan was giving, astonished he'd tell it to *nuns.*

When I was a kid Pelikan told me the Mississippi River was

America's alimentary canal, running right down the middle, draining everything . . . "and, Charlie, you know what's at the lower end of the alimentary canal, we're talking about the ass, the anus, the Mississippi Delta, muddy and nasty and fertile and stinking as it spreads out into the ocean like shit into a big toilet called the Gulf of Mexico, and here we stand above that delta, and if America is a woman, which of course she is, Charlie, then you know what's above her ass, which is *pussy* . . . sweet, warm, wet, tropical, fishy, Big Easy, Crescent City, New Orleans is America's pussy, just take a whiff," Pelikan instructed me when I was here as a teenager and thought this stuff was cool, "take a whiff and tell me you haven't ever smelled *that* on your fingers . . . it's the smell of New Orleans, Charlie, warm and wet and joy giving, wide open and ripe, mankind's most valuable renewable resource, lovely and luscious, fat and happy, the Big Easy and the Crescent City, sweet cunt of the South, New Orleans."

Whatever version he was telling the nuns, I think there was a language problem because the double set of big and little nuns just looked confused. The tall Janet Reno nun, however, must've understood because she was blinking maniacally behind her large glasses. She started to say something to Pelikan, apparently couldn't find the right words, and settled for shooing the other four sisters away from him, like schoolgirls being hustled away from a flasher.

"What was that all about?" Renfrone asked.

"I have no idea," I lied.

Without ever looking our way, though I suspect he knew we were there all along, Pelikan ambled off after the fleeing nuns . . . and I asked the detective, "What'd you want to show me?"

"*The nuns.* I told you they were hanging around your uncle, now do you believe me?"

"So?"

"*So,*" Renfrone demanded, "what's the connection?"

"Between what and what?"

His mushy features went red with anger and frustration, but before he could vent the steam, Renfrone noticed my finger and asked what happened.

"Pelikan," I said.

He nodded as if this proved his point. "You're going to take the fall for Three Jacks, you're going to take the fall for the job your old man and Pelikan were planning."

I told Renfrone I still had no idea what he was talking about.

He looked upriver, looked downriver, then, grunting with his stomach, he bent over. I thought he was going to attempt tying a shoe except his shoes were loafers with tassels, not laces, and what he was really doing was positioning himself to deliver an uppercut between my legs, dropping me to the ground with pain . . . it felt like really mean guys had tied twine all around in my lower intestines and now they were trying to pull everything out through my scrotum . . . I was gasping and holding myself and wishing it was ten or twenty minutes in the future when this would still hurt but not a crippling pain that promises to prevent me from ever standing straight again.

"*Now* I'm interrogating you," he said.

13

STILL MAWKISH
AFTER ALL THESE YEARS

This is the part where, if I had a saxophone and any talent, I'd be blowing the blues. I'm in jail and I think my balls are broke. The finger Pelikan bent still hurts and in a larger sense I'm feeling sorry for myself, being stupid enough to come back to New Orleans and let all this unfold, also my daddy's dead. I'm pathetic, wretched. If I had a thesaurus I'd be even more miserable.

Mean Gene Renfrone brought me to this holding cell but didn't charge me with anything. I wasn't booked or fingerprinted, just shoved in here where Renfrone could question me hard, not about Three Jacks's murder, though . . . Renfrone was interested mainly in what Pelikan and my father had been planning and why hadn't the burglary occurred yet and, now that my father was dead, what role was I playing. In response to being shoved around and having questions hollered in my face, I kept saying the same thing over and over: I want a lawyer. Renfrone called me a fool for being loyal to Pelikan who was ratting me out, setting me up . . . and I replied, I want a lawyer. Renfrone finally left me alone without indicating what would happen next, would I be booked or released?

My old man taught me years ago to give the cops nothing, just keep requesting a lawyer no matter what you're asked. Good advice. I wondered where he was being buried and if I should call my sisters to find out when the funeral was . . . would I be able to attend?

When I lived with my mother and three older sisters in Connecticut, during summers we'd go to a lake in the Adirondacks for a whole month. Time seemed in endless supply, those summers blissfully uneventful . . . narrative without plot, I was treading time back then.

Then I came to New Orleans and spent three fast, decadent adolescent years in the French Quarter with Pelikan . . . and after that, the rest of my life seemed slow and clumsy by comparison. I had become jaded before I got my driver's license.

A few years ago I was at a family gathering in Connecticut, watching videos with my mother's cousins' children, kids still in college, and I was fascinated by how impatient they were, fastforwarding through the opening credits and then through any part of the movie that failed to hold their interest . . . when a car ride went on too long or there was dialogue nonessential to the plot or if more than a few seconds were spent on showing a plane taking off or a character walking through the airport.

I think that's what New Orleans did to me, made me want to fast-forward through boring parts, impatient with anything slow or subtle, unappreciative of life's patterns and routines, plunging into relationships and affairs and engagements, changing jobs, moving at the end of every lease, always searching, never satisfied. I think I was finally getting over this adolescent restlessness, was building my business and finding some serenity in life's routines . . . when the old man sends me back *here*.

I don't want to be in New Orleans, I don't want to be in jail. I want to be in a little log cabin by a mountain lake—I guess this is the saxophone part—where I can sit and watch the water, go to bed early, no radio or television, and the only books I'll read are those without violence or depictions of oral sex, containing no plot surprises or scenes considered shocking.

The cell door is opened and in walked Amanda. "I understand you need a lawyer."

I gasped and blinked and tried to think of something cool to say.

"You remember me, don't you, Charlie?"

"Twelve years," I finally said.

"Has it been that long?"

I asked her what she was doing here.

"Offering you my legal services."

"You're a lawyer?"

Amanda laughed and said yes, she was a lawyer.

"Where'd you come from . . . I mean, where's your office?"

"Right here in New Orleans."

"Wow. I didn't know."

"I know this is a lot to spring on you—"

"You look . . . good." Amanda was turning forty, a woman of substance and dignity with thick dark hair, broad open face, wide hips, and a bosom shelf like Sophia Loren. When I hugged her I felt like I was getting my arms' worth. She wore a purple dress printed with white lilies, black high-heel shoes, and she was carrying a heavy leather briefcase. "You look better than good, you look fabulous."

She laughed and said, "I've put on twenty pounds since you saw me last."

I kept smiling, at a loss what else to say to her. I used to carry around in my head heavily rehearsed and hotly enraged speeches I intended to deliver if I ever met her again, but I wasn't angry now, I just wanted to keep looking at her.

"I've arranged an informal hearing," she said, putting the briefcase on the metal cot that I'd folded down from the wall.

I asked her what she was talking about.

"Charlie, do you want me to represent you?"

"You really are a lawyer?"

She laughed and touched my face. "Yes, I really am."

"How'd that happen?"

"Well, after our . . . *incident* here . . ."

Which was when I stopped smiling and thought: you mean when I brought you down for Mardi Gras and you ended up fucking my uncle?

". . . I stayed on awhile," she continued, "thinking about things, my life and so on, because I was approaching thirty then . . . and teaching literature had sort of run its course for me. Long story short: I fell in love with New Orleans, moved here, enrolled in law school, and now I'm a defense attorney, which I understand you need."

"Pelikan send you?"

"Does it matter—"

"Yes," I said, speaking too quickly, too sharply, that old anger burping up from twelve years ago. Amanda taught English lit at NYU, where I attended classes during the day, drove a cab at night, trying to pretend I was a Beat poet who'd missed my decade by a quarter century. Although I never took Amanda's class, there was still something vaguely illicit and exciting about dating a professor. Were we really dating? We went out for drinks and coffee, talked books and movies, but usually other people were with us. Maybe the love affair was all in my mind, it was certainly never consummated even though at evening's end I frequently talked myself into her apartment, where I would paw and hug and beg, getting nowhere, convinced I'd made such an ass of myself that she'd never agree to see me again. But then I'd call and she'd say sure we'll go out for a beer, see a movie. During our spring break, when I found out she'd never been to Mardi Gras, I pestered her to go to New Orleans with me . . . promising to give Amanda her very first oyster-flavored kiss, which I never got around to doing.

She sat on the edge of the cell's metal bunk. "James Joseph saw you get assaulted by Detective Renfrone, saw you being cuffed and led away, so, yes, he asked me to come down here and offer you my services."

I stood there cross-armed and glaring at her.

"Do you want me to represent you, yes or no?"

"You and Pelikan—"

She got up and brushed by me, calling at the cell door for the turnkey to come let her out.

"Wait a second," I said.

"Why?"

I didn't have a ready answer. We both waited but the jailer didn't appear and Amanda didn't call for him again.

"Charlie?" Looking into her brown eyes reminded me of when I was in love with her. "Charlie?" When I still didn't answer, Amanda said, "I'm not going to discuss, rehash, or analyze what happened between us. I know this is awkward, my showing up without warning and offering to represent you when you didn't even know I lived here or had become a lawyer. But we don't have a lot of time. I know a little of your situation and I've arranged for us to meet with a judge and even though it'll be an informal, unrecorded meeting, at least we'll have told someone in authority what Renfrone did to you."

"You know what I should've said when you first came in? I should've said, of all the cells in all the prisons in the world, you walk into mine."

She smiled and I remembered something else . . . what a great mouth Amanda has, voluptuously lipped and big enough for a fist.

"If you want me to represent you, you'll have to say so."

"Yes, I want you to represent me."

"Good, let's talk about what's going to happen when we meet the judge."

"Amanda."

"Yes?"

"We're simply not going to discuss *us,* is that the plan, just pretend it never—"

"We're going to pretend it's twelve years in the past and we both got over what happened, *that's* the plan."

"Pretend huh?"

She made a point of checking her watch. "We're meeting with the judge in half an hour."

"I thought I was so cool going out with you . . . a professor, an older woman, lifelong New Yorker, smart and beautiful and funny. I felt so *hip* taking you out for a drink, kissing you in that cab . . . and when I found out you'd never been to New Orleans—"

"Charlie, let's not do this *now.*"

"Why'd you fuck him?"

She held up both hands as if helpless to change the course we were on. "He gave me a bath."

"Gave you a bath? Where was I?"

"It was one of the afternoons when you'd passed out."

"So as soon as you hear me snoring, you jump in the tub—"

"There'd been a lot going on between me and Pelikan."

"You'd just met him, for godssake!"

"Tone control, Charlie . . . or I won't have this conversation with you, not now, not ever."

Tone control is what Pelikan always said to me when my voice got snotty . . . but I didn't point this out to Amanda. "Go on."

She exhaled like someone trying to extinguish a candle, then said, "He gave me a bath, shampooed my hair, washed my feet . . . I'd never been bathed like that, he cleaned my teeth with his finger, he even rubbed the roof of my mouth—"

"Right now I feel like putting a *bullet* in the roof of my mouth, is what I feel like."

Amanda glared and said the topic was closed.

"Not before you apologize."

She looked bewildered.

"Okay, an explanation . . . at least you owe me that."

Grabbing my shoulders like I was an obstinate child who needed a good talking-to, Amanda lectured, "Charlie, in the next one minute, you have to decide what you want from me. I can be the woman who did you wrong and maybe someday we can rehash that whole incident over lots and lots of drinks, assuming of course that you ever get of jail alive . . . *or,* I can represent you as an attorney, get you released, make sure Renfrone doesn't assault you again. Your decision, Charlie, tell me what you want."

"I want you to unbreak my heart."

14

GAG ME

Amanda leaned forward and put two fingers at her lips, pretending she was gagging . . . and then looked at me to laugh along with her.

I stood there stone faced.

"Come on, Charlie, that's from a song, isn't it . . . unbreak my heart, I mean, really."

I remained stiff and unamused.

"Look, even if I *done you wrong,* it was twelve years ago, we weren't lovers, at least not technically."

"Technically? Amanda, I was in love with you."

"I know you were, Charlie, and what I did with James Joseph was bad form."

Bad form?

"I should've stayed with the guy what brung me . . . but *unbreak my heart?* After twelve years?"

Now we were both angry . . . but then a transformation began because as she stood here in front of me, Amanda was apparently losing her proportions as the great lost love of my life: I could feel myself unknotting inside, no longer harboring those dark, adolescent sentiments of betrayal . . . is this how it felt to be an adult finally?

"Amanda?"

She glared, no patience left for any of my bullshit.

"Get me out jail."

• • •

On the way to the judge's office I hurriedly explained what'd happened since my arrival in New Orleans, omitting any references to robbing the Louisiana Repository, of course. She advised that as a witness to a murder I was legally obligated to come forward and tell police about the woman who killed Three Jacks but we could set that aside for a moment and file complaints against Renfrone for battery, for various violations of my rights.

"This meeting with the judge will be informal, as a personal favor to me he's agreed to talk with us. When he advises us to follow official channels in filing complaints against Renfrone—which is exactly what the judge will advise—that's when I'm going to slip it in that you were witness to a homicide but are reluctant to come forward because of the way the police, in the person of Detective Renfrone, have treated you."

"Who's the judge?"

"Julian Borders, he's honest . . . a notorious flirt, but here in New Orleans that's still considered just boys being boys." I noticed she pronounced it *N'awlins,* in that exaggerated drawl Northerners use when they move down here and lay claim to this city.

After reaching the judge's office, off a crowded corridor in a low-ceilinged, orange-carpeted modern building, the antithesis of what you'd think a New Orleans courthouse would look like, we were told he was tied up still hearing arguments and might be awhile, we should wait here in the hall. Amanda and I ran through my options a second time. Then we talked about weather, food, and all the reasons Amanda loved New Orleans.

Still no judge.

With no seats available we had to stand at the wall. In the flow of litigants and lawyers and cops traveling this corridor, Amanda and I were repeatedly buffeted against each other, smiling our pardons like strangers, and then after one particularly long silence she asked, "Do you remember hitting me?"

I felt like I'd swallowed ice.

She said, "I didn't think you remembered."

"When?"

"You were massively drunk, you'd already stormed out, back an hour later, out again—"

"After the blowup about—"

"After you found James Joseph and me together, yes . . . and when you returned a second time, even drunker, I tried to get you to lie down, but you were spouting off all your complaints about me, then you demanded sex, then you hit me. Hard, on the side of the head."

"Jesus. Did I . . . were you injured?"

"It rang my bells, gave me a headache that lasted several days, which worried me enough that I went to a doctor for tests. Turned out nothing was wrong, no permanent damage."

The public nature of this setting prevented me from expressing how I really felt. Turning slightly to the wall to hide my face, I told her, "I grew up in a household of women, raised by my mother and three sisters . . . Jesus, Amanda, I'm sorry."

She touched my arm. "It was the first and last time I'd ever been hit. I never saw myself as the kind of woman who gets hit by a man. I wanted to have you arrested but got talked out of it."

"By Pelikan?"

She nodded. "When I told you earlier to let go of all those bad feelings from twelve years ago? That's good advice for me, too, but I guess I wanted you to know, since you didn't remember . . . wanted you to know why I didn't exactly feel obligated to fall to my knees and beg forgiveness, I had my grievances too."

I wanted to go back to jail, I felt so bad.

"Your uncle . . ." She paused, unsure whether to continue. "Did you know that James Joseph was an addict?"

I shook my head.

"I don't know if he *still* is." To protect the privacy of our conversation, Amanda was looking at the floor as she spoke . . . and finally noticed my ruined finger. "What happened there?"

"Pelikan did it."

She didn't ask why, didn't act surprised. "He's a strange combination of vulnerability and mayhem . . . eaten up with disappointments. James Joseph believes in the myth of the perfect family, that unattainable goal of the happy family where Mom and Dad are still in

love with each other after all these years, Sis wants to learn to bake a
pie just like Mom and grow up to marry a guy like Dad, and brother
Bud is a real cutup who makes everyone laugh, takes after his old
man, and brings Mom flowers for no reason except he loves her.
James Joseph believes all that really exists . . . somewhere outside the
French Quarter. The danger in this myth is that when we compare it
to our own families, we despair. I practiced family law. The myth can
be especially crippling during the holidays. I spent a Chrismas with
James Joseph . . . after that, I stopped being close to him.

    "Since he's never been in a family, all he knows is what he learned
from TV, which is why he's so deeply infected with the happy family
myth. This one Christmas, the one I was invited to, James Joseph de-
cides he's going to get a tree, decorate it, have some people over for
dinner . . . apparently the first Christmas tree he's ever had, the first
Christmas dinner. I think there were six of us, maybe eight. He had a
real Christmas tree with the usual decorations, except James Joseph
got this idea in his mind that it would be really neat . . . I don't know
if he saw it on TV or what . . . but he acquired eight or nine small
birds and put them on the limbs of the Christmas tree, tied them in
there with string around their legs."

    "Live birds?"

    "Yes! Parakeets, canaries, a couple little parrots. But instead of
the birds peacefully sitting there and singing like I suppose he
thought they would do, maybe like they did on TV, the birds became
panicked about being tied down and kept trying to escape, falling
from the limbs, hanging by their legs from those string leashes, fluttering, screeching in terror, knocking off decorations. It would've
been funny if it hadn't been so tragic."

    "Did you have to untie them?"

    "I wanted to, we all did . . . but James Joseph told us to leave the
birds where they were. He was going to have this perfect, birds-
singing-in-the-tree Christmas even if it killed the birds, which it did."

    "It did?"

    "During dinner. The rest of us were unable to eat, James Joseph
saying nothing, just sitting at the head of the table and grimly forcing
himself to take bite after bite of his Christmas dinner, no one speak-

ing . . . the birds tied to the tree in the other room are now in a wild panic, feathers everywhere, breaking their wings as they're trying to escape. I found out later that of course James Joseph didn't walk into a pet shop and buy the birds, he'd never do anything as square as that, he got them off somebody who's stolen them out of people's houses . . . these were *pets* and a few of them were screeching words and phrases they'd been taught . . . we're in the kitchen trying to pretend it's Christmas dinner and in the next room there's this avian carnage, the birds literally killing themselves trying to escape, one of them actually pulled a little foot off, and the parakeets or parrots are calling, 'Pretty bird! Pretty bird! Hello! Pretty bird! Hello!' I remember one of them chirping in this tiny pathetic voice, like dying words on a battlefield, 'Margie, Margie, Margie.' One of the men at the table said he was going to untie the goddamn birds, he didn't care what James Joseph said, but when this guy stood up, James Joseph told him if he untied even one bird, James Joseph would make him eat it, feathers and all . . . and from his demeanor, God, you knew he wasn't bluffing. Eventually we all got up and left. A couple of the birds were dead by then, the rest were either hanging upside down or grasping sideways to a branch, their little beaks open in exhaustion . . . I remember as I was going out the door, one of the parrots was screeching, 'Good-bye now, good-bye now!' Over and over. I had the sense it was desperately trying to be a good bird by doing what it had been taught, saying good-bye when someone was going out the door . . . being a good bird hoping that some human would take pity and reward its good behavior by setting it free, untying the goddamn string."

Before I could respond, a secretary came out from the judge's office and told us he'd be here in a few minutes, we could come in and take a seat.

Amanda picked up her briefcase and I was just putting a hand to the small of her back, to let her enter before me, when I glanced down the corridor and saw a familiar face . . . familiar but from where? Familiar, familiar . . . Jesus, it's the naked woman who killed Three Jacks. She's got clothes on now, of course, a white blouse and black skirt, but *it's her.*

I grasped the back of Amanda's dress to stop her from entering the judge's office. She looked back at me wondering what's wrong.

I'm trying to decide if I should I run over there and grab the woman or attempt to explain the situation to Amanda first.

The killer saw me, we exchanged *It's you!* looks, then she walked quickly away.

When the woman turned around and saw me coming she walked faster, while I ran, dodging people, knocking them back against the wall, attracting the attention of half a dozen cops. I heard Amanda shout my name. I caught up with the woman and grabbed her around the waist, lifting her off the floor as she dropped the papers she'd been carrying and screamed.

A cop jerked me from behind, ordering me to let the woman go. Before I could attempt an explanation, a second cop had my arms, a third pushing the first out of the way to put me in a choke hold.

I managed to holler, "She killed Three Jacks!" That sounded stupid enough, but then I got more deeply muddled trying to explain: "Three Jacks On The Floor, she was naked and—"

Further idiocy was choked off by the cop's forearm squeezing my throat.

Meanwhile the woman was insisting she wanted to press charges . . . which apparently emboldened one of the cops to use pepper spray in my face. I was released to squawk and flap around on the floor like those birds Pelikan tied to his Christmas tree . . . and when the entertainment value of my performance waned, another police officer stepped up to jump-start the party by kicking me repeatedly in the small of the back.

15

AM-BUSHED

I wanted to remove my eyeballs and hold them under fresh cold clean running water but had to settle for leaning back in a chair so Amanda could administer a wet Kotex.

I explained to her why I'd grabbed that woman—she's the one who shot Three Jacks. Was I sure? Amanda asked. Absolutely positive . . . the same short blond hair, the same blue eyes, no fishhook through her lower lip, but *it's her.*

"Can you see?" Amanda asked. Since the cops weren't interested in getting me treatment, Amanda was improvising with the contents of her briefcase which fortunately included bottled water and the aforementioned sanitary napkins.

We're in the judge's chambers. With us are the woman who killed Three Jacks and two of the cops who beat, choked, and sprayed me. I'm the only one cuffed, two pair of bracelets for a dangerous guy like me, each wrist cuffed to a rung of the chair.

"Take off the cuffs so I can check my eyes," I tell the cops who are standing between me and the young woman, to protect her, I suppose, in case I try to bounce this chair across the room and attack with my feet.

I'm surprised when one of the officers comes over and uncuffs my right hand.

Amanda thanks him, I don't. When I have kids I'm going to tell them if they ever get lost in a mall or somewhere on the street, don't go to a cop for help, in fact if you see one, run the other way, find anyone else, a dirty old man in a raincoat if you have to, but stay away from cops, they're not your friends. And also, kids, don't ever go in the French Quarter, in fact keep out of New Orleans and Louisiana altogether. Go to Cleveland instead, or Yellowstone, or Canada. Visit one or more of Minnesota's ten thousand lakes. Stay north.

A door in the corner of the room behind the desk opens and a fierce gnome in a black three-piece suit stares out at us, apparently not liking what he saw. Humpbacked and pigeon breasted, this little man whom I take to be Judge Julian Borders lurches from the doorway like a sailor on a rolling deck, making his way unsteadily toward the massive desk, oak and cypress, large enough to house children, worn but still dignified, much like the judge, dignified in spite of the peculiar way he was forced to walk on hips that weren't centered correctly, leaning heavily to the left when taking a right step, leaning to the right when bringing his left foot forward. (Amanda told me later that as a boy the judge was thrown from a horse and broke his back.)

Finally reaching the desk, grabbing it like that sailor might reach for a storm line, the gnome-judge drilled another savage look our way, daring someone to comment on his condition. He stood a moment like a turtle forced up on its hind legs, like a fat apple propped up on two Popsicle stick legs.

And then he sat . . . and when he was settled behind that big desk, he was transformed: from the neck up, Judge Julian Borders was a handsome man of sixty years, square faced and strong jawed and finely nosed, a shock of silver and black hair, widely set green eyes lit with intelligence, a broad mouth and big teeth like Teddy Roosevelt's. Maybe the whole reason he became a judge was so he could sit behind a bench with only that handsome Borders head visible, only his intelligence on display.

"What the blazes is going on here?" he asked angrily, jabbing a finger at Amanda. "You first, Miss Allfriend." He had a broad and practiced accent, *You fust, Miz Awfriend.*

"Judge, before I can explain, I'm going to have to request that you ask the police officers to step out into the hall."

"Why? I was told your client assaulted a woman . . . presumably this here sweet young lady." He nodded at the murderer, who turned her face down but looked up with her eyes, that universal expression of feminine availability, followed by a killer smile that immediately softened the judge's ferocious expression.

Amanda continued: "I give you my word, Your Honor, that I can explain everything. Part of that explanation, however, involves the Police Department, and although I am not accusing these two officers of anything, I don't think I can speak frankly in their presence about one of their colleagues."

I wanted to say, *Go get 'em, girl,* but Amanda had instructed me earlier to keep quiet regardless of provocation.

"He's handcuffed to that chair, Your Honor," she added while Borders was making his decision. "Hardly in a position to harm anyone."

"All right." He told the two cops to step out in the hallway and wait, thanking them for their quick-thinking action in saving a young woman from harm during an assault by a crazed assailant, me.

When I guffawed, Amanda squeezed my shoulder to tell me *shut up* as the judge shot me another of his mean looks.

"And *you,* young man," Borders warned as the cops were leaving, "had better mind yo' manners." From under his suit coat he pulled out a stainless steel .44 Magnum revolver, a cannon of a gun, and laid it *clunk* on the desk. "Or I *will* shoot you 'tween the eyes." Then, returning to the standards of judicial decorum, the judge nodded at Amanda. "Miss Allfriend."

"First of all, Your Honor, I apologize for my client's behavior in grabbing this woman, but I think you'll understand why when I tell you that Mr. Curtis here is an eyewitness to a homicide—"

He held up a hand. "Wait a second . . . has Mr. Curtis gone to the police and reported this here homicide?"

"Your Honor, my client was assaulted by a Homicide detective, cuffed and jailed without being booked or read his rights . . . he's reluctant to discuss *anything* with the police."

Amanda had conveniently omitted the time sequence, that I was assaulted by Renfrone an entire day after I fled a murder scene.

Borders smiled thinly. "Amanda, let's drop the *Your Honor* protocol and just chat here a moment. If yo' client witnessed a homicide, he must report to the police, y'all know that . . . end of *dis*cussion. If he has a complaint of *po*lice brutality, there are channels for that to be reported also. Why are you discussing this with me and what does any of it have to do with your client grabbing this here young woman out in the hallway?"

Three Jacks's killer again smiled come-hither at the judge and he grinned back.

Amanda said, "I admit it's an awkward, unorthodox situation we have here, Julie, but Charlie recognized this woman out there in the corridor and he felt obligated to make sure she didn't escape because she's the woman who killed Karl Gruber."

"What?"

The young woman was shaking her head. "I never killed anyone, Judge, I promise you." Her blue eyes were open and sincere and if I hadn't known the truth I would've believed her. In fact, I felt no animosity toward the woman. After all, she didn't shoot me when she had the chance. I just wanted off the hook.

"This has to be taken to the *police*," Borders was saying. "I can't even ask this young woman a question, not even her name, and neither can you, Amanda . . . anything that happens here could jeopardize a homicide investigation. Young lady, if you need to speak to an attorney—"

She smiled. "No, Judge . . . I haven't done anything wrong. If this guy thinks I killed someone, he's either nuts or it's a case of mistaken identity . . . I've never seen him before in my life and to my knowledge he's never seen me."

She stood and when the judge appeared disinclined to stop her from leaving, I finally had to speak. "She killed Three Jacks . . . Karl Gruber . . . and I can prove it."

Borders told me to take my proof to the police.

"Ask her if I ever saw her naked."

"I beg pardon?"

"He never saw me naked," the woman volunteered. "He's got me mixed up with someone else."

The judge wanted to know where I was going with this "line of inquiry."

"It sounds bizarre," I admitted, "but she was naked when she shot Three Jacks, that's Karl Gruber's nickname, Three Jacks On The Floor . . . so I know what she looks like in the buff and I can describe some very distinguishing characteristics."

"No, he can't," she insisted.

I wiped my eyes with a Kotex and turned in the chair to face the woman. "What I want to know, how'd you get out of that swimming pool? I stayed there and timed it, more than seven minutes, no way you could've held your breath—"

"What swimming pool?" Borders asked . . . then decided it was better if he didn't know, and told me to leave the woman alone.

But she said, "If he thinks he's seen me naked, let him prove it."

"See that little white mark under her lower lip?" I said to the judge. "That's where she was wearing a fishhook."

"A fishhook?"

"That's right, she said it discouraged blow jobs."

The judge's eyes got big, Amanda nudged me not to go in that direction, and the woman touched her lower lip and insisted, "I got that scar falling off a bicycle when I was twelve years old . . . and I certainly never said anything to anyone about discouraging blow jobs, in fact I quite enjoy oral sex, both giving and receiving." She sounded perky and formal, like a Miss America contestant during the interview portion.

Borders took out a handkerchief and wiped at his handsome face.

"And what's my scar got to do with his claim he saw me naked?" the woman asked.

"Good question," Borders said.

"I'm just getting started, Judge. She's got tattoos on her breasts, a little red devil about the size of a quarter on her . . ." I brought up a mental picture to make sure I got it correct. ". . . right breast and a little blue angel, same size and same inside position on her left breast. And, Your Honor, if I never saw her naked, how do I know that?" Perry Mason nailing another one.

Borders turned to the young woman. "Could he have seen you, I don't know . . . maybe topless on some beach . . . have you ever been . . . an exotic dancer?" I detected a hopeful tone.

But the woman said no. "Furthermore, I don't *have* tattoos on my breasts."

I told the judge she was lying. "Now we got her on perjury."

"This isn't a legal proceeding," he reminded me.

"Oh for crying out loud," she said, standing and reaching for the top button of her blouse.

"You don't have to do that, young lady," Borders said reluctantly.

"I don't mind showing *you,* Judge."

I watched with reddened eyes as they exchanged another round of flirtatious smiles, then I said to the woman, "Go ahead, I dare you."

"You're in no position to dare anyone," Borders warned me. To the woman he suggested, "You really should discuss this with an attorney."

"I'm not going to spend money on a lawyer when I can show you right here and now this man is either crazy or he's got me mixed up with someone else. Besides, if I had killed someone and knew he saw me do it, would I have insisted, out there in the hallway, that I wanted to press charges?"

The judge looked at me but I didn't have an answer. Why *did* she take a chance by sticking around here, talking with cops and judges, when presumably she could've told the police she didn't want to press charges and then just walked away? I looked at her carefully to make sure I was right . . . same short-short blond hair, big white-toothed smile, the mark where that fishhook had been embedded, the same Mary Poppins perkiness. I didn't know what her game was, but there was no doubt in my mind she was the woman who shot Three Jacks.

"It's her, Judge . . . I'll stake my life on it."

"As well you might."

"Ask him to move back from your desk," the young woman requested, and Judge Borders started shooing away me with both hands.

Since I was still cuffed to the chair, Amanda had to help. When we had moved several feet from the judge's desk, the woman took a position between us and Borders. She stepped closer to him than I thought necessary, but the judge, eyes wet with anticipation, obviously had no intention of waving her away.

I remembered that Three Jacks had introduced her as Maria. "Hey, Judge, ask if her name is Maria."

She was blocking his line of sight so the judge had to lean and look around her to instruct me to keep quiet.

She told Borders she had no intention of letting me know her name. "He might be a stalker or something."

"You don't have to tell him anything," he assured her the way you might a child.

"And I'm certainly not going to show him my breasts, maybe that's the whole entire reason he's doing this, to get me to strip."

"Entirely possible," the judge cooed.

I said, "I can see tits anytime I want, sister, don't flatter yourself."

Borders peeked around her again to point a finger at me, then his face disappeared once more to watch the show.

From behind the woman and unable now to see the judge, Amanda and I watched as Maria, if that was her name, lifted hands to throat, starting at the top buttons, taking her time as she worked down, at one point giggling a little and telling the judge she was so nervous she might have to ask him to help her with the buttons, and he laughed softly and told her he was there to assist any way he could, the important thing was to get to the truth.

I looked at Amanda and repeated the *Gag me* gesture she used when I asked her to unbreak my heart.

After removing her blouse, the woman laid it on the judge's desk before reaching behind her and undoing the bra clasp . . . but then, still holding the bra on, she said in a little girl voice, "Judge, I'm so embarrassed."

"Call me Julie."

"Julie."

"I could ring for a matron," he offered unconvincingly . . . he was probably shaking his head *Please no* as he spoke. "She could take you in the ladies' room—"

"I want to get this over with right now."

"Whatever you wish."

From behind, Amanda and I watched as the woman swept her bra away (I think I heard the judge gasp) and then we waited for the verdict. I was thinking what a nice back that young woman has, white and unmarked and tapering to a waspy waist before flaring out into a womanly set of hips . . . how do I get her to turn around?

Borders took a long time, as if he wanted to make sure his decision wouldn't be reversed on appeal . . . then finally his chiseled features made a sweaty appearance around the side of the woman and he said to me, "No tattoos."

"That's impossible, let me see."

"She doesn't have to show you."

"She killed Three Jacks and she's got tattoos on her tits."

"Are you saying *I'm lying?*"

"Maybe you're part of the . . ." I didn't want to call it a conspiracy, final refuge of nutcases. ". . . maybe you're one of the people trying to set me up—"

"I'll have you on contempt!" He seemed to be looking for a gavel to bang.

"This isn't a legal proceeding, remember, Judge?" I said.

"Why, you little twerp . . ." Instead of a gavel, Judge Borders lifted the big revolver, and I thought, oh no, this is the part where Chekhov says I get shot.

The woman might well have saved my life when she turned to face Amanda and me, showing us her tits.

"See?"

I'll be damned, no tattoos.

Amanda looked at me for an explanation and all I could do was shrug . . . but I was more than ever convinced this was the woman who shot Three Jacks because I remember those sweet little chubby breasts topped by big ice cream scoops of grape purple nipples. Yet, no tattoos.

Seeing my confusion, the judge said, "Mistaken identity, it happens all the time with eyewitnesses. Now I think you owe this young woman an apology."

"No . . . it's her . . . I remember those big purple nipples—"

"Oh sure," the woman said, almost stamping her little foot. "Easy enough to describe my nipples after you already *saw* them!"

"Listen, *Maria,* you and I both know you shot Three Jacks, so why don't you stop lying and—"

The judge warned me to back off.

Then from Amanda: "Maybe the tattoos Charlie saw at the murder scene were *temporary*."

The woman gave Amanda a hateful look and, between closed teeth, said, *"Shut up."* Her tone and attitude were strange, almost as if the woman felt Amanda was betraying a confidence.

Temporary tattoos made perfect sense to me. "Judge, there are places in the Quarter where you can get a beautiful temporary tattoo, they use ink but not the needle, you either let the tattoo fade or take it off with—"

The woman, who still hadn't put her bra or blouse back on, interrupted me to say this was ridiculous.

And Borders said he couldn't agree more . . . although he apparently was in no hurry to dismiss the issue and tell the woman to get dressed.

We held our respective positions in this pregnant silence until I remembered that the woman was shaved between the legs, which was something that *could not* be faked . . . so I blurted it to the judge, "She has no pubic hair!"

"What?"

"She was waxing Three Jacks's stomach, that's the scam she used to get into his penthouse, free wax job. Look at her, Judge, she's virtually hairless herself, that burr cut, no hair on her arms, and I'm telling you she definitely has no pubes. That can't be faked, Your Honor. Get her to lift her skirt and drop her drawers."

Borders told me to shut my filthy mouth, then he assured the woman, "Young lady, I am *not* going to ask you to remove any more of your clothes."

"Good, because I won't," she said petulantly.

"Of course you won't."

"Of course you won't," I mimicked. "Because if she *does*, it'll prove I'm telling the truth."

This time it was Amanda who told me to shut up.

I did . . . and once again we all waited in the silence.

"I notice," the judge said very carefully to the woman, "that there is no hair on your arms, not that this means anything, of course."

"Judge, he can—"

"Julie."

She smiled. "Julie, he can make up any story he wants about why there's no hair on my arms or how I got this scar under my lip, but he still hasn't told you anything about any part of me he didn't see before I took my blouse off."

"True, true."

When I started to speak, Amanda put her hand over my mouth.

With her back to us, the young woman began softly weeping and I knew I was sunk . . . but then, incredibly, she leaned over and grasped the front hem of her skirt, telling Borders through crocodile tears, "Julie, I'm doing this only because I can't stand the idea *you* might think something bad about me." And with that she lifted the skirt's hem all the way up to her chin.

From behind, Amanda and I saw she was wearing stockings and garter belt, no underpants.

I wondered how the judge was faring . . . still able to breathe, no heart attack or burst blood vessels yet?

Once again he took his sweet time, another long judicial review before looking out at me from around the woman.

Imagine a warden leading you to the death chamber and you ask if there's been any word yet from the governor and the warden shakes his head sadly *no* . . . that's how Borders shook his head at me.

Except the judge's eyes were still bright from what he saw: Maria's Crescent City, positioned now just across the desk from him, as easily within reach as that .44 Magnum and just as dangerous.

Before I could ask to see for myself, the woman sighed and told Borders, "I might as well show *him* too." She put the hem of the skirt in her mouth and turned around with both arms outstretched in shameless revelation. It was a great raised-skirt image . . . saucy young woman in stockings and black satin garter belt, the hem of her skirt held naughtily between a set of white teeth as those Cadillac blue eyes looked out over the roof of it all . . . but I was too surprised for tumescence because from thigh to thigh, deep dark auburn and curly, the woman was fully bushed.

PART TWO

NUNS, NAZIS & ORAL GRATIFICATION

16

DOCTOR CREOLE

Gallier—Dr. Philippe Blanchard Galvez Gallier—sat in the farthest backseat of a ridiculously large white limousine parked on Orleans Street just off Bourbon. He was listening to a tape of Edith Piaf leaking tears from her soul, perfect accompaniment to how Gallier felt this evening . . . a troll taking bites from Gallier's heart. See, that's my problem, he smiled to himself . . . dead French singers, overly ripe images, obscure literary references—too many shiny facets for this dull, flat world. Cranking the volume on the Little Sparrow, Gallier closed his eyes and raised one small hand to keep time . . . this bittersweet moment interrupted by rude cheering.

A block behind the limousine, in Cathedral Gardens, also known as St. Anthony's Garden, a statue of the Sacred Heart of Jesus stood with arms raised to beckon and bless sinners. Illuminated from below with powerful spotlights, the Sacred Heart of Jesus cast a massive shadow on the back of St. Louis Cathedral. The disturbance that bothered Gallier was caused by a passing group of drunken college students who, seeing this looming shadow with upraised arms, had begun mocking its pose and chanting, "TD, TD, TD!"

Gallier—*Galley-ay*—turned in the seat to look out the one-way glass. Seeing the drunken college kids, Gallier whispered one contemptuous word, "Kaintocks." Then he switched off the tape . . . the moment had been ruined for him. Maybe, he thought, I should invite one of those oafs to come in here and sit with me. *Young man, can you say "bilateral orchiectomy"?*

He opened a small compartment next to the seat and withdrew a pad of paper, made a notation, put the paper back, closed the compartment just as one of the college kids came up to the limousine and slapped a darkened window with his meaty hand, drunkenly shouting, "Hey, who's in there . . . you a movie star?" The kid was quickly hustled away by security men, but Gallier was seething once again.

He was sure his ancestors, the French and Spanish Creoles who settled and civilized New Orleans, felt exactly this way when they were being overrun by the American frontiersmen and river-barge riffraff who came streaming into New Orleans even before that runty peasant Napoleon sold Louisiana. Americans from Kentucky, *Kaintocks,* Celtic drunkards and braggarts . . . Gallier *knew* how his ancestors must've reacted upon encountering one of these ruffians, oblivious to the requirements of honor, puffed up in their buckskins and ignorance, bellowing about being half gator and half snapping turtle, three-quarters bobcat, weaned by an ol' momma bear, egging all comers to fisticuffs, knife fights, pissing contests. A Creole gentleman, insulted as he might have been by this crude behavior, could never have challenged these brutes to a duel because the *Code Duello* required that in matters of honor, challenges be issued to or accepted from only those individuals one would invite to one's home as a guest. The Kaintocks obviously didn't qualify. Better simply to shun the beasts. Or take them out and shoot them as you would a mongrel dog.

Somehow, in spite of their obvious inferiority, the Kaintocks had won New Orleans . . . Gallier's sad conclusion as he stared out the limousine's windows at the parade of tourists slouching down Bourbon Street. Look at them, Kaintocks, look at the way they dress, the men in baggy shorts and black socks, triple-X-large T-shirts emblazoned with moronic slogans as if their lack of refinement needed to be further advertised: I have no self-respect, I'll wear *anything*. And marry anything too, their fat wives in tracksuits, polyester uniforms chosen to expand and stretch over sagging guts and fat-rubbing thighs.

Just look at them, shuffling along flat footed, holding plastic bags full of trinkets—more T-shirts for the Kaintocks back home—their corpulence banded with camera straps and fanny packs that bounce along as they pass up the finest cuisine in America to search dull eyed and fat soaked for another hamburger and fries, another pizza, more grease, more dietary fat— Oh look at that one, *that huge one* raising a great whopping hot dog to his mouth, stuffing it in like a ramrod down the barrel of a cannon, dripping ketchup and relish on his shirt as his equally fat wife laughs her foolish, overly permed head off, she thinks it's *funny,* for the love of God.

Gallier imagined himself lowering the window and calling the man over. *Friend, how about if I take out several yards of your intestines, speed that hot dog on its way, what do you say?*

He opened the compartment and made another note.

Unable to watch any more of that fat tourist impaling himself with frankfurters, Gallier turned to look out the limousine's other row of windows . . . the view here more interesting, young women gathering. They always did. Gallier had purchased this preposterous vehicle specifically to appeal to the unrefined tastes of young women. Long enough for five large windows down each side, the limousine's gleaming white exterior was appointed with small mirrored lanterns twinkling in alcoves along the side windows, an overabundance of chrome, uniformed chauffeur, bodyguards in tight-fitting black suits and wraparound sunglasses even at night. Oh yes, must be someone *famous* in this limo. Gallier pondered choosing one of the girls for an evening of entertainment. *His* entertainment, of course . . . what he had in mind, a girl wouldn't find at all entertaining.

Gallier closed his eyes. It wasn't just tourists causing him to despair . . . tonight it was the calendar that put ice in Gallier's heart: he was turning forty tomorrow. And, considering his family history, forty was a birthday of terrible significance. His father had died at forty-nine, his mother at forty-eight, one grandfather at forty-five, the other at forty-three, and a great-grandfather at forty, Gallier's age tomorrow.

The joke about Creoles—was it Judge Borders who first told him this, years ago?—is that they're like the Chinese—they eat a lot of rice and worship their ancestors. Gallier's family tree had of course been thoroughly traced and his family history was well known to him. From his father's side he inherited a tendency toward heart disease, and from his mother's, a propensity for sudden, fatal strokes.

People fawned over Gallier because of his smooth good looks and well-bred manners, because they thought he was wealthy and interesting, a nonpracticing physician.

People were wrong on almost all counts. He wasn't rich, the family fortune all but gone. And Gallier had left the medical field before getting his license because while he enjoyed the art of medicine, in its practice he was forced to deal with patients who turned out to be common, often fat, and so tediously *ill.*

Gallier's defining quest was collecting art: a quiet, dignified pursuit, and if you operated at the right levels, the peasantry was excluded from participation. The problem with collecting art was *money.*

Gallier didn't have enough of it . . . another brutal fact of modern life upsetting to him as he turned forty. If he had been born a hundred and fifty years ago, money simply wouldn't have been an issue, his family had been fabulously wealthy. Even the prospect of dying relatively young wouldn't have seemed so tragic because a Creole aristocrat in New Orleans would've packed a bountiful life into four decades.

He turned Piaf back on but very low so as not to interfere with his time travel, which Gallier did frequently. Being his age a hundred and fifty years ago he probably would've already killed a few men in duels. He would've had a quadroon mistress with skin the color of coffee and cream . . . he might've met her at a quadroon ball, where the woman's own mother would've arranged terms with Gallier under a system of *plaçage.* Right here on Orleans Street was the site of the old Quadroon Ballroom, where masked Creole gentlemen, after being introduced to quadroon maidens, were soon negotiating with the young ladies' mothers. And as a *gentleman,* Gallier would've continued supporting his mistress and their children even after he had married a proper Creole woman and started a recognized family with her. His wife would never acknowledge the mistress publicly, of course, but both women would've accepted the situation without acrimony because that was simply the way the world worked when it was civilized by Creoles here in the Vieux Carré. And if Gallier were to have died in his forties, his wife would've arranged a discreet moment for the mistress to view the body and say her final farewell, after which Gallier's wife would see to the continued financial support of her husband's other family, ensuring that all his bastards finished their education, that his other widow would never have to take in laundry, which would've brought shame on both families.

He leaned forward and poured brandy from a crystal decanter. Remembering something that happened last week, Gallier smiled.

During the very early morning hours when tourists and drunks are still abed, he enjoyed walking the streets of the Vieux Carré. (Gallier refused to call this original site of New Orleans the French Quarter, not only because his ancestry was both French *and* Spanish but also because the Spanish influence here was equal to the French, especially in architecture: the Spanish controlled the city when it was rebuilt following two great fires and two devastating hurricanes, in the late 1780s and early 1790s. In point of fact, only one original French building—the Ursuline Convent—still stood in the Vieux Carré: the Old Square, a name more accurate and formal, which is why Gallier insisted on using it.) During his early morning walks, Gallier was occasionally solicited by beggars, whom he simply did not acknowledge . . . except for the chap last week, a toothless little man who came up to Gallier and said, "I need fifty bucks for a good bottle of brandy." Gallier was so taken by this audacity that he surprised himself—and the beggar—by handing over $100 and telling the man, "Get yourself an *excellent* bottle."

In the finely upholstered and softly lit backseat of the limousine, Gallier sipped his brandy, allowing it to flatten out across his mouth before slipping down the back of his throat. He knew how much this brandy cost . . . and that was another crippling aspect of being born too late and in reduced circumstances, he was forced to track money, keep tabs on its sums and subtotals, allowing it to take up space in his mind and all-too-short life.

If Gallier had been born into his family in the early 1800s, wealth would've been available to him as readily as oxygen in the air. Certain

Creole families, Gallier's ancestors included, had concentrated such wealth that grand gestures become commonplace. One family, upon learning they would receive royal visitors from Europe, had an entire collection of tableware cast in solid gold. At the conclusion of the royal dinner, every golden plate and each golden goblet, all the solid-gold knives and forks, were tossed into the Mississippi—a beau geste indicating no one else would ever be sufficiently worthy to eat or drink from the tableware used by that single, august dinner party.

If that royal dinner were given by my family these days, Gallier thought bitterly, I'd be diving in the river trying to salvage gold from mud, that's how desperate I've become about *money*.

Two years ago Gallier thought those money worries were over, his uncle having left him an estate low on cash but so rich in artwork and antiques that Gallier could've sold off selected pieces and lived well the rest of his life, never to fly coach again . . . but he made the mistake of putting his uncle's collection on view at a private showing where an obnoxious professor recognized certain *objets* and later opened his big mouth about the murky origin of those pieces, then here came the Jews whining about this painting belonging to their grandfather, that armoire being the property of a grandmother or great-aunt. The case went to court, where it has been lodged ever since. In spite of his connections throughout New Orleans, Gallier hasn't been able to sell a single piece from his uncle's estate, the legal fees slowly soaking up whatever modest assets he owned before his uncle died. Even the Catholics got in on the effort, Gallier's inheritance turning into a grab bag for anyone who lost something to the Nazis . . . that vulgar Bulgarian Karl Gruber having contacted his sister, a nun, which led to a goddamn convent from France claiming the Edessa was theirs. Who's next, Gallier wondered . . . the godforsaken Armenians?

He closed his eyes. He felt more put upon than Edith Piaf sounded. One good thing only has come from all this: after all these years, Gallier was contacted by James Joseph. They'd been such fast and famous friends, the highborn Creole and the lowborn hustler . . . my, my, the trouble we got ourselves into, Gallier remembers. I was going to medical school and James Joseph always called

me Doctor Creole. One of the many times they stayed up all night
partying, dawn found them at the Mississippi River where James
Joseph gave a speech about the river being the country's alimentary
canal, New Orleans as America's sweet, fecund pussy. They watched
as tugboats down by Governor Nicholls worked to get a big navy ship
away from dock and into the river's current . . . and James Joseph told
Gallier that the tugs were like Indian elephant handlers who are trying to rouse their biggest and most lethargic elephant for a day's work
in the teak forest. Gallier watched and it was true, the tugs like busy
little people pushing and prodding the huge warship that just didn't
seem ready to go anywhere this early in the morning. "Now watch,"
James Joseph said, "as soon as they get that elephant pointed right,
he's going to bellow and trumpet and take off as fast as he
can . . . fainéant no more." And James Joseph was correct again because when the tugboats had the navy ship in the channel, the ship
directed all engines full speed ahead, black smoke bellowing from the
stacks and sirens sounding as the ship, so sluggish just moments before, now raced downriver for the Gulf of Mexico. "Fainéant, James
Joseph?" Gallier had asked. "Where did we come up with that word
this early in the morning?" Pelikan smiled. Gallier thought this older,
lowborn man was enormously attractive, which nudged him into
making the friendship-fatal mistake of trying to kiss James Joseph
there by the Mississippi River.

Recalling this awkward moment, Gallier opens his eyes and sees a
pirate.

After Gallier touches a button to unlock the door, the pirate gets
in, the door closed behind him by a security man, who then resumes
a sober scan of the crowd.

"You look ridiculous," Gallier said. The man was in his early thirties, hairy and unkempt, dressed as always in pirate costume. Tonight
it was a red bandana around his head, wide leather belts crisscrossed
over his chest, a silky red shirt, blue pantaloons, and a black patch
over his left eye.

"I be Zane," the man intoned. "Pirate king!"

Gallier smiled, showing teeth that were white and even but unusually small, like a child's milk teeth . . . one of the two physical as-

pects of himself that caused regret, the other being his male-pattern baldness. "You're not Zane," he told the pirate. "You're Zany."

Zane grinned nervously.

"And you're not a pirate either, you're a Gypsy."

"No, my family—"

"Gypsies," Gallier said without changing the tone of his voice.

Zane furtively picked at his face before slipping a finger under the eye patch to scratch there.

"It's obvious what you are. If someone shows me a dalmatian, I don't have ask about its family, I say, 'That's a dalmatian.' If I see a mule, I don't ask after its parentage, I say, 'That's a mule.' And one look at you, *Zany*, and I say, 'That's a Gypsy.' "

The pirate had thick black hair and a bushy mustache, his facial features blunt and his eyes—or at least the unpatched one—so dark you couldn't make out the pupil. He tried to amuse Gallier by offering a bad Long John Silver impersonation. "Regardless of what I be by blood, sur, by destiny I be the pirate king, Zane."

"King Zany."

Zane didn't correct him.

"And on the streets," Gallier asked, "what do they call *me?*"

The weirdo in the limo, Zane thought . . . and also the mad doctor . . . the little shrimp who dresses funny . . . the pervert. Not that Zane was going to offer any of these as his answer, of course. Other people might mistake Gallier as a fop because of the mincing way he sometimes acted, occasionally dressing in velvet suits and ruffled shirts, a lacy handkerchief up one sleeve, little pointy shoes highly polished. And others might also underestimate him because he was a short, slight man who seldom raised his voice, who looked delicate with his soft skin and long eyelashes and large doelike brown eyes. But Zane knew firsthand what the man was capable of and told Gallier, "Sur, they calls you *the Creole.*"

This pleased Gallier even though he didn't believe it. "Now tell me . . . success at the courthouse?"

17

BATHING AMANDA

At her apartment that evening, Amanda stripped in the bedroom and walked naked to the bathroom, where she turned on spigots and waited for the temperature to moderate . . . a nice cool shower to wash off the sweat and dirt and worry of the day. While soaking in the stream, Amanda thought back to what happened twelve years ago when Charlie brought her here for Mardi Gras.

He was such a *boy* back then, hot to show off and in a hurry to get drunk, and while Amanda found his exuberance amusing, even endearing, she wasn't in love with him. She came along with Charlie to Mardi Gras because he described New Orleans in loving detail, his enthusiasm infecting her . . . and also Amanda was looking at thirty and not particularly liking what she saw, so why not an adventure south with this wild boy?

Then she met his uncle, who was a man. Pelikan must've been around forty at the time and Amanda thought that if James Dean had lived to that age, hadn't been killed young in the pearl gray Spyder, the resemblance might've been startling.

It was Amanda's third night in New Orleans, Charlie passed out in the bedroom of the flat Pelikan had arranged for them and Amanda soaking in a tub when Pelikan somehow got the bathroom door unlocked and walked in on her.

She slid deep into the water and told him to get out.

He slouched there in his blue jeans and black T-shirt, barefoot and sleepy eyed.

"What do you want?" she demanded.

He announced he was going to bathe her.

"No you're not."

He rolled up his sleeves and began to suds a washcloth, and after a few more protests that both Amanda and Pelikan knew were issued just for the record, she cooperated and he washed her face and rubbed her earlobes between his finger and thumb like a tailor examining the quality of fabric. Pelikan shampooed her hair and massaged her scalp and washed each of her fingers and all her toes, Amanda had never had her digits washed individually, she didn't even do that herself. Then he made her get over on hands and knees so he could wash her nasty hole, that's what he called it, though his bathing of her never seemed salacious, she didn't sense he was copping feels, more like Pelikan was an acolyte washing celebrant Amanda in preparation for whatever ceremony came next. At the end of the bath, Pelikan had Amanda stand so he could fill a pot with clean warm water that he poured over her. He said it was very important to wash off all the soap. He got out a fresh fluffy towel and dried her, rubbing briskly, then he brushed her teeth telling her when to spit. He wiped the folds of her ear with Q-Tips and dusted her with baby powder before dressing Amanda in an old soft clean white cotton shirt of his, pulling her hair tight and tying it with string. Just as Amanda was luxuriating in the feeling of being safe and comforted like a child, Pelikan said he wanted to watch her pee.

"I beg your pardon."

"I want to see you pee."

She considered it, glancing down at the dark blue tattoos covering his forearms and thinking of Queequeg in *Moby-Dick,* because this man here in New Orleans was as exotic to her as the tattooed cannibal from Kokovoko . . . Amanda steeling herself to touch one of Pelikan's tattoos and ask him, "Is it true?"

He looked at the tattoo as if not remembering what it said: *I will fuck anything.* "Oh yeah," he promised her. "Now pee."

"Why?"

"When a woman's a virgin or at least doesn't have sex very much, her urine stream comes out like a man's in a neat pencil stream, but a sexually active woman will pee in a wide, fanlike stream."

Amanda was astonished. "You want to determine if I'm sexually active?" she asked incredulously.

"Charlie said he hasn't screwed you."

"You're a jerk."

"Does that mean I can't watch you pee?"

"And a pervert . . . let me save you the trouble." She was trembling with anger. "I screw around all I want, none of Charlie's business and certainly none of yours."

"You screw around but not with my nephew?" Pelikan asked.

"He's a nice *boy.*"

Pelikan took her hand and led her to a bedroom, they both heard Charlie snort-snoring in the room where he was passed out.

Pushing Amanda onto the bed, Pelikan removed her soft cotton shirt with one swift yank.

Not bothering to cover up, she warned him that if he touched her she'd scream.

"Whatever," he said, taking off his clothes. He was pale white, which Amanda had expected because he worked day and night in various bars, but she was surprised his body was so muscular with lean, long arms and big hands, and the thickest cock she'd ever seen . . . probably shorter than average but clublike: thick, veined, hooded, and profane as it rolled oily from one testicle top to the other like something from underground brought recently to light.

But it wasn't his cock Pelikan was proud of, lifting a foot up on the edge of the bed and telling Amanda to feel because he had very soft-skinned feet that were so perfectly formed they could be used as models for a sculpture called *Perfect Feet.*

She felt his foot, it *was* soft.

Pelikan said, "If Michelangelo was around and wanted a model so he could sculpt perfect feet, he'd come to me."

"I see."

He sat on the bed to show her both feet. "They match. And my little toes there?" he asked as he lifted both little toes above the rest.

"Yes."

"Sometimes I have them take a bow." He wiggled his little toes. "Because they work anonymously and need the attention . . . see how proud they are to get noticed."

She laughed.

But he didn't seem to be joking. "Kind words go a long way," James Joseph insisted.

He lay next to her and eventually, with Charlie sleeping it off in the next room and Pelikan hard and tattooed, Amanda was well used and rode hard and hurt good . . . even days later her little clit still felt like it had been knot-tied.

Some hours later. there was a scene, *the* scene: Charlie caught them in the bedroom getting dressed and he went into an explosive, furniture-kicking rage, left the apartment, got drunker, came back, kicked and cursed, left again, returned again, and hit Amanda before he passed out on the floor. Throughout it all, Pelikan remained a maddeningly neutral observer.

After recovering, Amanda returned alone to New York, settled her affairs there, then moved to New Orleans. For nearly a year and in spite of his emotional neutrality, Amanda dated Pelikan . . . maybe because being on James Joseph's arm was such an intense way to experience New Orleans, he squired her around like a king his consort and introduced her to treats and delights, from smoky jazz clubs to Maylies's Restaurant. He gave Amanda her first oyster-flavored kiss, Pelikan slurping an oyster and then tongue-kissing her, slippery and fishy and good and one of those experiences you don't get anywhere else in the world.

They went for long walks along the river and, one afternoon, watched a yuppie couple having trouble with their toddler, who was screaming and crying, overly tired as he fidgeted in his stroller, and no amount of pleading or promising from his parents could get the kid to shut up. Pelikan walked Amanda over to the couple and told them all to follow him . . . the couple did, but reluctantly, wary that they were being set up for a New Orleans street hustle, and Amanda, not knowing what Pelikan had in mind but aware of what he was *capable* of, was unable to reassure them. After talking briefly with a street musician, an old black man who played the tenor sax and wore a yellow sports coat and black vest, Pelikan directed the couple to bring the stroller and screaming kid close . . . the musician playing "Rock-a-bye, Baby" in a way that Amanda had never heard before: soft and soothing but also embedded with jazz riffs and blues references, so delightfully hypnotizing that the toddler stopped screaming, stared at the saxophonist the way a cobra watches the charmer, and eventually the child's eyes closed, his head rolling, then he released himself to a deep and peaceful sleep. Having arranged all this, Pelikan now waited for the couple to fork over a fat tip for the street musician, but they scurried away, apparently relieved that their child hadn't been kidnaped, and it was left to James Joseph to produce a sawbuck for the saxophonist. Modest dramas like this were played each time Amanda went out with Pelikan.

He knew everyone in the Quarter, especially people who worked in the bars and performed in the streets, and he introduced Amanda to bartenders and bouncers and clowns, puppeteers and zydeco singers. She always felt protected, watched over, in Pelikan's French Quarter. For that first year she was deeply in love with him even after they stopped sleeping together. Although Pelikan was technically proficient as a lover, sex with him eventually became like screwing a robot. Other men she'd slept with might not have had Pelikan's experience and technical skill, but at least they were spontaneous in bed and sometimes funny . . . but James Joseph wasn't in bed for laughs, he was there to deliver the goods. She complained once that maybe they could slow down and quietly enjoy one another without all the athletics . . . and he never touched her after that.

This emotional coldness ran so deep in James Joseph that Amanda had to consider he was a sadist, first enticing her to love him and then withholding that love as punishment or dark amusement.

Like other men who came of age in the fifties, Pelikan apparently thought it was uncool to say, *I love you.* (By contrast, Charlie, on his very first date with Amanda back in New York, was brimming with love and moon and stars and forever.) When Amanda told James Joseph that she loved him, he'd wink and point and say, "Right back at you, babe." Or he'd toss out a line from some old song . . . even if the ship was made of paper I'd sail the seven seas for you.

She got a tattoo for him. Pelikan used to call her his little girly gator so, high on the inside of her left thigh, Amanda had a small green alligator tattooed along with the words *Girly Gator* in curlicue. She considered it their romantic secret but sometimes in bars Pelikan would be talking to a stranger and then suddenly raise Amanda's skirt to show the tattoo, either insensitive to her embarrassment or not giving a damn.

Surprised that recalling these old frustrations and contradictions could still cause her chest to tighten, Amanda turned off the shower and began drying herself . . . remembering now the late-night phone calls that Pelikan was famous for, calling her after midnight when she was asleep but his work had just begun, asking how she felt . . . was she blue. Occasionally she was. I'm blue, she'd tell him. Maybe leaving New York was a mistake, I'll never become a lawyer or get married, I'll end up alone, with cats . . . I'm fat. He'd say all the right things about how smart and beautiful she was, tell Amanda stories about what was happening at the bar that night, who came in, what they said . . . and she would drift to sleep with that reassuring James Joseph whisper in her ear. More than once she awoke later to hear his voice from the phone on her pillow, still talking to her, describing what was on TV, who was in the bar, what they were saying. It was such a comfort when she was blue . . . and difficult for Amanda to reconcile this soft-talking man with one who lifted her skirts in bars, who tied living birds to a Christmas tree.

Pelikan's contradictions could be found in his eyes too. If he'd had a driver's license (Amanda never knew Pelikan to drive) the eye color would be marked *blue*, but they were more than blue, they were slate and green too . . . eyes of a sentry never off duty. If a bar fight was brewing or some other danger lurked, Pelikan's eyes would strafe a room in a way that left no one untouched. Even the way he walked and lounged and sat and smoked all began with the eyes: cool and ever watchful. James Joseph prowled like a leopard who pretended he wasn't hungry, but if you looked closely in his eyes you saw the truth, the man was always ravenous. However: on certain nights (she found out about the drugs much later) she would look into those eyes and *not see him there,* which unsettled her.

He was cool, knew a hundred tricks with cigarettes, flipping them

to catch between his lips, blowing perfect smoke rings, round or figure eight, telling stories that involved a cigarette and two paper
matches, holding a lighted cigarette inside his mouth . . . one morning
she caught him practicing flipping cigarettes to his lips and without
embarrassment he told her it takes discipline to be casual.

Amanda dressed in a heavy cotton robe James Joseph gave her
years ago, probably stolen from a luxury hotel. In her kitchen, she
poured a glass of wine and thought that she and Charlie were both
lucky that Judge Borders hadn't sent them to jail . . . Borders so be-
fuddled by Maria's striptease that he didn't object when Amanda
blustered something about Charlie having mental problems, very
sorry to have troubled you, Judge, but Charlie apparently is delu-
sional and didn't witness a homicide after all, I need to get him psy-
chiatric care. Get out, get out, Borders had ordered . . . which is
exactly what Amanda and Charlie did. And since Charlie was never
officially booked into jail, the bureaucracy wasn't likely to come after
him for being *out* of jail. Detective Renfrone was another matter entirely.

I should call Gallier about him, Amanda thought . . . but then
Gallier will ask questions I don't want to answer or he'll insist I take
a ride with him in that ridiculous stretch limousine. Amanda decided
she'd wait until morning to call Gallier, hope to get his answering machine.

Because she was looking at her telephone when it rang, Amanda
was so startled she spilled her wine . . . cursing as she picked up the
receiver and snapped, *"Hello?"*

"I need a gun."

"I beg your pardon."

"A gun."

"Sister Margaret?" Another client Pelikan had arranged for
Amanda to represent, the tall nun everyone said looked like Janet
Reno.

"Yes."

"I don't understand what you mean about the gun."

"Hog-leg, *pistole,* gat, sidearm, what part don't you understand?"

"The part about who the gun is *for.*"

"Me!"

"Sister, you don't need—"

"We need to resolve this matter is what we need, and it's obviously not going to be resolved in the courts . . . you're dragging your feet."

"I'm not even being paid for this, how dare you—"

"Christ dares me, Holy Mother Church dares me. Nearly two thousand years the sacred Edessa was under our protection, then lost, now found . . . but *still* not returned to us. Do you call that justice . . . well let me tell you, if the courts won't give it back, we'll *take* it back."

"Whom do you intend to shoot?"

"Whoever gets in our way."

"What about *Thou shalt not kill?*"

"We'll wing 'em. Now, can you get me a gun or not?"

"Most certainly *not.*"

"Then I'm sorry but the convent of Limoges no longer needs your services as an attorney."

"Sister, what you *don't* need is a gun."

"We'll see. God bless you."

18

SEND IN THE CLOWN

On Royal Street a movie crew was shutting down after filming nighttime exterior shots. Fans at the barricades had been told that no famous actors were involved in tonight's filming, but people continued milling around in vain hope of seeing stars . . . one young woman stood at the ropes fantasizing a cliché about being plucked out of the crowd and put in the movie. To encourage this fantasy she wore a silky floral print dress with big white buttons up the front. Her father was a dentist in California, she was of peasant stock with thick hands and wide hips, but she also possessed three sought-after assets: thick, dark luxurious hair, nearly flawless white skin, and she was nineteen years old.

The air tonight is apparently too thick and damp to move anywhere else, staying in the Quarter out of lethargy and wet weight, the entire evening simply standing here refusing to do anything . . . and in this oppressive stillness people wandered, sweated, stank, drank. Some were stone-stumbling drunk though you could hardly distinguish them from the sober, equally dazed. A hooker and a clown approached the crane that had been leased by the movie company. Operating the crane was a man named Tom Indering, who in the old Louisiana tradition was open to consideration.

"You know what really frosts me about this?" the hooker, Diane, said to the clown, Sad Bob. "I don't mind bribing this guy with a blow job, that's my contribution to the cause . . . I told James Joseph I'd do it and I'll do it. But I have to supply the hundred dollars? A blow job's not enough, I got to pay him too? Does that seem right to you?"

The clown looked at the hooker with genuine sympathy. She reminded him of Joan Crawford at forty. Diane "Knees" O'Rourke had wide shoulders and a narrow waist. No part of her face had been left untouched: she'd shaved her eyebrows and then painted them in with high arches, she'd stuck on long thick lashes, she wore a blaze of red lipstick, and atop the foundation that covered her entire face like a base coat on a canvas, she had added an eye-popping variety of shadows and blushes. Joan Crawford was Sad Bob's favorite . . . and he told Diane the hooker, "I have twenty dollars to my name, I'd be happy to contribute it."

She smiled and patted him carefully on the cheek so the greasepaint wouldn't come off on her hand. "You're sweet . . . but I told James Joseph I'd pay it, so I will, I just think it's unfair. I should've been asked to pay the bribe or give the blow job, not both, that's all I'm saying."

"If James Joseph had the money, he would've given it to you."

"I'm not saying he's trying to cheat me, I just wish he would've made it clear from the beginning where the hundred was coming from. Forget it. You look nice tonight."

Sad Bob thanked her and said she looked nice too . . . Diane wearing a silver-shiny top with shoulder pads, black toreador pants with a wide patent leather belt, and spike high heels. She had wild red hair that wasn't like Joan Crawford at all but somehow worked with the rest of the ensemble.

"Do you recognize my character?" he asked.

She said she didn't.

"Well, last week I was the Harlequin—"

"When I went to the circus as a kid," she interrupted, "the clowns were my favorite act . . . clowns and elephants."

"Actually, Diane, the Harlequin is based on the commedia dell'arte, from Italian theater in the sixteenth century. Harlequin began as victim of Brighella but eventually evolved into master with his own victims, one of whom became the whiteface—"

"Oh Bob," she laughed.

He looked surprised, then nodded. "Yeah, I know . . . stop trying to be the smartest kid in the class. But I thought you might recognize me tonight because this character is from television, though before your time." Sad Bob was fifty-five.

"Sorry," she said, "I don't know any television clowns unless you mean like David Letterman, he's a card."

"But not a clown."

"Not officially, I guess, no."

"I'm . . ." Sad Bob paused here for dramatic effect. "Clarabell."

"Sorry," she said.

"Howdy Doody."

"Howdy Doody to you, too, Bob, but I don't have clue one what the fuck you're talking about."

"I know it was way before your time, but I thought surely you'd heard of it, a classic show . . . Phineas T. Bluster, Flub-A-Dub, the Peanut Gallery, and of course, Buffalo Bob."

"Is that how you got your name, from Buffalo Bob?"

Sad Bob could only sigh in the face of such ignorance.

"Well, I'm sorry," the hooker apologized, "but I never heard of no clown Buffalo Bob."

"Honey, he wasn't the clown, he was Howdy Doody's— Never mind. Anyway, Clarabell was the famous clown on that show . . . this zebra-striped costume I'm wearing and which I made myself, I'm proud to say, the ruffles around my neck, the bald head with topknot, and these hair fluffs by my ears, the classic rectangles above the eyes—"

"Bob."

"Sorry. Clarabell never spoke, he had an ooga horn and he was notorious for spritzing people with seltzer water and he had this box, see here, attached to the front of him, and on the show the box had his name on it but I didn't want to violate any trademark rights so I didn't put *Clarabell* on my box, I put *Sad Bob* . . . but of course you can see that, can't you . . . am I rambling again?"

She assured him he was but added, "Clowns are your business, I can't blame you for being obsessed."

"For five or six years Clarabell was played by the man who later became Captain Kangaroo."

"I never heard of that clown either."

"Captain Kangaroo wasn't a clown."

"With a name like that? Listen, Bob, can we talk about something else?" They were waiting for the movie crew and fans to leave, giving the hooker and clown the privacy they needed for dealing with the crane operator. "Where are you going after the job," Diane asked, "you made up your mind yet?"

Sad Bob nodded eagerly. "Oh I knew exactly where I was going as soon as James Joseph said that leaving the country was part of the deal . . . France."

"Me, I'm going back to Ireland and find a little thatched roof cottage to live in which I'm going to call Apple Tree Cottage and I'll raise a little garden and have white chickens—"

Sad Bob was sniffling.

"Don't," she told him coldly.

"Apple Tree Cottage sounds so charming, and then I was thinking about cute little baby chicks . . ."

The hooker was adamant. "Don't start one of your crying jags tonight, we got too much work to do."

He said okay.

She watched for tears, then continued, "Now where was I . . . raise a garden and mind my chickens and live in Apple Tree Cottage and never ever suck cock again . . . that's got to be one of the advantages of living in Ireland, not having to suck cock."

"Well, I'm going to France and I guess you can't say that about France but I don't care, I'm taking the pledge right along with you, girl, retiring from oral sex and affairs of the heart . . . too much sadness down those roads. You know the story of how He Who Shall Remain Nameless left me high and dry?"

"I know the story, yeah, you told me the story more than once."

"He came home one night with a man he said was an old school 'friend.' "

"Yes—"

"And we sat around drinking margaritas and smoking a little grass, everything very mellow when He Who Shall Remain Nameless asked if I'd get dressed in one of my costumes and then let him and his school 'friend' both go down on me at the same time."

"You told me—"

"So like the fool I am I agreed and eventually they're down there snickering and making little remarks about blowing a clown when He Who Shall Remain Nameless asked his school 'friend,' 'Does this clown taste funny to you?' Which got them both laughing like hyenas, actually rolling around on the floor . . . and the harsh reality hit me right between the eyes—"

"He'd been laughing *at* you all those years, not with you," the hooker said, finishing Sad Bob's story for him. "I know, you told me already."

Sad Bob sniffled. "The French love clowns, the French consider clowning an art form."

"Let's not talk for a while," she suggested . . . so they stood together in the French Quarter's steam bath, Diane puffing a cigarette, Sad Bob trying to stay out of the slipstream of her secondhand smoke.

He couldn't stay quiet for long though. "The show, *Howdy Doody,* was on for more than ten years and Clarabell never said a word on air that whole time."

"Bob, you could maybe take a hint from Clarabell."

"Rumor was . . . I never saw the last show, but the rumor was, on the very last show, Clarabell came close to the camera and after a decade of silence looked longingly and lovingly into the lens and said, 'Good-bye, kids.' "

"Longingly and lovingly?"

Sad Bob was softly crying.

"Oh Bob," said the hooker.

He shook his Clarabell head. "I know I'm being silly."

"You can't get through a single fucking night without bawling?"

"I'm *sorry.*"

It's how he got his name, Sad Bob . . . he cried a lot. Almost anything could make him cry . . . puppies out in the rain for sure. And Bob was gone before Hallmark commercials were half over, weddings and funerals got him weepy even if he didn't know the people involved, and little kids at airports looking frightened were enough to make Bob sob.

After his break up with He Who Shall Remain Nameless, Sad

Bob suffered a decade-long depression punctuated by bouts of such self-loathing and paranoia that, like Kafka in "The Burrow," building the Castle Keep, Sad Bob would repeatedly run into the walls of his apartment and hit forehead first. It was drywall so he seldom drew blood himself, but still, irritating for the neighbors. He's better now. In fact, other than the crying affliction, Sad Bob could honestly say life was good. He took clowning very seriously and once gave a class at a junior college, maybe the proudest day of his life. Sad Bob had the kids cheering, "Greasepaint with Attitude" was the name of his presentation, even thinking about it now could cause him to weep with pride. He makes okay money here on the streets of the French Quarter, though Sad Bob tends toward classic clowning routines, which don't get the kinds of tips he could harvest by blowing balloons into animals and using props such as gag string. His mom died last year and left him a house, all paid for, and although he doesn't have anyone special in his life right now, Sad Bob's fine, thank you for asking.

If he could just stop crying! It's so embarrassing. Sad Bob thinks he knows when the affliction struck . . . back during that awful winter following the breakup with He Who Shall Remain Nameless, Sad Bob shared an apartment with a professor who insisted he wasn't gay, har, har. Anyway, this professor knew a whole collection of sad stories: Father Flanagan, the corduroy wedding dress, the little boy lost in the airport, dogs in heaven, dozens of stories that he'd tell Bob of an evening, stories *so* terribly, mawkishly, dramatically *sad* that Bob just seemed to acquire the habit of crying.

And now he's Sad Bob.

When the movie crew had gathered up the last of the cables, Diane "Knees" O'Rourke told Sad Bob it was show time. "Is your truck in position, is that machine thing ready to be lifted?"

Sad Bob assured her everything was in position and ready. "By the way, it's an industrial air compressor."

"To me it's a machine thing."

"And to me, Diane, it was a holy quest."

He had spent the better part of three days traveling, though not costumed as Clarabell, of course, through the bayous and around the bays and into the swamps, following Pelikan's elaborate directions about what could be traded with whom, eventually ending with pickup truck and industrial air compressor. Pelikan had made all the arrangements but Sad Bob had to do the legwork.

He tried complaining to Diane but she said, "Your job was to get a truck and machine thing, now my job is to blow that crane operator and give him a hundred dollars of my own money . . . who do you think's getting the dirty end of the deal?"

He laughed and told the hooker, "Come on, girl, strut your stuff."

She nodded, putting on her smiling game face, making that curly red hair shake all over her head . . . Diane walking carefully on very high heels to the cab of the crane. "Hey, up there!" she shouted. "Is Tom in there?"

A round, florid face showed at the window. "Whatta you want?"

"You Tom?"

"Whatta you want?"he asked again.

"Did you talk to James Joseph Pelikan yesterday?"

"Ohhhh," he crooned, opening the door to the crane's cab. "I most certainly did."

"Well, give me a hand, Tom."

He helped Diane up a ladder and into the cab with him. Then, looking down at Sad Bob standing there in the street, Tom asked her, "Who's the clown?"

She was tired of discussing clowns. "That's Sad Bob, Buffalo Bob, Clarabelly, Flub Your Dub, Captain Zebra, I don't know who the fuck it is, Tom, are you going to put our machine thing where we want it, or not?"

He said he would, as promised. "Where's my two hundred bucks?"

"Nice try," she said, giving him the hundred.

He smiled as if to say, hey, I took a shot. "And one more thing that's part of the deal."

"Yeah, yeah, I know."

But when she reached for his fly, Tom pulled her close and whispered something in her ear.

"Are you serious?" she asked.

He nodded like a naughty little boy who's just made a nasty sug-
gestion to the little girl living next door.

Diane laughed and looked out the crane's window, down at Sad
Bob . . . who looked up at her and said, "What's wrong?"

"Well, Tommy boy here has a fantasy . . ." She laughed again. "It
has to do with watching as a clown face—" But now she was laughing
too hard and gestured *wait, wait* to Sad Bob, she'd have to come down
there and tell him, she couldn't shout it out the cab like this.

When she was finally on the ground, Diane tried not to laugh as
she told Sad Bob that Tom wanted to get blown by a clown.

"You're not serious," Sad Bob said.

She assured him she was.

"Well Jeez-bees!"

"Hey," Diane said, "we both told James Joseph we'd do whatever
necessary to get the job done."

"*Shit.*" It was about the worst curse word Sad Bob ever used.

"Come on, you gotta do it," Diane encouraged. "Strut your
stuff."

Clarabell's shoulders sagged.

And now here's Tom again: the crane operator's big red face at
the crane's window as he croons, "*Send in the clown . . .*"

19

THE PELIKAN GANG

I'm trying to sleep but it's too hot. Pelikan didn't tell me that the air-conditioning in this apartment was one of the systems being renovated. Lying here on the bed in a pair of undershorts, I keep looking at the ceiling as if to will cool air from the air-conditioning duct right above me . . . and I still hear the cockroaches. I haven't moved the bed yet, it's too hot to move furniture. It's probably not too hot to watch TV but there's no TV in my little roach-infested slave cottage. I tried reading a book but the pages felt mushy in this humidity. About the only thing that would heal me of this heat is a red Popsicle, I don't care much for them unless they're red, but the Popsicles are downstairs in the refrigerator and it's too hot to go downstairs. I remember from when I was a kid how this wet New Orleans summer heat seems to have actual weight, like someone sitting on your chest and you keep telling them get off, get off, it's not funny anymore, please get off, but the heat doesn't get off, it bears down all the more . . . I'd like to call Amanda and ask her to come over here and screw me to make up for what I missed out on twelve years ago, but it's too hot to screw unless she lets me be the one on the bottom so I can just lay there and sweat and watch her do all the work. I reach a hopeful hand down in my shorts but it's too hot to—

Someone here . . . I pull my hand out and scramble up near the headboard . . . *Jesus, you scared me,* I say to Pelikan, embarrassed he caught me with a hand in my pants (how long had he been standing there at the foot of the bed watching?). "How'd you get in, I locked the outside door."

"To every lock, a key." Pelikan sat on the bed. He wore sneakers, blue jeans, and a white dress shirt that seemed amazingly fresh and unwilted.

"Doesn't that long hair bug you," I asked, "in all this heat?"

No reply.

"I'm getting dressed," I said.

But he wouldn't move to let me off the bed. "When you were a little boy, three or four years old, I think, well before I ever met you, of course . . . your sisters would dress you up in different outfits and then you would act out little stories for them, related to the outfit you had on. If they dressed you up like a cowboy, you'd tell a story about chasing bad guys and reaching for your six-shooter . . . I think they had a double set of holsters for you to wear, silver six-shooters. Of if they dressed you in a miniature astronaut outfit, you'd walk around with your arms out to your sides and taking real high steps, faking the moon's lesser gravity because you were very smart as a little boy and already knew about things like gravity . . . and you'd tell your sisters stories you made up about being a spaceman."

"Where are we going with this?"

"I wish I could've seen you growing up spoiled rotten by your sisters. I've never even met them, my nieces, much less their kids. I hope someday when you have kids—"

"That I'll send them down here to meet you? I'll have their legs broken before I let them come to New Orleans."

He used his large hands to finger back his hair. "Your eyes are all bloodshot, not getting enough sleep?"

"I was pepper-sprayed in the courthouse—"

"I know, I heard about it."

Then why did he ask if I was getting enough sleep, why didn't he just come out and say he'd heard I'd been pepper-sprayed in the courthouse? "I saw the woman who killed Three Jacks. Do you know about that too?"

He didn't answer.

"Now get this, her tattoos are gone, and remember how I told you she was shaved between the legs . . . well it grew back. The tattoos could've been temporary ones that she washed off, but how did she regrow a bush overnight? I've been thinking about it, maybe she has a twin sister who's got the tattoos, who's shaved between the legs, and it's that twin, the evil twin, who killed Three Jacks, because if two different women aren't involved, how else do you explain that bush?"

Pelikan murmured something I didn't catch . . . *murky* or *merlin?* He always talked so quietly that you had to listen carefully or miss half of what he said unless you leaned close. I asked him to repeat it, but he shook his head and said, "Do you have a lawyer?"

"Of course I have a lawyer . . . you sent her to see me, didn't you?"

"Amanda."

"*Yesss,*" I hissed in frustration. He could be the most maddening man in the world.

"Come downstairs, I want to show you something."

"Do you think you can find me an apartment with air-conditioning and a TV, maybe a place without so many cockroaches? This building is infested."

"Come on," he said, walking toward the circular stairs.

Wondering if I should get dressed, I asked him if we were going outside. Pelikan said no. He went circling down the wrought iron staircase and I followed, arriving at the first floor in nothing but my undershorts, to find everyone staring: five nuns, a clown, and a streetwalker.

Mumbling apologies, I hurried back up. Did Pelikan do that as a joke? I didn't hear any laughter behind me, but I was angry and embarrassed. Things like this don't happen in Connecticut, in Connecticut we are reasonable people who seldom have nuns and hookers and clowns in our homes. Tempted to stay upstairs and lock myself in the bathroom, I took a long time putting slacks and a shirt on, hoping they'd all leave, but everyone was still in place when I returned downstairs.

Pelikan acted as if unaware he'd done anything wrong, taking my elbow to escort me around the room to the various characters sitting on boards balanced across sawhorses or, in the case of two little birdy nuns, kneeling on the floor fingering beads.

"This is my burglary team," Pelikan said with quiet pride.

"You're shitting me."

He grabbed my bent finger.

"Jesus Christ." All the nuns looked. "Don't do that," I told Pelikan, "it hurts."

"Then please moderate your language."

When I promised I would, Pelikan let go.

"Can I talk to you?" I asked him. *"Upstairs."*

"No secrets in this gang, Charlie."

"Fine." But then I didn't know what to say, finally sputtering, *"What* are you doing with these people?"

"Waiting for a storm, then we're breaking into the repository and—"

"Nuns?" They were the same five who were with Pelikan down by the river when Renfrone hit me in the nuts before dragging me off to that holding cell. *"Nuns."*

"The sisters have a huge stake in this operation, Charlie."

"This isn't really a burglary, is it . . . you're all involved in some sort of performance art, right?"

He led me to the tall, craggy nun who, when I saw her and the four other nuns with Pelikan, reminded me of Janet Reno . . . her big black-framed glasses sitting so far down on her nose that only the tip showed, like a little red knuckle.

"This is my nephew Charlie," Pelikan told her. Then to me, "Charlie, this is Sister Margaret, she's from a convent near Limoges in France."

"Enchanté," I said.

"You got to learn to hold your mud, cowboy," she replied roughly, shaking my hand as a man might.

"Sister Margaret grew up in Montana," Pelikan explained.

"Where I learned how to shoot," she said.

Pelikan smiled at her but shook his head. "I told you before, that's not going to happen."

I didn't know what they were talking about, some bone of contention.

Next he took me over to the two big nuns, they had to be pushing three hundred pounds each, a lot of that weight in their upper bodies. Their faces, straining out of their stiffly starched coifs, were heavily boned with deep-set eyes behind the black eyeglasses that fit them perfectly. They both sported sparse but dark mustaches. I even wondered briefly if they were men dressed up like nuns, the way so many guys do here in New Orleans during Mardi Gras and for Halloween or on a Wednesday. Later on I'd have a difficult time telling these nuns apart because not only were they dressed and shaped the same, they moved in the same galumphing manner . . . hippos in habits, an uncharitable person might say.

"These two sisters," Pelikan was telling me about them, "are from Bulgaria originally . . . you might be interested to know that in the year five oh two, the Bulgars ravaged Thrace."

"Really." I didn't have a clue what that meant.

"All these sisters are from the same convent," Pelikan said. "The Limoges convent in France. This one is Three Jacks's sister."

I took her hand and offered condolences about Three Jacks being killed.

"They don't speak or understand English," Pelikan said.

We moved down the line. "And these two *praying* sisters"—he indicated the little nuns kneeling on the floor—"are from the Philippines. They're my little pinkletinks, aren't you, girls? I call this one Tiddlywink and this one Tickledpink."

They looked up. Unlike the Bulgarians, who were being squeezed by their wimples, these two seemed to rattle around in there, the Buddy Holly glasses overwhelming their faces.

Next the clown. "This is Sad Bob."

I tensed.

The clown stuck out his hand but I didn't take it.

"Nephew . . . ," Pelikan said warningly.

"That'll be the day when I shake a clown's hand."

"It's perfectly all right," Sad Bob said with a catch in his throat. "There's a certain portion of the population that's clown phobic, and who can blame them . . . probably sometime in your life, Charlie, when you were a little baby, some well-meaning person thrust you toward a clown at the circus or some party and the very sight of that painted face and big hair is enough to frighten any little person. There's a lot to like about clowns but—"

"You know what I like about clowns, I like to knock them down with heavy blows to the head is what I like about clowns."

He sniffled and wiped a smear of greasepaint from around his eyes. "I don't blame *you*, Charlie. Society is to blame, there's a whole evil clown genre that poisons people against us . . . and then you get someone like John Wayne Gacy, it's a wonder more people don't hate clowns. All I can do to rectify that is to be as good as I can every day, as kind as I can in every way."

"I think you should change your name to Unctuous Bob."

He spoke brightly through his tears. "See, it's working, I got you making jokes already."

I turned to Pelikan. "Is he going to come in *uniform* when you rob the repository?"

"Costume," Sad Bob corrected.

"He's a clown," Pelikan said, "so he dresses like a clown, what do you expect? Tonight he's Clarabell."

"Thank you for noticing, James Joseph," Sad Bob said, putting a sincere hand on Pelikan's forearm and telling him, "James Joseph, not for the world would I hurt your feelings . . . but the truth is, and maybe you haven't even noticed it about yourself, when I'm *out* of costume, you don't give me the time of day."

Acknowledging this with a noncommittal nod, Pelikan turned to the woman who either was a streetwalker or had dressed like one for tonight's party . . . she had frightful red hair, her makeup troweled on. She smoked a cigarette and chewed gum at the same time, her jaw muscles so pronounced as to make her resemble a chipmunk.

"And *this*," Pelikan announced proudly, "is Diane O'Rourke."

"Howz ya momma and 'em sisters?" she asked.

I turned to Pelikan. "Why is everyone asking after my mother and sisters?"

The woman answered for him. "Because James Joseph regales us with stories of how them women spoiled you as a little boy."

Pelikan said, "Diane is the woman who started it all."

"Started what?" I asked.

"I don't mean disrespect," he replied, throwing a look back at the nuns before continuing in his quiet voice, "but Jesus said Peter was the rock he would build his church on, and this little lady's talent is what I build my whole entire business on . . . she is without doubt or question, unparalleled, unchallenged, and undefeated, the number one best cocksucker in the world."

"Oh James Joseph," she said shyly as if he'd just complimented her skills as a cellist. "There're probably better ones somewhere . . . in Vegas, I bet."

He told her, "*Nonsense.* If I had a dozen like you working for me, we wouldn't have to break into the repository, I could buy it."

Grinning, she slipped a heroin-skinny arm around his waist. "Okay, that's enough now."

Peeved not to be a part of this love fest, Sad Bob popped up and said, "Except I'm the one who had to *bribe* the crane operator."

"Duty," Pelikan told him sternly.

"Yeah, I know . . . anyway, I'm seeing him later on this week, call me crazy—"

Pelikan interrupted the clown by turning to the others and saying, "Duty . . . ladies and gentlemen, be you nun, hooker, clown, or nephew, I expect each to do his duty."

I stood there with my mouth open . . . who the hell does he think he is, General Lee preparing troops for the battle of Gettysburg?

"Everything's in place," Pelikan was saying, "the last of the equipment went up today. Sister Margaret, the two Bulgarian nuns, Diane, and Sad Bob will all be up on the roof helping me break through. Charlie, you stay on the ground . . . your assignment is to drive the rescue truck."

"What rescue truck?"

"Once we have access to the interior vaults from the top of the building, we're bringing everything back up to the roof, then lowering the loot over the side in sheet-covered stretchers, which we'll load into the rescue truck, equipped with full lights and siren for smooth passage. The law will be distracted by the storm, and no one's going to stop a rescue truck. Any questions?"

Even though I had no intention of joining this mad enterprise, I was the only one to ask anything. "What loot, where's it going?"

"Pass Manchac. Papa Gator will load his boat with everything we've liberated, then—"

"Who's Papa Gator?"

"Another member of the gang."

"Sounds reassuring. What happens if the city gets lucky, no severe storms this summer?"

"We got that covered."

"How?"

"Tiddlywink and Tickledpink are praying for a storm, that's their only assignment on this job. You could say they're the most important members of the team."

20

THE DOCTOR'S IN

Pelikan and the gang are gone, I'm back in bed sucking on a red Popsicle and listening to the scratching in the vent and thinking maybe it's not cockroaches, maybe a rat's trapped in the ductwork gnawing its way through that vent to drop onto my sweating stomach . . . I really should get up and move the bed.

The others went out to eat, Pelikan saying it was dangerous for me to come along . . . I should stay in the apartment and not even answer the door. Downstairs I find that Pelikan has stocked the kitchen with cans of chili, boxes of macaroni and cheese, and a locally prepared dish in a carton with an overly clever label: *Red Beans Anne Rice*. But I want a restaurant meal and a real drink and mainly I want to leave this oppressive little cottage.

It's cool walking through the stone corridor, but when I open the door to the sidewalk, it's even hotter than it was in the apartment . . . across the street there's a guy dressed like a pirate and when he sees me he takes off running, probably to go tell Pelikan I'm breaking the rule about not leaving the apartment.

I've walked a few blocks when a huge white limousine glides up beside me, a darkened back window coming down and the guy inside calling pleasantly, "Charles? Charles Curtis?"

I stop.

"I knew your father," the man in the limo said, pushing open the door. "If you would consent to sit with me a moment, I'd like to offer my condolences."

He didn't look dangerous . . . slightly built and elegantly dressed in a dark suit and stiff white shirt showing a lot of cuff and collar, gold bracelet on his thin wrist. I got in, the limo smelling of spicy apples, and sat facing rear, opposite the man, smiling widely, showing small white teeth. Though he was almost bald on top, the hair at the sides and rear of his head was long enough for a ponytail. He had big brown eyes like a deer and when he leaned down to speak in an intercom telling the driver to proceed, I noticed his eyelashes were unusually long and thick. He looked like a fey version of one of those old-line mafioso types who sit for an hour or two in the barbershop to get styled and shaved, manicured and powdered and primped.

"Do you wear lipstick?" he asked.

"What?"

"Your mouth is red."

"Oh . . . a Popsicle."

"Popsicle," he chuckled, offering a small hand. "My name is Gallier . . . Dr. Blanchard Gallier."

Oh shit.

"Is something wrong?"

"I just remembered . . . I have to go." I braced for an attack.

"Of course." Gallier leaned forward again to speak in the door-mounted intercom. "Edward, pull over please." Then to me, "I'm sorry we can't spend a little time together, there's so much I was hoping to tell you."

I scooted to the door.

"When I introduced myself," he said, "you look startled . . . if I may ask, did your uncle say anything about me to you?"

"No," I lied, grasping the door handle. I didn't believe Pelikan when he told me there was an evil doctor who removed somebody's kidney in a hotel room but now this little guy looks weird enough to do it.

"Are you sure you can't stay, I have a full bar back here."

He wants to drug me. "I have to go."

"Of course." Still smiling, he continued considering me. "The rea-

son I asked if your uncle ever mentioned me, he has told people incredible stories, that I'm a madman who goes around cutting my victims open and stealing their body parts . . . which is a well-established
urban myth here in New Orleans."

With my hand still on the door, I hesitated. "Yeah, I've read
about them."

He nodded encouragingly. "At one point the myth was sited in
Las Vegas, some gambler engages the services of a prostitute and ends
up having his kidney removed in his hotel room, a morality lesson for
our times, I suppose. But now the myth has this happening in New
Orleans . . . our police force gets dozens of calls about it, people wanting to know if it's safe to travel here. Of course the story's not true,
never happened, not here, not in Las Vegas either. Pablum for the
gullible. Your uncle uses it to slander me."

"Why?"

Gallier smiled as he glanced at my hand still grasping the door
handle. "That door is unlocked, you may, of course, leave anytime
you wish . . . however, I'd be most grateful if you could spare a few
minutes."

I released the handle.

"Thank you. And you do have my condolences for the death of
your father. I knew him through James Joseph; he was a good man,
your father."

I thanked him.

"James Joseph did tell you that I was the evil kidney remover,
didn't he?"

I shrugged.

Gallier *tsk*ed. "I'd really like to have a word with the author."

"Who?"

"The person scripting my life."

I didn't understand what he was getting at.

"I am devoted to art and beauty, but do you see what role I'm cast
to play?" His soft eyes turned upward in plea. "Have I really been reduced to this . . . this *cliché*, the evil doctor?" Gallier sighed dramatically. "What you must think of me."

I said nothing.

Pulling down the seat back to reveal a large compartment with bottles and glasses, Gallier asked again if I'd have a drink with him. "I'm indulging a brandy."

Feeling foolish for being so timid with this little man, I said a drink sounded great . . . did he have ice?

"Yes, of course."

"A gin and tonic, then."

"Excellent choice. Tanqueray, wedge of lemon?"

"Perfect."

He fixed the drink, handed it to me, we toasted . . . I no longer felt threatened. Gallier seemed genuinely pained that Pelikan was spreading stories about him and eager to correct the bad impression I might have gotten.

"James Joseph and I were once close and famous friends," Gallier explained. "None are so bitter as enemies who once were friends."

"What happened between you?"

"I won't bore you with the details except to say that, because of this repository job, I *thought* James Joseph and I were going to bury the hatchet and work together again. But apparently not." He pursed his lips, shook his head. "I don't suppose James Joseph has been entirely forthcoming with you, so let me explain my situation. My uncle died and left me an estate rich in artwork and antiques, an inheritance that unfortunately has been tied up in the courts for nearly two years.

"My uncle, Dunbar Gallier, acquired a great deal of artwork and many antiques during tours of Europe with the army following the Second World War. Dunbar had a great eye for art and, frankly, for bargains too, but he was meticulous in ensuring that each piece he bought came with a provenance detailing *and legitimizing* the item's ownership and sales history. As I said, I inherited everything two years ago and was rash enough to put the collection on display, only to be betrayed by one of my guests, who recognized a few things as possibly belonging to family or museum collections looted by German troops. Maybe it's true in some cases, but everything my uncle bought was purchased in good faith . . . at what point do we stop going back in history to readjust ownership? Shall we return North

America to the Indians, give Texas back to Mexico . . . where do we draw the line?"

"Wherever you draw it, Doc, it has to include returning Nazi loot to the original owners."

"Please don't call me Doc. And the original owners are dead, it's a bunch of relatives who are after my uncle's estate."

"The owners are dead because the Nazis killed them . . . is that the kind of loophole you're looking for?"

He stared at me for an uncomfortably long time, then asked, "What's your profession?"

"I deal in collectibles."

His eyes and smile widened. "Truly? I'm a collector myself. Wonderful." Gallier's smile was genuine now, not that unctuous grin. "You see how simpatico we are, Charles . . . we simply must spend some time together, I have a quirky little collection of eighteenth-century watercolors that I'd be privileged to show you. What are your specialties?"

"Baby Boomer memorabilia, lunch boxes and toys from their childhoods, some political stuff too."

His crest fell. "Lunch boxes and political stuff?"

"Yeah, political campaign buttons."

"Like . . . *I Like Ike?*" He laughed contemptuously. "Here, let me freshen your drink."

"No thanks." He was pissing me off. "I have to go."

"Oh look, I've upset you. I do apologize . . . sometimes I'm not very good with people. One of the reasons I no longer practice medicine, the milk of human kindness often curdles in my mouth." He took my glass and mixed another gin and tonic.

"If you have any misanthropic tendencies at all," he said, "here's a story you should enjoy . . . a party of French explorers, searching for the mouth of the Mississippi, needed local Indians to guide them, but the tribes were suspicious and refused all contact. Hoping to prove how generous they could be, the explorers captured an Indian who was crippled. The Frenchmen constructed an enclosure to protect the Indian from the weather, filled the little hut with various treasures, then tied the Indian inside and built a campfire to keep him warm.

The explorers retreated some distance. The theory was, the other Indians would see how royally their comrade was being treated and come out of hiding to meet with the explorers." Gallier began to laugh. "But the campfire caught the hut on fire . . . and the captive Indian along with all the gifts were burnt to a crisp." He put a little hand over his mouth to hide his Chiclet teeth while he continued laughing. "God, I love that story."

"I really have to go, thanks for the drinks."

"Always trying to rush off, can't you stay just a little while longer? Charles, listen to me. I think your uncle might be planning to betray you."

"Yeah?"

"He needs someone to take the fall for the repository burglary."

I kept a poker face.

"James Joseph is setting you up as a patsy . . . by the way, *patsy* is from the Italian *pazzo,* fool."

Detective Renfrone had claimed the same thing, Pelikan was playing me for a fool, letting me take the fall for Three Jacks's murder.

Gallier apologized. "I shouldn't malign your uncle, not even with the truth. Family loyalty is supreme. In fact, Charles, I admire your restraint because if someone claimed that *my* uncle was betraying me I would tell the accuser, *'Allons sous les chênes!'* "

When I didn't reply, he translated, " 'Let's go under the oaks.' It was a classic challenge to duel under the oaks of the Louis Allard plantation, now City Park, where a thousand duels were held . . . ten on a single Sunday in eighteen seventy-three, three of them fatal." His eyes glistened as if he was sitting there watching men shoot each other. "Dueling became so *bustling* that participation had to be codified, the *Code Duello.* A hundred and fifty years ago, if a man dishonored you, you didn't turn to the courts, you went under the oaks. Opera fans challenged critics, fathers dueled sons, and brothers challenged brothers, the most common combination being father-in-law against son-in-law. The code required that participants be of the same social class, of course. A man back then was measured by his skill, courage, and honor . . . people back then didn't mistake delicacy for weakness. If you did, the consequences could be deadly. Gilbert Rosière arrived here from Bordeaux and within a week was challenged seven times, Rosière so refined and tenderhearted that he wept openly at the opera . . . and then dueled and killed those who mocked his weeping."

Gallier's attention snapped back to me. "My problem, Charles, is that I was born in the wrong century. Life now has become coarse, lacking in civility. Mardi Gras, once a stately festival rich in tradition, has in many areas deteriorated into a unseemly drunken display . . . most especially here in my beloved Vieux Carré. Your uncle is part of the problem, a major contributor to the coarsening of life here . . . the drinking, the prostitutes." He raised a small padded hand and waved it back and forth as if to ward off an airborne pest, then continued in genuine sadness, "Life was better in the past. Do you realize that even early in this century middle-class families could routinely afford live-in servants, that until well after the Second World War service stations still hired uniformed workers to fill your tank and check your fluids, that I can remember a time when air travel was gracious, the men dressed in suits, the women wearing hats and gloves, the service personnel polite and well trained? I wish I could afford to fly first class or, even better, could own my own aircraft . . . today, one suffers endless indignities that begin upon arrival at the airport . . . is the airline industry the only business in the world wherein all the employees actually detest their customers?"

"Prostitution."

He looked surprised then smiled, again showing those little white teeth. "Exactly. That air hostess standing at the door saying *bye-bye* to the passengers holds within her the same duplicitous contempt as a prostitute telling a client what a hot lover he is. Charles, you are an insightful man. Maybe you're the one to help me."

"How so?"

"As I mentioned before, James Joseph and I were once great friends, then he misinterpreted something . . . thought I was making a pass at him, which is ridiculous. This happened years and years ago. There were charges and recriminations. I arranged for investors to buy a bar that James Joseph thought was going to be his—"

"You're the one who was behind that?"

"Mmm, yes, I'm afraid so . . . a terrible and destructive feud I've been having with your uncle. James Joseph retaliates by spreading these awful rumors about me, that I removed organs in hotel rooms, that I have ambitions to become the Vieux Carré's Jack the Ripper. He won't let me near him, that's what hurts most of all. Now there's the matter of the Edessa."

"What *is* it?"

"Part of my uncle's estate, being held at the repository. The nuns want it."

"Stolen from them during the Second World War?"

"So they claim. James Joseph is supposed to *remove* my uncle's entire estate from the repository, take a few items for himself as compensation, I'll let the Edessa go to the nuns, the remainder returns to me . . . hardly a crime in the larger, moral sense, because it's my rightful inheritance."

"You're in on the burglary, is that what you're telling me?"

"In on it? I planned it, I'm financing it. James Joseph and I had an understanding, alliances and compensations were made, but now he pursues other agenda. James Joseph is apparently reneging . . . no burglary, no word from him why. You're my last best hope, Charles . . . talk to your uncle on my behalf, find out why he hasn't performed the break-in yet."

I said nothing and Gallier continued, "I was told he was waiting for you to show up, to take your father's place. Well, you're here, what's the delay *now?*"

"I don't know—"

"Charles, stop playing games, I'm in on this deal with James Joseph, I'm financing it, I supplied him with repository blueprints, showed him the vaults where my uncle's estate is housed. And now I'm being honest with *you*, warning you that your uncle is planning to set you up . . . can't you return the favor by being honest with me?"

"I have to go."

He tossed his head. "Well for chrissakes *go*, you've been grabbing for that door handle like a schoolgirl on her first date. Leave, just leave. Pelikan and that woman, Amanda, played you for a fool twelve years ago, they're doing it again, but you're too—"

"What do you mean?"

He smiled.

"What do you mean?" I demanded.

"That young woman who shot Gruber—"

"Maria . . . with the tattoos that disappeared—"

He nodded. "She's a whore who used to work for your uncle . . . why don't you ask him."

"I will."

"You're the *pazzo*."

I sat there fuming.

"Poor little Charlie."

"Fuck you."

He smiled. "I can be a powerful friend. I can get you off the hook with the police, make sure you're allowed to leave New Orleans in time to make your father's funeral."

I didn't believe him but was intrigued with the possibility.

"You can't conceive that your uncle would betray you," Gallier said. "Yet, twelve years ago he betrayed you with Amanda."

"How do you know about that?"

"He told me . . . he told everyone. How he bedded a woman his nephew couldn't—"

"Through the roof."

Gallier was startled. "I beg your pardon."

"He's got the equipment up there already . . . going to drill, cut, chop through the roof."

"Won't that cause quite a commotion?"

"Not in a storm."

"He's going to commit the burglary during a storm?"

I nodded. "A storm will cover the noise, divert the cops, ground the helicopters. Pelikan's waiting for a storm."

Gallier reached across me to push open the door. "Get out."

"What about being my powerful friend, getting me off the hook with the police?"

"I could never be friends with someone who would betray his own blood," he said, insisting he was sick of the sight of me.

I got out and the air-conditioned limousine glided away leaving me to suffer in heat, humidity, and guilt.

21

VULTURES AND VAGRANTS AND OL' PAPA GATOR

A pirate came to the apartment where Pelikan was living this month, Pelikan opening the door to find the man rubbing his nose. "What do you want, pirate?" Pelikan asked though he knew the answer because a bartender and a mime had already told him that nephew Charlie was seen getting out of Gallier's limousine.

Said the pirate: "The good doctor knows everything now and he says, *by the end of the month* . . . or he's putting his own crew on the job . . . and then he's going to begin harvesting your nephew's body parts, starting, I believe he said, with—"

Pelikan interrupted by asking, "How's piracy?"

Zane reached under the patch covering his right eye and said, "Bountiful." Back in the old days, one of the things Zane enjoyed about working for Pelikan was that the man treated you exactly like what you were, clown or pirate . . . unlike Gallier, who didn't take piracy seriously.

As if knowing what the other man was thinking, Pelikan said, "You're always welcome to come back."

The pirate began nervously picking at his face, shaking his head. "Be it France or be it England, the pirate king goes to the highest bidder but calls no flag his master save the skull and crossbones."

"I understand," Pelikan told the pirate, then closed the door and went to a bathroom where he pulled back his long hair and tied it with white string before bringing out his works. Simply unfolding the leather pouch brought him peace . . . soon, soon. But now he's refolding the leather and putting it away because first he has to find Charlie and do what's necessary. This makes him sad.

Pelikan, in blue jeans, long-sleeved white shirt, engineer boots, and hair pulled tight for action, made his way toward Jackson Square . . . traveling the Quarter for him was like walking through an outdoor house where he'd lived his whole life. There's the alley two men took him in when he was ten . . . and over there, I used to live in that building, and that one and that one . . . there's a stoop where a man sat one whole evening and night and it wasn't until the next morning that people realized he wasn't just sitting very still, he was dead. Pelikan crossed the street. I knew a woman who lived here. And there, my mother took me for a lovely meal in that restaurant when I was ten years old.

In Jackson Square, Pelikan will find his agents: jugglers and clowns and clarinet players, assigning them to watch for Charlie, come get me when you know where he is. But before he's able to issue this assignment, Pelikan meets an old street person he knows as Father, a name that came from English tourists who took to calling the man Father Christmas. Pelikan hadn't come across Father for some time and sees now he's a mess.

"What's happened to you, Father?"

The other man looked up with an absent expression . . . maybe in his sixties, but the ravages of living on the street made him appear much older. He had long unruly hair and a bushy beard of the same dull yellow color and where these two crops of hair met, at Father's jawline, they blended so perfectly you couldn't tell one from the other. At this moment, however, both were filthy: greasy and tangled and matted with food, tobacco, bits of leaf, and the general junk you'd pick up sleeping on a sidewalk. His face was dirty too, that ground-in grime that looks like a blackened tan. The bridge of his nose seemed to have disappeared, leaving a fat bulb sticking out above his mouth, lips cracked and dirtier than the rest of his face, though his hands were filthiest of all. The only aspect of him that seemed clean and bright were his eyes, blue. He wore a flannel shirt, torture in this heat, but Father wore what was given to him, a pair of brown corduroy trousers held up with a rope. On his feet, those plastic flip-flops you wear to the shower. He's got a big belly but he's not nearly as heavy as he was back in the days when he was called Father Christmas. He stinks, he reeks.

Take a step back and look at those trousers: starting at an apex by his groin, a large dirty yellow stain fans down the inside of his thighs, rolling outward, reaching all the way to his knees. Although the underarms of that flannel shirt are also stained, the shirt is clean compared to his urine-soaked-and-caked pants, repellant to see and stomach-turning to smell.

Pelikan asked again what's happened to him. "Where're your teeth?"

He spoke perfectly well without them: "Stolen from my mouth . . . ah it's you, James Joseph, I thought I recognized a sweet voice in a sour world."

"We have to clean you up."

"Let me look at you," Father said . . . he liked looking at Pelikan's face, pacific and serene and wise, it had a calming effect on the old man, like medicine. Then he remembered he was hungry. "Take me for a shrimp po'boy."

"I can't, Father, they won't let you in . . . I'll fix you something to eat at my place."

"Banana and peanut butter sandwich."

Pelikan grasped the old man's shoulder and turned him toward home. "I don't know if I have any bananas."

"Yes we have no bananas today."

"I'll stop at the A&P."

"Marshmallows too, the little ones."

"All right. Where's your stuff?" The older street people always carried a kit, their treasures and necessities, but Pelikan didn't see Father's.

"Stolen out from under my head, thieves in the night."

It was more likely, Pelikan thought, that the old man walked off and left his kit somewhere . . . much of the time Father was mentally sharp, but on occasion he departed for elsewhere.

Tourists stared as Pelikan guided Father across Jackson Square, occasionally a tourist child pointed at the urine-stained trousers and alerted his appalled parents . . . Father was oblivious to all of this, but of course Pelikan noticed, he saw how even polite and dignified people crinkled their noses in disgust. Six college kids bumped into one another to spread the word, look at that old guy with the beard, *look at his pants,* and then the three boys grabbed their crotches as if to pee in *their* pants while the three girls laughed to see such a thing. Tourists supported the French Quarter generally and Pelikan specifically, so he could never hate them, as a shepherd wouldn't hate his flock . . . but a sheep's ignorant bleating can sometimes get on the nerves of even the most caring shepherd. Pelikan *dealt* with tourists but didn't befriend them. To bar workers and clowns, Pelikan could speak of many things, reveal personal secrets, but when tourists came around he always put on his game face and showed them nothing intimate . . . which is why he was embarrassed on Father's behalf, not that the old man had fouled himself but that *tourists saw it.*

With Father shuffling, the trip home took a long time and Father wet his pants at least once on the way. When Pelikan got him inside the smell was worse, fresher, and the crusty stains on the corduroy had turned darker with the wet.

"Into the bathroom," Pelikan ordered . . . and the old man meekly obeyed. Once in that little room, even with the door left open, the smell went higher. "I'm going to bathe you."

Father immediately assumed the arms-stretched, head-back, eyes-closed pose of a little boy about to be undressed by his mother.

"Let's wait until I get the tub full," Pelikan said, turning on the taps. "Then you can step right into the tub and I can take your clothes out back to the trash."

"I won't go naked on the streets," Father insisted.

"No, I have things you can wear."

"As nice as these?"

"Nicer."

"Deal."

Pelikan sat on the toilet lid while the tub filled, the old man remained standing.

"Why do you pee your pants, Father?"

He had an answer ready. "Rebellion."

"Against what?"

"Incivility. No one'll let me use a bathroom. Surely that violates some basic human right. Even in a chained prison gang where I once served with distinction, the road boss would turn away and let you take a slash in private . . . but not here in the French Quarter. The Quarter's motto should not be *Let the good times roll,* it should be *Bathrooms for customers only.* They won't let me use facilities in their bars or restaurants, their shops or drugstores or groceries, I can't get in antique stores or art galleries, museums or movie houses, public custodians even stop me at the door of public restrooms and deny me entry, claiming I seek to loiter."

Pelikan smiled because Father was enjoying one of his lucid periods . . . *seek to loiter.*

"Still wishing to be a responsible citizen," Father continued, lifting both arms and raising one foot as he warmed to his story, "I searched out small places well away from foot traffic, but now the gendarmes have launched a reign of terror they call 'no public urination' and when I'm caught in an alley or too tightly against a building, the law descends with truncheons."

Pelikan checked the water flow to make sure it wasn't too hot, though the way this old man smelled he seemed to need boiling. "They never hit you, did they . . . the cops?"

Father had to admit they'd never actually struck him for public urination. "But I'm taken in, I'm *processed.* Don't you see, if I wanted to be *processed* I'd still have a job and wife, I wouldn't be living on the streets."

"You have to stop peeing in your pants, that's why you're being hassled."

"I told you, son, it's rebellion, I pee in my pants as an act of freedom. Deny me even the most basic of human needs? Then I rebel against that denial by pissing where I stand. Turn away a pilgrim requesting only that he be allowed private relief? Then I declare my freedom from that tyranny . . . and pass urine while sitting on a park bench. It takes a bit of concentration, but once you get the hang of it you can even piss while walking."

Pelikan reached over and shut off the taps. "It must be uncomfortable, wearing wet pants?"

"If the price of freedom is wet pants, then gladly I pay it . . . as my ancestors paid freedom's price with frozen feet at Valley Forge. As a rebel, now I walk by their smug little shops with my head held high, I no longer *need* their toilets, I thumb my nose and with hands in pockets I shake my dick, keep your precious pissoirs, drown in your trough urinals, I don't need them anymore, I piss in my pants, I am free, thank God, at long last I . . . am . . . free!"

"Put your arms down," Pelikan told him. When Father did, Pelikan began unbuttoning the shirt, wincing a little as the previously captured odors began seeping out from beneath the flannel.

"If it's bothering you already," Father said, "you're not going to survive when the trousers drop."

Pelikan laughed softly, put Father's shirt on the floor, then rolled up the sleeves of his own shirt and sat again on the toilet seat.

The old man's belly was protruding like a woman eight months pregnant . . . sores and boils pocked his skin. Though Pelikan had seen much worse on other street people he'd cleaned, it was the belly that concerned him. When Pelikan palpated Father below the ribs on the right side, the old man said, "Hey don't get fresh."

"You have cirrhosis."

"And I just used mouthwash too."

"No, it means—"

"I know what it means," Father told him. "Time for the pants, then?"

"Kick off your flip-flops."

The old man did, balancing himself with a hand on Pelikan's shoulder as Pelikan pulled the rope loose, undid a button hanging by its thread, and tried to lower the zipper, only to find that it had rusted tightly in place.

"I can just pull them down," Father offered, which he did. The yellow-brown underwear had rotted to his skin.

Acrid odor made Pelikan's eyes tear as he stood to guide Father over to the tub, helping lift one leg, then the other, balancing the old man to stand there in the warm sudsy water. Here's what you see now: starting at his groin and duplicating in size and shape the stain on his pants, a yellow protein crud lay across Father's legs like a terrible skin affliction . . . little chunks and flakes of dried urine clung like mites to the old man's leg hairs and his graying pubic hair was matted with crumbling cloth from the disintegrating underwear, the head of his little hooded penis crud-stuck over on one leg.

"Sit in the water and soak," Pelikan said. "I'll get a soft brush."

When he returned he saw that Father's blue eyes were full of tears.

"Don't cry," Pelikan told him. "While you soak, we'll start with your hair, get your face and beard clean too."

Distraught with humiliation, Father turned to anger. "Goddamn it, I don't want you washing my face with the same goddamn water my ass is sitting in!"

Pelikan got down on his knees close to the tub and placed a soft hand to the old man's starkly white shoulder. "Then, sir, shall we begin with the anus?"

Which caused Father to laugh and weep until he lost his breath and coughed, gagged, got his breath back to laugh and weep all the more, telling Pelikan through the tears that he'd wash himself, please leave, it's too embarrassing to have someone else touch him when he's this disgusting.

"Nothing about you embarrasses or disgusts me," Pelikan assured him.

"I'm a bum. I reek to high heaven. God himself wouldn't bathe me."

"Nonsense . . . in thirty minutes you'll be as clean and fresh as a baby."

". . . who's been pissing in his diaper for the last two weeks. I sicken myself, don't tell me this doesn't bother you."

"Do you know Papa Gator?"

Father shook his head and wiped his eyes . . . but then began nodding because suddenly he *did* remember. "The old Cajun?"

"That's right, ol' Papa Gator. I tell people I never been out of New Orleans, it's my cradle and it's my coffin, but truth is I left New Orleans one time when I was a boy, went to live with Papa Gator out in the swamps . . . he was a friend of my mother's and he didn't think it was right that a boy grow up without ever stepping foot out of the city. Papa Gator said I needed swamp time."

"He used to come in and get drunk."

"Yes, that was Papa Gator's recreation once a month. I won't lie to you and say that I adored living with him out there on that stilt house you had to reach by boat, give me the French Quarter any day of the week, but my swamp time was illuminating."

"Eat muskrat and nutria?"

"That man would eat anything that didn't eat him first. He'd serve things on the table that I thought should be sent out to some laboratory for more study . . . but Papa Gator was a bug on not wasting food, so whatever was put in front of me, I ate, even if I had to swallow it without chewing so as to avoid the taste. Back then I had a phobia about getting a hair in my mouth, I guess you could call it a phobia, nothing disgusted me like seeing a hair in what I was about to eat. One day in Papa Gator's cabin he served something decent and recognizable for once, grits I think it was, and just as I was about to take my first forkful I see a big black hair sticking out of the grits, I think it was from one of the hounds. So when I figured Papa Gator wasn't looking I sneaked my plate over and dumped those grits in the dogs' bowl but I got caught and Papa Gator was cranking mad, demanding to know why I was feeding good grits to the dogs. I told him a hair was in my grits. 'So?' he says. I said a hair in your food is disgusting. 'Disgusting?' he says back to me like it's a bad word. Then he tells me to put on my shoes and follow him, which of course I did.

"We take the boat to a strand some distance away and follow it awhile on foot, then Papa Gator tells me to climb this certain tree and up there I'll find a couple nestlings which I should grab by the legs and bring down without injuring them. I'm happy to do something useful after getting him mad at me over a hair in the grits so I shinny up that tree and sure enough there's two young birds in a nest . . . they were really big babies and, good Lord, ugly, they stank, I didn't know at the time they were baby vultures. The parents had flown off, they usually won't defend a nest, but those babies were vicious. They put their little heads down and hissed like snakes and the breath that came out, I swear to you, Father, I was skunked once while living out there with Papa Gator and the breath of those vultures was worse, far worse than any skunk. Vultures have such strong stomach acid they can eat any kind of dead animal and no bacteria or virus will survive their digestive tract, so of course all that rotting meat being worked on by that powerful acid produces a wicked odor . . . which nearly knocked me off the limb. When Papa Gator hollered up what's wrong, I hollered back down, 'They're hissing at me.' Also, they had their wings out, elbows down to look all the meaner, doing these mock charges, and believe me it was working, I was plainly scared of them. But Papa Gator said, 'They can't hurt you, they're just babies . . . now grab 'em by the legs and bring 'em down.' I knew the man didn't take no for an answer, I could either bring those stinking creatures down out of that tree or I could stay up there on a limb until I rotted and the birds would eat *me* as carrion. So I screwed up my courage and reached in to grab and when I did those birds performed two other defense mechanisms that I knew nothing about but which ol' Papa Gator was well aware of . . . they vomited all over me. You can imagine what that smelled like, if their breath was worse than skunk . . . well, just imagine. It was so bad I vomited too but by comparison mine was sweet nectar. The second thing they did in fear and defense was shit all over their own legs which made grabbing and holding them all the slippier and more disgusting. I got 'em down, though. It was a hell of a struggle but I got both of them nestlings down, holding them by their legs like chickens. When I tried to present them to Papa Gator, he backed off and held his nose. I asked, 'What should I do with them?' He said I should take them back up the tree and put them back in their nest and make sure I don't hurt them either, they're the most valuable birds in the swamp. I'm wondering what the hell this is all about but I do exactly as he says, glad to be rid of the nestlings because for a while there I thought Papa Gator was going to make me bring them home with us and pluck them for dinner. Once I'm back down from that tree I head off the strand to find water so I can clean up but Papa Gator tells me to leave it and even after we're in the boat he won't let me reach in the water to wash. Once we're home though, he says, 'Go clean up, then come here, I want to tell you something.' I cleaned myself two or three times, using turpentine on my hands because the odor of turpentine was better than smelling that mixture of vulture vomit and vulture shit. Then I present myself to him and ol' Papa Gator says, 'Now *that* was disgusting.' "

Father nodded. "He was telling you that a dog hair in some grits isn't really disgusting."

"That was the lesson, hard learned."

"So I guess the point you're making, giving a bath to an old bum like me doesn't bother you a whit."

"I like making people clean, it's the most satisfying thing I do . . . so are we over the tears and attitude, ready for a bath?"

Father agreed he was.

First Pelikan had to pick away the remnants of rotted underwear, telling Father that Viking warriors never changed the garment they wore next to their skin, they always allowed that garment to rot before replacing it.

Father nodded, weeping, not feeling at all like a Viking warrior.

Pelikan gently used brush and soap and cloth and shampoo, draining and refilling the tub several times, working carefully to clean the old man's legs without scratching open any wounds that might lead to infection. When all the encrusted parts were clean, Pelikan started anew up top. Portions of Father's hair and beard were so entangled Pelikan had to use scissors but when he finished, the old man's hair and beard were both the same bright clean yellow shade like gold, like sunshine.

Pelikan kept at the task, cleaning, scrubbing, washing until his fingers and the muscles of his forearms ached. He massaged the old man's scalp, scrubbed his face pink clean, washed under his arms and over his distended belly, between his legs, made Father go over on hands and knees to get his nasty hole washed—they made jokes about that—then cleaned Father's legs yet again. Finally, Pelikan spent a good ten minutes on each of Father's feet to make sure they were scrupulously clean, nails properly trimmed.

"Dispose of those clippings properly," the old man warned Pelikan. "I don't want some hoodoo queen getting her conniving claws on them."

Pelikan nodded and, as he was helping Father out of the tub, saw the ruined corduroys still there on the floor. "Should have gotten rid of these before," Pelikan said, picking up the pants. "You got anything in the pockets?"

Father said no but when Pelikan checked anyway he found the old man's teeth in a right front pocket. After disposing of the trousers, Pelikan used two toothbrushes and half a tube of toothpaste cleaning the teeth while Father sat there on the toilet lid with a large towel around his drooping shoulders. Throwing the toothbrushes away, Pelikan remembered that, when he was a boy, he caught one of his mother's clients using his toothbrush and told him never to do it again but the man just laughed and Pelikan later rigged a single-edge razor blade in the toothbrush. The next time this man came over, he was so drunk and the razor was so sharp that he sliced up his gums and got a mouthful of blood before he realized what was happening. This memory causes a great sadness to blanket James Joseph . . . when a life gets long enough it leaves such a record of regrets.

"What ever happened to ol' Papa Gator?" Father asked. "I remember him coming in to get drunk all the time, but it's been years."

Pelikan came over to dry the old man off. "Papa Gator stays out in the swamps these days, he told me he's about given up on civilization. He still lives alone but I don't know for how much longer, he drinks so much I bet his liver outweighs yours . . . I think soon ol' Papa Gator will go on the list."

"What list?"

"I keep a list of all the people I've ever known who've died, you want to see it?"

Father said he did.

"You finish drying, make sure you get between all the toes, I'll fetch a robe."

By the time Pelikan returned, Father had his teeth in place but unfortunately was losing mental acuity, gibbering something about how riding boxcars will make you piss blood because there's no shock absorbers, it's steel on steel, lads, better to find yourself a nice grain car, but watch for the chutes. Then he slipped into a language like twins or foreign spies use to exclude the rest of us, and finally into a silence you couldn't really call contemplative.

Pelikan put the robe on Father and waited for him to return, the first of these trips usually never lasted long. While he waited, Pelikan brushed Father's yellow hair and yellow beard until they glistened like the mane on a pampered horse.

Finally the old man came back from his wanderings and looked up to see who was working on him. "James Joseph."

"Yes."

"You forgot the bananas."

"You're right, I did . . . we never stopped at the A&P."

"Marshmallows too."

"You're going to have to settle for peanut butter and a bowl of soup."

"No hair in it, though." The old man laughed.

"You still want to see my list?"

"Let's go sit down at a table."

They went to the kitchen where Pelikan brought out a sheet of heavy linen paper, much folded, and showed Father how he had named in ink everyone he could remember whom he'd known and who had died. "See, there's Momma on top of the list and then all these others, it goes to both sides . . . there's Linda Green, who had red hair in spite of her name, and, well, you don't know any of them but there they are. When I go through the list, one by one, I recall something good about each person."

"Will you put me on your list when I die?"

Pelikan smiled because a lot of older people asked him that. "Of course I will. See here at the bottom, that's my brother who just died. His son is here in town working with me, my nephew."

"It's good to have family."

Pelikan nodded. "My nephew, his name is Charlie, he grew up in a house without a father around much, that father being my brother who just died, a gambler, a schemer, and a dreamer. I didn't know my brother growing up but we got real close later on and did a lot of jobs together, I miss him dearly. Anyway Charlie is my brother's son and Charlie was raised by his mother and three older sisters. When Charlie was a little toddler, the girls would race each other home from school because the first in the door would get to be first to hold Charlie on her lap. She'd kiss him and hug him and smell him behind the ears while the other sisters begged and begged until the first sister finally had to pass him off to the next sister who would do the same thing, hugging and kissing and tickling, and finally the third sister got her turn for more of the same. Charlie's sisters also took turns giving him a bath, then afterwards all three sisters would cooperate brushing his hair and powdering him and making sure his little pearl ears were clean, brushing his little white teeth while telling him when it was time to spit and then putting him in a little set of cotton soft pajamas. Charlie was supposed to sleep by himself in his own bed in his own room but there was hardly a night he didn't end up with one of his sisters who'd pet and cuddle him like he was her teddy bear and of course Charlie took all this as his due, he didn't know any different, coddled and stroked and loved like a princeling pasha potentate."

"James Joseph, what're you afraid of most?"

Pelikan looked at the old man, wondering if Father had heard anything Pelikan had just said about Charlie.

"What *I* fear most of all in life," Father said, "is dying cold. I used to be afraid of dying while employed but I took care of that, now it's the cold that scares me. I move south in front of cold fronts, scared to death someday the cold'll catch me."

"I'm afraid of ending up alone when I'm old," Pelikan said. "End up on nobody's list."

"Like me, you mean?"

"Not exactly . . . you have me, don't you? But who will I have? I've taken care of others all my life, when I'm old I want someone to take care of me, I don't want to end up dying on the streets where there'll be no one to put me on their list. I don't suppose I'll ever be invited to come live with one of my nieces, seeing as how I never even met them . . . their mother was a bear about them never coming to New Orleans, Charlie's father arranged for him to come here when Charlie was a teenager. Then Charlie stayed three years, partly to defy his mother, all that adolescent rebellion, and partly because he was at an age where he just couldn't get enough pussy no matter how much I sent his way. So I had all my hopes and dreams pinned on that boy . . . for when I got old, figuring by then he'd be married and have a nice family, a big house with some property to it. I want to eat dinners with the family—at the dinner table, in the dining room—but I plan to live in a room over the garage so I can have my privacy or maybe a little cabin out back if he's got that much property. I'd tell the kids stories but Charlie and his wife wouldn't have to worry, I'd tell only the clean ones." Pelikan thought of all the clean stories he could tell children. "But I don't suppose any of that's going to happen, not now."

"You're a young man, you got plenty of time."

"I was trying to set it up but—"

"When I'm dead and get put on your list and you go through thinking good things about everybody, what're you going to think about me?"

Pelikan touched the old man's head. "I will recall that you had the most beautiful yellow hair I've ever seen on man or woman . . . and that you were a rebel who struck a blow for freedom by peeing in your pants, a true American."

Father got weepy again, telling Pelikan, "I hope it works out with that room over the garage, your nephew sounds like he led a sweet life with those sisters spoiling and pampering him."

"I think so too, Father. But I wonder . . . if his life was so sweet, why'd he turn out sour?"

22

THE BLACK DOG

If I watch a movie that shows a member of some group acting on his conscience by breaking ranks to reveal the group's secrets, I hate the rat . . . and even if the movie shamelessly celebrates this individual for coming forward to do the right thing, I still think he should've kept his cheese-eating mouth shut, that's what I was taught by my father and my uncle about loyalty. But now, since I've betrayed Pelikan tonight, I have to face the possibility that I am what I hate most, a rat, that treachery is my character. Unable to face this all by myself, I will need half the gin in the French Quarter and a mood meaner than any black dog that's ever bitten a feeding hand. Let's get started.

Bourbon Street is a good place to walk the black dog, look how everyone's face is shiny with sweat and skin oils, bright and expectant . . . already I'm starting to hate them nearly as much as I hate myself.

I stop in bars, drink, leave, stop in others, the bars getting more crowded and stranger as the evening progresses, though you could hardly call it progress, people pressing so close you can smell their beer breath and sweat, their perfume and cigarettes. Sex was in the air too but it came with trouble intertwined, couples tongue-kissing one moment and arguing the next when someone came back from the toilet to find someone else tonguing where he or she had just been tonguing. In the Fatted Calf we heard a rumor that there was a pet monkey loose on Bourbon Street, attacking people, going for their eyes. Cops were trying to shoot it, the monkey had jumped a police horse, which panicked and ran over a bunch of drunks who were taken laughing all the way to the hospital and still the monkey is loose, working its way along balconies, always a threat. Some people left to see it, others stayed here and drank even more. Music got louder, driving out sane thought. If a drink got passed from the bar back into the crowd, people would steal sips along the way, enraging whoever had ordered the drink. Scuffles broke out, there were shoving matches and dark threats.

I stop in at The Old Absinthe House and manage to score a stool at the bar, have a few more gins, listen to the blues sung by a Caucasian female who went to junior college, her blues don't make me feel any bluer with each song, the thrill is gone . . . you don't know the half of it, white girl . . . I'd like to fuck her. And as soon as that thought forms in its particular manner, whole and profane, *I'd like to fuck her,* then I know me and the dog will make a night of it.

Bourbon to Iberville, back down Royal, the plan now is to stop at any bar where there's room to get a drink without waiting. A gin here! Tonic? I don't care. And another, another. Where's Henry the bartender. Oh, Henry! Another of the same! Why is he ignoring me . . . *oh, Henry!*

Conti to Chartres to Jackson Square, where I come upon two teenage lovers snuggling close on a park bench, staring into each other's eyes in that Vulcan mind meld of love. I see the exact moment when they apparently receive a signal from the mother ship because suddenly their faces leap forward—it's a wonder teeth weren't chipped—to engage in a twisting lip lock, almost like they're fighting rather than kissing, like they're birds trying to feed each other by regurgitating and eliciting regurgitation . . . Jesus, look at them, mouths gaping open, tongues down each other's throat, was I ever in love like that, yes, dozens of times, it's repugnant, I want it, want to be in love again . . . like I was with Amanda, like I was with that bartender Lauren who gave me the oyster kiss, like I was with the young woman who dressed like a nun for my sinful pleasure. I used to love being in love, Pelikan thought it was idiotic, an affectation. He came into the apartment where I was living with my father back then and caught me at the kitchen table, eating chocolate ice cream with a fork while staring blankly into the middle distance, and he knew I was once again brokenhearted over some woman, James Joseph kneeling next to me and saying, *Charlie, it's only pussy.* I hated him.

Now these Jackson Square lovers repulse me and I walk over to kick the bench, causing their wet mouths to part with a smack and their equally wet eyes to look at me . . . whereupon I toss 'em a twenty and say, "For chrissakes, get a room."

As I leave they actually thank me, wish me a good night . . . if I had a gun I'd shoot them both in their swollen hearts and then kill myself with a bullet to the brain stem.

I walk. There's a lonely clown dressed as Emmett Kelly's Weary Willie, standing like a sentry wistful for something he's lost, perhaps what he was supposed to guard, holding a poster with a message felt-tipped in flowery letters: STOP THE VIOLENCE, NOT THE LAUGHTER. Little happy faces and daisies adorn the sign and I want to choke Weary Willie until his tongue is forced to protrude from between his fat painted lips . . . but I resist the urge and continue over to the downriver side of Jackson Square where there's not nearly as many people but I can still find a bar a block. Give me a gin. No, screw the tonic, did I ask for tonic? Now give me another. Hey, am I invisible, I said *another.*

After the second bartender in three stops asks me to leave, I head up Barracks to Bourbon again, down through the queer section and into the heart of the postmidnight craziness . . . a guy standing on his head is drinking a red drink and another guy, this one dressed up like Jesus Christ, is walking down the middle of Bourbon Street dragging a cross, a couple of young drunk college kids talking to him. I overhear Jesus telling the kids he came in from Baton Rouge with the cross, I didn't catch whether he meant came in dragging it or did he drive a pickup with the cross in the back? The two college boys, earnest in their inebriation, offer theories and feelings and personal opinions about religion and sin . . . Jesus finally says he's got to be going, not even Christ our savior has the patience for talking to drunks.

I take the black dog over to Canal for some greasy food, then right back into the breach, lads, to the fray, down Bourbon, stumbling.

All through the Quarter but especially here on Bourbon and then over at Jackson Square, lost children that the locals call gutter punks are begging quarters, living on the streets, heavily pierced and tattooed and purple haired, they stay ganged together for the sense of family they apparently didn't get at home. Wearing oversized denim and tight leather, some of them carry plastic cups to ask for a splash from anyone with a go-cup, they don't care what they're drinking. They smoke like children pretending to smoke, they beg cigarettes. Many of the girls wear dead black lipstick. In another grasp for companionship, these kids travel with animals, the dogs most pathetic of all, just like their owners: skinny and droop tailed and looking nervous about being left behind again . . . there's also a girl with a snake and one with a possum-sized iguana on her shoulder, the iguana staring into the girl's ear as if expecting food to emerge . . . and here's a skinny blond nineteen-year-old girl wearing a dirty tube top and holding a fat white rat in both hands, lifting the rat to her mouth, I gotta stop and watch this . . . while the rat is sniffing at this gal's lips she opens her mouth and sticks out her tongue, the girl has a silver tongue stud and the rat puts its little pink paws on the girl's chin to lean forward, lean *into* her mouth, and nibble around the tongue stud, eating bits of food stuck there.

A spike-haired sixteen-year-old punk in black leather and chains sees me staring at the girl and comes over to stand too close and ask, "You think you could do something like that?" And I tell him you bet your ass I can, just get the fucking rat out of the way, I'll suck that girl's tongue stud clean as a whistle . . . the kid backs off with a queer grin showing bad teeth.

I'm horny now, drunk and horny . . . what woman wouldn't love me in this condition? Me and the black dog want to fuck somebody . . . I wonder why these street girls are carrying around so many reptiles, do they love cold-blooded creatures and if so, why not throw me a mercy fuck, I'd accept one with grateful humility.

Now I'm off Bourbon Street again, through the residential neighborhoods with their soft-brick, rotting-wood charm, mold growing wherever the sun doesn't shine, Formosan termites eating unseen like cancer, and eventually I'm sitting in a relatively quiet bar where I am drunk but acting relatively civil when I remember what my father told me in the hospice. *Born in shit.* Did I need to know that? Born in shit. I call the bartender over, a bald man in his sixties who looks like the captain in the original *Love Boat* show. "Yes sir?" he says. "I was born in shit," I tell him. He nods, apparently he's heard it before.

Back on Canal I come to this vagrant who's trying to push-drag *three* shopping carts full of his various treasures, cans and overcoats and blue tarps and boxes of bottles, plastic milk jugs tied to the outside of the carts. One cart he's pushing in front of him, the other two are tied together and he's trying to drag them but their wheels keep going funny. I ask him, "What's the point of being a vagrant if you have all these *things?*" I see myself, all those collectibles in my warehouse, struggling with the weight of their debt the way this guy is struggling with shopping carts. "If you want to own things," I tell him, "if you feel compelled to amass possessions, get a job and move to the fucking suburbs like I did . . . you're supposed to be a goddamn vagrant!"

"Please don't hurt me."

I guess I was talking too loud.

Canal to Decatur, I'm heading down to Mother's and maybe if Pelikan's there I'll tell him I sold him out, tell him right to his face . . . but I'll also make sure he knows I had my reasons. Somewhere around Bienville I get stopped by two black teenagers who are smiling and telling me welcome to New Orleans, one of them admiring my fine shoes and the other saying he bets me ten bucks he can tell me where I got my shoes. He is about to launch what might be the longest running street scam in New Orleans, the con being that he's not going to tell me where I bought my shoes, he's going to tell me that I "got" my shoes on Decatur Street, where I'm standing at the moment. Amazing how often it works, you can watch it being pulled on Bourbon Street every night, the tourists actually paying off, perhaps out of amusement but more probably from the intimidation of angry young black men demanding money they claim was won fair and square.

I should've, could've walked on, these two guys wouldn't have bothered pressing the matter, they were in their late teens, not drunk or drugged, just working the scam . . . but the black dog was prodding me, so I took the bet. They couldn't believe their good luck, another sucker. One of the young men triumphantly said, "You *got* your shoes on Decatur Street, New Orleans, Louisiana. Now pay up." But I told him right back, "No I *got* my shoes on my feet." After a bewildered pause, he insisted I pay off, ten dollars on the line, a bet's a bet, *ten dollars on the line.* I suggested he could bite me. He muttered a name, I called him one back, we got chest-to-chest like a pair of fighting cocks . . . and meanwhile his partner's checking for patrol cars and potential witnesses because it's clear to all three of us that they're going to beat the shit out of me, black dog or no, but then miraculously I'm saved when the other guy grabs my opponent's shirt and says, "Oh shit, Larry, *look!*"

Larry looks and I do too: three nuns in full black habit and Buddy Holly glasses running toward us.

It's Janet Reno holding a silver six-shooter and flanked by thundering Bulgarians galloping not like horsemen of the Apocalypse but like the horses themselves.

We stand there frozen, the two black guys and me . . . it's a Catholic school kid's worst nightmare come true and I guess they went to Catholic school too because when the nuns start screaming like Bedouin, all three of us take off.

The blacks peel off toward the river while I stay on Decatur, lungs heaving and heart walloping by the time I reach Jackson Square and look back . . . no nuns.

Their appearance would've been more amazing and mysterious to me if I'd been sober, but my thoughts are gummy with alcohol. After catching my breath I continue across Jackson Square as if nothing strange and wonderful had just happened, without even asking myself, why did *I* run from them?

"Read your fortune?" asks a fortune-teller . . . with a flick of one foot I kick over his little table and then stand there daring him to make something of it. He doesn't because he's too fat and ridiculous, wearing what looks like a goddamn tent made out of shiny silver-gray material and, on his head, a pointy turban.

"I guess you didn't see that coming, huh, fortune-teller?"

He doesn't respond, it's an old line he's sadly heard too many times before.

I keep stumbling down Decatur and whenever I catch anyone staring I demand, "What're you looking at!" But they never answer the goddamn question.

Mother's is packed . . . I don't see Pelikan, no clowns either, thank God for little favors. I make my way to the bar through jugglers and jazz musicians but can't manage to squeeze in anywhere until I see an empty spot next to Fat Elvis. I take a seat and try to catch the bartender's eye. Jesus, but Fat Elvis really stinks, an industrial case of body odor arising from under that fake leather white jumpsuit that's missing about a fourth of its sequins. I read somewhere that Elvis practiced such poor hygiene, Priscilla had a series of water jets, covering from head to foot, installed in his shower to make sure the King at least got wet all over . . . so maybe Fat Elvis standing here next to me isn't a pig in his personal habits, he's just being terribly authentic. Drinking some sort of frappé that puts a white mustache on his upper lip which might've curled seductively at one point in his life but now looks fat and slack. If his mother were here she'd say close your mouth. A layer of fat is humped like a bedroll across his shoulders, where the inadequate cape has been sewn on in afterthought. I can't wait any longer to order a drink, I have to leave, Fat Elvis smells too bad . . . no wonder there was an empty spot next to him, Jesus.

In the narrow corridor between the regular bar and the little shelf bar against that mirrored wall, I push my way past girls and boys and wonder when did I get old enough for all of them to appear under-age? I'm only thirty-three and Jesus died young. I smile and nod at a woman wearing a beret but she rolls her eyes and looks away, am I that obviously drunk, I guess I am. Onward then to the back wall where I see Fifties Elvis, black slacks and white T-shirt, playing the pinballs while two girls watch from either side.

Lean and sleepy eyed, hips and pelvis, he's got all the moves, playing that machine like dancing a sexual ballet, the girls keeping tabs on him, not the score, his black hair unfolding to fall over his forehead . . . he looks potent enough to impregnate the girls just by slow-dancing "Unchained Melody" with them.

I get a brainstorm and go up to him and say there's someone I'd like him to meet, come up front with me. He doesn't want to leave the machine and girls but I implore and he's too polite to say no to his elders even when they're shitfaced, so he tells the girls he'll be right back and then trails me as I work once again through the crowd.

I'm thinking, this is going to be rich . . . I'll introduce Fifties Elvis to Fat Elvis and then scream at both of them, *Shame on you, shame on you!* I'll berate them for what they've done to each other, telling Fifties Elvis, *The way you're living right now leads to THAT,* and then tell Fat Elvis, *Look what you ruined.* I'll make them stand close together, before-and-after style, so I can laugh at them.

But by the time I've fought my way to the front, Fifties Elvis has slipped behind me and I hear him say to someone, "Who the hell was that?" Then he returns to pinballs and girls.

I feel defeated. Also, I must be doing something wrong because I'm still sober enough to remember all of this, realizing now that the black dog is no longer with me, the cur must've taken off during the nun attack, now I'm on my own and can't get a drink. I think the bartenders are ignoring me on purpose.

Back outside, Jesus, it's hot . . . walking, needing to piss, not sure where I am, keep walking. Here's a bar on a corner, lots of red neon, which is always a good sign, so to speak . . . I come rushing in, my bladder slopping over full, and as I quick-walk the length of the bar, a bartender calls to me: "Hey, toilets for customers only!"

Without stopping I take out a twenty and wad it up and throw it in his direction. "Give me that many gin and tonics, put 'em all right there on the fucking bar, I'll be right back."

I return from the can and after drinking my $20 worth, *finally,* I remember nothing more. Until memory like a mule kicks back in at some dark hour to find me standing out in a downpour watching gutter punks copulate in the street.

23

DUSTIN HOFFMAN, WINONA RYDER IN <u>LIMOUSINE</u>

"What's taking her so long?" Gallier asked, his head leaned back to rest on a small velvet pillow, his girlish eyes closed . . . turning forty was on his mind again, irritating him. Money too. Charles was also on Gallier's mind.

"She's probably doing girl things," Zane said. "You know how they are before a big date."

Gallier and Frank Zane, the pirate, sat in the limousine parked near St. Louis Cathedral, waiting for a woman named Maria who had a new outfit to model.

"Say, Creole man, how's about we let one of these sweet young things come and sit with us, while away the time?" the pirate said, referring to the young women standing about twenty feet from the limousine, speculating who was inside.

Gallier glanced out the window at the giggling girls, who're being kept back by his security men. "Which one appeals to you?"

"That pigeon-chested blonde there, the one in little white shorts."

"Well, she would appeal to you, wouldn't she?" Then he said nothing more, leaning back in the seat and despairing of ever being happy or seeing fifty.

"Ain't we going to get one in here?" Zane asked.

Gallier sighed and looked again out the window. *That one,* he chose, flicking his wrist. With the dark Spanish hair and milky white skin and old enough to vote but barely. He lowered a window to speak to a bodyguard, who went to the dark-haired woman, whispered in her ear, then led her to the limousine. Before getting in, she looked back at her friends, who were wide eyed with envy.

"Wow," the young woman said as she was seated next to Zane, across from Gallier. The limousine's interior was every bit as rich as she'd imagined, low lighting and plush seats and lots of gadgets and compartments, but the two occupants were a complete surprise . . . the guy sitting next to her was dressed like a pirate, eye patch and all, leering at her, his thick hair and mustache bushier and curlier than a black sheep's wool, she didn't like him at all. The man in the facing seat was kinda interesting, though. Kinda old and balding a little bit but he was dressed real nice, fancy, and he was handsome in a Latin way with real nice, soft brown eyes.

"Would you care for a drink, my dear?" Gallier asked as he opened a compartment of crystal decanters and elegant stemware.

"Sure, thanks." Nineteen years old, thick dark hair, flawless white skin, brown eyes like Gallier's, this college sophomore was glad she had dressed up tonight, had decided on the spur of the moment not to wear comfortable shorts like her friends but to put on a dress, summery and silky and buttoning all the way up the front with big white buttons . . . she was sure it was the dress that caught this gentleman's eye.

"Brandy?"

She couldn't remember if she'd ever had brandy but she intended just to sip anyway, didn't intend to let these guys get her drunk no matter *who* they were. Accepting the glass from Gallier, she thanked him and asked flirtatiously, "Should I know you?"

"I would certainly hope so," he replied, leaning back in the seat and holding the brandy under his fine nose to sniff.

The girl sniffed at her brandy too, was there something wrong with it? "You *look* familiar, are you with that movie they're shooting over by Royal Street?"

"Fellini," he said, coming forward to offer his limp hand. "And you are . . . let me guess, Debbi or Poopsie or—"

"Betsy."

"Ah, like the cow."

Zane hadn't said anything, hadn't been offered a drink, he just sat there staring at Betsy's breasts.

"Fellini the movie director?" she said by way of confirmation.

Gallier smirked.

"Wow, I *thought* I recognized you. You're making that movie here, we saw the trucks and everything earlier on."

Gallier nodded and confided to Betsy he was having a problem. "One of my film's supporting actresses, a small but critical part, was sent home with an unfortunate outbreak of vaginal warts, leaving me with one of two choices. I either return to Hollywood for a replacement, go through the tiresome routine of negotiating with agents . . . or I try to find an unknown who could step into the part immediately. That's what I'm doing now, scouting for that young woman who woke up this morning as an unknown but will go to bed tonight a star. How do you find the brandy, dear?"

She was so excited she hadn't even taken a sip yet. Now the overpowering taste of the brandy wrinkled that cute nose her father the dentist had paid for so dearly. She waited to make sure her voice worked, then told Gallier, "Mmm, good."

He smiled little white teeth at her discomfort. "Have you had any acting experience?"

Until that moment she didn't dare believe that Mr. Fellini was actually, really considering *her* for the part. Betsy now became so worked up that the brandy snifter shook in her hands. "Yes," she finally managed to gush. "I mean, that's practically the whole reason I'm here, I had a role in *The Streetcar Named Desire,* which is set here in New Orleans—"

"Yes, I know."

She laughed nervously, her face reddening like a tomato. "Of course you do, you're a famous director. Anyway, the part I played—"

"*A Streetcar Named Desire.*"

"Yeah, the play by—"

"You said, *THE Streetcar Named Desire.*"

"Right, by Tennessee Williams."

"You ignorant cow."

"What?"

He shook his head and smiled. "It's an Italian expression of fondness."

Zane chortled.

"Please continue," Gallier told her.

"Okay, well, being in that play made me fall in love with New Orleans and this is my second trip here, the first time was—"

"I'll have to see your breasts."

When the pirate hooted laughter, Betsy leaned away from him as she looked across at the famous director. "Excuse me?"

"Your breasts, I'll take a look at them *now* if you please."

"I don't *think* so," she replied huffily . . . and thought, I should just give this brandy back and get out of here right this minute. Betsy glanced through one of the windows to see her friends standing there expectantly.

"The most famous and talented and critically acclaimed actresses in the world have employed nudity as one of the arrows in their artistic quiver," Gallier was saying. "But you consider yourself what . . . better than those actresses, more moral? Or . . . is there something wrong, amiss, with your breasts?"

Her head was spinning. "Mr. Fellini, I know I should be grateful you're even talking to me about a part in your movie, but this is all happening a little fast."

"You want stardom to come more slowly?"

"No . . . all my life I've wanted to be in a movie."

"Well, my dear, ultimately you are in control of your own destiny. Thank you very much for coming, we'll contact you if we need to see you again." He reached over and removed the brandy glass from her startled hands.

"Wait. It's not that I *won't* . . . it's just, well, you know, here in a limo and all, it's kind of weird, isn't it?"

"Shall we go check into a motel, just you and me in a cheap little motel room, is that what you're angling for, is *that* how you intend to win this part?"

"*No!*" She was desperately trying to sort all this out in her mind. Although she'd never seen a Fellini movie she knew he was a famous

director from France and isn't this how stars are discovered, somebody famous sees them and—"

"Don't call us," Gallier said, reaching for the door handle.

"Wait, I'll . . . well, you know . . . if nudity is required for the part,
I can understand how you'd have to see . . . but . . ." Her voice lowered conspiratorially as she leaned across the aisle and whispered to
Gallier. "Could it be just you and me, could you ask *him* to step out?"
Betsy didn't like the way the pirate continued leering, saying nothing,
just staring as if he could see her breasts right through the dress's floral print.

Gallier feigned indignity. "You want me to ask Dustin Hoffman
to step out of the vehicle?"

"Dustin Hoffman?"

Zane nodded. "Hey watchit, huh, I'm trying to walk here!"

Betsy looked at him with widened eyes, wondering what that out-
burst was about . . . was he going to attack her? "He's not Dustin
Hoffman," she told Gallier.

"A master of disguise," Gallier assured her. "You saw *Tootsie?*"

She admitted she hadn't.

"If you've never seen Mr. Hoffman's work, how can you—"

She remembered one. "He was in that movie with Tom Cruise."

"*Rain Man.*"

"Yeah."

Gallier looked over at Zane, who took the cue and put his hands
high on his chest, looking down at his fingers as he spoke. "Definitely
have to see your breasts, yes, definitely, see your breasts for the
movie, have to see them, for the movie, integral to the part, your
breasts, definitely have to see them."

She was shaking her head. What the pirate had just mumbled
made no sense to Betsy, who again insisted to Gallier that the man
sitting next to her wasn't Dustin Hoffman.

"Well," Gallier said with a show of exasperation, "I suppose I
could send Mr. Hoffman back to makeup and have him restored to
his natural self just to satisfy your suspicions . . . but then why should
I give in to the demands of an unknown hopeful who's only experience is in a college play, the name of which she can't get right!"

"High school," Betsy admitted in the voice of a little gray mouse.

"I think it's time for you to leave. I require an actress, not a prima donna."

"I've never been stuck-up in my entire life!" Betsy protested. It was what she was known for in high school, not being stuck-up even though her father was a dentist.

"Who's on first?" Zane mumbled.

Betsy *tsk*ed and with trembling fingers began undoing the big white buttons on the bodice of her dress, Zane watching now with one wolfish eye.

"There," she said dramatically, holding the bodice open for a few moments and then dropping her hands to let the dress fold back over her bare breasts.

"You don't wear a bra . . . slut," Gallier said.

"I beg your pardon."

"I don't want to be *flashed,*" he snapped.

"What do you mean?"

"I mean I have to study your breasts the same way I studied your face before selecting you. I am an artist, you are my canvas . . . now please cooperate or *leave.*"

Tears welling, she reopened the bodice and slipped the dress from her shoulders.

"Two of them," Zane said, "definitely two of them, one-two, there's two, yes, definitely two."

Gallier laughed softly . . . he remembered now why he'd hired this face-picking Gypsy who not only supplied inside information about Pelikan but could on occasion be mildly amusing.

Wanting to cover up again, Betsy asked, "Okay?" in a Valley girl whine.

Gallier told her no, it was not okay. "I don't think they're real."

"What?"

"I won't have plastic tits in my film."

"I beg your pardon, these are *mine.*"

"You mean they're all paid for."

"No I mean—"

"This'll have to be confirmed."

"Definitely have to confirm it," Zane added eagerly. "I get my boxer shorts at Kmart." He reached over and grabbed her right breast, squeezing it several times before Betsy managed to slap his hand away. "Uh-oh, uh-ho!" Zane squealed in mock alarm. Then to Gallier, "Definitely real, no silicon, definitely no silicon, they're real."

"That's not Dustin Hoffman," she told Gallier.

"Pinch your nipples," he ordered. "I want to see how they look *erect.*"

"Erect," Zane said. "Definitely erect."

Betsy lifted her dress back in place and began rebuttoning, she was openly crying now, which caused Gallier's large eyes to glisten with excitement. "Do you have an agent?" he asked her.

She smiled warily through her tears. "Are you serious, I could get one."

"Good, the part's yours."

Her mouth and eyes both went big as she reached across and shook Gallier's hand, then turned to Zane, "I'm sorry, Mr. Hoffman, but your makeup is so incredible."

"I'm an excellent driver," he told her, reaching over to rub her breasts through the dress.

"Come on now, Mr. Hoffman," she said with good cheer as she gently removed his hand from her chest. "Enough of *that.*"

"In the scene we're shooting tomorrow," Gallier told her, "you and Mr. Hoffman have just returned from a costume party—hence the pirate outfit."

"Okay, well *now* I understand."

"Mr. Hoffman's wife catches the two of you together, the wife will be played by Winona Ryder."

"Oh wow, I like her." Betsy looked out the window and waved at her friends, who of course could not see her through the heavily tinted windows.

"Do you want to rehearse this part," Gallier said sharply, "or do you want to go out and play with your little friends?"

"Sorry." She looked over at Zane and gave him a knowing wink . . . these directors are tough, huh, Mr. Hoffman . . . Dustin . . .

"Your line in this scene is, 'Who are you?' You'll be speaking that to Winona Ryder when she catches you with her husband, Mr. Hoffman here."

Betsy nodded as she carefully memorized the line . . . who are you, who are *you,* who *are* you, *who are you?*

"Ready?"

"Yes sir." Who *are you* . . . would Mr. Fellini appreciate it if she put a little twist on her reading of the line . . . Who are you *anyway?*

"Okay, put Mr. Hoffman's dick in your mouth."

"Excuse me?"

"The scene is, Winona Ryder comes in and catches your character giving Mr. Hoffman's character a blow job, so you take his dick out of your mouth and say your line, 'Who are you?' But of course you can't take his dick out of your mouth until you first put his dick *in* your mouth."

Zane was working furiously on his pantaloons, which had a complicated fly, using an intricately laced string, while Betsy, coming late to full realization, finally told Gallier, "You're not Fellini." She tried to hold his stare, to shame him, but his eyes were too intense.

He said, "You worthless . . . hapless . . . ignorant . . . *cow.*"

Zane said, "Moo."

There was a knock at the window nearest Gallier, who touched a button unlatching the door. A young woman in an incredibly tight, short red dress bounced onto the seat next to Gallier, then looked curiously at him, at Zane, and at the woman in tears next to Zane. "I interrupt something?" the newcomer asked. She had yellow blond hair barely half an inch long.

"Thank you for coming, Winona," Gallier told her. "I almost gave this unknown *cow* a part in your new movie, but she didn't have what it takes."

Betsy moved to get out the opened door, her mind scrambling to compose a withering exit line that would devastate them, make them feel terrible for what they'd done to her. Looking at the blonde in the red dress, Betsy saw she had a fishhook sticking out from just under her lower lip. "You're not Winona Ryder," she told the woman, then Betsy left the limousine, to their acid laughter.

Gallier brought the short-haired blonde onto his lap and openly fondled her. "You're wet."

"It's raining," she said.

24

A REASON TO WAKE UP IN THE MORNING

For Father's supper Pelikan made soup, Campbell's beef (with vegetables and barley), using only half a can of water to create a heartier and less filling meal; he also gave the old man fresh bakery bread slathered with butter but with the crust removed because Father's teeth were loose. Afterward, Father, who hadn't eaten a substantial meal in two weeks, said, "I hope I don't belch, because if I do it'll all come up."

Pelikan urged him to resist belching.

When that danger had passed, the old man leaned back expansively, like a steel baron after a big club steak at Delmonico's, and asked Pelikan if the house happened to have a wee drop available. Pelikan said alcohol didn't contain the kind of nutrition Father needed. "How about that peanut butter sandwich?"

"Without a banana, I don't think so. You got any Kentucky bourbon, it's very nutritional . . . a pork chop in every glass."

Pelikan said he'd look, maybe the people who owned this apartment had left something behind.

"You don't drink, do you?" Father said as Pelikan searched cabinets.

"I guess I had too much when I was too young, and also it's in my genes that alcohol isn't good to me, makes me sick in the gut and sick in the head . . . here's something." Pelikan brought down a squat bottle with a long neck and asked Father, "Do you drink port?"

"Son, I drink Sterno if it's all that's available, now what do you think I'm going to say to a little glass of port after a fine meal, let me answer that question for you, I say yes."

Pelikan poured a glass, the smell instantly transporting him back to when he was a kid, with his mother. This memory dazed him for a moment, Pelikan not knowing if he was going to retch or rejoice because so much about his mother was a comfort to him and so much wasn't.

"Thanking you kindly," Father said as he lifted the glass of port, checked its color, then downed it with a single smooth motion followed by a smile. "Another?"

Pelikan poured another.

"I remember Bourbon Street," the old man said as he again lifted the glass, "when it was entertainment for adults, not like it is now, a place for college kids to get drunk and throw up. I remember the 500 Club, the Dream Room, Sam Butera and the Witnesses, and Galatea, 'The Statue Brought to Life By Love.' She was a stripper, son . . . so was Redi Flame, 'The Fire Ball That Causes Spontaneous Combustion.' I saw 'The Dance of the Wandering Hands' and 'Evangeline, the Original Oyster Girl.' Yvonne Adair had a parrot who undid Yvonne's sarong. I don't know, James Joseph, the world seemed grander back then, more grown-up . . . now it's all amateurs who are too young and don't know from nothing. I heard The Old Absinthe House was going to become a tropical drinks stand . . . it's enough to make you cry. Why, I remember . . ."

As he continued smelling the port, Pelikan also remembers . . . his mother massaging his feet and telling him he had perfect feet, not broken-arched old bricks like her feet, *his* were beautiful and without flaw. The only time she ever showed a maternal spark was when she rubbed his feet of an evening.

"Another taste of port," Father said, "and I shall recall even more for your benefit and edification . . . *homo memor,* man the rememberer, that's Latin, son, evidence of a classical education. Why, I remember . . . you're not pouring my port?"

Pelikan shook his head no and led the old man to a bedroom where large cardboard boxes of used but clean clothes were arranged in neat order . . . he dressed Father in a nice pair of moleskin trousers that must've cost a small fortune new and a similarly once-expensive blue oxford shirt, long-sleeve because Father said he didn't like his arms exposed even in the heat of a New Orleans summer. "Are you sure you don't want underwear?" Pelikan asked and the old man assured him he didn't, he was done wearing underwear after that last pair rotted the way they did . . . Viking warriors be damned. The shoes Pelikan found for him, black wing tips, were used but in good repair and perfectly polished; the socks, one pair of white under one pair of black, were brand-new.

"You look good," Pelikan told Father when the old man was finally dressed.

"I feel good."

"All dry and clean and fluffy."

"Thanks to you."

Pelikan gave him twenty bucks, two fives and ten ones . . . more than that might've endangered the old man either by making him a target of thieves or by financing a liver-rupturing binge. "Anything else you need?" Pelikan asked as he walked Father to the door.

"A reason to wake up in the morning."

"Don't we all." But Pelikan in fact had his reason to wake up in the morning, it was wrapped in a black leather pouch hidden away in the bathroom. He'd known several men and at least two women who lived to old age with nearly lifelong habits, junk is benevolent in that sense, though of course the old addicts hadn't led long and *productive* lives, just long and busy ones. A habit keeps you busy and that's the entire point, using addiction to galvanize your life, providing motivation to work or thieve, whatever it takes to finance another dose: a reason to wake up in the morning. Even now, simply thinking about unrolling the soft leather pouch and gazing upon his shiny clean outfit made Pelikan stomach-tight with anticipation. Here's how that first dose will hit his heart: as if a big man had cut Pelikan's aorta, put it in his mouth, and blown hard . . . making Pelikan's heart feel suddenly large and soft like a pillow.

"I'll see you around," Father said as he set off down the walk at a slow and hobbled pace. "Don't forget about putting me on your list."

Standing at the door watching him, Pelikan promised he wouldn't forget . . . *homo memor,* man the rememberer, and now that the smell of port had caused Pelikan to remember his mother and how she massaged his feet but did nothing else like a mother should, never hugged him or sat him on her lap to tell bedtime stories, was never a mother to him beyond the biology of it, Pelikan remembering how he bathed his mother when she reeked of port, despising himself for arousal at the sight and touch of her wasted body . . . remembering all this, Pelikan wanted to shoot a dose that not only would inflate his heart like a pillow but would cause it to burst open and bleed away memories.

"Hey, James Joseph!" Father called as he turned around, about twenty-five feet away, raising both arms.

Pelikan watched the old man and wondered why had he called out, what was he doing with his arms up?

Concentrating.

Pelikan saw a stain spreading down the inside right thigh of those lovely moleskin trousers, the wet reaching almost to the knee before Father shuddered and cried, *"Freedom!"*

Pelikan nipped back the initial aggravation he felt toward the old man and gave him thumbs-up . . . Pelikan just then feeling something on his face and looking up: Father's trouser stains wouldn't be noticeable much longer, it had begun to rain.

25

NIGHT RAINS

Memory tapes began again with me on Bourbon Street, aslosh, at what must be 5 A.M. or thereabouts, in a steady rain that has already soaked me to the skin and filled gutters with streams of water, bearing trash. Because of the rain this famously crowded street is finally deserted except for a small group I seem to be part of . . . I don't remember joining, how I got here, what if anything has been said among us. Three men stand with me, they are older, fatter, but no drunker or wetter than I. Like the four points of the compass we stand around two street kids, gutter punks, teenagers tattooed and heavily pierced, and both of them are wearing similar tops, red shirts from which the sleeves have been inexpertly scissored, and both of them are naked from the waist down. They are copulating in the street.

I have a can of beer in my hand, strange because I don't drink canned beer, it gives me a headache . . . the other three men are holding cans of beer and probably offered me one when I joined their group.

The street kids we're watching are zonked on something, I'm not sure if they're aware of our presence or simply don't care . . . I think it's the latter. They're both emaciated with fish-belly white skin that doesn't look clean even when washed by this downpour. They aren't just humping-rubbing against each other, this is sexual intercourse . . . occasionally they roll to change who's on top and you can see everything.

I realize my shoulders hurt from keeping them hunched up against the deluge . . . but this isn't Pelikan's storm, in which to burglarize a building, because there's no thunder or wind or lightning to knock out electricity and divert cops.

Except there are no cops here, maybe the rain *is* keeping them away.

I feel dirty watching. Did the other three men pay these kids to do this, or did the three men—and I—just happen upon it? I can't see the men's faces, the rain's too heavy, it has plastered their shirts against their whopping large bellies . . . I loathe them as perverts.

Yet here I stand with them. I should drop this beer can on the street and walk on. But I don't.

The two kids are literally in the gutter now, having rolled out of the street and up against the curb, water splashing over and around them the way a river flows against and over its rocks. The girl's on top.

I should drop this can of beer and walk on. But I don't.

The girl is on bottom now, her many-ringed fingers on the boy's bony shoulders and her skinny white legs locked around his thin waist as they go at each other pneumatically . . . the rain suddenly harder, the gutter streams widening until they almost meet in the middle of the street, making a river of Bourbon. Water in the gutter becomes so deep that the girl, on her back, can't keep her face out of it, she's thrashing, releasing the boy's shoulders to use her hands trying to raise up out of the water because she can't breathe and is panicking, but the boy, oblivious, continues his methodical pounding of her until one of the fat-and-fifty men grabs the kid by an underarm, effortlessly hauling him off and out of the girl, who sits up wide eyed, gasping.

I drop the beer can and walk on.

Now that I'm away from it I feel as unaffected by that display of screwing in the street as I was about the nuns rescuing me from a beating . . . I must be dead inside.

Suddenly the water begins falling not simply as rain but in cascades, shooting out of gutters as if pressurized, pouring from roofs onto balconies and from there in wide sheets to the street. The buildings seem to be *producing* water rather than shedding it, as if the interiors of these old structures are filled with massive hydromachines vomiting water by the millions of gallons, by the acres, the buildings too small to contain the water they produce so it comes gushing out of windows, running down the sides of the buildings, off balconies, splashing from sills and doorways, drowning thresholds, flooding stoops.

I have to keep my head down to breathe. Walking, unable to see where, I get the sense that something's gone horribly wrong with the world, rain this intense could not have been produced in the normal course of weather . . . we've been hit by a meteorite, volcanoes are erupting in the middle of the Gulf of Mexico, it's the night of reckoning, Rapture.

I think I'm going the wrong way, not toward the apartment on St. Peter Street. I walk faster ending up in Jackson Square, and rush to the Pontalba Apartments, which flank the square and provide balconies deep enough to get out of the rain or at least some of it.

Exhausted, hungover yet still drunk, I'm miserable and wet like a masterless dog.

An old guy sitting up against the building is staring at me . . . I've seen him before because I remember that perfect yellow beard and those clear blue eyes.

I go over and collapse next to him, he's the one I saw here my first night back in New Orleans . . . the man who looks wise and knowing enough to be God.

"Are you God?" I ask him.

He doesn't reply . . . but then, God wouldn't, would he?

"If you are, on behalf of mankind in general and the French Quarter specifically, I apologize for our behavior."

He's not looking at me but even in profile his face exudes the serenity of an all-knowing God.

"I've had a rough couple days," I tell him, not knowing where to start, choosing a random page. "I saw a woman shoot Three Jacks and she was shaved between the legs but when I saw her the next day she had a full bush and also I don't know how she got out of that swimming pool."

If he's God, he'll know what I'm talking about.

"I need some help here," I plead.

Nothing.

"I saw your son earlier, he was on Bourbon Street talking to drunks . . . brought the cross in from Baton Rouge."

When I don't get a reply to that either, I move to the front of God so I can look right into his face . . . which is when I smell urine.

"You pissed your pants," I tell him unnecessarily.

"Up the Irish," he says, or at least that's what I think he says, his voice is quiet and slurred . . . apparently God also gets drunk when visiting the French Quarter.

I don't think he's going to answer any of my questions but I try again. "How could she grow her bush back overnight . . . do you believe in evil twins?"

He says something I don't catch.

"What?"

"Merkin."

"What?"

"Merkin."

The urinal smell clinging to him repulses me so I stand and walk out from beneath the deep balcony to discover it has stopped raining. Amazing. The way it was coming down I thought it would never stop.

Idiotically I bring out my handkerchief to dry my face, the handkerchief so thoroughly soaked I can wring it like a full sponge.

The hour must be later than I thought because it's getting light. When I look toward the river I can see where the sun will rise . . . and like a vampire I'm in mortal dread of this coming light, please, God, don't let me be caught looking and feeling as I do now: wrecked, wet, corrupted. Don't let tourists see me. I must hurry back to my slave quarters on St. Peter Street and stay there in little coffin rooms until I'm dry and it's dark again.

Shoes squishing and pants legs slapping, I pass the front of St. Louis Cathedral hoping I don't bump into early morning worshipers . . . but I do: around the side of the cathedral I come upon Pelikan down on hands and knees, using a toothbrush to clean cracks in the sidewalk.

26

MORNING REDEMPTION

When I was living here as a teenager, Pelikan went to St. Louis Cathedral very nearly every morning, he said that for him walking to the cathedral was nearly as redeeming as the rite of confession . . . because it is early morning when the French Quarter is washed of last night's sins.

Every night Bourbon Street is a carnival where revelers drink and smoke and dance and create a gigantic mess: beer bottles and go-cups, napkins and newspapers, cigarette butts everywhere like confetti . . . vomit splashes (red ones from hurricanes the most vivid), spilled beer, runoff from bars, piss and spit. The smell gets in your lungs and lingers on your clothing, while gum wrappers and cigarette butts stick to the soles of your shoes.

Then comes morning when street filth is washed away, water trucks followed by mechanized cleaners with big whirling brushes, while in front of all the bars rubber-booted workers use an array of hoses and wet brooms to scrub away last night's sediment. In Jackson Square, inmates on community time wrestle firehoses spewing powerful streams to force away the trash while people living on second floors come out and wash their balconies with garden hoses and plastic buckets, all this runoff joining up on sidewalks and streets, flushed down drains, until the whole of the French Quarter becomes dripping clean. Shopkeepers open shutters on windows which are then assiduously shined pane by pane. Last night's bad odors are replaced in the morning by smells of bread baking, coffee brewing with chicory, and flowers put out for sale or display, growing in pots or cut into long stems leaning in white buckets. Walking by these flowers is like passing a woman wearing fragrance, you turn around to see what smelled so sweet.

But of course this early morning cleansing of the French Quarter is less like confession and more like a smoker washing last night's ashtray, wishing he could cleanse his lungs but settling for using soap and water on the ashtray before putting it to use again.

Here I stand soaking wet in the morning sun, watching my uncle, barefoot and shirtless, crawling along next to St. Louis Cathedral. I guess he didn't make it to confession, apparently trying to achieve redemption this particular morning by cleaning sidewalk cracks with a toothbrush . . . as all around him clowns have gathered, attempting to talk to Pelikan, find out what's wrong, urging him to get up off his hands and knees.

"Oh Charlie," says one fat clown dressed all in red, wearing a plastic flowerpot on his head with a big fake daisy rising from the pot and, on the daisy, a sneering plastic bumblebee the size of your fist . . . I don't know this clown, why is he calling me by name? "Something's wrong with James Joseph, he won't answer us, do you see what he's doing with a toothbrush, he's never been like this before."

"Oh yes he has," said a Harlequin in red and green tights, an older man with a pinched face and a little pouch of a stomach. "You don't remember when his mother died, he went around cleaning the sidewalks for days on end, higher than a kite." Then, sotto voce to me, "He's been a drug addict most of his life."

But when I leaned down to Pelikan, I smelled alcohol, sick-sweet and winelike. I'd never seen him drunk before.

"We have to *do* something," said a worried clown in a bright green costume that was stretched around the waist by a large hoop, giving him the appearance of a fat toy you could tip over on its side and roll along the floor. "I heard that cranberry juice was a natural antidote for most drugs, we should go over to the A&P and buy some."

"He's not on drugs," I said, standing. "He's drunk."

"James Joseph doesn't drink," insisted several of the clowns.

I told them I know drunk when I smell it and he's drunk.

"We got to help him!" one of the more emotional clowns cried.

"Someone find his shirt!" another shouted.

"Leave him where he is," I said, looking at Pelikan's ropy back muscles scrunch up and stretch out as he scrubbed, my uncle working in total seriousness, no symbolic act this, he was trying to get the goddamn sidewalk clean.

When the clown with the hoop around his waist tried to lift Pelikan by the upper arm, I shoved him away and insisted they all leave Pelikan alone.

"Charlie," said the clown with the flowerpot on his head, "tourists are coming!"

I nudged Pelikan's left wrist with the toe of my wet shoe. "Hey, asshole." He didn't respond until I pointed my shoe at a piece of flattened gum. "You missed a spot." Pelikan quick-crawled to the gum and began furiously trying to remove it with that toothbrush, which by now had lost nearly all its bristles.

"Why are you being so mean to him?" the clown with the flowerpot whined, placing a hand on my forearm.

I told him not to touch me. "Surrounding me wherever I go," I warned them all as I moved my arms in a wide arc, "is a no-clown zone . . . like an invisible shield, a force field that no clown must ever attempt to violate."

"Oh Charlie," cried the clown, "he's your uncle."

"And last night I betrayed him." I said it for Pelikan's benefit, my begrudging confession.

"Charlie," the clown told me snippishly, "I'm going to get him on his feet, I don't care what you say."

Which is when I took a swing, intending to knock the clown's flowerpot off . . . but I was still drunk enough to miss by a wide margin.

The clown cringed back out of range. "Why'd you do *that?*"

I went for him a second time but a clown wearing a fireman's hat and smoking a cigar stepped between us. "Listen, you two, stop it . . . we have to get James Joseph out of here before those tourists cross the street."

"You can't let tourists see him," the Harlequin agreed.

I looked to where a young couple and their two kids were watching us. "Come on over!" I called to them.

This horrified the clowns, who rushed en masse to collect Pelikan, raising him to his bare feet while I wailed in among them, pushing clowns right and left, knocking two of them to the ground, kicking the fat flowerpotted one in the balls, coldcocking the old Harlequin.

"*Daddy,*" said a little boy from the family that had indeed crossed the street to watch, thinking perhaps we were a street troupe giving an early morning performance, "that man's hurting those clowns."

"Hmm?" the father hummed.

"He's hurting *clowns,* Daddy, do something!" cried the boy's little sister.

"I think it's part of the act," their father replied hopefully.

Once I'd beaten back the clowns, I grabbed Pelikan, pulling his left arm around my neck to drag him away like predator with prey.

Back in the apartment on St. Peter I wasn't able to get Pelikan up the circular stairway and threatened to drop him on the floor and cover him with construction rubble unless he walked up those stairs. Still without speaking or making eye contact, he started up the steps, but went so slowly I had to push from behind.

I finally got him to bed but he was lying flat no more than a minute when he rushed to the bathroom, dropping to his sidewalk-stained knees in front of the toilet. I came in and held his forehead while he vomited, though very little came out beyond a sour smelling phlegm stained a deep red. He continued retching. I've had the dry heaves before but never like what Pelikan was suffering.

When it was over, I used a wet washcloth to clean his face, then hauled him back to bed.

Finally he talked to me in his usual calm, soft voice. "I don't want to lay down, margrave . . . it'll make me sick again."

"What the hell you been drinking?"

"Port. My mother drank port and tonight I got a case of the bad memories. I should've taken a lid of smack, I would've been better off . . . alcohol is so mean."

"You're shooting up and getting drunk when you're supposed to be getting ready for the biggest burglary job of your life?"

"You don't look so businesslike yourself. Did you spend the night drinking gin and listening to the blues and crying in the arms of a clown . . . I've had nights like that."

"The gin and the blues I might admit to, but I wouldn't let a clown put his white-gloved mitts on me, you know that."

Yes, he said, he knew that.

"Listen . . . about betraying you—"

"Yeah, I know all about it."

"No, you don't. Jesus Christ, you always act like nothing can surprise you. When I was living here, I could've come in and told you there was a grizzly bear whistling Dixie and riding a white horse down Bourbon Street and you would've said, 'Yeah, I know all about it.' Well, you don't necessarily know all about everything, you don't know who I talked to last night or what I said."

He had no energy for arguing with me. "I think I'll try laying down again." He did, putting a hand over his eyes. "I'll tell you what I know, princeling . . . I know you're blood and nothing you did can change that."

"Are you planning to set me up?"

He removed the hand from his eyes to look at me.

"Setting me up so I take the fall for Three Jacks," I continued. "And the repository job, too, that's what I've been told."

"You don't believe it, do you?"

"I'm asking, ain't I?"

He looked stricken.

"Just tell me the goddamn truth, Pelikan."

He put his hand back over his eyes and said, "Oh Charlie," with such anguish I had to leave the room.

After showering I put on jeans and a shirt stinking of my sweat and tobacco smoke from all the bars I'd been in. I wanted a cigarette. Had I started smoking again? I checked on Pelikan, he was sleeping dead to the world, so I left the little brick cottage intending to go for a long walk and clear my head, get something to eat, then return and, like Pelikan, sleep until I was cured.

I lingered in the stone passageway, thankful for this last bit of coolness before stepping out into a sun that would already be too hot. Opening the door onto the sidewalk, I was met by a group gathered there like starstruck fans waiting for their idol to emerge from the stage door. It was the repository gang: nuns, clown, hooker. But I wasn't the idol they were waiting for, of course.

"How's he making it?" the Janet Reno nun asked.

"Sleeping," I told her. Remembering last night's nun rescue, I felt blood warming my face with embarrassment.

"We heard what happened, James Joseph caught by tourists," sobbed Sad Bob the clown, who was wearing a shiny blue-black jump-suit, a brown derby, and a big red nose the size of a navel orange. "It's his favorite," Sad Bob explained when he saw I was staring at the huge honker.

The whore, Knees O'Rourke, asked me where I was going.

"For a walk. If I give you a key to get in, you'll all have to stay downstairs so Pelikan can keep on sleeping . . . which is what I'm go-ing to do when I get back."

There was general agreement that I should turn the key over to Sister Margaret. When I realized the two little nuns were missing I asked her where they were. She pointed up the street . . . Winklewoes and Tiddlepink or whatever it was Pelikan called them were on their knees, hands folded in front of their faces, eyes squeezed tightly shut.

"They got it in their heads," Sister Margaret replied, "to stop and kneel every fourteen paces like the Stations of the Cross . . . that's what took us so long to get here, we keep waiting for them to catch up."

"Are they still praying for a storm, or is it Pelikan they're praying for now?"

"Emily."

"Who?"

"They're praying for Emily," she said.

"I don't know who that is."

"And I think," the sister said, "there might be such a thing as praying *too* hard."

27

MERKIN MODEL #289

I'd gone a couple blocks when I remembered something I wanted to ask Sister Margaret. Returning to the St. Peter Street address I saw Knees O'Rourke on the sidewalk standing in that peculiar smoker's pose, left forearm parallel to the waist, left hand cupping right elbow, right forearm straight up with the right hand holding the cigarette near her mouth.

"Forget something?" she asked.

"I got a question for Sister Margaret . . . what, they won't let you smoke inside?"

"They don't say not to, but when I light up there's a lot of hand waving and nose wrinkling . . . you don't smoke either?"

"No . . . but I'll have one of those if you can spare it."

"Sure." She unbent her right elbow to hand me the works, a pack of Kools and book of matches.

"I hate menthol," I said, lighting up.

"Beggars . . ."

"Yeah, I know."

As we smoked I took opportunities to glance at the thin, red-haired hooker, trying to imagine what she'd look like if she hadn't shaved her eyebrows and drawn in fake ones, wasn't using long thick eyelashes, didn't wear so much mascara, lipstick, foundation . . . but ultimately I was unable to find a real face hidden under that painted one.

She asked me what question I had for the sister.

"Just wanted to see if she knows a word I heard last night."

"What word?"

"Merkin?"

She laughed and flicked her cigarette in a high arc into the street, and it was while she was laughing that I finally caught a glimpse of what her real face might look like: Appalachian angles, thin nose, prominent pointy chin, high forehead, never considered cute, maybe not even as a child, but I bet someone along the line thought of her as a handsome woman. Hell of a set of jaw muscles. She was wearing turquoise pedal pushers that had to have been in a closet for the past thirty-five years and a white sleeveless blouse buttoned all the way up to her thin neck . . . and on that neck I could see a line where the makeup stopped.

"What's so funny?" I finally asked.

She produced a Kleenex from some pocket I didn't know pedal pushers had and blew her nose. "Now why in the world would you want to ask a nun what a merkin is?"

I wasn't about to tell her that this guy I met last night in Jackson Square reminded me of what God would look like, that he said something sounding like *merkin,* which I think is the same word Pelikan muttered to me, then wouldn't explain. "I dunno, Sister Margaret struck me as a pretty smart cookie . . . maybe it's not even a word, or maybe I'm saying it wrong."

"No, you got it right, Charlie. You have a pen on you?"

I patted pockets and said no.

"That's okay, I can tell you how to get there." She gave me directions to a shop on Governor Nicholls Street down by the French Market.

"What's this got to do with—"

"Just go there, ask for a woman name of Harmony."

"I still don't see what this's got to do with—"

"Merkins . . . Harmony sells them."

I found the shop Knees told me about, but it was closed, according to a scrawled sign on the door, until after lunch.

I went up Decatur to a little bar and ordered Cuban coffee. Four husky men in their thirties and forties were getting an early start with tequila shooters and bottled beer . . . they wore rugby shirts and shorts, their thick arms deeply tanned, but their legs were so white you had to wonder when that skin was last exposed to sunlight. They were from Canada, they told the bartender, a dishwater blonde whose odometer was way past what it should be for her model year. "A single, lone tavern in our town," said one of the men. "A town so small, our village idiot is actually kinda bright." Which made his chums laugh and throw down their shots and order more. "Back home we couldn't be enjoying this breakfast of champions. The tavern doesn't open on Sunday," said another, "and during the week it closes at ten, then on Saturday it closes at midnight . . . but it never opens before noon." He drank deeply before continuing, "We just flew in, stored our tackle boxes in the hotel room, having told our wives it was a fishing trip." One of his accomplices picked up the narrative. "You'll be honored to hear this is the first tavern we've visited, and what we're wondering is . . . please tell us you don't close at midnight." The bartender gave them a hard look to make sure they weren't pulling her leg, then informed the lads, "We never close." It was their turn to look skeptical. She assured them she was serious, "If you can stay conscious, you can sit there drinking shooters and beer twenty-four hours a day all week long, *we never close.*" The awed Canadians lifted their glasses and chanted quietly in unison, "God bless America."

I wanted another cup of coffee, but our neighbors from the North were trying to get me to join them in a round of shooters and dirty songs about Sam McGee, so I excused myself, forced to shake each hearty hand before departing, then went to a little market a few doors away and bought a muffuletta and a Dr Pepper, taking them across the street to a park bench. Unable to finish the muffuletta, I folded it back in the paper wrappers and placed everything on the ground. Leaning back to close my eyes, I was gone.

To be awakened by a nightstick tapping just a little too hard on one knee.

"What?" I asked straightening up, blinking in the hot bright sunlight.

"That your trash there on the ground?" the cop asked . . . he was
a tall blond kid, I don't think his uniform had been washed the first
time yet.

"Yeah, so?"

"Pick it up, put it in the trash receptacle."

"Receptacle?"

"Do it."

"I'm not finished."

"Pick it up, put it in the receptacle."

"I *said* I'm not finished eating."

"Then hold it on your lap."

I started to take this discussion another step down the path, but
I'd already been beat up on—ball-kicked, finger-bent, pepper-
sprayed—plus, I still wasn't sure of my status as a murder suspect . . . so I said, "Right away, Officer," and picked up the paper
wrappings, the empty can.

He walked on. I was tempted to dump everything back on the
ground but carried it to the nearest trash can, then returned to the
shop, which had its door open.

I couldn't tell you what kind of store it was, stuffed animals shar-
ing shelf space with jars of olives and canned beets . . . no customers
and no prospects. I asked the old lady sitting behind the counter if
she was Harmony and she shook her head, pointing at the ceiling. I
looked up, just a regular ceiling. "Is Harmony here?" The old lady
pointed at the ceiling again. "What are you trying to tell me?" I
asked. She rolled her eyes and said, "Second floor."

"Oh." I didn't see any stairs. "How do I get there?"

She pointed this time to the back of the store, where, in a corner
and behind a green curtain, I found the narrowest set of stairs I've
ever climbed in my life. If my shoulders had been an inch wider they
would've rubbed both sides . . . also the risers were unusually short,
leading me to alternate between taking two at a time and stumbling.

At the top of the stairway was a small room, not much more than
ten or twelve feet to a side, with windows all along the front and back
walls and a wide variety of small cabinets hanging on the other two
walls, some of the cabinets handsome, handmade of oiled woods, and

others just old tin medicine cabinets with mirrored doors. With all those curtainless windows letting in the sun, the place was suffocatingly hot. In the middle of the room was a plain kitchen table on which stood some kind of holder made out of smooth wooden dowels like a bare tree with a thick center shaft from which the nine or ten wooden dowel limbs stuck straight out parallel to the ground.

"May I help you?"

This apparently was the shop's proprietor, though I still had no idea what was sold here, saw no product being displayed. She looked to be in her eighties, white hair and sensible shoes, five and a half feet tall, wearing a standard-issue old lady's dress, appearing cool and collected in this stifling heat. I remember thinking at the time, here at last is someone *normal,* a granny.

"I was wondering about a merkin."

She kept looking at me with that pleasant, I'm-waiting-for-you-to-say-something stare . . . was she deaf?

"Are you Harmony?"

"And you are?"

"Charlie, my name is Charlie."

The old lady shrugged to show my name meant nothing to her.

"Pelikan . . . James Joseph is my uncle."

Her whole manner changed, relaxed and friendly now as she walked over and took my hand. "Why didn't you say that in the first place . . . Harry, was it?"

"Charlie."

"Of course. Now what can I do for you?"

"A merkin?"

"Of course, how old is your friend, what's her coloring?"

I smiled the way I would with my very own grandmother. "What friend are we talking about?"

"The one who needs a merkin, don't you have a lady friend who needs a merkin . . . I'm confused."

I told her I was too. "You're Harmony?"

"I am."

"I asked someone what a merkin was and that person told me you could explain."

"I see." She stood there squinting as she searched my face. "*Charlie* . . . I remember you from years and years ago when you lived here as a boy."

"I was in my teens but, yes, I lived in the Quarter with my father, Pelikan's half brother."

"Of course . . . you and I had sex once."

I laughed like a hyena, then nearly choked trying to stifle that laugh. "No, I don't think so."

"You probably don't remember, that's all right, I'm not offended."

"But we never—"

"Your uncle James Joseph was setting you up with all kinds of different women, he thought the world of you. You and I had sex one night in the back room of—"

"No." I put up both hands as if to ward off the accusation. "Definitely not, I would've remembered."

"I would've been only in my sixties then. You were such a nice shy boy . . . you held hands with me, don't your remember? I guess I was a little lighter on my feet back then, had the henna hair . . . remember?"

"No," I said. "No."

"Well, I'm out of the business now anyway."

"Good."

"Why good?"

I didn't know. "I mean, as long as you're happy, right?"

"Happy? I'm eighty-three," she said as if that closed the subject. "So, you want to buy a merkin?"

"No, I want to know what a merkin is."

"Well, Larry, when a woman gets older, several interesting developments occur to her genitals."

"Charlie," I corrected her. "And please, ma'am, I don't want to hear this."

"Squeamish?"

I admitted I was.

"The aging vagina—"

I raised a hand. "Please don't."

"Lubrication problems can be easily corrected with the help of Kenneth Young."

"What?"

"Maybe you know him by his initials, K.Y." Another of those ridiculous winks, this one accompanied by a soft nudge to my side. "Age shrinks a woman's vagina and causes her to lose pubic hair, so in some ways the older woman's genitals begin to resemble those of a girl—"

I was reaching behind me for the stair railing. "Okay then, well thank you for your help." I turned to go.

"Sometimes an older woman is sensitive about losing pubic hair." Harmony stepped toward one of cabinets on the wall. "Or she's taken on a younger lover who likes a woman fully bushed."

I turned back to see her open one of the wooden cabinets, revealing inside a set of pegs from which hung a dozen of what looked like scalps taken from people with short, curly dark hair.

"Merkins?" I asked.

Harmony smiled like granny with the grandkids at Christmas. "Which one would your lady friend be interested in, do you think?"

"No, I didn't come here to buy . . . I want to know if you sold one of those to a *young* woman."

"That wouldn't be out of the question, I get the younger crowd on occasion, especially the *professional* woman who keeps her bush very short and well clipped, nothing more irksome than getting a pubie pulled in and out with each stroke . . . but sometimes these pros acquire a steady beau who doesn't like to be reminded why his lady fair is poodle-cut down there for quick action, so she'll come in and buy a big hairy—"

"Ma'am—"

"On the other hand, sometimes a young woman who isn't in the business will meet a man that's a connoisseur of a particularly thick or especially extensive or specifically colored—"

I tried speaking more loudly. "Have you sold any to a young woman recently, can you just tell me that, *please?*"

"Also I sell to the Sapphos . . . they have a keen interest in the undergrowth." She took one of the merkins down from a peg and carried it over to the table, placing the little pelt on a limb of that tree of dowels. "This is the Bella model. As you can see, it—"

"Please." I felt like crying, screaming with frustration. "This young woman I'm looking for has very short blond hair . . . on her head. I mean extremely short, like a burr cut. You'd remember her. She's in her early or middle twenties, bright blue eyes."

Harmony seemed troubled. "I think it must be private information, who I sell to . . . can you imagine if a woman had a lover who adored her rich, full, curly, soft bush . . ." With the backs of her fingers, Harmony stroked the Bella model as she spoke. "And then I revealed that the woman was wearing a merkin. Why, it could destroy a relationship, I might be sued, it's like violating the sacred trust between doctor and patient, lawyer and client, priest and—"

"Fifty dollars?"

She jerked her hand away from the Bella model and thrust that liver-spotted mitt at me, palms up.

I mined a few pockets and offered Harmony some crumpled bills without bothering to count them.

She looked down at the money, then up at me . . . and snatched the dough, becoming all business. "Give me a description."

"Like I said, she's in her early or mid-twenties, very short blond hair, attractive, petite, not much taller than you—"

"No, describe the merkin . . . she was wearing one, right?"

"I guess so because one day she was shaved bare between the legs, the next day she had a bush."

"Describe it, please, I remember my merkins better than I do the customers."

"Okay, it was curly—"

The old woman laughed. "Well *that's* a big help."

"Curly and dark but not black, almost a deep, dark auburn, and really full—"

"Sounds like our Dolly model number two eighty-nine."

"Does that ring any bells with you?"

"It might."

I waited and sweated in the overbearing heat while Harmony stumbled along her memory banks before finally asking me, "This young woman, did she have a fishhook through her lower lip?"

28

DEVIL IN THE RED DRESS

"Maria," Harmony said after I confirmed the fishhooked lip. "That's her," I said.

"In fact I just saw Maria," Harmony told me.

"Where?"

"She was having lunch at Mother's."

"Do you think she's still there?"

"I don't know. No, wait. She was telling some pirate about taking a walk up Bourbon Street, you might be able to catch her if you hurry."

"Okay—"

"You won't be able to miss her . . . considering what she was wearing."

I waited, then had to ask, "What's she wearing?"

"A short tight red dress with red high heels, an outfit that'd make a Quaker quake."

"Thank you." Hurrying for the narrow staircase, which proved more difficult going down than coming up, I heard Harmony calling behind me, "Charlie, we did have sex, you and me."

"No we didn't!"

She cackled.

I didn't know how much of a head start the shorn blonde had, I'll hurry toward the end of Bourbon Street then backtrack, hoping to meet her on the way.

Running up Decatur to Jackson Square, I didn't see God as I fast-

walked under the Pontalba Apartment balconies, took a left on
Chartres, right on Toulouse, stopping to rest at Bourbon Street, not
crowded and loud yet but getting that way. A midget barker was trying to convince tourists to come into his club while across the street a
giant barker was telling people to ignore the midget and come in *his*
bar . . . the midget would on occasion bend over and look up a skirt,
which got a laugh from everyone, even the giant across the street.
Among all these characters would I be able to spot the woman who
killed Three Jacks?

Answering my question, she strutted by on the opposite sidewalk:
same short blond hair, same sweet face, fishhook in place under her
lower lip, and wearing a knockout of a dress: tight, low, short, red.
She didn't see me but everyone saw her. Men stopped to watch her
approach, then turned around to watch her walk away. The younger
men grinned, the older ones sucked in their stomachs. She wore spike
high heels, red to match the dress, and she walked in a quick, diddily-
bopping way that made her ass shake and breasts jiggle . . . that ass
barely covered by the dress, those breasts threatening to jiggle out the
top and expose fat purple nipples I've seen when she killed Three
Jacks and again in Judge Borders's office. She walked the way Ali
fought, pure and exuberant . . . she carried nothing, no purse, all her
effort concentrated on walking, no distractions, her arms swinging
free, she walked like honky-tonk music sounds. Men and women in
conversation would stop talking as she neared them. And when four
college boys saw her, they all assumed silent, rigid poses like
weimaraners freezing at the sight of quail.

She was walking so fast—walking like Tina Turner dances—that I
had trouble keeping up, especially when I got caught behind the PG-
rated tourists coming in this time of day, before dark, trusting sunlight to keep them safe in sin city, strolling along in that maddening
tourist crawl, get *outta* my way.

The four college boys were following her too, nudging one another and laughing. I wondered what kind of disturbance she
might've caused if she walked like this down Bourbon Street past
midnight when everyone was drunk . . . in my condition last night,
what might I have done?

When she turned off Bourbon, the college boys ducked into an upscale strip joint while I kept trailing Maria, down Iberville, watching as she slowed to a normal pace and stopped swinging her groceries. The dress was still too short and tight and red *not* to get noticed, but the pedestrians she passed now didn't gawk the way people did back on Bourbon. It was all in the walk.

She slipped into a little alley off Iberville and turned it back on again, strutting for a private audience of one. From where I stood across the street I couldn't see who the lucky guy was, someone in black slacks and red shirt, blondie giving him an eyeful as she swayed and shook and shimmied and did everything she'd done on Bourbon, except now she was doing it nice and slow.

When they met near the alley's back end they went into a full-body embrace, mouths locked.

I gave them a few moments, then entered the alley, which had only one way out, past me.

Black pants and red shirt saw me first, immediately taking the Maria's arm. In the little alley with them, I could see that this person was a woman. Short and thickset with cropped black hair and a piggy expression, she had shoulders as wide as mine and biceps thicker . . . and beneath her lower lip were *three* fishhooks, you had to wonder how they can kiss without getting their barbs crossed.

"Show's over, asshole," said the fireplug dyke, taking me for a horny tourist who had followed her girlfriend here from Bourbon Street . . . but Maria knows who I am, her eyes wide with a big question: what's going to happen now?

"So she gets a whole streetful of men hot and bothered," I said to the dyke, "and then rushes here to tell you all about it, making *you* hot and bothered."

Like a junior sumo wrestler, the dyke assumed a wide-legged stance.

"Does it turn you on," I asked, "knowing that you got the girl all the boys want?"

From behind, Maria whispered something in her girlfriend's ear . . . ID'ing me.

"You need to leave right now, mister," the dyke said with less bluster, more intent.

"I'll go when your hot little friend there tells me why she killed Three Jacks On The Floor, who arranged it, who's she working for . . . tell me that and I'm out of here."

"She's going to tell you shit." The dyke looked to be in her early thirties, her plain face untouched by makeup, the tip of her nose turning up in an unfortunate manner that exposed her nostrils . . . which, along with her small eyes, gave her that piglike appearance.

I said, "Three Jacks told me those fishhooks are worn to discourage blow jobs—"

"That's right, asshole, no more blow jobs, never again," she said, stomping toward me, apparently ready to kick me in the balls or grapple or duke it out, however dykes fight.

"Sad words," I told her with complete sincerity. And then, as abruptly as a sneeze, I started to cry.

She stopped her advance, asking me what's wrong.

"No more blow jobs," I said, my voice catching. "Is it true?"

She insisted it was. "Blow jobs facilitate the degradation of women, another way for men to keep women silent, gagged, and on their knees."

I told her I was sorry and then took out a handkerchief, blew my nose, felt silly for having cried. "Blow jobs feel good."

"The larger issue has nothing to do with pleasure," she explained. "A blow job is a political act, an act of oppression. Can a woman speak to you when you're getting a blow job, can she look you in the eye as an equal?"

"No," I admitted. "But I *like* blow jobs."

"Of course you do, you're one of the oppressors. But the oppressed are getting up off their knees and speaking with one voice, *No more blow jobs.*"

"No more blow jobs . . ." I felt my shoulders slumping, my entire self sagging . . . I was exhausted, had been through too much, betrayed my uncle, I needed sleep, I wanted to make amends with Pelikan by agreeing to help him rob the repository, I wanted to be forgiven . . . and now I have to deal with *this*? "No more blow jobs," I whispered like a little boy who's been told that someday there won't be any more ice cream, no more hot dogs, all baseball games canceled forever.

The fireplug dyke stepped closer, speaking in a whisper. "You know, if you really loved a woman and she loved you and you two were in a relatively equal relationship, though some say that with the power a man holds in this society, any relationship he has with a woman is inherently unequal—"

I wiped at my face and looked at her. "What the fuck are you talking about?"

"There might be blow jobs in your future *if you treat women with respect and dignity.*" And then to punctuate this, she slapped me across the top of the head.

"Ow! What was that for?"

"If you treat women with respect and dignity."

"Okay, I will. Now can I ask Maria just one thing . . . who's setting me up, is it Pelikan or is it that weird guy in the limo, Gallier? Which one of them arranged for you to kill Three Jacks so I'd get blamed for it?"

The two women conferred briefly, then Maria told me, "Gallier."

"Why?"

"He and Pelikan had a falling out, Gallier is using you to get back at Pelikan. Gallier never had anything to hold over James Joseph, to threaten him with . . . until you showed up. Because James Joseph thinks the world of you."

"He does?"

She said he talks about me all the time. "Howz ya momma and 'em sisters?"

I told her they were fine.

"James Joseph can't ignore Gallier because Gallier is threatening you," Maria explained. "It was Gallier who had me go to the courthouse because he knew you'd be there, he wanted to get you in trouble, keep the police on your ass. He bought me this dress and sent me looking for you last night and again today, first I went to Mother's, then I walked up Bourbon."

"I know, I was following you. How'd you get out of that swimming pool, I must've waited there seven or eight minutes."

"I swam and hid behind the waterfall."

"I'll be damned."

"Soon as you left the patio I got out, grabbed my clothes, hid in a bedroom while the police were let in by the manager . . . when they all went out to the patio and stood around Three Jacks's body is when I left. Gallier made me kill that man, I had to get high to do it—"

"Why did he want Three Jacks dead?"

"I don't know, something about being double-crossed." Maria and her girlfriend conferred again, making pigeon sounds to each other.

"What's Gallier got on you," I asked Maria, "that you would commit murder for him?"

"It's Wendy." She stroked the dyke's shoulder.

Wendy?

"She got arrested for dealing drugs and was looking at a mandatory twenty," Maria continued. "I couldn't live without her, Gallier talked to some people in the court system, then got us a good lawyer, the same one you're using, Charlie."

"Amanda?"

She looked up at me with a sad smile. "Promise me you won't say anything to Gallier. If he knew I talked to you like this, he'd cut my heart out."

"I won't say a word. But you're telling me that Amanda works for Gallier?"

Maria nodded.

"One last thing," I said. "Gallier had you wear that red dress and go trolling for me . . . I follow you into this alley, what was the plan after that?"

"I'm sorry, Charlie, I really am . . ."

I didn't know what she meant until I turned around to see Detective Mean Gene Renfrone coming for me, he's still wearing that yellow satin, blue-trimmed windbreaker in all this heat . . . and holding what looked like a nightstick, but when he pressed a button, bright blue sparks crackled up and down the length of the club, one of those million-volt stunning wands.

"What's Gallier got on *you,* Gene?" I ask him.

Holding the stunning wand the way you might an Olympic torch, eyes dead above that mushy potato nose, Renfrone came straight for me. I fake right and go left but he caught me on the arm with sufficient volts to make me drop to the pavement. Renfrone steps close and holds the wand to my mouth.

"Please don't," I beg.

He does. It's the worst thing that's ever happened to me, physically, in thirty three years of life. I felt the shock through my teeth, down my spine, out my ass, the length of my dick . . . in a spasm I curled up to a tight fetal position. If you've never had a high-voltage, low-amp shock, it's hard to explain the effect . . . not pain as you normally think of it, worse than normal pain because the shock hurts *and* it produces a sensation that's profoundly unpleasant . . . something so odious you're certain that you never, ever want it to happen to you again.

Renfrone held the wand to my neck and shocked me again.

Another fetal spasm, mentally begging him not to do it again.

He did it again.

I wet myself, not a total emptying of the bladder, but I felt hot piss spurt out with the shock. If I'd been offered a deal right then . . . my soul spending eternity suffering hellfire in exchange for not being shocked again, I would've taken hell in a fluttering heartbeat.

I was saved from another shock when a big white limousine turned into the alley and used a soft bleat of the horn and quick blip of the headlights to call off my tormentor.

29

DOCTOR, DOCTOR

"It's like the Waltons, all together, one happy family," said Gallier, squatting toadlike in the far backseat of the limo. The pirate I'd seen around was here too, wearing a black hat with the brim turned up and a patch over his left eye. Renfrone, still holding his magic wand of pain, sat on the other side of Gallier. In the facing seat were Maria and the spectacularly misnamed Wendy, clinging to each other like newly orphaned children. I was on the floor.

"Charles?"

"Yes," I said warily . . . caring about nothing except avoiding another shock.

"Detective Renfrone tells me you were having a *chat* with Maria, what were you two discussing?" He grabbed my hair and made me sit up so he could see my face.

I didn't hesitate: "She said it was Pelikan who sent her to kill Three Jacks . . . Pelikan making me the patsy, the *pazzo,* just like you told me."

He let go of my hair and looked for someplace to wipe his hand, finally using the pirate's blouse and telling me I needed to shampoo . . . I readily agreed and then we all waited, none of the others saying a word, afraid to distract Gallier, afraid if he turned his attention from me he might start in on one of them.

"Charles, knowing now you've been betrayed by your uncle, will you come work for *me*?"

"Absolutely."

"Even if it means you'll have to kill James Joseph?"

I gave a nice long dramatic pause, then said yes . . . I was able and willing to kill Pelikan.

Gallier signaled Renfrone, who reached into the windbreaker and brought out a .38 Special snub-nose revolver. "Use that," Gallier said as Renfrone handed me the revolver.

The same one that killed Three Jacks?

Feeling a lot better with a gun in my hand, I asked Gallier, "What's wrong with Mean Gene? He hasn't said a word."

"Oh he's having a crisis of conscience." The doctor looked at the detective. "Aren't you, Gene?"

Renfrone raised the stun wand and made it dance with blue sparks.

Gallier laughed softly.

First thing I'm going to do, right now, is shoot Detective Renfrone to ensure he can't use that sparker on me ever again, one shot to his fat neck, get him choking on his own blood and ruin that windbreaker. Then the good doctor gets a bullet in the center of that starched white shirt. If the pirate, whoever the hell he is, makes any noise, he gets it too. Whatever shots are left I'll use on the security guards up front . . . how many I don't know, because I'm down here on the frigging floor.

Before opening fire I have the presence of mind to check the cylinder: *empty.*

"Oh, Charles, that *was* unfortunate."

"What?" I asked, eyes wide in pretended innocence.

"It was a little test," Gallier said. "If you tucked the revolver in a pocket, maybe you could be trusted. But if you checked to see if it was loaded because you intended to shoot me right here and now, then *no.* Actually, I was hoping you'd point the gun at me and go *click, click, click.*" The doctor laughed. "Oh, Charles, I was cast out and now I must punish him by hurting you."

He signaled Renfrone, who laid that *cursed* electric club on top of my head and made it zap down through my brains . . . putting me into a miniseizure right there on the floor, while Gallier jabbed a hypodermic needle through my jeans and into my ass.

30

MYTHS AND KIDNEYS

I t was like being drunk the previous night, at some point memory went blank . . . though I do recall being dragged-carried between two men while other people looked at me with disgust and I remember voices, a woman's voice begging and pleading and promising (for herself or on my behalf?) . . . and hospital smells, I remember those too.

And a dream: several people are working furiously near me, they must be tired of hearing my complaints about the heat because they're packing ice around me and at first it's wonderful, I'm cool, after the smothering summer heat of New Orleans, finally I'm cool . . . I'm Sasquatch running naked through the snow, but then, too quickly, that pleasant sensation deteriorates into an awful one, hunters have shot me in the side and I'm lying wounded in a creek, the water freezing, I'm cold and bleeding, going numb, parts of me are actually being frozen and I imagine my flesh turning hard like bloodred Popsicles from the deep freeze.

The dream must've arrived just before I awoke . . . in a bathtub of frigid water. Some ice is floating but most of it is packed in plastic bags along my left side. I need to get out of here before I freeze to death. But before I move I see on the white tiles above the bathtub spigots a message written in what appears to be lipstick or blood, dark red: *TO LIVE, CALL 911.*

The ice water I'm lying in is tinged pink.

There's a phone on the edge of the bathtub . . . when I reach for it, pain rips up and down my left side, stinging like wasps beneath those bags of ice. I put a hand there, under the ice, terrified what I'll find: my fingers come back red.

PART THREE

LOVE AND REDEMPTION: GOD'S BREATH

31

THE WIND GOES TOWARD THE SOUTH, AND TURNS ABOUT UNTO THE NORTH.

—ECCLESIASTES

Odds were ten to one against her survival when she was born in a depression several weeks ago over the Atlantic Ocean off the coast of Africa, north of the equator, her birth hot and wet as she inhaled a beginning breath of blood-warm wind blowing over ninety-degree water. Her chances were so slim that at birth she didn't have a name, not even a number, not yet.

Of the hundred tropical disturbances arising each year over the heated Atlantic, a dozen become organized storms designated with numbers. When their winds top forty miles per hour they are christened with names, but only about six in a season make it all the way to hurricane status, with winds seventy-four miles per hour and above.

What happens to the rest of them? Hot, wet wind is pulled into a low pressure trough, where the air rises and releases its moisture and energy in the form of tropical storms. When the rising air can go no higher, bumping its head against the stratosphere, the air spreads out and cools, then falls back to the ocean to repeat the cycle. But with each pass the air is less heated, less moist . . . and without these fuels—heat and moisture—the system eventually dies out.

Which would've been Emily's fate, to die cold and dry, if she hadn't met someone who took her breath away. A high-altitude, high-

pressure system parked itself on top of Emily and forced away her rising columns of cooling, drying air . . . allowing fresh fuel to be sucked
into the low-pressure heart of Emily. And when she depletes *those* new
winds of their energy and when they have been forced away by the
upper-level high-pressure system, Emily can eat again . . . and again
and again, she can feed on a whole ocean of wet heat, enough to sus-
tain a hurricane.

The Coriolis effect, caused by the earth's rotation, puts Emily in
a counterclockwise spin, which further organizes her pattern: winds
sucked in, carried up, blown away over the top to make room for new
wind, more energy.

Faster and faster she spins, growing larger, nudged slowly west
across the Atlantic by the same trade winds that carried the *Niña,
Pinta,* and *Santa María* to the Caribbean, where Emily headed when
she was barely a week old.

From Africa, Atlantic hurricanes generally travel north and west,
toward the Caribbean, Florida, and the southeast coast of the U.S.,
but often making hard turns to the north before touching land, blown
then by westerlies back across the Atlantic toward England and Scan-
dinavia, arriving out of breath, just enough fury left to be considered
severe storms . . . which is why, before Europeans began exploring the
New World, hurricanes were unknown to them.

Predictions from hurricane watchers had Emily traveling from
Cuba, across the Gulf of Mexico, eventually making landfall in an
area that centered on Matamoros, Mexico, near the southernmost tip
of Texas. But halfway there, Emily hangs a dramatic right turn as if
she suddenly changed her mind about Mexico . . . as if she were a
mighty warship abruptly called off course to join battle
elsewhere . . . as if something north summoned her.

A PELIKAN, A CLOWN, A HOOKER, AND FIVE NUNS

They've been here most of the previous day, all of last night, and now today . . . in this small, brick, former-slave-quarters cottage scattered with construction debris, no air-conditioning, only one bed, which is upstairs, and in it James Joseph Pelikan lingering in some catatonic state, staring up at the vent over the bed. He's not drunk or whacked, but lost in some deep well of melancholia.

"Can I get you anything?" Sister Margaret asks him as she has dozens of times before. The nun has been at Pelikan's bedside nearly the entire duration, speaking softly to him in her flat, no-nonsense, Montana voice. "Tell me what you need."

I need a call to courage now that life has withered hope . . . but he doesn't speak this aloud—who would?

"Do you think it's wrong we've gone to all this trouble for a relic?" she asks, not expecting him to answer. "Americans don't understand, when I was growing up on the ranch I wouldn't have understood . . . I was taught to worship God in my heart and by my actions, no mention of holy *things* beyond the Bible itself, and even then it was the contents we considered sacred, not the physical book. I didn't grow up Catholic, we thought Catholics were weird with all their symbols and ceremonies. But since I became Catholic I realize, of course, we don't worship the Edessa, we *venerate* it, and for a thousand years, until it was stolen from us, we had the sacred responsibility of *protecting* it . . . and that's something even an old Montana cowgirl like me can appreciate, *duty*."

Pelikan continued staring up at the ceiling vent as Sister Margaret continued trying to rouse him.

"The order at Limoges is dying out. We try to recruit from all over the world but it's getting harder and harder. Who wants to join an order whose raison d'être was stolen sixty years ago?" It sounds jarring to hear her say "raison d'être" in that Western twang . . . what must the people of Limoges think of her speaking their language? "Did you know that once our order was known as God's guards? It's never been a job for the timid. From the very beginning, the order has made use of strong women, married to God, well versed in his defense. Raids on the Limoges convent were attempted, repulsed. But even before the convent was built we were protecting the Edessa, transporting it in wooden carts pulled by ponies or by the sisters themselves. Then, during the Second World War, after France fell, the sisters couldn't hold out against the Nazis and the Vichy. Did you know, James Joseph, that three-quarters of the sisters at the Limoges convent did not survive the war? Some of them died of untreated illnesses, some of them killed outright. I'd like to honor those sisters by returning the Edessa to Limoges . . . but to do that we need your help. Will you be ready by tonight? James Joseph? We don't have much time left, Emily's coming."

He said nothing.

Downstairs, in spite of the language gap, Diane "Knees" O'Rourke and Sad Bob the clown were holding forth on their respective areas of expertise. Sad Bob had cornered the two little Filipino nuns and was telling them about his college days.

"A lot of people think they can put on a red nose, blow up a balloon, and call themselves clowns, but it's not that easy, not if you do it right. I was one of thirty-three applicants picked out of *fifteen hundred* for Clown College down in Sarasota, and I'm proud of being chosen, proud of the work I did, everything I learned . . . six days a week, fourteen hours a day for two months, but it was worth it. I was awarded the respected BFA. You probably don't know what that is."

As Sad Bob prattled on, the two nuns Pelikan called Tiddlywink and Tickledpink concentrated on keeping their big brown eyes open . . . they'd only recently been pulled off prayer duty and were exhausted, had already removed their glasses, which were weighing down oppressively on their small faces. Not knowing how to convey to the clown that they wanted to be left alone to sleep, they patiently sat and stared and listened to what they could not understand . . . thinking it odd that a clown could act so serious when dressed so ridiculously . . . Sad Bob in his blue-black jumpsuit with fuzzy red balls where the buttons should be, wearing a brown derby and oversized clown shoes and an absolutely huge red nose that almost blocked his view, it was that big.

"It's a bachelor of fun arts degree . . . BFA? Did you know that the clowns William Kemp and Richard Armin were two of twenty-six principal actors in a troupe called Lord Chandler's Men? Guess who was the playwright for Lord Chandler's Men? Give up? A guy you might have heard of . . . William Shakespeare?"

No reaction.

"What I'm trying to say, for me college wasn't all juggling bowling pins and getting pies in the face . . . I grew, I *learned.* I bet I can give you a hundred synonyms for clown. *Fool, jester, zany* . . . you know, of course, that *zany* is a noun too? *Harlequin, merry-andrew, buffoon, idiot, driveler, fool* . . . did I already say *fool*? *Fool* fits me all right, complete fool, born fool, fool for love . . . I don't know if I ever mentioned He Who Shall Remain Nameless, but . . ." Here's where Bob lost it, putting his upper teeth on his lower lip and biting down fairly hard, but still unable to hold back the single sob that brought forth in its wake a summer storm of weeping, blubbering, whimpering . . . the tears of a clown.

Tiddlywink nudged Tickledpink . . . or maybe it was the other way around.

"James Joseph is always embarrassing me with that thing he says about me being the foundation of his success," Knees O'Rourke was telling the two Bulgarian nuns, who sat, each on her own barrel of nails, like large square blocks wrapped for industrial shipment in heavy black material . . . Diane fascinated with how their coifs fit so tightly that their large faces looked as if they were being squeezed by hydraulic pressure. "I mean, yes, I do my best, I always have, but I'm uncomfortable being given *all* the credit, James Joseph has had some great and talented women working for him over the years. Men too, don't want to leave the boys out. All I'm saying is, I'm not claiming any greatness for myself. I guess, if anything, I just wanted to prove to the world that an Irish girl from Boston can suck cock with the best of 'em."

Their names were Sofia and Katrina, friends who came to Christ together but relatively late in life . . . they met years ago while living in the Soviet Union, where they worked construction and became experts in building demolition . . . they have no clue what this woman in the pedal pushers and white blouse is saying, but they think she must be a clown like that other one in the room, over there talking to Theresa and Marina, because this woman's makeup is vivid enough to be seen from the highest row of seats under the big top.

"James Joseph is so proud of me that he arranged I should teach a class, did I tell you about this before? He advertised a class for married women who were interested in keeping their husbands interested, that's how James Joseph billed it, 'Interested in Keeping Your Husband Interested?' We had thirty-two women show up for the first class, I think they were under the impression it was going to be about reverse psychology and interpersonal relations and all that . . . but it was just me and a few props up there in front of all those women, trying to teach them how to suck cock. James Joseph figured that since nine out of ten married guys who visit hookers are looking for blow jobs, if those guys got their blow jobs at home, they'd *stay* at home. I know what you're thinking . . . wasn't James Joseph undermining his own livelihood by showing women how to stop their husbands going to hookers? He didn't care, it was for the greater good . . . and also we charged fifty dollars for the class. I started out trying to be scientific, told the ladies that nothing I was advising would poison them, I wasn't suggesting they swallow Drano. I mean, if you look at it scientifically, it's potassium, sodium, fructose—that's a naturally occuring sugar—along with amino acids, citric acid, phosphorus, calcium for strong bones, zinc, sodium, did I already say sodium, yeah, it deserves being mentioned twice, magnesium, and the ever-present mucus. When my so-called students finally clicked what I was referrring to, some of the women wanted their money back, but most of them just left without saying anything. I think I ended up giving the class to about six women. The others were offended, their loss."

Large hands on large knees, Katrina and Sofia lean forward as if listening intently . . . actually they're trying to deconstruct Diane's makeup, all the various layers and shades and borders.

"I liked being an educator, I was thinking of going to college when I retire. I mean, get my GED, then go to college to become a teacher in Ireland, teach at a school within walking distance of Apple Tree Cottage, I think I got the knack for it. Of course, when I was teaching those wives I couldn't give out all my trade secrets, got to be careful about competition, but I wouldn't mind telling you two exactly what I do that's made James Joseph so proud of me. You want to hear a real honest-to-gosh trade secret? I realize you're nuns and you're not going to be doing any of this *personally,* but maybe you want to get a little sense of what kind of teacher I was . . . just a little bit of that class I taught, what do you say?"

From Diane's perspective, they were staring at her the way statues do.

The scene upstairs could've been from 150 years ago, a nun at the bedside of a heartsick man. "When Katrina's brother introduced us," Sister Margaret was saying to Pelikan, "I knew right away you were the one. Karl . . . what's that you called him, Three Aces In The Hole? He said you could be strange and moody at times but that no one knew the French Quarter better. It wasn't your knowledge we wanted, it was your heart. You're a good man. Do you have it in your heart to go out into a hurricane tonight?"

Pelikan lay there like Lincoln on his deathbed, a great man fading . . . except Pelikan kept his eyes open.

"The Edessa is the reason our order was begun . . . I know you've seen pictures of it but the day you open that reliquary and see it in person is a day you'll not forget the rest of your life." She held her hands out, thumbs and forefingers creating a circle. "Beautiful, gleaming gold, perfect in every detail, can you picture a golden crown of thorns?"

Whether Pelikan was picturing it, Sister Margaret could not tell . . . his expression so utterly blank she wondered if he had suffered a stroke.

"Thracians were the greatest goldsmiths who ever lived, many of their techniques for working gold have been lost to time. Crusaders invaded Edessa in ten ninety-seven, and that's when our order began. Can't you please put aside whatever you're suffering and help us get it back, help us now, tonight . . . James Joseph?"

Sister Margaret removed her heavy black glasses and rubbed her weary eyes, determined not to cry.

"Loser, failure, dimwit, sot, stooge." Sad Bob continued to list synonyms as he openly wept, greasepaint smearing, the huge red nose slipping as his own nose ran with the wet effects of sustained blubbering. *"Bungler, dunderhead, dunce* . . . I was all that and more, how in the world did I let myself become so vulnerable to . . . well, you know who I'm talking about, of course, it's an old song I apparently can't stop singing, ode to He Who Shall Remain Nameless . . . nameless but not forgotten, not by this old *mooncalf . . . ninny . . . goose . . . nincompoop."*

The Filipino nuns covered their little mouths with tiny paw hands to stop themselves from yawning.

Sad Bob apologized and removed the nose to blow his nose. "And here I was trying to give you some respect for clowning, but instead I end up making a fool of myself . . . *ignoramus, dimwit.* You see this little hole here?" Showing them the big red nose, Sad Bob pointed to where a small hole, no bigger than a pencil lead, had been drilled into the top of the nose. "That's one of our trade secrets. Watch this." He produces a long, wide turkey feather from a pocket in his jumpsuit and works the sharpened quill into the nose's hole, then puts the nose back on and stands, throwing both arms out, pretending to balance the feather, which teeters this way and that but never falls off.

The nuns are delighted with the trick, applauding the clown, their little hands beating like the wings of hummingbirds.

"Premoistened towelettes?" Knees was asking the Bulgarian nuns. "Do you have those in your country? When they first came out I considered them a godsend. My father was a carpenter and he always said a clean workshop is a happy workshop. Okay, but that's not the trade secret I was telling you about . . . I guess if there's any one, single thing that's responsible for my success, it's what I do at the moment of climax. First you have to figure out when that moment is coming, so to speak, but that's largely a matter of experience, just don't always expect a polite little tap, tap on the top of your head, more often than not you don't get any warning at all. Okay, but when it finally does come, so to speak, here's what I do, the trade secret, the key to my success . . . I suck real hard, I mean *real hard* . . . I pull a vacuum that makes my eardrums feel like they're turning inside out, and what that suction does is, it *yanks* the cum out, and I'm here to tell you, men love the sensation, they love it a whole lot. I've had clients tell me it feels like someone is yanking a fat wet string all the way from their balls, right out their cock. Like *whoosh*. Drives 'em crazy. They'll be back for more, guarantee it. Now I know a lot of hookers you talk to say they got various techniques and tricks, butterfly kisses and love bites, but after nearly fifteen years of sucking a mile of cock—I figured it out once with a calculator—I'm here to tell you that men are interested in one thing only: something wet, warm, and tight around their dicks, the wetter, the warmer, the tighter, the better . . . and that's it, the whole of it, all the rest is just vamping till ready. Well one other thing, some of them adore making a mess. 'Can I come in your hair, can I come on your face, can I come in your shoes?' Jesus . . . oops, sorry. But in the end, the customer's always right, you heard that expression, haven't you? So when a client asks if he can come all over me, I figure to give him his money's worth and what I'll do is, I'll pull my mouth away at the moment of climax and let him shoot way up in the air, then I'll go after that flying wad like a terrier after a spurting garden hose."

The big nuns remained blank behind their black-framed glasses.

"Do you guys have *any idea* what I'm talking about?" Diane finally asked. "Blow job? Suckee dickie . . . I don't know how to say it in your language . . ." To demonstrate, Diane leaned forward, made her hand into a fist, and then moved that fist rapidly up and down in front of her opened mouth.

Katrina remained clueless, but Sofia, who spent a week in Milan when she was nineteen and under two hundred pounds, blushed vividly red and repeatedly crossed herself . . . all this happening as Sad Bob is stalking around balancing a feather on his nose to the applause of Filipinos.

"The points," Sister Margaret is telling the unresponsive Pelikan, "are sharp beyond what seems physically possible. You cannot hold it in your bare hands because if you do, the points will sink into your skin no matter how carefully or softly you try to cradle it . . . points sharper than hypodermic needles, it's incredible."

He placed an arm over his eyes.

Which encouraged Sister Margaret. At least he was moving. "I've taken Theresa and Marina off prayer duty . . . for obvious reasons. Did I tell you what a kick they get out of hearing you call them Tiddlywink and Tickledpink? James Joseph? *Hey.* Are you listening, can you hear me? We're going to have to do it tonight, tomorrow will be too late . . . Emily's on her way to New Orleans."

33

EMILY SETS HER HEART ON
NEW ORLEANS

Emily has swollen up like she's pregnant, her low pressure having caused water to rise within her, in effect the surface of the ocean being sucked up as Emily travels over it, creating a huge dome of water fifteen miles in diameter and ten feet high. If Emily comes ashore she'll carry this water dome with her, giving birth to a storm surge that can flood everything for miles, ultimately responsible for ninety percent of the death and destruction Emily causes: hurricanes have killed more humans than any other type of natural disaster, and it's the storm surge that does the killing.

At the National Hurricane Center in Miami, meteorologists are now betting—though not yet officially predicting—that Emily *will* hit the Gulf Coast, perhaps following in the steps of her 1957 sister Audrey, who kicked up fifty-foot seas, then gave birth to a killer storm surge topped by twenty-foot waves. Striking near the Texas border, Audrey spared New Orleans.

Will Emily? Ever since she made that weird ninety-degree turn north in the middle of the Gulf of Mexico, she seems to have her heart set on the Crescent City, though she is traveling slowly now, under six miles per hour, taking her time getting stronger with each hour spent over those warm gulf waters. Right now she's a category three hurricane on the Saffir-Simpson Scale, with winds of 120 miles per hour and a predicted storm surge of ten feet. If her winds top 130, she'll make it to category 4 . . . and if she blows past 155 miles per hour with a predicted storm surge of over eighteen feet, Emily will join the small, elite, deadly sisterhood of category five . . . one of them, Camille, hit Louisiana in 1969.

A hurricane's landfall can be a siege lasting twenty hours or more, ten of those hours brutal beyond imagination . . . she can blow beach sand that will skin animals alive (almost all human victims of hurricanes are found stripped naked by the wind), she can drown people who've climbed twenty feet up in trees. When Camille flooded Highway 90, which leads into New Orleans from the south and west, the road was under ten feet of water . . . earlier storms have flooded the entire city. New Orleans is now surrounded by protective dikes, but all hell breaks loose if they're breached . . . Bourbon Street is ten feet *below* sea level, you have to walk *up* from the French Quarter to see the Mississippi River.

But even with Emily possibly just three days from here, the people of New Orleans remain unworried. Many hurricanes wander this way, few score direct hits, and the ocean is fifty miles away. The biggest concession people have made to Emily is creating room on their refrigerators to post the Hurricane Checklist and Tracking Map published by the *Times-Picayune.* The tracking map shows the Gulf of Mexico marked off in grids, and the checklist is organized in four categories: When Hurricane Threatens; If Evacuation Is Advised; During the Hurricane; After the Hurricane. So far Emily's status is in the first category, When Hurricane Threatens, with the advice being to stock up on supplies, fill containers with water, and make sure the car's got gas because you might have to get out fast. But if you're one of the city's hundred thousand people without personal transportation, you'll have to be evacuated by bus . . . and there are only two major highways going north from New Orleans, only two ways out for 650,000 residents, and whatever number of the 10 million tourists a year who happen to be in town on the day of departure.

It's estimated that Charleston, South Carolina, has a clearance time (how long it takes to evacuate a city that's in a hurricane's path) of twenty-three hours; for Mobile, Alabama, it's twenty hours. The clearance time for New Orleans? *Three days.* Which is why evacuation is such a major undertaking here and a tough call for officials to make . . . Emily could still miss the city completely, maybe miss the state, could turn and head back out to sea.

Even when a hurricane is only twenty-four hours away from land, the best meteorologists can do is call landfall within three hundred miles, so anything can still happen to Emily, but here's the latest best guess: she'll come ashore somewhere from Apalachicola, Florida, to Houston, Texas, with the center of that range being Grand Isle, Louisiana, fifty miles due south of New Orleans. Grand Isle is where another sister, Betsy, made landfall in 1965, arriving on 160-mile-per-hour winds and a storm surge of nearly sixteen feet.

Grand Isle is also the stomping grounds of the Millerd brothers, Wilfred, age ten, and Sebastian, just turned twelve, notoriously known throughout their parish as bad boys with sticks . . . aka ridge runners, swamp rats, fire starters, habitual truants, terrors to cats everywhere. *The boy throws the rock in jest, the frog dies in earnest* was coined in anticipation of Wilfred and Sebastian . . . mean little boys with nasty personal habits. Unlike everyone else in Grand Isle, the Millerd brothers are actually hoping for Emily.

Storms have always been good for them. Storms wash up muskrats and other little animals that Wilfred and Sebastian can then chase with sticks. The Millerd brothers have a reputation for being willing to pick up *anything,* dead or alive, and in the aftermath of storms they are suddenly in demand to come get a raccoon out of a garage, a snake from under a back porch couch, lizards from kitchens, gators from little ponds where back lawns used to be.

Wilfred and Sebastian are tracking Emily, rooting her on as they spread a map on the floor of the emergency storm shelter where they're staying, a brick school building, and upon that map they place a ruler along the course Emily has followed ever since making that right turn north, and with dirty fingertips they follow that ruler as it runs right through Grand Isle . . . the Millerds thrilled with the possibilities.

If you continued following the Millerds' ruler, its path would lead you past Grand Isle to New Orleans and through the heart of the French Quarter.

34

A CALL TO COURAGE WHEN LIFE
HAS WITHERED HOPE

"Uncle?"

When Pelikan opens his eyes and sees me there by the bedside, he says, "Charlie Chan." Then tells me, "Your father is being buried today."

I take his hand as he sits up to lean against the bedstead, looking back and forth between Sister Margaret and me.

"Sister," I said softly. "We're breaking into the repository tonight, as soon as it's dark . . . that is, if the conditions are right, if we have a sufficient storm."

"Sufficient?" she asked.

"Yes." I tell her I think there's a big storm brewing . . . I haven't heard a forecast but the sky looks ominous. "Beautiful too . . . like shiny fish scales."

"You don't know?" she asked. "You haven't listened to radio, read a newspaper, talked to anyone?"

"None of the above," I admitted.

"I'll go downstairs," Sister Margaret said, "and tell everyone to get ready, we go tonight."

After she left the bedroom, Pelikan patted the sheet next to him and I sat there.

"What happened?" he asked. "Where have you been?"

I told him about being shown merkins by the old woman Harmony, following Maria, being shocked into submission by Renfrone,

taken into a limo and drugged by Gallier . . . then waking up in a
bathtub of ice, bleeding from my right side.

"The *crapaud* operated on you?" Pelikan asked incredulously.

Operated on . . . when I brought my hand out from under those ice
bags and saw the blood, I was convinced that Gallier, the toad, had
removed one of my kidneys. My mind couldn't get around the enormity of it . . . moaning, I reached for the phone that had been left on
the edge of the tub, but in my panic I knocked it to the floor and had
to lift myself partially out of the tub to retrieve the phone, wincing
from the pain, then I called 911 and said I think I might be dying, I
needed a doctor and ambulance. The emergency operator asked me
where I was, I didn't know . . . but the phone number was there on
the telephone and I gave it to the operator and pleaded with her to
find the location, it looks like a hotel bathroom, I said, I'm bleeding,
I said, please hurry, and she told me to stay on the line, which I did.

But as I waited I realized that, although it had hurt when I
reached over the side of the tub, the pain wasn't really that bad. If I'd
just had surgery, I wouldn't be reaching for anything, would I? I
wouldn't be wincing from the pain, I'd be screaming. Maybe I was
still under the influence of whatever drugs Gallier had given me, but
I didn't feel woozy.

Gingerly, I reached again beneath the ice bags and found the incision, probing gently . . . it felt like a cut you get from thorns, a deep
scratch rather than an incision. And although the cut was still bleeding, I wasn't losing much blood.

I slowly stood . . . the cut hurt when I moved but the pain was
manageable, if I hadn't been so totally concentrating on how it felt, I
don't think I would've categorized it as true pain, just discomfort.
Standing, I was able to see myself from the waist up in a mirror over
the bathroom's sink, visually tracing the vivid scratch from under my
right arm, around under my ribs, and to my stomach, then down
from there. *Just a scratch,* a long but shallow slit that wouldn't need
stitches, wouldn't even require a dressing unless I was worried about
the wound weeping onto my clothes.

Wondering where those clothes were, I got out of the tub, shivering as I stepped from the bathroom, seeing my shirt and jeans and underwear on the floor, next to the bed. As I was dressing I remembered the 911 call and quickly returned to the bathroom and picked up the receiver, the emergency operator saying "Sir?" over and over, asking if I was there, informing me she had traced the number to a hotel room, the emergency crew and police were on their way. I didn't want to try explaining any of this to the police so I hung up on the operator's pleas, toweled off, and got dressed while still shivering, though now from fear more than cold.

I was in the lobby by the time the police and medics arrived. As soon as I got outside and oriented myself, I walked here to the French Quarter, amazed to find the streets all but deserted.

"What's this about the weather?" I asked James Joseph.

"Emily," he said. "A hurricane named Emily."

"You're kidding . . . you're not kidding. Jesus, we have to get out of here, you got any idea what'll happen to the Quarter if a hurricane hits?"

"It's perfect for the—"

"No it's not. A severe summer storm might've been good cover for the job . . . but it would be crazy to try anything during a *hurricane,* we're agreed on that, aren't we?"

He didn't commit, but fingered back his hair and asked if he could see the shallow wound Gallier had given me.

I took off my shirt and turned.

"It's where an incision can be made to remove a kidney," Pelikan told me. "So the message is, I'd better cooperate with the toad or else next time he'll do the operation for real. It's the same thing the pirate told me."

"Yeah, there was a pirate with Gallier."

James Joseph nodded.

"If I had stayed in the tub until the police arrived, they might've started questioning me about Three Jacks's murder . . . I'd be in jail right now."

He asked me to hand him his clothes. "Which also would've been okay for Gallier, he's got Renfrone working for him . . . having you in jail would've been like putting you in safekeeping while I did the job."

I put my shirt back on. "Gallier told me the two of you used to be friends."

Pelikan nodded.

"And that you'd agreed to break into the repository *for him,* that you were partners."

James Joseph nodded again. "That was the original plan. Your dad and I would pull a quick in-and-out, Gallier gets his inheritance, we get paid."

"But then the nuns showed up?"

"Yes. Three Jacks knew about the Edessa from his sister Katrina, she's one of the Bulgarian nuns."

"I know, you introduced me."

"And Three Jacks introduced me to Sister Margaret, who made an appeal . . . and your dad gets the cancer, and then, I don't know, Charlie, it turned into this big thing. Three Jacks got greedy, sold information to Gallier."

"I told that idiot doctor how you were planning to break in—"

Pelikan held up a hand, said he didn't blame me for anything. "And Gallier's not a doctor, he never finished his internship or got a license."

"Another reason I'm glad he didn't operate on me."

We sat awhile in silence, neither of us sensing any urgency about the approaching hurricane, the possibility we were going to break into a building tonight. Pelikan asked me if I knew anything about his mother, my grandmother.

"Things have been said . . . Renfrone said she had a jones for cognac."

"Port. I told you that, Charlie . . . don't you listen to me?"

I didn't answer.

Before Pelikan looked away, I saw his eyes were weary. "Cheap port. You ever smell port the day after the night before, when it comes sweating out of a person's pores and stays on their breath too . . . I'd say it was disgusting if someone hadn't taught me once, years ago, what's *really* disgusting. Remembering her, my mother, your grandmother, is what led me to get drunk . . . she rubbed my feet and said they were perfect but that's the only thing good I ever got from that woman . . . not counting life, of course. So I drank port and ended up by the cathedral, cleaning that sidewalk with a toothbrush and embarrassing myself in front of tourists." When he looked back at me his eyes were dry. "So don't apologize for saying anything to Gallier, Charlie . . . if we start trading mea culpas we'll be here all night."

I nodded, wondering why I felt relieved when, in fact, nothing has been resolved. "Do you think the police are looking for me about Three Jacks?"

"I think Emily will blow away all your problems, is what I think."

"We have to get out of town."

"No, we're going to pull that job tonight . . . just like you told Sister Margaret we would."

"I said that before I knew there was a hurricane coming. Listen, why don't you go downstairs and tell the others the job's canceled until after the emergency? At the very least, tell Pinkletink and Winkledink they can stop praying for a storm already."

"They stopped praying for a storm the minute we heard about Emily."

"No, they're still praying . . . on my way through downstairs I saw the two of them going at it hot and heavy, hands folded, heads bowed, lips moving."

"Yeah, but what they're praying for now is that Emily should turn and miss us."

35

EMILY'S FIRST CASUALTY

Following recommendations from a hurricane preparedness book-let published by the federal government, a woman living in a fine house on St. Ann Street began collecting important documents such as birth certificates and passports and insurance papers that she would take along for safekeeping when she and her husband left that afternoon for Monroe, Louisiana, up in the northern part of the state, where the woman had family, a sister who would put them up until the hurricane danger had passed. The woman living on St. Ann Street didn't have children, her sister had four, three girls and a boy, and the woman was looking forward to seeing her nieces and nephew.

Her husband usually took care of paperwork but he had to run to his office in the Central Business District and finish some deal he was working on before the hurricane hit, so the woman has taken this task upon herself. After removing the relevant documents from a small safe kept at the back of a walk-in closet in her husband's study, the woman began searching for a rubber raincoat she was almost sure her husband still had from his navy days. It would no longer go around his fat belly but it might fit her. Instead she came across a briefcase she didn't remember ever seeing, locked and heavy with contents. It eventually yielded to the woman's efforts with a paper clip. She wasn't sure why she was taking time to snoop around like this when a hurricane was on its way except maybe she did know and refused to admit it to herself. The briefcase contained photographs of

women . . . and letters to her husband from these women, which troubled the wife (why was he keeping them?) but didn't enrage her because the contraband predated their marriage. Except for one picture,
one letter. This one picture was of her sister naked but for a pair of
black underpants, sitting on the edge of a bed and kind of leaning forward, her hands under her heavy breasts as if offering them up to the
photographer. The contrast between her sister's big tits and the
woman's own small breasts constituted a family joke. The woman
long suspected her sister was delighted with the comparison because
sometimes if the men of the family didn't bring the topic up, her sister would. The letter accompanying this titty picture was written by
the woman's sister to the woman's husband. She had to sit down on
the closet floor to read the letter five times . . . the first time just to
take it all in, the second time didn't count because the woman was
crying too hard, the third and fourth readings were required to understand more the enormity of what was being said, and she had to
read the letter a fifth time because she still didn't want to believe it:
her husband was the real father of her sister's son, the woman's
nephew. Maybe everyone in the whole family knew. The woman
burned to think how they'd been laughing at her all these years. But
what turned her temporarily insane, at least this is the argument her
lawyer would eventually use, was realizing her sister's son was con-
ceived while she, the woman living in this fine, rich house on St. Ann
Street, was fighting cancer that resulted in a hysterectomy. Also, the
bed her sister was sitting on while holding those big tits was the same
bed the woman and her husband slept in back when the photograph
was taken and ever since, including last night. Another case tucked
away in the husband's closet contained a .45 semiautomatic, which
her husband had also kept over from the navy . . . cartridges were
locked elsewhere, in a cabinet in the bedroom. The woman was a
daughter of the South, she knew how to load a .45, she knew how to
shoot it, and with that loaded pistol in her lap she sat there on the
bed, *the bed,* and waited for her husband. The letter and picture were
on the bed next to her. The woman practiced different versions of
what to say to him when he came in . . . did you screw (have an affair
with, fuck, impregnate) my sister (my bitch of a sister, that whore
who calls herself my sister) and is Robert (Robbie, that little bastard

son of hers) yours? Even though she knew the answer, the woman wanted to see if her husband would compound his sin by lying to her face. She'd already made up her mind: If he lied, she would shoot him in the heart. If he told the truth, she would shoot him in the heart.

Moving slowly but getting stronger, Emily stayed on course for New Orleans by way of Grande Isle . . . and four hundred miles away, already indirectly responsible for one death in the French Quarter, she'd been upgraded to a category four hurricane, winds of 140 miles per hour and an estimated storm surge of more than fifteen feet. This could be the Big One, as disaster commentators like to say when speculating on the possibility of a hurricane virtually destroying a city like New Orleans. When Emily was still a category three, damage could be expected to some buildings, rivers would overflow, and there'd be coastal flooding, but with a category four hurricane, "extensive" structural damage is expected and anything within ten feet of sea level will flood. If Emily makes it to category five, all roofs will be lost, buildings will go, everything below fifteen feet will be underwater, and massive evacuations will be required.

At her current rate of travel Emily is still more than sixty hours away from New Orleans, but predictions remain speculative because Emily could easily double her rate of travel, which means that destructive winds could start whipping through New Orleans in only six hours. Or she could simply stop out there in the Gulf of Mexico, go a different direction, or even blow herself out . . . anything's possible.

The hurricane's eye, a circle of calm in the middle of all that fury, averages about fourteen miles in diameter and is surrounded by a cloud wall, beyond which blow the storm's most furious winds, thunderstorms, and tornadoes. A hurricane's position is given at its eye, landfall is called when the eye comes ashore. But determining the hurricane's *outer* edge, where wind speeds die away to normal rates, is less precise. For example, the winds now rushing through the New Orleans are from Emily's outermost boundary, so in one sense you could say the hurricane is already hitting the city.

Everyone living south and east of the city has been ordered to evacuate, and evacuation is being *recommended* for New Orleans residents too.

Gases normally trapped in the soil are being released by the unusually low atmospheric pressure. Smelling these gases has made animals in the area act screwy, horses running up and down fences, cattle huddling in open fields, dogs whining.

Near Grande Isle at a junior high school building that's serving as a rescue center, people are worried about animals they left behind. These refugees are also hoping that the brick school building will be out of Emily's path, will be high enough not to flood, strong enough not to topple. Everyone is praying that Emily goes elsewhere, everyone except Wilfred and Sebastian Millerd, who have been banished to a detention room (during their brief stay here they've flooded toilets, stolen shoes, written misspelled obscenities on several chalkboards) and are still rooting for the hurricane to hit here and hit hard, they'll make money looting and also get paid to remove wild animals out of people's houses and will generally have tons of fun in the storm's aftermath.

Meanwhile the black cats that live all over the French Quarter have come out of their alleys and crawl spaces to populate the streets, crisscrossing everyone's path with bad luck.

36

THE GANG'S ALL HERE

Pelikan's gang has gathered here on the ground floor of the slave quarters, standing around a table made from a sheet of plywood laid across sawhorses . . . waiting for Pelikan, who's gone back to his apartment to pick up "the plans." Feeling dazed, my false incision itching, I'm sitting on an unopened five-gallon bucket of white paint, where I watch the others as if they're onstage.

Diane "Knees" O'Rourke went home and changed into what I guess she considers her Cat Woman outfit, a tight-fitting, fake patent leather jumpsuit with oversized silver zippers, but at least she's wearing sneakers and not high heels.

Incredibly, Sad Bob the clown is undertaking tonight's assignment wearing a clown outfit: baggy red pants with wide red suspenders, a blue shirt with multicolored balloon bouquets printed on it, an orange fright wig, and full makeup, except this time he's simply painted his real nose red, he's not wearing a prosthetic . . . also, like Knees, he's had the good sense to show up with reasonable shoes.

After a confusing debate in which no one understood anyone else, the Bulgarian nuns were finally convinced to replace or cover their habits with zippered overalls Pelikan apparently got from some auto mechanics . . . big mechanics. The sisters insisted upon retaining their coifs and their classic nun shoes. The mechanic overalls are light blue denim with a heavier blue vertical stripe and a name in red script over the left chest pocket. The one Bulgarian nun is wearing overalls that apparently belonged to a *Dave,* while the other has on overalls donated by or stolen from *Bubba.* Now I can finally tell the big nuns apart.

Sister Margaret has changed out of her nun garb and is wearing black slacks and sweater. She looks tall and strong . . . like one of those women from the forties who could do a man's job and everyone called her Slim.

The two Filipino nuns, still dressed in full black-and-white nun attire, are still praying hard, eyes closed and lips mumbling a mile a minute . . . praying now, so I've been told, for Emily to go away or at least hit New Orleans only a glancing, nonlethal blow.

It's a motley and whimsical crew for which, to my chagrin, I'm feeling affection and even envy . . . after all, here are people comfortable in their faith, loyal enough to go out in a hurricane . . . if Pelikan asked them to sea tonight in paper boats, they'd set sail for Emily's eye.

He returned a little past 7 P.M. letting in a vicious wind that blew sawdust and drywall chalk, making us all squint until Pelikan managed to get the door shut behind him.

He's brought a large portfolio similar to what an artist might use to display drawings, which he dropped with a thud that shook the plywood table. I guess the portfolio contains "the plans." I closed my eyes and lectured myself not to make fun of these people. Back in the suburbs my friends and I ridiculed everyone, I think it was our main style of recreation . . . watching television or in restaurants, making fun of accents and dress and most especially of anyone overly earnest. We all spoke with great animation and that glibness that comes from a lifetime of watching entertainment, but little of what we said carried substance or passion. If one of our group had ever stood and made a declaration of what he or she truly believed in, was willing to die for . . . the rest of us would've used that occasion for months of gossip and laughs. But now I'm in a room with people—whores, clowns, nuns, all ripe for ridicule—who intend to wager their lives for what they believe in or out of loyalty to Pelikan. I've decided not to laugh at them anymore.

"How bad is it out there?" I asked Pelikan.

"Not bad," he said unconvincingly. His long hair had been tangled wild by the wind, making him look like a crazed prophet blown in by a sirocco. Knees O'Rourke in her shiny jumpsuit stood behind him and worked on his hair.

"I got two pieces of good news," he said, looking at each of us in turn, including those who didn't speak English. "And two pieces of not-so-good news, which do you want first?"

I said let's hear the bad news but Knees and Sad Bob and Sister Margaret all asked for the good news first.

"The Quarter is shut down, closed up, just like we wanted it," Pelikan said. "No tourists, no bar workers or shop owners, no cops except for a few riding around in patrol cars, using loudspeakers to tell any stragglers they should leave. The second bit of good news is the storm . . . it's perfect, enough of a wind to drown out sounds and discourage patrols but not so much you can't work in it . . . and very little rain."

I pressed for the bad news.

"Well, first, the power is still on, obviously," he said, glancing up at the lights. "We really need the electricity off because we want the dark to cover our movements. Also, without electricity some of the security measures will be disabled. But don't worry, electricity is always turned off in advance of a hurricane."

"And the other piece of bad news?"

"The National Guard's been called out . . ."

I kept my mouth shut, expecting the rest of the English speakers there at the table to express outrage or disappointment, something.

"They're posted on most of the street corners," he continued, "guarding against looting, I suppose, you know with all the bars and restaurants being closed."

Like Islamic suicide soldiers, the others stood there looking at Pelikan as if waiting to be told how many National Guardsmen they were expected to take with them when they died for the greater good.

"Okay, then," Pelikan said, turning to thank Knees for having fixed his hair in a ponytail, then facing the table again and opening the portfolio's front cover. "Here's how I see the—"

I said *whoa*. "The National Guard? Near the repository?"

"Four of them stationed in front of it."

"When we start lowering the loot over the side, you think the soldiers might ask us what we're up to?"

"I thought we'd wait until the National Guard left." Although Pelikan wasn't smug in saying this, both the hooker and clown looked self-satisfied on his behalf. "My understanding is, once the hurricane's imminent, the Guard is pulled out and no one else comes in, no rescue crews, no cops . . . no one is allowed to reenter until after the hurricane has passed."

"I hate to keep harping on the negatives," I said, "but if soldiers are ordered to leave and no one is allowed in, the *reason* is, a hurricane will kill anyone caught out in it. In fact"—I looked up at the ceiling—"I don't know if this place is safe or where we could go to be safe. If the hurricane hits here, the entire Quarter could be ten to twenty feet underwater. Does this building have an attic?"

"Charlie, New Orleans is protected by a whole series of dikes and levees—"

"And when they're breached it'll be like filling a teacup."

"It's going to be fine, I was just out there and everything's dry in the Quarter," he said, trying to reassure me in that soft, comforting voice. "You'll see when you go—"

"I think you should return to your original plan, wait for a nice *normal* storm—"

Pelikan told me it was now or never. "Gallier isn't going to let this linger any longer . . . next time he gets his hands on you, you'll be missing a kidney."

The others stared at me, wondering what that meant.

"I'm counting on you to drive the truck," Pelikan said. "That rescue truck is going to transport everything, including us, out of the city. I want you to wait in the hotel garage, the truck is all gassed up and ready to go, then when I call you on the walkie-talkie you drive over to the repository and we start lowering things to you.

"Okay, then," Pelikan said to the others as he brought out a pair of half glasses. "Let's get on with it." He opened the portfolio. "Here's the repository, here's a cross-section drawing of the roof." He turned one of the large pages. "Now we've all been through this several times, let's do one last review. Here I've pictured some of the equipment that's already in place on the roof."

Looking like a hip professor in those glasses, Pelikan continued lecturing as Dave and Bubba, the Bulgarian nuns, frequently grunted in recognition . . . apparently they were familiar with the drills and saws and compressors and pumps and pulleys that Pelikan had painstakingly detailed in the portfolio. Later he explained how the repository's roof would be breached. "You see here, the first layer on the roof is just poured asphalt, old shingles under that, flat tin, then the original wooden roof, which has been supported by retrofitted steel trusses, but we can fit everything between those trusses, we don't have to take the time trying to cut through them."

The drawings in the portfolio were beautifully detailed. I asked Pelikan if he did them and he said he had . . . worked on them with my father.

"Getting through the roof isn't going to be a problem," he continued, pointing to relevant drawings as he spoke. "But the ceiling of the vault is made of steel plating in between layers of reinforced concrete, it's going to be a trial breaching it. Fortunately, the really thick stuff is at the front, on the door, they don't expect anyone to come in through the roof. I calculate it'll take us an hour, once we're on the roof, to get all the equipment working."

I asked how he planned to get everyone on the roof of a four-story building.

"It's being renovated, remember . . . there's scaffolding—"

"Scaffolding in a hurricane?"

"It's been attached to the side of the building, in a protected niche, it'll hold."

The others nodded agreement, I was the only one shaking my head.

Pelikan continued, "Okay, an hour to get the equipment working, an hour to cut our way through the roof, then two to three hours to hack through into the vault . . . an hour to find everything and lift it back up through our access holes, half an hour to get it off the building and into the rescue truck. I'm figuring seven hours maximum, if we get the breaks it'll be closer to five. We need to be *gone* from the

French Quarter before dawn . . . which means if we start by ten tonight we should have plenty of time. Charlie, I got a map of the area here, I'll show you where to drive the truck after it's loaded . . . the interstates to Pass Manchac, between lakes Maurepas and Pontchartrain. There are three bridges over the pass, we'll wait on the old highway bridge, that's where Papa Gator will meet us. We'll be going by boat into the swamps."

"I'm going by foot to bed."

Sad Bob started singing a little ditty under his breath but loud enough for me to hear. *"Every party needs a pooper, that's why we invited you . . . party POOper."*

I slapped his orange wig off, the clown bawled like a baby.

Pelikan came around and I thought he was going to read me the riot act, but instead, he put a hand on my shoulder and laughed. "Charlie, such a vendetta you got against clowns." Still laughing softly, he retrieved Sad Bob's orange hair from the floor . . . the clown brushing it off and giving me a hurt look. Pelikan told me it was a good idea I should go to bed, get some sleep. He turned to the others. "Everyone should try to get a couple hours sleep before we have to leave . . . once the power's off and the National Guard is gone, we go. I'm sorry we don't have beds for everyone, there are some blankets upstairs, you'll all have to do the best you can finding someplace to sleep. It's a big queen-sized bed upstairs, maybe Charlie will share it with one or more of you . . . except not you, Sad Bob, Charlie is surrounded by an invisible no-clown zone . . . and he can't be trusted with nuns either."

Sister Margaret chortled.

"So I guess that leaves you, Knees," Pelikan continued. "You go on up and get some shut-eye in the bed there with Charlie."

"She can have the bed," I said. "I'll sleep on the floor."

"You take the bed," Knees insisted, no more pleased than I with Pelikan's matchmaking attempts.

Before going upstairs I told Sister Margaret not to let the two little nuns go out in the wind wearing those habits. "They'll be blown away . . . you understand what I'm saying, little Tinkerbell and Winkerdink will literally go airborne, I'm serious."

37

DIVINE WIND

Kublai Khan, Mongol ruler and grandson of the Genghis Khan, was called Setsen Khan, the Wise Khan, by the Mongols. He established a glorious capital city (present site of Beijing) where he received and then employed for seventeen years the Venetian explorer Marco Polo. Kublai Khan would eventually serve for thirty-five years as a ruler wise in domestic affairs (importing experts from Egypt to improve the refining of sugar, for example, and storing crops as protection against famine) and bold in matters of war. But not all of Kublai Khan's ventures were either wise or successful: he led a half million soldiers into Vietnam, where guerrillas virtually annihilated the entire army . . . and he mounted two disastrous campaigns against Japan.

In the first Japanese invasion, nearly thirty thousand troops were landed at Hakata Bay on October 19. A month later, when a typhoon (the name for hurricanes in the Pacific) threatened as the invaders were preparing to march inland, naval commanders convinced army generals that soldiers would be safer aboard ship than exposed on land. After the army reboarded, the typhoon hit . . . and two hundred of Kublai Khan's ships went down, drowning thirteen thousand men, halting the invasion.

The second effort was mounted seven years later, in 1281, employing a thousand ships, fifty thousand Mongol troops from Korea, another hundred thousand from China. These invaders were still near shore areas when, on July 29, another typhoon struck and drowned half of Kublai Khan's army. The Japanese defenders had waited in bunkers, then came out when the storm passed and fell upon the typhoon's survivors, killing more than fifty thousand. After this, the Japanese began referring to typhoons as divine winds, or *kamikaze*.

Emily apparently is in a sudden hurry to get to New Orleans, having almost tripled her rate of travel over the past eight hours, her eye less than 150 miles from landfall at Grand Isle, which has been evacuated. Her change of pace is well documented by National Oceanic and Atmospheric Administration aircraft that have been dropping sixteen-inch tubes all around Emily, the tubes parachuting to the surface while taking measurements of wind direction and speed, temperature, humidity, barometric pressure. Emily's pressure is rising, good news for anyone in her way because a hurricane's intensity is driven by the vacuum caused by the low atmospheric pressure at the hurricane's center . . . the lower the pressure, the faster the winds. Maybe Emily is passing over cooler waters now or perhaps more air is dumping inside her eyewall, creating greater pressure there and destabilizing the system . . . Emily is dying even as she rushes to land.

But like a wounded animal she's still dangerous, having already blown over trailers and flooded roads and sunk boats where the Mississippi River delta reaches into the gulf and also over near Grand Isle where an old Cajun woman, Belle Foger, missed being evacuated, and now her trailer is torn from its foundation. Belle is forced to wade knee-deep to a tree she must climb to avoid rising water, quite a feat for a sixty-three-year-old woman, but her grandkids play up this tree and have nailed in steps where there aren't enough limbs for climbing. Belle finally struggles twenty-feet up, where the kids have put a platform she can sit on while hugging the tree's trunk like it was her second husband, the one she loved more than the other two combined.

Although Belle hasn't seen them yet, bodies are floating near her tree. Because of the high water table around here, most people are buried in crypts . . . but there are still some underground graves and when they're flooded the coffins come floating to the top, where low air pressure pops open their lids.

Latest bulletin from the National Hurricane Center is that Emily has been downgraded to a category three hurricane, but she holds that status tenuously with wind speeds of 112 miles per hour, and a predicted storm surge of nine feet. At her current rate of travel, Emily will make land in ten hours and if she continues her current course she'll enter New Orleans around dawn. The abiding question now is: how strong will she be when that eyewall passes over the city . . . how much of a *kamikaze*?

38

RAINING COCKROACHES

"It's time."

Pelikan was trying to wake me, his softly insistent voice in my ear . . . until my conscious mind suggested it's better to wake up and face reality rather than continue wallowing in yet another squalid Sasquatch dream.

"Charlie, it's time."

I opened my eyes to the dark room.

"Were you having a nightmare?" Pelikan asked.

"I dreamt I was Big Foot and ravens warned me that people with guns were hunting me, intended to butcher me alive, but the worst part was the looks on the hunters' faces, I was such an abomination in their eyes."

"And you say *I'm* strange?"

"I have strange dreams," I told him, "but you lead a strange life, that's the difference."

He softly laughed. "When you were a little boy and one of your sisters missed an evening of television for some reason, she had to do homework or went out on a date, the next day you'd tell her the plots of all the shows she missed."

I didn't remember.

"The trouble Rusty got into on *Make Room for Daddy*," Pelikan was saying, "or what that old blowhard, Principal Osgood P. Conk-

ling, said to our Miss Brooks. You were smart as a whip and could remember all the plots and a lot of the dialogue too. *Mr. Peepers* and the
rest of them."

Pelikan has fantasized for so long about my supposedly perfect
childhood that he has mixed it up with his own, because I never saw
any of those shows, they were all before my time.

"He was so gentle and good with people," Pelikan said as he sat
there on the bed.

"Who?"

"Mr. Peepers, the schoolteacher at Jefferson High, remember how
he'd get all flustered around the school nurse, Miss Remington?"

"No I don't—"

"He had a lot of inner strength, Mr. Peepers, and sometimes I
used to think that if you died and went to heaven, the first angel you
should meet, the one assigned to taking you in and making sure you
weren't scared . . . should be exactly like Mr. Peepers, soft but not
weak. Mr. Peepers was a kind and generous soul, I always wanted to
grow up and be like him."

Pelikan, who killed a man by stabbing him in the face with an ice
pick, who hustles blow jobs to tourists, who has a tattoo declaring he
will fuck anything . . . this is the man who wanted to grow up to be a
gentle Mr. Peepers?

"I have it all written down here," he said, handing me a sheet of
paper . . . then a set of keys. "The big key fits the first garage door you
need to open to get to the rescue truck, the small key is to the pad-
lock that's on the second door, the other two keys are for the truck,
one for the back door, one for the ignition. On the paper there I've
written directions where you drive the truck after it's loaded. You're
going to take the truck on the elevated highways west of Lake
Pontchartrain, get off at Pass Manchac . . . it's all there in the paper.
The garage is just a block from the repository, I want you to stay there
with the truck until I send someone to tell you we're ready. Got it?"

"What about walkie-talkies?"

"They don't work in this storm. I'll send someone."

"We shouldn't be doing this."

"We're already doing it. I left some rain gear downstairs, also a
couple of flashlights."

I was so tired . . . I think this is how people get when they confess to crimes they didn't commit, how a woman feels when she agrees finally to unwise sex, how you make up your mind at long last about killing yourself: you're so tired you do whatever is necessary just to get it over with.

Pelikan was fingering back his hair and pinching the crease in his jeans. He said he was sorry about Amanda.

The apology surprised me.

"This'll help," Pelikan said, trying to hand me something.

It felt like a communion wafer. "What is it?"

"A tab."

"A tab of what?"

"The crankster gangster . . . help you get through the night."

"Meth?"

"I gave it to the others."

"You passed out *meth* to those nuns?"

"Knees and Sad Bob too, they're all cranked for this job."

"I bet."

"Get up and get dressed."

"What time is it?"

"Ten. The others have already headed over there. Four hours from now, two A.M. I want you by the truck in the hotel garage, waiting for word from me."

"How bad's the storm?"

"Blowing hard, pasha." He got up from the bed and left me in the dark listening to the wind trying to rip off the roof . . . I can hear the lumber, wood squeaking against wood . . . and then something was dropping on the bed, landing on my face and arms. At first I thought pieces of plaster had been knocked loose but then I felt them scurrying over my hair and across my arms, hundreds of cockroaches falling through the vent and landing all over me.

I grabbed my clothes off the floor and went into the hall to dress, shivering with disgust as I vigorously shook each article of clothing before I put it on . . . then rushed downstairs, where I found the flashlights and two pieces of rain gear, a pair of heavy rubber pants with suspenders and a matching yellow rain jacket like firemen wear. I put everything on and told myself, don't think about it, just go.

Outside in the tiny courtyard the wind was so vicious I had to lower my head and feel along the wall, pushing myself along until I reached the stone corridor leading to the street. Momentarily protected, I paused to catch my breath and wonder how bad the streets were flooded, water already coming in under the door to the sidewalk. Stop whining and worrying, I told myself . . . be like Pelikan, *do it.*

The moment I unlatched the door, it was blown out of my hand and slammed back against the stone wall.

I covered my eyes and lunged into the storm.

39

EMILY'S DYING TO REACH
NEW ORLEANS

Life's funny, thinks Belle, the sixty-three-year-old Cajun woman who's twenty feet in a tree, the sea flooding halfway up to where she is sitting on that platform her grandkids made . . . funny because her second husband was the kindest by far of the three men she was married to but he's the one she treated worst of all. Walter was his name, he died of a heart attack. Maybe because I broke it so many times, Belle thinks. She cheated on him and could be hateful in his presence, yet Walter always handled her like she was a baby bird he found on the ground. Walter never raised hand or voice to Belle and gave her the paycheck, never cashing it to have a good time on his own. Husbands One and Three were bastards, One was a drunk with a roving eye and never held a steady job, while Three was mean and stingy and also a drunk . . . but during those two marriages Belle treated her husbands with deference, making sure their meals were on time and the house always clean and she never cheated on either of them or gave cause for heartache. Yet she was so mean to poor old Walter, who treated her like spun gold . . . life's funny that way, and unfair.

Belle is hugging this big tree as if the trunk were Walter, whom she fell in love with posthumously . . . each year that passes, she finds more reasons to love him.

If she's crying, you wouldn't be able to tell in all this rain . . . the woman keeps her face close to the tree trunk to prevent flying debris from blinding her. Whenever she does venture a look, she sees a crazy world, as if this tree and two growing near it have sprouted in the middle of the ocean, wind-whipped water ten feet deep in all directions and every manner of thing floating in it . . . refrigerator, propane tanks, shed, roof, barrels. And over there is what Belle at first thinks is a mannequin from some department store but sees now is a man all dressed up in a nice dark suit, was he caught and drowned on his way to a party? And another body, this one a woman in a pretty ivory-cream dress, she must've been the man's date. But then the woman's body floats near enough to the tree for Belle to make out its features and recognizes Martha Treymorris, who used to do Belle's hair, poor Martha . . . what party was she going to? Belle didn't remember any talk of a party being given around here. Then she remembered that Martha Treymorris died months ago.

Belle hugs the tree more tightly and puts her face to the rough bark like it was Walter's unshaven face . . . has she lost her mind?

Emily is dying, her condition downgraded to category one, with ninety-miles-per-hour winds and a five-foot storm surge compounded by high tides . . . she might not even be a hurricane by the time she reaches New Orleans, though with winds near seventy-five miles per hour plus all the flooding, she'll be one hell of a tropical storm.

But even as she's dying, Emily is traveling at nearly thirty miles per hour, twice the top speed that most hurricanes achieve. If she keeps this up, she'll make landfall in just three hours and then race over bayous and up the Mississippi to reach New Orleans two hours after that . . . around three in the morning instead of dawn as the forecasters had predicted when Emily was traveling at a more normal pace, when she wasn't racing her heart out for New Orleans.

40

HURRICANE HEIST

In the street I could barely make headway against the wind which seemed to consist of something heavier and more substantial than air . . . and when I turned around and tried walking backward, my leg muscles burned with the effort, like pushing against a boulder. I made for the buildings that fronted directly on the sidewalk and, head down, pulled my way along St. Peter Street to Bourbon. If you've ever been out in a severe storm you know how the wind will suddenly gust, threatening to lift you off your feet, then die down a bit and you can recover your balance . . . but this wind remained at a steady howl as if produced by a massive machine that never varied its output.

Both hands over my face, I lifted my head and spread my fingers enough to glimpse up a flooded Bourbon Street, the first time in my life I'd ever seen it dark and abandoned, the street a raceway for wind debris that turbocharged toward me . . . here comes a galvanized metal garbage can flying fast and low, burging down with a splash every thirty or fifty yards, must be going sixty miles an hour. I can't hear it because the wind's too loud, hurting my ears, popping from the low pressure. As I watch, the garbage can veers off the street to hit a metal pole supporting a balcony, knocking the pole out from the bottom, shearing the bolts that were holding it. The balcony sags threateningly. If the can had hit me I'd be dead: decapitated or crushed.

That's going to be the danger, I thought as I pulled myself along the buildings, each bit of debris is a potentially fatal missile. There goes a metal street sign, here comes a bicycle tumbling down the street as if thrown from a terrible accident, a piece of tin, a garbage can lid.

The roaring noise remains as constant as the wind's velocity and when I turn and press against a building for protection, I cover my ears with both hands.

Glass is everywhere, in fact the only sound I consistently hear above the wind is that of breaking glass, which is also flying through the air, each shard a potential killer. It occurs to me that if glass was invented now, the government would never allow it to be released to the public, much too dangerous, such a brittle substance, so easily broken into pieces that are so deadly sharp . . . you wouldn't permit something like that into your home, certainly wouldn't pour milk into it and hand those potential knife shards to a child, and no one would be so foolhardy as to install glass in *windows,* where it could be blown out and broken up and made into missiles by the wind.

My wet shoes crunch on that glass as I bend to the wind, reaching Royal Street and turning right . . . the wind even worse here, I don't know how I'm going to make it four or five blocks to the garage where that rescue truck is supposed to be waiting.

Jesus . . . I'm standing here holding on to a balcony pole when a *No Parking* sign, about three feet tall and a foot and a half wide, hits another pole right in front of me, the metal sign folding in half like a sheet of paper. If it hadn't struck that pole first, the sign would've wrapped itself around my head.

The flooding seems less intense here, the street full from curb to curb but the sidewalks still above water. I should duck into one of the buildings, head for the upper floors, find a windowless interior room with a strong thick door, hunker down there, and wait out the storm.

But instead I push on under the protection of my new philosophy: get hit or get lucky. I try using a flashlight but the wind seems to blow the beam away, nothing beyond my reach is illuminated, though occasionally the street flashes bright blue, lightning, I assume, but can't hear the thunder, not over this wind, constant and terrible and with a power that seems impossible . . . something crashing from overhead, more glass or a complete building failure, I don't know, I just hunch my shoulders and wait to get crushed.

I make a few more feet before huddling in a deep doorway. Is this the actual hurricane, I wonder, am I in the worst of it, or is there more to come?

Emily is thirty-five miles from land, eighty-five miles from New Orleans, traveling now at a steady twenty-five miles per hour, wind speed ninety miles per hour, Emily still a category one hurricane with an eye that's predicted to pass right over New Orleans in under four hours. She's already flooded Grand Isle and most of the highways south of New Orleans . . . but Emily hasn't truly, fully embraced New Orleans, not yet.

On my way to the garage I hear what sounds like gunshots, cannon fire . . . thunder? Disoriented, I reach the repository on Royal Street without realizing it, then pause across the street from the building, a massive, four-story white marble structure that takes up the entire block . . . but I see nothing of Pelikan or his gang, hear nothing above the constant ferocity of this wind. I can't seem to think straight or get my bearings, if I weren't following a street I'd be lost . . . and if someone gave me a simple test right now, square pegs in square holes, I'd fail it. How can Pelikan and his crew be getting any work done on a roof where the wind must be even worse . . . maybe there's less debris flying around up there. Down here the barrage is so thick that I duck and crouch from doorway to doorway like a soldier trying to retake this street from an enemy with well-placed snipers.

I don't think the rain would amount to much in terms of inches but its horizontal velocity is stinging my face as I finally get to the garage, next to a hotel that apparently has been evacuated. I feel along until I start finding doors, but am unable to open the first three, drop the keys in six inches of water, kneel in the water and feel around until I retrieve them, but finally I find the right door . . . and the relief of being in this concrete structure makes me inhale great heaving breaths and laugh at the surprise and joy of being alive.

In here the flashlight proves useful, though the parking garage is a maze that takes me almost an hour to negotiate. I find a door that opens onto an area where there's only one vehicle, the rescue truck in water halfway up the wheels, but the diesel starts, the lights work, both fuel tanks are full.

I drive the truck to street level and park in front of a large overhead door, there's barely a foot of water on the floor here. Now I'm supposed to wait until someone comes and gets me, but after less than half an hour, restless, I leave the protection of the truck and slosh over to the big sliding door to make sure I can open it when the time comes. It's supposed to open from the inside without a key but I can't find what button or lever makes the damn thing unlatch. I use up nearly another hour and the last of the flashlight's battery power making a close search, discovering finally that I have to reach down in the water and unhook the door where it's latched to the concrete floor. When I open the door, wind explodes into the gap, flapping my wet pants legs so hard that my shins and calves sting like they've been belt whipped. I get the door closed and return to the truck, exhausted.

I wait. What's happening out there, has the whole world been blown away? After checking to make sure the second flashlight works, I take a deep breath and go back out into that warlike wind. A further drop in pressure has produced a screaming pain where I had that root canal before coming to New Orleans.

Holding a hand to the side of my face and heading to the repository, I stumble, trip, and fall, sliding on my stomach, making a grab for a balcony pole, then continue, reach the repository, climb through the hurricane-toppled cyclone fence that surrounds the massive building, crouch-walking around to the side where Pelikan is supposed to set up a winch . . . but I can't see to the roof, the flashlight's beam won't reach that far. They could be up there already, waiting on me. Do they know I'm here, can they see down to the street?

The scaffolding is miraculously still in place, in a protected niche between two wings. I scream for Pelikan, a foolish gesture. Then I grab the scaffolding and pull on it, seems solid enough. I don't know if I have the testicles to climb up on the roof and take the chance of getting blown off this scaffolding or riding it to the ground if it collapses when I'm halfway up . . . but I am desperate to find the others and kick the feeling of being the last person still alive on a self-destructing earth.

Moving like an old man, I finally reach the top where the scaffold ladder loops over the edge of the roof, the wind at this spot so vicious I wait for the inevitable, blown away, blown away. Inching my way over onto the roof, I grab a vent pipe and hold on, tucking chin to chest, working hard to breathe. The wind lets up slightly or I'm getting accustomed to it because eventually I'm able to crawl toward the center of the roof, where lights have been set up, powered by a gasoline generator. But no one's here, have they all been blown away?

The wind is shooting pea gravel off the roof asphalt, brand-new rooftop air-conditioning units peppered like road signs during hunting season. Staying low, I crawl toward the lights and scream again for Pelikan. I can't even hear myself, as if I'm miming a scream.

A big ragged hole, maybe six feet in diameter, has been gouged through the roof, a rigging of metal tubes braced over the hole with cable lines running through pulleys and down into the building. I'm nearing the hole as Pelikan is coming up the cable, controlling the electric winch with a black panel box about the size of a carton of cigarettes. When he is lifted into the wind, it blows him around and around in a tight circle but he's able to reach the rigging and stop himself, then step onto the roof.

He signals to me and we both get on hands and knees to crawl toward each other, keeping our faces down to avoid pea gravel shrapnel.

"What's wrong?" he shouts to be heard above the locomotive wind. "You didn't find the truck?"

"The truck's all ready to go, I was worried about you . . . did you think it would be this bad?"

"What?"

"IT'S BAD!"

"ARE YOU OKAY?"

I told him I was fine except a little seasick and my root canal felt like someone was driving a nail through my jaw.

"WHAT!" he screamed.

I pointed at my mouth. "ROOT CANAL!"

"AIR PRESSURE!"

"YES!"

Pelikan said something but I didn't catch it. He tried again, I shook my head. Finally, to be understood, he had to lean his head low and shout up under my armpit.

"We're almost ready to start bringing things out," Pelikan said, "but we can't lower over the side, the wind's too bad!"

"Are you in the vault yet?"

He indicated yes.

The wind, impossibly, was blowing stronger now and I didn't understand everything Pelikan had said but got the gist of it, asking him now how he intended to get the stuff out if he couldn't lower it over the side of the building.

"We're bringing everything down through the building . . . we were able to bust open the fire doors on the stairways."

I asked if that's where he wanted the truck, by the front, but Pelikan shook his head indicating he didn't hear me, so I tried again, "TRUCK . . . FRONT DOOR?"

"YES!"

"WHEN?"

"NOW!"

He crawled away, found a coil of rope, gave it to me, then crawled back to the hole . . . maybe I was supposed to use the rope as a safety line by tying myself off as I went back down the scaffolding. Why didn't he take me with him back through the roof?

Wishing I was anywhere but back on the scaffolding . . . when halfway down, I am marveling at the strength and staying power of this pipe scaffolding, it begins to shiver and shake in a start-slow, end-bad toppling that's thrill and terror, which I celebrate by screaming unheard into the wind.

No one can hear the dogs howling. Animals by the tens of thousands are being moved, displaced, killed by the hurricane . . . and since pets aren't allowed in evacuation shelters, evacuees have tearfully left hundreds of terrified dogs and cats at home alone, the city of New Orleans alive with their calls . . . where are you, where are you! Wild creatures face deadlier fates than abandonment, drowning in the floods or scrambling up trees and onto floating debris only to die of thirst and shock or at the hands of boys with sticks. Thousands of birds have been caught in the eye, forced to travel along with the hurricane . . . cattle egrets originally reached Florida this way, force-flown from Africa. Birds unable to keep within the storm's center will be caught and blown apart like paper bags in the eyewall, where the most ferocious winds and spinning tornadoes reside . . . or, still in the calm of the eye, birds will drop exhausted to the ocean, where huge sharks, swimming along under Emily to feed from her scraps, take them in single bites. Weeks from now, eight-foot hammerhead sharks will be seen swimming in the Mississippi River near Baton Rouge. In the swamps and bayous of southern Louisiana, ten thousand adult alligators will be displaced by the hurricane, a few of them forced into residential areas, where home owners will kill them with clubs and guns, even run over them with pickup trucks. Before it's over, however, these gators will eat dozens of small yapping dogs . . . an ill wind that blows no good.

Landing in mud after dropping off the scaffolding just before it crashed to ground, I was rolled across the repository grounds and blown against the fence, bruised, scratched, battered, but apparently not broken. I make my way once more toward the garage and the rescue truck.

If I were able to surrender right now, if had someone to submit *to*, I would, but no one is offering me a chance to give up, so I drive the truck out of the garage and down Royal Street, headlights on bright though I still can't see more than a few feet, wincing each time the truck is hit with a piece of rubble, and twice I put my right hand over on the seat when I thought the truck was about to be toppled. Then suddenly out of the darkness I'm hit from behind by a black sport utility vehicle.

I stop. The black van stays glued on my back bumper. I honk the horn, urging the other driver to back off, but the van just sits there. What the hell? I pull over, right up onto the sidewalk, and the van creeps by me: I look in, no one driving, the damn thing is being blown down the street by the storm. Jesus.

Proceeding to the repository and driving up the steep grade in front of the building, I park close enough to the middle set of front doors that we should be able to load the truck without getting blown away.

Inside the lobby I'm greeted by a sight weirder than a whole fleet of driverless ghost vehicles: although the repository building is several feet above street level, there's still water here on the first floor and my gang members are perched up on counters or chairs, all of them soaked and dirty and exhausted around the eyes, suffering physical and mental fatigue and total methamphetamine collapse.

I wade across to the bench and ask Pelikan what they're waiting for.

"You," he says simply.

"Did you get everything out of the vault?"

He points. "There on that low table . . . just to the right of the door."

The only object I see is a small square white chest, a cube two feet high, two feet long, two feet wide, ornate with carvings, supported by four perfectly round feet the size of baseballs, also of white marble.

"That's everything?" I asked Pelikan. "I thought you were bringing out Gallier's entire inheritance."

"That's all we managed," he said.

"The Edessa is a marble box?"

"No, the box is called a reliquary, the Edessa is inside."

"In perfect condition," Sister Margaret said.

I looked toward the front of the building, listened for a moment, then turned back to the two of them. "You hear that?"

They listened, shook their heads, Pelikan asking me, "Hear what, Charlie?"

"*Nothing.*"

They listened again and understood what I meant: no wind, no rain, nothing.

• • •

Now that she has reached the city of New Orleans, Emily's forward movement has all but stopped and she whirls down like a huge merry-go-round slowing to let riders off. In the hour before Emily's eye touched New Orleans, her overland winds were eighty-three miles per hour but as that eye creeps across the city, her wind speeds reduce, soon to be under seventy-five miles per hour, when she'll no longer exist as a hurricane. By dawn her worst winds will be force six on the Beaufort scale, hardly strong enough to turn an umbrella inside out. But before she dies, Emily conjures some magic for anyone caught in her eye.

In a night full of events that were incredible, I step outside the repository building to witness yet another: the space between buildings flanking Royal Street is full of birds, most of them huge white birds flying *softly, slowly* below rooftop level, trailing their long legs behind them . . . and among these large flyers a fluttering of smaller, more colorful birds dart like nervous fighter planes escorting the big slow bombers. While looking up to watch the armada pass, I see in this windless, rainless, still night an entire skyful of bright stars.

Pelikan came out to stand with me.

"I've never seen stars from the French Quarter," I told him.

"Me neither . . . too much electric light."

"*Of course*, the power's out."

"Charlie," he said, keeping his head leaned way back so he could continue looking up, "I've never seen stars before, not in real life, only pictures of them on TV and in the movies."

"You've never seen stars before?"

He turned a circle and whispered *wow*. "So many of them. And you know what, Charlie . . . they look brighter in real life than they do on television."

I asked him if he knew what the smell was . . . he didn't. "Like after lightning," I said.

"Ozone?"

"Maybe . . . God, I love the way it smells right now, don't you?"

He said he did. I felt inexplicably happy. Pelikan kept his head back because he couldn't get enough of the stars.

"Some of them are planets," I told him.

"Never knew they looked like this." He brought his head down to look at me. "What else have I missed, Charlie?"

Before I could speak . . . here come the Bulgarian nuns, "Dave" cradling the heavy marble reliquary and, right behind her, "Bubba" carrying, swear to God, a big white porcelain sink with a few inches of galvanized pipe still attached.

"Did you tell them," I asked Pelikan, "to bring everything including the kitchen sink?"

He seemed as mystified as I was.

With the nuns waiting at the back of the rescue truck, I hurried over and opened the door for Dave, who eased the reliquary carefully to the floor, where a stretcher would normally go. Dave then helped Bubba with the big utility sink, which they turned upside down to place it *over* the marble reliquary as a heavy protective dome.

"I'll be damned," I said, giving the Bulgarians a thumbs-up, which they acknowledged with the first smiles I'd seen on their thick-featured faces . . . and then in unison they turned and slammed the door.

Pelikan was looking at the sky again.

"James Joseph, I'm assuming this is the eye of the hurricane."

"Yes."

"Okay, how long you figure we got before the back end hits?"

"I don't know, half an hour, forty-five minutes . . . depends on how fast the hurricane is traveling, how big the eye is . . . Charlie, point the Big Dipper out to me."

"Hey, James Joseph."

He brought his head forward, a goofy grin on his face.

"If we're going to try to leave the city before the rest of the hurricane hits," I said, "shouldn't we get back in the vault and clean out as much as we can?"

He draped an arm over my shoulder. "Let's go talk to the others about it."

We went inside and Pelikan was asking everyone to gather around when the double doors opened behind me and James Joseph muttered, "Johnny *Crapaud.*"

I turned to see Gallier standing between two men with guns. He was wearing a black cape over a dark suit, like he was on his way to a costume party. To his right was that nervous pirate with bandoliers crossed over his chest, a blue kerchief tied around his head but no eye patch, a big revolver in each hand. On Gallier's left stood a more serious man, one of the limousine bodyguards, wearing a brown leather jacket and a grim expression. Resembling a weightlifter with thick neck and tiny ears, the bodyguard held a semiautomatic pistol in a steady and apparently practiced hand.

"I want to thank you, Charles," Gallier said in his soft, mocking voice. "Your information on James Joseph robbing this place during a storm was obviously accurate . . . but a *hurricane,* who knew, hmm?"

"Up yours, *Doc,*" I told him.

He *tsk*ed, then spoke to the others, who were all behind me. "Ladies and gentleman, whores and nuns, fools and clowns . . . we need *quickly* to take advantage of this lull in the weather, so here's my first, last, and rock-bottom offer . . . give me my possessions, my inheritance, my *things,* or die."

No one spoke until Pelikan said: "The Edessa is out in the truck, under a sink."

I turned around but couldn't read his blank expression . . . was he hoping to prevent anyone from getting shot, had he lost his nerve? Sister Margaret was also staring at Pelikan's face, trying to figure it out.

Gallier wasn't sure either, telling his armed companions, "I'll go look . . . if any of them move, shoot to kill, is that clear?"

The bodyguard nodded solemnly, the pirate yelped, "Aye, aye, Cap'n!"

After Gallier was out the door, Pelikan started forward.

"Hey," the bodyguard said, "hold it right there."

"You *will not* shoot me," Pelikan ordered, lifting his arm to point at the bodyguard's eyes.

"Stop!" the pirate screamed, raising his twin revolvers and holding them sideways like he'd seen in the movies.

"Shut up, Zane," Pelikan told him. "You're not going to shoot me either."

"I will, goddamn it, I WILL!"

Pelikan shook his head and kept wading through the water.

"Stop!" demanded the bodyguard, taking aim.

"Stop right there!" echoed the pirate, holding the revolvers so high now that he had to point them *down* at Pelikan.

James Joseph continued to wade slowly but steadily for the door

while the bodyguard and pirate took backward steps to stay in front
of him as they shouted more loudly and insistently, their eyes white
and wide with the anxiety of what was about to happen, becoming
so aroused that they both began making small back-and-forth
movements with their weapons as if those firearms were remote-con-
trol devices, the bodyguard and pirate desperately trying to change
channels.

I was amazed at his performance, Pelikan apparently *did* have su-
pernatural powers, able to will those men not to shoot him.

But when someone *outside* fired two shots, the bodyguard and pirate were jarred into firing on Pelikan, who went down hard on one
knee before toppling over sideways into the water.

I ducked just as someone began shooting from behind me.

Crouching, I looked back to see Sister Margaret in the classic
stance, legs at shoulder width, her old-fashioned six-shooter in both
hands cup-in-saucer style . . . she let off four or five rounds, one of
them catching the bodyguard in his right leg and the other shots so
frightening the pirate that he dropped the revolvers in the water and
covered his face with both hands.

The next several moments gave over to chaos . . . the little Filipino nuns and I were pulling Pelikan's head out of the water trying
to determine if he was alive . . . Knees O'Rourke was collecting guns
the pirate and bodyguard had dropped . . . Sad Bob wailed the same
question over and over ("Is he dead, is he dead, is he dead?") . . . Sister Margaret came to kneel by me and say something about aiming
only at their legs, having no intention of killing anyone . . . then I
was taken by the arms and propelled out the front of the building by
the big Bulgarian sisters who obviously wanted me to stop Gallier.

I didn't see him. The rear door of the rescue truck was open, the
large sink had been turned on its side to expose the reliquary, which
was still closed.

The wind was picking up again as I went around to the front of
the rescue truck and saw a Hummer, the commercial version of the
Army's humvee, parked in front of my truck.

Too pumped now to worry about getting shot, I ran over and got
to the door of the Hummer just as it was opening . . . Amanda.

I dragged her by the front of her raincoat as the big nuns pulled me away and Pelikan shouted from the repository building, *"Charlie!"*

Sad Bob and Sister Margaret were holding Pelikan, who called my name again and said, "She's working for us, Charlie . . . has been all along. Amanda was our spy, told us everything Gallier was up to. Charlie, you hear me?"

I looked at Amanda, who said, "I know, it's all very confusing . . . I was representing the nuns in their legal claims against Gallier's uncle's estate too, then James Joseph had me go to Gallier and pretend to give him information so I could keep tabs on what he was up to."

"Where's Gallier now?"

"He came out of the building and opened the back of that rescue truck, then he hurried over here to the Hummer and wanted to get some tools . . . but I kept the door locked."

"Good for you."

She pointed at a window. "He tried to shoot me."

I saw now that the thick glass had been spidered by two bullet holes.

"You okay?" I asked Amanda.

She said she was. "I ducked down."

"Where'd he go then?"

She looked across the street. "I think he broke into Brennan's."

At the rear of the truck Sister Margaret was reclosing the lid of the reliquary, telling me, "He didn't get it."

"Good," I said. "Let's load James Joseph and *go.*"

Saying *go* was like a signal for Gallier to open fire on us from across the street . . . quickly proving himself a good shot. Gallier's first rounds hit both of the Bulgarian nuns, who threw their heads back and shouted words I didn't understand, then went to their knees in the water.

"Get behind the truck!" I hollered, trying to herd everyone around it as Gallier let loose another volley, this time dropping one of the Filipinos and neatly creasing Sad Bob's right ear.

"Everyone inside!" Pelikan shouted. "Except you, Charlie . . . get the hell out of here!"

Sister Margaret told me to leave *now . . . go!*

While the others dragged and hobbled into the repository, I

slipped into the truck and started the engine while Gallier ran into the street, hollered my name and something about making me rich.

I tried to keep focused on Pelikan's instructions—Interstate 55 north between Lake Maurepas and Lake Pontchartrain—and made better progress than I dared hope, my route never completely blocked as I drove through what appeared to be collateral damage from a great war. I was steering around a double-door refrigerator when my headlights caught a huge black Angus bull running steadily but not particularly fast in my direction. I waited to see what would happen next. Apparently a bull on a mission, he jogged past without a look. I went on.

Although the wind became steadily stronger as I picked my way out of town, the back end of the storm didn't approach the ferocity of its front end. Encountering no cars and very little flooding, I was on the elevated interstate and just about to congratulate myself on a clean getaway when I ran over a chunk of metal that sounded as if it had torn out the bottom of the truck.

I got out, walking back to see what I'd run over . . . a piece of farm equipment, part of a plow, I think, maybe a cultivator . . . why was I standing here in the wind and using dwindling flashlight power trying to figure it out? Just as I shut the flashlight off, something caught my eye, a light in the distance behind me . . . another vehicle? Maybe a power line sparking, I'd seen several of those. I waited and watched, saw nothing more, and returned to check the damage. Down on my back, I slipped under the truck and turned on the flashlight, its beam initially strong and white but deteriorating within seconds to a weak yellow that was close to useless. I waited a few minutes and tried again, the same thing happened. I smelled diesel fuel, but if it wasn't leaking too severely, maybe I could still make it . . . though I didn't hold out excessive hope when I returned to the driver's side and stepped into diesel fuel that had pooled there.

The truck started. Driving slowly, I concentrated on watching the highway in front of me for more obstacles and keeping an eye on the fuel gauge . . . ignoring my rearview mirrors until I saw headlights. How long have I been followed?

Gallier? I didn't think so, the headlights weren't positioned right for a Hummer. Then again, Amanda might've taken the Hummer's keys, forcing Gallier to find another vehicle.

Trying to watch three things now—the road, the fuel gauge, the rearview—I fell into that sustained concentration that becomes trancelike, losing track of time and distance . . . startled back to reality when the truck began bucking: one fuel tank empty. I switched to the other tank and decided to get off this elevated highway, make a stab at hiding from whoever was following me.

I took the next exit and pulled under the elevated highway, water halfway up my tires as I parked near a little boat dock that was covered with debris. While I was sitting there with the engine idling, my second tank ran dry too, drained by the leak.

I saw the headlights above me on the highway, watched them drive slowly past the turnoff . . . then brake lights went on and the car began reversing. Apparently having trouble with this maneuver, it stopped frequently, occasionally going forward a bit before reversing again.

When the headlights came down the ramp, I climbed out of the truck, thinking I could take off on foot if it came to that . . . though it looks as if there's nothing on either side of the road but swamp and floodwaters.

I think it's a beat-up old Buick, hard to tell in this half-light, pulling a small boat on a trailer. No wonder he had trouble reversing. It's not Gallier, he wouldn't drive around in an old Buick. Maybe it's Pelikan's friend, that Gator guy, who's supposed to meet me up at Pass Manchac . . . but when the driver gets out I know instantly who he is.

41

GOLDEN DAWN

I was leaning against the back of the rescue truck doing an imitation of casual.

"Hey, Chaz," he said, walking toward me, stopping ten feet away.

"Mean Gene," I replied. His pumpkin profile was unmistakable, and Detective Eugene Renfrone was also wearing his trademark yellow satin jacket, I wonder if he took it off in bed at night. "That jacket give you any protection from this wind?"

He looked down as if he'd forgotten he was wearing it, then up at me. "Hell of a hurricane, wasn't it?"

"The back end's coming through."

"I heard a weather report that it's not even a hurricane anymore." To light a cigarette he cupped one fat hand to the side of his face, then turned back toward his car. "And if it does flood, we can always take the boat."

Renfrone was referring to the fifteen-foot open boat sitting on a trailer behind his Buick.

"Yeah, I saw that, Gene . . . I was wondering if you came out here to go fishing."

"Always be prepared, so say the Boy Scouts."

"You follow me all the way from the Quarter?"

Renfrone snorted. "Not that difficult, Chaz . . . you're driving the only other vehicle on the road and it happens to be a big-ass ambulance, where'd you steal it?"

"Pelikan arranged for its use."

"Yeah, I bet he did. Did you see that bull in the road?"

"Hell of a thing," I said, wondering how long we were going to chat like this before he started muscling me.

"And that piece of metal you ran over, what was it?"

"Part of a plow, I think."

"Busted your fuel tanks? I stopped and took a look at it . . . smelled the diesel and knew you were wounded."

"Yeah, I'm empty."

He laughed and came a little closer, tossing away the cigarette that had proved impossible to smoke in all this wind . . . it was also becoming difficult to hear each other and the rain had begun again. "So, Chaz, tell me, what you got in the back there . . . not hurricane victims, I bet."

"I was sent out here as a diversion, all the loot's still in the Quarter with—"

Renfrone stopped me with a raised hand. "Come on, Charlie, what you got for me? Maybe we can split it."

"Down the middle?"

His fleshy face brightened. "Maybe, depends on how much there is."

"How come you're working for Gallier, he doesn't seem to be your type."

The light went out of Renfrone's face and his eyes narrowed into those sinister slits. "What the hell's that supposed to mean?"

"I always thought of you as one of us, my dad, Pelikan, you . . . we'd all hang out back when I was staying here as a kid, get drunk, go fishing. Somebody like Gallier would've never been part of our group, how'd he get a piece of you?"

"Little by little, Chaz. Gallier loans money to cops, and whenever I came to him he acted like it was his *privilege* to lend me some cash, acted embarrassed that his accountants and lawyers made him get a signed note from me. Those notes added up and payback's a bitch."

"You owe the guy some money and that's excuse enough to nearly kill me in the alley with that goddamn zapper?"

"Forget Gallier, I'm working for myself now. Open the truck, let's see what you're hauling." When I hesitated he reached into the yellow jacket and pulled out the shocking wand. "This the zapper you were referring to?" he asked.

"You're not going to use that on me, never again."

"All you got to do is cooperate."

Turning to open the truck's rear door but frequently looking back to make sure Renfrone didn't sneak up and zap me, I told him he was a real bastard.

His feelings apparently weren't hurt. "Get out of my way," he said, coming to the truck.

I stepped back.

"Get out of my way."

"Okay, okay," I said, reversing farther from the truck. "There's nothing in there but that sink and an old chest."

"Chest?" he said, looking at it. "Containing what?"

"I don't know, Pelikan told me to take the chest and the sink somewhere and dump them."

"You're full of shit, Chaz . . . how does it open?"

"I don't know." Which was the truth.

He grabbed a handhold to lift his bulk into the truck. Renfrone's mushy face was red by the time he hauled himself in and sat on one of the bunks with the reliquary there at his feet. "What is this thing?" he asked when he'd caught his breath.

I said I didn't know.

Pissed him off. "I oughta come down there and zap your ass just for lying to me."

I told him I could outrun him. "It's not like when you snuck up behind me in that alley, here I can just take off running down and you'll never touch me with that goddamn cattle prod."

He pulled out a nine-millimeter semiautomatic. "Outrun *this,* asshole?" Renfrone put down the zapper so he could light a cigarette, then leaned forward trying to figure out how the reliquary's lid opened.

"It belongs to the nuns," I told him.

"What does?" he asked.

"That box."

"So?"

"Remember how squirrely you were about all the nuns hanging around Pelikan, that box is the reason. Didn't you tell me your father fought Nazis in the Second World War? The Nazis stole that box from the nuns, Pelikan arranged to get it back for them. You got no business interfering."

Panting and sweating from the effort of leaning over on his potbelly to examine the marble reliquary, Renfrone straightened up and said, "All that trouble for this little box made out of white stone? No, I don't think so, Chaz . . . I want to see what's inside."

"I'm telling you, I don't know how it opens."

Flipping his cigarette at me, Renfrone cursed and puffed his way back out of the truck while I prayed like a Filipino not to get zapped again. The detective pulled the reliquary to the edge of the truck's doorway so he could work on the lid with an oversized pocketknife.

"I don't think you should open it," I told him. "There's a curse on all who—"

"Shut up, Chaz." He used the big blade to probe beneath the reliquary's lid, leaving me feeling weak and stupid in the wind and rain, watching him gouge away at the marble box that might've been a thousand years old.

"Hey, Gene, don't scratch at it like that . . . what happened to Gallier?"

"He's an idiot. Planned his attack on you guys like he was Napoleon or somebody . . . holding me in reserve, he said. Reserve, my ass . . . if I'd been inside that building, Pelikan would be dead and you would've never got out of town with this truck. Gallier and Pelikan both, they *play* at things."

"But where is Gallier *now*?"

"You wouldn't believe me if I told you."

"Try me."

But Renfrone just shook his head and continued working on the lid. "There!" he exclaimed, opening the reliquary and reaching in to move aside a white linen cloth. "Good Lord," he whispered. "Is it real?"

I came closer to see a thorn crown made of gold like gold I'd never seen before, warm and rich as if it must be producing heat. Each golden thorn, two or three inches long, ended in a needle point.

We stood silent for a long time . . . and when the sunlight came through clouds it cast yellow light on my face and his.

When he reached in to pick it up, several of the golden thorns immediately impaled their needle points into his hands. Renfrone cursed and stepped back, pressing his hands against the jacket, getting blood everywhere, cursing again and leaning forward to hold his bleeding hands against his wet Big Boy jeans.

With Renfrone distracted, I lunged into the truck and grabbed the zapper and his semiautomatic pistol, both of which I pointed at him.

He remained unimpressed, telling me, "You ain't going to do anything with either of them."

But I was exalted, finally owning the upper hand, shouting happily at Renfrone, "Don't try me!"

"*Watch,*" he said, returning to the back of the rescue truck, where he took off his jacket. "You ain't going to shoot or zap nobody, it ain't in your character." Renfrone folded up the jacket to use it like oven mitts for protection from the thorns.

I asked him, "How can you try to steal something like that?"

"Chaz, I ain't *trying* to steal it, I *am* stealing it." Carrying the crown like a heavy wedding cake, he walked toward his car. "I guess you're not going to open the door for me, huh?"

He was right about my inability to shoot him, not in cold blood. If he tried to rush me or took a swing, then I could pull the trigger . . . and he knew this too, which is why he didn't provoke me. He would just get in the car and drive away, leaving me standing there fully armed but impotent.

Or maybe not. When Renfrone set the jacket-covered crown on top of his car so he could open the door, I stepped past him and shot out the rear left tire with two rounds, quickly moving behind the boat to the other side of the car, where I did the same to the right rear and front tires. I asked him how many spares he had, then came around front and shot the fourth tire to make it unanimous.

"Well, Chaz," he said after a long pause, "if I'm ever attacked by radials, I know the man to see." He carried the crown to the boat, placing it on a seat, then strolled to the back of his Buick, where he began unhooking the trailer hitch.

None of this was working out like it was supposed to, not even when I was the one with all the weapons. "What the hell you doing *now?*"

"Give it a guess," he replied, looking out at the flooded swamps on both sides of the highway. "By the way, there's one round left in that nine-millimeter, so you still got the opportunity to kill me."

"I wouldn't push it, if I were you."

"I'm pushing it, I'm pushing it," he laughed, lifting the trailer's tongue and guiding it backward off the highway, toward a launch site next to the small, debris-covered dock.

I waded over and put the last round in his outboard.

He dropped the trailer tongue and hurried back to the little engine, looking at the bullet hole to see if I'd hit anything vital. Then he quickly pushed the trailer the rest of the way to the water, where with practiced hands Renfrone unhooked straps and lifted the tongue, sliding off the boat. He waded into the water and clambered over the side of the boat with an agility that surprised me.

As he sat in the stern seat and fiddled with the outboard, I came closer and told him, "It ain't going to start with a bullet hole in it."

He pulled the rope, the engine started.

Apparently as surprised as I was, Renfrone looked at me and laughed, then came forward, stepping over the crown on the middle seat as if it was nothing more than a tackle box. He motioned that he wanted to say something.

"What?" I asked.

"If it was me with the gun, you'd be dead by now." Renfrone twisted the accelerator and forced the little boat to squall around in a tight half circle to face out into the flooded swamp. Lifting the jacket-covered crown onto his lap for safekeeping, he raced for a gap in the trees.

"Bastard," I muttered, leaning back to throw the zapper, thinking what sweet poetic justice it would be if I managed to hit him right in his fat head but my aim was wide and the heavy zapper landed in the water several feet off Renfrone's port.

He glanced at the splash, looked back at me, and waved . . . turning around again just in time to see—but too late to avoid—a half-submerged refrigerator, avocado in color. The collision was dead on the bow at a good clip, flipping the boat and tossing its captain into the flooded swamp.

42

ALL'S LOST

With the boat upside down and the propeller out of the water, that little outboard went screaming off into rpm oblivion . . . then all was quiet.

I went over and waited on the dock for Renfrone to show himself . . . had he managed to hold on to the crown?

When he surfaced he was floating faceup and I thought he'd made it okay, just resting awhile before swimming or wading back to land. His arms were grasping that yellow jacket, still folded around the crown. But something was wrong, is he dead? He *is* dead. Dead but still holding on to the crown? Then I realized that the impact of the crash had driven those gold needle thorns through the jacket and into Renfrone's flesh, sticking the crown to his arms and stomach like a golden burr.

While I stood there mesmerized his body went facedown, Renfrone's broad back floating like a manatee until the body bobbed lower and lower and sank out of sight.

Now what? The capsized boat drifted slowly out of sight, pulled away by the floodwaters draining back out of this swamp . . . I should've taken a better mental fix on where Renfrone had sunk. I looked for the avocado refrigerator but it was no longer visible either. The crown must've acted like ballast, first turning him over, then sinking him.

Leaving the rain gear on the dock, I waded in up to my knees.

The bottom felt solid as I continued until I was in over my waist . . . which is when I saw the first alligator.

I thought it was a little log but wondered why a two-foot log was floating my way, against the current . . . when I saw that the log had eyes I began a panicky calculation on how big a gator would be if its head is two feet long. I turned toward land . . . there, hidden in debris on the berm no more than a few yards from where Renfrone had launched his boat, four coal-black alligators about five or six feet long were lying (in wait?) with their tails toward the road and their heads—and eyes—pointing at me.

Get out of the water . . . I waded fast and at an angle away from the alligators on land and the one behind me in the water, expecting any moment now to feel jaws. I'd been told that if a gator isn't protecting a nest or being cornered it won't attack an adult person, won't come after anything it doesn't think it can eat . . . this knowledge providing me exactly zero comfort as I held elbows high for leverage and churned mud.

As soon as I stepped onto relatively dry land, the four alligators resting near the road went tail-thrashing back into the water joining their now-submerged colleague . . . giving me at least five excellent reasons why I couldn't attempt a recovery.

I climbed into the rescue truck, shut the door against the possibility of climbing gators, and lay on the floor next to that kitchen sink to await whatever might happen next.

Exhausted, I expected to drop like a stone into deep sleep, but each time I closed my eyes I saw the nuns' Buddy Holly glasses and, behind those glasses, earnest eyes asking what I'd done with their holy crown . . . so instead of sleeping I practiced excuses and apologies.

I couldn't stop Renfrone from taking it . . . can you ever forgive me? . . . I would've had to kill him and I just couldn't bring myself to do that . . . please accept my sincere apologies . . . I didn't have the nerve to shoot him . . . I'm sorry . . . I should've tried wounding him, should've hit him over the head or gotten in the boat with him . . . I'm sorry . . . I wasn't thinking straight . . . I'm sorry . . . I failed you . . . I'm sorry . . . I'm sorry . . . I'm so very sorry.

Hearing a diesel in the distance, I got out to see a military vehicle approaching fast on the partially flooded two-lane road that parallels the elevated interstate . . . either this is a real humvee from the National Guard or it's Gallier's Hummer though I think the latter. Is he coming to put a bullet in my head? Or is my ragtag gang driving out here to collect the Edessa crown . . . which was given to me for safe-keeping? I think I'd prefer Gallier's bullet.

It turns out that the Hummer is carrying my gang . . . or what's left of it: Knees O'Rourke driving, Sister Margaret and Amanda in the back with Pelikan, who's covered with blankets and blood.

"How is he?" I ask Knees as she steps out.

"Not good, Charlie."

"Where're the others?"

"Cops and soldiers came into the Quarter after you left. We barely got out in time, took the wounded ones to the hospital, even Sad Bob, who just had a scratch but insisted on going so doctors could 'save' his ear, he said."

"You look beat."

She nodded. "You too . . . you been in the water?"

I glanced down at my muddy pants, then asked her what happened to Gallier.

"He let us use his Hummer to come check on you."

"He *let* you use it?"

Knees nodded and looked toward Pelikan. "We tried to make your uncle go to the hospital with the rest of them, but you know James Joseph, there's no forcing him to do anything once he's got his mind set. Let's go around back."

Knees opened the rear door, Amanda looking out at me while Sister Margaret gently placed a pillow under Pelikan's head so he could see where I was standing.

"Hey, pasha," he said, speaking softly as always, though I got the impression that a soft voice was all he had left.

"James Joseph . . ." His face seemed elongated, pulled down, made heavy with pain and reminding me of something famous I'd seen. "How're you doing?"

"I'm fine."

He wasn't fine. His face reminded me of the outline on the shroud of Turin.

He told me I was a hero.

Shame rendered me speechless.

"Why'd you stop here on the highway," Pelikan asked, "why didn't you go all the way to Pass Manchac?"

I looked at his smiling face and bit my lower lip.

"Charlie?"

"I ran over something, lost all my fuel."

"It's okay, we'll use this Hummer and— Who's that old Buick belong to?"

I said there was something I had to tell him.

"Yeah?"

Then couldn't bring myself to say it.

"Charlie," he asked, "what's wrong?"

I waited, speaking finally in smallest words I could find: "I lost it."

Pelikan stared at me without changing his expression, Sister Margaret looked bewildered, Amanda averted her gaze . . . Knees was behind me so I don't know how she was taking it.

"Tell me exactly what happened," Pelikan said.

I did, including the parts that made me look bad . . . having a gun on Renfrone but unwilling to shoot him, too frightened by gators to go in the water.

Sister Margaret took off the heavy glasses and rubbed her eyes. Amanda put a sympathetic hand on my arm.

Pelikan asked me, "Are you sure Renfrone drowned holding the Edessa?"

"Yes."

"Positive?"

"I watched Renfrone's body floating . . . first faceup, then facedown, then he went under and sank."

"Holding it?"

"Yes, stuck to him, the needles impaled in his arms and belly. He still had it wrapped in that yellow satin jacket he's always wearing."

"Given to Gene by his lover boy."

"Lover *boy*?"

Pelikan opened his eyes. "That was one of the swords Gallier had hanging over Gene's head, the fact Gene had a boyfriend." James

Joseph asked Sister Margaret and Amanda to help him sit up, and when they did, he sucked in short, gasping breaths that made me wince in sympathy. Settled now in this more upright position, his gray-blue eyes looking old and worn out, Pelikan finally said the words we'd all been waiting for. "Okay, here's what we do." He looked at me first. "Charlie, I want you to go over and stand by the water and fix in your mind exactly where Gene went under . . . and I mean *exactly*. Take as long as you need. Find reference points. Mark the ground. Whatever it takes. Also make sure you can locate this exact spot, I'll need you to be able to return here." He turned to the women with him there in the Hummer. "Sister Margaret and you, Amanda, I want you to get out and wait here with Charlie while he zeroes in on where Gene Renfrone drowned. When Charlie's got it fixed in his mind, then the three of you can go back to the Quarter. Walk up on the interstate there, someone will be along who can give you a ride."

"Where are *you* going?" Amanda asked him.

"Knees will be driving me somewhere."

"Better be to a hospital," Amanda said.

"I'll be back in three days."

Amanda shook her head. "James Joseph, you've been shot in the stomach, if you don't die of blood loss, the peritonitis will kill you before three days."

Ignoring her, he told me, "Charlie, exactly three days from now, at dawn, I want you to be in this precise place."

"Doing what?"

"Waiting for me, I'll be along."

"Should I have a boat, are you going to try recovering—"

"Bring the others, any of the others who are well enough to come along." He looked back and forth between the two women. "Amanda . . . Sister Margaret . . . go on out there with Charlie now. Knees, you're doing a great job driving this thing, let's go."

She asked where.

"I'll tell you on the way. Charlie?"

"Yes?"

"Wait here with me a minute, I want to ask you something. . . ."

After the others walked away from the Hummer, I leaned

in . . . maybe this would be the dressing-down I was expecting, I deserved.

"You know constellations, Charlie?"

"Constellations?"

"Don't you remember all those stars we saw?"

"*Constellations* . . . sure, I know some of them."

"See, what I was wondering . . . Well, over the years I've heard the names of a lot of strange-sounding constellations . . . the Bear, the Archer, the Water Bearer. My question is . . . and I'm a little embarrassed to be asking this, at my age."

"It's all right."

"When you look up at a constellation, Charlie, does it appear right there in the sky like its name says . . . Charioteer . . . or do you have to use your imagination?"

I couldn't find the voice to answer him.

"It's not like I haven't seen *pictures* of constellations, but the pictures have lines drawn between the stars," he continued, "and I was wondering what it all looked like in real life, without the lines. After tonight, seeing those stars, I kept thinking maybe if you live someplace where stars are out like that every night, all you got to do is look up and right there across the sky is Orion the Hunter made out of stars, like a picture in the sky . . . or do you have to use your imagination to see him?"

I told Pelikan you have to use your imagination.

"Yeah, I figured you did." He closed his eyes and said nothing more as I watched to see if the blanket covering him was still moving up and down with his breathing . . . or had he died?

I gently shook his foot.

"Hmm?" he replied dreamily.

"Let me take you to a hospital."

"No, Charlie . . ." His voice trailed.

"Please—"

He opened his eyes and smiled down at me. "There's somewhere I got to go. Just remember. . . . take care of your feet . . . as wet as they got tonight, they'll be ripe for funguses if you don't take care of them. Wash them especially between the toes when you get back, soap and hot water, then dry off real well, again making sure you get between all your toes."

"I will."

"It wouldn't hurt to sprinkle on some medicated powder, not too much, though."

"Okay."

"Then thick dry socks, white cotton . . . don't try to put shoes on for a while, give your trotters a rest."

"All right . . . and you'll be back here when you said?"

"Three days at dawn."

I asked him to promise.

"It's a promise, Charlie."

But I knew better. "You're not coming back, are you?"

"What's that?"

"You're going off somewhere to die alone. It's not right to leave your friends like this . . . to leave *me,* I'm your blood."

"Come on now . . . you're too old to cry."

After Knees drove off with Pelikan, I stood at water's edge fixing in my mind where I thought Detective Renfrone went down . . . but the longer I stared, the less sure I become. Amanda went up on the highway to flag a ride, Sister Margaret waited down here with me.

The nun hadn't uttered a single word since hearing me say I'd lost the Edessa. And now she approached from behind. I hoped she wasn't going to holler at me . . . but I also hoped she wouldn't lie and tell me everything was okay.

Sister Margaret did something worse: first a strong arm around my shoulder to turn me in her direction, then a nun's all-powerful and forgiving embrace.

43

EMILY'S WAKE

Lead sentence to one of the dozens of human interest stories published in the *Times-Picayune*'s special section called "Hurricane Emily": "The day after disaster swept through this sleepy area of bayous and swamp hamlets, two young citizens went out in a boat, recovered a precious thing, and came back home as heroes."

The hurricane was a short-lived boon to these heroes, Sebastian and Wilfred Millerd. A woman by the name of Nancy Clanton was the first to pay them for an activity they would've gladly done for free: five bucks to remove a snake she found curled obscenely in her underwear drawer. Mrs. Clanton placed two conditions on the Millerd boys: they couldn't kill the snake while it was still in the drawer or anywhere in her house, they had to take it outside, and second, they were to keep their filthy hands off her underwear. When it came to animals, Sebastian and Wilfred were fearless, so grabbing that big ol' rat snake and carrying it out to the backyard to stomp it to death was no problem, but Mrs. Clanton's second condition proved harder to meet. Wilfred did a lot of underwear touching and Sebastian—bolder, older, hornier—stole a pair of red knickers with Santas on them, kept way at the bottom of the drawer and presumably brought out just once a year, Sebastian figuring his theft wouldn't be detected for four months at least ... but he was wrong because Mrs. Clanton pulled an inventory right after they left.

Their animal removal business ended a few hours later when Sebastian was caught carrying a possum *into* someone's garage while Wilfred—younger, cuter, and a better liar—was at the front door negotiating how much Millerd Brothers would charge to *remove* the possum from that garage. When word of this scam and the underwear theft spread, the Millerd brothers took to the swamps in one of many boats Emily had orphaned.

Sebastian and Wilfred had heard there was treasure just waiting to be found in the bayous: paper money floating everywhere, men's wallets scattered like leaves, women's jewelry hanging from trees, folding knives, fishing gear. But after three hours of rowing, Sebastian and Wilfred hadn't found anything interesting beyond a few old T-shirts and six single shoes, five of which were lefts. They hadn't even come across any swimming animals to beat with their sticks and were planning to turn around and row home when they saw a peculiar sight in a clump of trees.

Although the flooding had mostly receded, the water here was still four or five feet up the trunks, and in the trees' crowns were three bodies, two of them wearing the remnants of fancy clothes.

The boys sat slump shouldered, slack jawed in their boat for the longest time, just looking . . . dead bodies fascinated them, they were always being chased out of funeral homes.

"Musta climbed up durn da hurrcane den got drownded in da flood," said Sebastian, who was listed on census forms as English speaking.

"Figger we shin up an' search 'em?" Wilfred asked.

"Might be a idear, pockets'll be full, betcha," Sebastian replied.

They sat awhile contemplating the upcoming thrill of searching dead bodies, then Wilfred asked, "You feel any wind?"

"Nary a trace."

" 'Cause that one body up there in the tree by itself, sittin' on that board, looks like the wind is a-causin' its arms to flap."

Both boys sat there watching, Sebastian finally urging his brother, "I say if a corpse starts a-lookin' like it's a-wavin' atcha, it's time to leave."

Wilfred agreed and rowed well for a boy his age, when both brothers froze on hearing a voice calling unmistakably from the tree where that arm-waving corpse was lodged: "*Wilfred Millerd,* where in God's name do you think you're going!"

He stopped rowing and asked his brother, "When a dead body calls to you, shud you answer?"

Wide eyed, holding to both gunwales, Sebastian was fully prepared to throw his younger brother overboard, because if dead bodies were calling Wilfred by name, who knew what came next, them bodies might start climbing down out of the trees and swim over to this boat. Sebastian saw something like that once in a movie he sneaked in on . . . then *his* name gets called out by the dead.

"*Sebastian* Millerd, I know that's you there with your brother, now row over here to this tree and pick me up . . . this instant!"

"Should we?" Wilfred asked.

"We dare not disobey a dead body," Sebastian replied. "Or else they'll come callin' of a night."

Searching for heroes in the wake of Emily, the news media would eventually settle on these two most unlikely candidates, who bravely rescued sixty-three-year-old Belle Foger (in the future, whenever she took people to show them where she'd been stranded during the hurricane, Belle would refer to the tree, which had saved her life, as Walter). Mrs. Foger, who suffered exposure and animal bites, would've died for sure if those brave lads hadn't come along. The Millerd brothers told reporters that's what they'd been doing since the hurricane passed, looking for old ladies to rescue.

Final paragraph in the *Times-Picayune* story extolling the Millerd brothers: "Who knows how this adventure will affect them? Can we hope for future heroics and good deeds from Sebastian and Wilfred Millerd?"

No.

Amanda took me home to her apartment, on the fifth floor of a Central Business District building unaffected by the hurricane, and there I went to bed, sleeping dead and dreamless for eighteen hours. When I finally got up, Amanda had bagels and cream cheese and coffee with chicory ready on the table even though it was past midnight, but I couldn't eat. She offered to give me a bath, I said I'd take a hot shower instead and then go back to bed. When I came out with a towel around my waist, Amanda was stripping the bed and asked me to wait a minute while she put on clean sheets.

"I got them filthy, didn't I . . . I was too tired to shower . . . I'm sorry."

"It's all right."

"No, it was thoughtless of me, I should've showered first . . . I'm sorry."

"Don't be silly."

"Sorry."

The next day, when she took me to see the nuns in the hospital, I kept apologizing to them too . . . I was sorry they got hurt, I was sorry I lost the Edessa. Only one sister had been admitted to the hospital, the others were there visiting her, the Filipino who'd been shot in the abdomen . . . and I was especially apologetic to her.

That night when Amanda and I sat in her apartment I said I felt like getting calling cards that carried my full name along with an apology so I could pass them out wherever I go. "I'd use the best card stock," I told her, "and the finest ink in the fanciest script. My name printed with different apologies. *I'm Sorry. Can You Ever Find It in Your Heart to Forgive Me? I'm So Very, Very Sorry. Please Accept My Apologies. Sorry.*"

Amanda brought me a glass of wine and said we should talk about something else.

"Anything but clowns."

She laughed. "Why do you hate them?"

"They're always playing with string."

"What?"

"And tend toward perversion."

"Oh Charlie."

I asked if she thought Pelikan would be there by the highway the morning after next . . . and Amanda said no, she didn't think he would. "You didn't see how he was shot, Charlie. Maybe if he'd gotten to a hospital right away, taken immediately into surgery, *maybe* he would've made it. But I don't think Knees was taking him to a hospital, do you?"

"No . . . but where, then?"

"I have no idea." Amanda asked if *I* thought he was still alive.

"No. In the back of that Hummer, he was saying good-bye, I'm sure of it."

"James Joseph thought the world of you."

"He had strange ways of showing it."

"He always told people he'd never end up old and feeble on the streets because he had a standing invitation to go live with his nephew."

"We never discussed that."

"More than once I heard it, James Joseph telling people that his nephew Charlie had promised him he'd always have a room waiting anytime he wanted it, a room over the garage. Or sometimes when Pelikan told this story, it was a little cabin on the back of your property. And when he came to live with you, James Joseph's only jobs were going to be working in the garden and keeping an eye on your kids."

"It's pathetic, isn't it?"

"Pathetic? I don't think so."

"James Joseph always had his plots and plans, none of them connected very tightly to reality. When I was here as a kid he would send me everywhere as an emissary, delivering messages, checking out plots and rumors. He wouldn't survive anywhere in the world except the French Quarter." I told her about Pelikan giving me an assignment to collect objects I thought a pygmy would find soothing and Amanda told me about late-night phone calls when Pelikan would talk to her even while she fell asleep to his voice. This is what we do when someone dies, remember them.

Amanda said, "You know who you should go see, Sad Bob . . . he's feeling sorry for himself because no one's been around to sympathize with him about being shot in the ear."

"He's a clown."

"You're not serious about hating clowns, are you?"

I told her I was. "And besides, he was *creased* on the ear . . . scratched . . . such a crybaby."

"Charlie."

"I know, I'm sorry."

The next morning I read the paper for news of the repository heist but found no mention of it. On TV there were strange tales, including one of an eight-foot bull alligator on Bourbon Street, harassed by news crews pointing cameras and National Guardsmen pointing rifles . . . it was later reported that the gator hadn't slithered to Bourbon Street on his own, but was transported there in the back of a pickup by country boys with too much time on their hands.

"No news about the repository," I said to Amanda when she joined me at the breakfast table. "What do you think's going to come of it?"

"We already talked about this."

"I know . . . sorry."

"No more apologizing, Charlie."

"I won't say I'm sorry for apologizing."

"Good." She poured coffee. "No one knows for sure, but I think the repository robbery will be an open case for a while and then just die from lack of interest. If the audit is honest, it'll show only one item of significance taken, the Edessa crown, which was being stored in the repository because two parties were claiming ownership. One party, the nuns from Limoges, obviously aren't going to demand that the robbery investigation be pursued. And as we both know, Gallier, the other party claiming ownership, was overwhelmed by James Joseph."

"Overwhelmed?"

Amanda smiled. "How would you put it?"

"I guess *overwhelmed* is about right."

After I left the Quarter the night of the robbery, Pelikan, even though he was seriously wounded, went to talk to Gallier. Amanda has had to tell me the story several times because I still have a hard time believing it: she and the others watching from the repository as the two men talked, then James Joseph suddenly embraced Gallier and they remained in each other's arms for what Amanda called an unusually long time. From then on, Gallier couldn't do enough, lending the Hummer and helping transport the wounded, nuns *he* had wounded, to the hospital.

"Meanwhile he gets away with murder," I said.

"Maria too," Amanda reminded me.

"But Gallier forced her to—"

"We don't want to open that can, do we, Charlie . . . especially since you were a witness and never told the police."

"I guess not."

"New Orleans is a gumbo," she told me. "Everything's all mixed up together, obligations and alliances, plots and counterplots."

"Yeah, I know, that's what people here keep telling me, like they're proud of it. But it gripes me that Gallier gets away with everything he's done . . . and all for nothing because I lost the Edessa. Do you think we could dredge for it?"

"The nuns won't allow that, too much chance it might be damaged."

"There's no other way to recover it. That area's too muddy to see anything . . . dredging would be the only—"

"It's not going to happen, Charlie. I've already discussed this with Sister Margaret."

"Then it will stay there with Renfrone's body rotting around it."

"Maybe Pelikan has a plan."

"You said you thought he was dead."

"You think he's dead, too, don't you?" she asked.

"Yes."

"But we're both going to be by that highway in the morning, aren't we?"

"Yes."

44

MAMA TURTLE AND OL' PAPA GATOR

A couple hours before dawn, I started gathering what was left of our gang. Amanda and I took her Ford Explorer to pick up three nuns at the Ursuline Convent. They were standing on the curb in the dark, dressed in crisp fresh habits, wearing their Buddy Holly glasses: Sister Margaret and the two Bulgarians, one of whom had a cast on her right arm, the other with her left arm in a sling. The Filipino nuns were still at the hospital, one of them as a patient and the other on prayer duty. I drove across town to pick up our final passenger, but he wasn't standing outside his apartment as promised, and after waiting fifteen minutes I asked Amanda to go up and see what's wrong. She returned to report that Sad Bob was crying his eyes out because he couldn't decide whether he should come as a clown or not ... if Pelikan was there waiting for us, Sad Bob wanted to be dressed as the kind of happy clown Pelikan loved, but if he didn't show up, if James Joseph had died, then Sad Bob didn't want to be dressed as a happy clown while the rest of us were crying and mourning. Amanda suggested I go up and talk with him ... I said my protective no-clown zone prevented me from entering Sad Bob's apartment. In the end, Sister Margaret went to fetch him, the clown dressed in white satin costume with big red dots, a matching dunce cap with fluffy red ball on top, huge floppy clown shoes. The sight of him annoyed me and I got further irritated when I realized he had a bandage around his head, a big pad over that scratched right ear, and was wearing one of those waist hoops that made his costume bulge out around the center . . . how in the hell was *that* going to fit in the car?

I ordered him to crawl in the back and stuff himself in there somehow, and he sobbed softly all the way to our destination.

When I pulled off the elevated highway to the little dock by the two-lane road, an ancient, rusted pickup was already waiting there. I parked behind it as the sun was clearing Lake Pontchartrain.

We sat a moment in the Explorer, all of us excited and anxious, not knowing if Pelikan was in that old truck, was alive or dead. I told the others to stay put while I checked it out.

As soon as I opened my door, the driver's door on the pickup also opened and out came a large, older man wearing dirty bib overalls with no shirt underneath. He stomped toward me like he was angry at something I'd done, and the closer he got the meaner he looked . . . in his late sixties but still straight, over six feet tall, big bellied and big armed, a full brambly beard, gray and black, and long hair equally tangled. On top of his unruly hair was perched a red baseball cap with black lettering: *Reliable Casket Company.* He wore work shoes, no socks, and when he opened his mouth I saw that his upper and lower teeth met infrequently.

"Where you from, boy!" he demanded.

"Who the hell are you?" I demanded back.

"Third time I ask the question, you're going to be answering it on your ass . . . now where you from?"

"Connecticut."

"Well, I don't know what they call dawn in Connecticut, but around here dawn is when the sun comes up."

"Yeah, that's what they call dawn in Connecticut too."

"Well, you were supposed to be here at dawn, now it's *past* dawn."

"I had to wait for a clown to get dressed."

His small blue eyes squinted to see if I was making fun of him. "I also ended up waiting for you after the hurricane and you never showed then either."

"Where's Pelikan?"

The man huffed and blew out a breath, then turned and walked toward his truck. When he saw I wasn't following he said, *"Well?"* So I went with him, and as we approached the truck, Knees O'Rourke got out the passenger side door and ran to hug me. I asked her the same thing, "Where's Pelikan?" She took my hand and led me to the back of the pickup . . . there on a bare mattress lay my uncle, dressed all in white . . . and his face in repose looked all the more like that outline on the shroud of Turin.

"James Joseph," I said quietly.

"Little potentate."

I did my best not to show any emotion in front of the fierce old man who now stood next to me.

Pelikan introduced us. "Charlie, this here is ol' Papa Gator. Papa Gator, this is my nephew."

We didn't shake hands.

"Well, Joey, let me tell you something about your nephew," Papa Gator said . . . he was the first person I ever heard call Pelikan *Joey.* "Your nephew's got dumb all over him."

When Pelikan smiled, his face seemed to hollow out . . . he looked small in the crisp white trousers and starched white shirt, both too large for him.

Had I brought the others? he asked.

They were watching from the Explorer but couldn't see Pelikan, so I turned and gave them thumbs-up, Amanda and the three nuns coming at a run. Sad Bob eventually came waddling over, too.

At the sight of nuns and then a clown, Papa Gator kept saying, *Jesus Christ.*

I stepped back to let the others swarm at the sides of the pickup and talk with Pelikan, hold his hand, touch his face, ask how he felt . . . Papa Gator meanwhile had gone around to the tailgate, looking at me with that ferocious expression of his.

"What?" I finally asked.

"Tailgate," he said as if it should've been obvious he wanted help lowering it.

Following his grunted directions, I helped him unload the truck's other contents: a strangely altered wheelbarrow full of blankets and pads . . . and a big plywood box, completely sealed, weighing two hundred pounds. Papa Gator took more than his share of the weight when we put the box on the ground.

Still without telling anyone what he was doing or if or how he needed help, the big man climbed into the truck bed and cradled Pelikan in his arms, moving him with surprising gentleness to the tailgate.

"Hey, dumb," he said to me and pointed with his chin at the wheelbarrow . . . then I realized what it was, a homemade wheelchair. The front had been removed and extensions added. Blankets and table pads lined the interior so that Pelikan could half sit, half recline.

I came over and accepted Pelikan from Papa Gator while Knees held the wheelbarrow-wheelchair steady, Pelikan surprisingly light in my arms as I lowered him to that nest of blankets and pads.

Once settled there, Pelikan started introducing Papa Gator to the others, but the old man got impatient and interrupted. "Joey, let's get this road on the show, we're burning daylight here." He turned to the rest of us. "Somebody move Joey down to the water."

The Bulgarian understood what was needed, the one with the good left arm picking up the wheelbarrow-wheelchair's right handle, the nun with the good right arm grabbing the other handle . . . and off they went, wheeling together like a matched pair of draft animals.

I was about to follow after them when Papa Gator said, "Come here, dumb." He wanted me to help him carry the box.

"What's in this?" I asked just before grabbing one of the rope handles and nearly putting my back out lifting the damn thing. "Feels like it's full of liquid."

Papa Gator didn't answer as we struggled—at least *I* struggled—to carry the box.

When we got there Sister Margaret was asking Pelikan a series of worried questions. "What's the plan . . . how're you going to be able to find it . . . you're not going to try dredging or dragging for it, are you?"

Pelikan said Papa Gator would explain everything.

Sad Bob came over to look at the box. "What's in it?" he asked, standing close enough for his waist hoop to bump into Papa Gator's belly, which nearly matched the hoop in circumference.

The old man put a sausage finger, dirty and broken nailed, in Sad Bob's vividly painted face and growled, "Back off, clown."

I was starting to like Ol' Papa Gator.

Sad Bob touched his bandaged ear and whined about being wounded in action.

"You don't back off, I'll rip your other ear right off that stupid clown head of yours."

"Your box stinks anyway," Sad Bob huffed as he hurried over to complain to Pelikan about how he was being treated.

The old man produced a big screwdriver from a back pocket and started prying off the plywood top.

"Papa Gator," Pelikan said softly. "Tell them how it's going to work."

"They'll see," he growled back.

"No . . . you tell them."

He threw a fierce look but it became clear, regardless of his huff, that like everyone else he would eventually do as Pelikan said.

"Okay then, listen up. I lived in swamps and bayous all my life, I'm half gator, half snapping turtle, and three-quarters bobcat, weaned by an ol' momma bear, meaner than a snake, and faster than lightning, I can outdrink, outfight, outsmoke, outlove, outrun, out-sleep, outeat—"

"Papa Gator, let's get on with it before the traffic starts."

The old fraud grinned at Pelikan and started over. "I live on what the swamp provides, ain't nothing I won't eat at least once. Years and years ago, I taught Joey there what's disgusting and what's not, didn't I, boy?"

"Yes, you did."

"Why, in my lifetime I've eaten so much swamp food that now my stomach rises and falls with the tide, I'm half muskrat and all grit." He looked over to see how this was going down with Pelikan before continuing. "One of my favorite of all meats is snapping turtle, tastes just like chicken." He looked around, then resumed his lecture. "Now the way you prepare a turtle before butchering is, first you put it in a barrel of fresh well water, keep changing the water until that ol' snapping turtle is flushed clean of all the swamp mud. Second thing

you do is starve the turtle until most of its fat is gone. How come?"
Papa Gator was looking at me.

"I have no idea."

He shook his head in disgust. "Fat is where an animal, any animal
including a man, stores all the poisons and toxins he's taken
in . . . which is why fat tastes so bad on a wild animal that's been living in the swamps. I like gator tail meat an awful lot, but if you happen to get a mouthful of gator *fat,* it's enough to gag a vulture. Do any
of you realize how much poison I got stored up right here?" he asked,
grabbing that massive gut beneath his overalls and shaking it with
both hands for our inspection and amusement and astonishment.
"Why, the toxins in this belly fat alone could poison half the people in
New Orleans, not that that would be a bad idea, I'm just saying the
whole entire reason I dare not lose any weight is, all the poisons in my
fat would be released, killing me deader than a rat in a trap."

Pelikan quietly urged him to show us what was in the box.

Papa Gator finished prying off the lid: the box was half full of water, the interior lined with heavy black plastic to make it watertight,
and at the bottom of the box, underwater, was a snapping turtle, a
foot and a half across the back of its shell and breathtakingly ugly.

"Now this here is an ol' momma turtle," Papa Gator told all of us
who'd gathered around to look in. "And she's ready to be butchered.
Not fed anything for a while, so her poisonous fat is about gone and
what's left will be easy to trim away. Underwater, she's gentle as a
spotted pup." To prove his point, the old man reached into the water
and tapped that monstrous head right on the nose . . . the turtle simply backed away from his touch. "But out of the water . . ." He
grabbed the stubby fat tail and, one-handed, swept the turtle out of
the box . . . as soon as the creature cleared the water it began hissing
and lunging for anything near its terrifying head.

We all gasped and stepped back. "It's the ugliest thing I ever saw
in my entire life," Sad Bob declared.

"Oh, I hold on to something a lot uglier and meaner," Papa Gator
said, "every time I take a leak."

When Knees laughed, her jaw muscles bunched up to make her
look like a squirrel with walnuts in its mouth.

Papa Gator lowered the monster back into the box and said, "Anybody tell me what ol' momma turtle's most favorite food in the world is?"

"Frogs?" Amanda guessed.

"Fish?" I offered.

"Fingers?" Sad Bob joked.

Sister Margaret said, "Carrion."

"You got it, Sister," Papa Gator told her, then he looked at me. "Figured it out yet, hotshot?"

"No."

He leaned over and brushed at my pants leg, telling me that I had so much dumb on me it was running down my leg.

I still didn't get it . . . then I did. "You're going to use the turtle to find Renfrone's body."

"Give the boy a Kewpie doll. We'll tie a rope harness around ol' mama turtle and let her lead the way, in fact I got to go back to the truck and get the rope right now. Hey genius," he said, referring to me. "You come with."

On our way to the truck I asked if he'd ever done this before.

"What do you think?" he snapped.

I didn't know . . . and didn't pursue it.

Papa Gator opened the passenger door and pulled the seat back forward, grabbing a Mason jar half full of a clear liquid I suspected wasn't water.

"Where's the rope?" I asked.

He patted his front left pocket.

"You came back for refueling, not for the rope."

"Another Kewpie doll . . . here, you have the first drink."

"No thanks."

"Why not?"

"It's barely past dawn, I'm not going to start drinking hooch."

"I *thought* I smelled pussy." He unscrewed the top and lifted the jar to his mouth, drinking slowly. When he lowered the jar again, his eyes were bright and wet.

"You hate clowns and talk mean to people," I told him. "I like that . . . a man after my own heart."

Raising the jar to his mouth again, he stopped to give me the evil eye. "A man after your own heart?" He resumed the jar's trip, took a slow slip, then grimaced and spoke in a strained voice. "Next thing you'll be suggesting, you and I should strip down and rub on Crisco so we can wrestle each other naked in front of the fireplace."

"It hadn't occurred to me," I assured him. "You drink a lot of that hooch?"

"Put it to you this way . . . all my male children were born with creases across their noses."

I watched him take another drink, the mouth of the jar leaving an angry red mark across the bridge of his nose.

"Sure you don't want a hit?" he offered.

I said I was sure . . . even the smell of it was turning my stomach.

"Let me ask you a question," he said. "You ever enjoy the services of that woman who brought Joey out to me?"

"Knees? No, I can't say that I have."

"Good."

"Why?"

"I don't like drinking with a man who's enjoyed the services of the woman I'm going to marry."

"You're going to marry Knees?"

"That gal sucks cock like Henry Ford made black automobiles . . . I'd be proud to call her number seven."

"*Wife* number seven?"

"*I'm* like one of them pony express riders, I keep needing fresh mounts 'cause I wear 'em out making deliveries."

"I see."

"Sure you don't want a drink?"

"No thanks—"

"Do you know why Joey made you wait three days before meeting him out here?"

"I suppose because during the past three days Renfrone's body has ripened considerably. If that turtle is hungry and if her favorite food is rotted meat, she should make a beeline for the body. Then you follow the rope you've tied to her, locate the body, bring it up, and give the Edessa back to the nuns."

"I think I'm going to start calling you Kewpie."

"If it works, are you going to let the turtle go?"

"Shit no, I've gone to a lot of trouble getting her ready to butcher . . . ol' momma turtle is this Sunday's dinner."

"But if she gets to the body and starts feeding—"

"I don't mind a little human flesh mixed in, tastes just like chicken."

"Give me a drink of that."

He was happy to . . . and although I took the tiniest of sips, it still felt like liquid fire being poured down my throat. When I was able to speak I told him, "I think you brought a jar of kerosene by mistake."

He took it and smelled. "You might be right. Let's not drink any more."

Back at the swamp's edge, where everyone was waiting, Papa Gator reached into the plywood box and fashioned a rope harness to the turtle's shell . . . she didn't seem to mind his touch as long as she stayed underwater, but when he wrapped the rope several turns around his thick wrist and lifted that creature into the air, she was once again transformed into a hissing, lunging, snapping she-devil.

Papa Gator carried momma turtle to the edge of the swamp. He stopped and asked me where Renfrone went under. I pointed and explained how far I thought it was, but admitted I was largely guessing and estimating.

"It's all right," he said, gentle with me now that we both had creases across our noses. "Ol' momma turtle will find him." He put her to the ground and she fled scampering into the shallow water while proud-bellied ol' Papa Gator stood there playing out line.

45

WHO'S SORRY NOW?

A fading handwritten sign behind the bar claims that Mother's never closed during hurricane Emily, no matter how hard the wind blew or high the water rose. I suspect that's not true, but as the months went on and increasing numbers of people bragged that they'd spent the hurricane drinking in Mother's, the sign eventually passed for true.

Tonight there's a private party here, you can't get in unless the man on the door knows you. He's a big guy with a beard and prison teardrops tattooed at the corner of his left eye, tonight he's dressed as Dr. Frank N. Furter, the Tim Curry character in *Rocky Horror Picture Show* . . . tight black vest, pearl necklace, garter belt, boa, the whole works. If you're a tourist he says, "Private party," then won't look you in the eye, but if he knows you, he'll flirt and say, "Come on in the lab . . . and see what's on the slab."

We're in the back celebrating the one-year anniversary of Emily, some of us also celebrating an event we can never discuss in public, the repository hurricane heist. As always, James Joseph is holding court . . . surrounded by clowns and mimes, hookers and lawyers, street bums and one nephew who has moved his business from Connecticut to New Orleans and now has an eclectic shop on Royal Street, you could stop in and see me next time you're in town.

Except for James Joseph and me, most of those gathered here are getting drunk.

Amanda is drinking peach schnapps and looking happy.

Knees O'Rourke, tipsy on champagne, is showing off her engagement ring . . . when Papa Gator gave it to Knees a year ago he told her he believed in very long engagements.

Sad Bob, sipping a beer, is equally proud of his "real" Purple Heart, which James Joseph bought at an army surplus store and pinned on the clown when the bandage was taken off his ear a week after the heist . . . and if you can see a scar, your eyes are better than mine.

Harmony, the merkin mogul, is doing tequila shooters and winking at me.

Zane, the pirate, has a mug of rum and a nervous left eye, his right one covered by a patch at which the pirate keeps picking.

That old guy who lives on the street and hangs out at Jackson Square, the man I thought looked like God with gold yellow hair and matching beard, is drinking bourbon with beer back and hasn't wet his pants, though the night is young.

Maria and Wendy are holding hands.

Gallier's not here, of course . . . it's not his kind of crowd. But Pelikan visits him, commiserates about the various lawsuits against Gallier's uncle's estate, and occasionally they go out to eat at the one of the Quarter's finer restaurants, where Pelikan picks up the tab.

Tonight's standard for intoxication has been established by Papa Gator, now lashed (maybe with the same rope he used on that ol' momma snapping turtle) to the jukebox in an effort to keep him upright and also prevent him from grabbing women. His intended, Knees O'Rourke, tied him there, the rest of us cheering her on.

As a result of his gunshot wound, James Joseph underwent a series of operations, never fully recovered even now, a year later . . . though you wouldn't know it by the happy way he looks tonight. In fact, tonight he reminds me a little of how profoundly buoyant he was when Papa Gator pulled the Edessa out of that swamp and returned it to the nuns. They're long gone, back to their convent in Limoges. The Filipino who'd been shot in the abdomen eventually recovered . . . good as new, Sister Margaret wrote to Pelikan.

Sometimes I tease James Joseph about botching the repository heist, getting away with not a single dollar in loot . . . no money for him, nothing to send Knees to Apple Tree Cottage in Ireland or Sad Bob to France, where he might finally be appreciated. James Joseph blames it all on Tiddlywink and Tickledpink, claiming they prayed too hard . . . all he wanted was a thunderstorm but they prayed him up a hurricane.

Papa Gator is now struggling against the rope and screaming for me, "Kewpie, Kewpie, please release me, set me free!" I take that as my signal to go and remind James Joseph that I have to open the shop early in the morning . . . a private showing to some well-heeled collectors from England.

We spent this past Christmas together and I told him that as soon as I was established here in New Orleans and could afford to buy a house, he's welcome to come live with me, there will be a room inside or over the garage, whichever he prefers. Hearing this, James Joseph nodded as if he wasn't surprised by my offer, as if I was simply repeating a proposal I'd made frequently over the years. He could still be maddening, the way he never acts surprised by anything.

When people see that I'm leaving they come around to say good-bye, it's like this every night I'm at Mother's . . . takes half an hour to get out of the place. I hug everyone, shake all the hands that're offered, and kiss all the cheeks, except I won't go near Papa Gator when he's in this condition and I still refuse on principle to embrace a clown.

But Sad Bob, bless his weepy heart, gives me a signal that I should turn around and look . . . something happening by the entrance and he indicates I won't want to miss it.

I turn and see that the encounter I'd been waiting for—and tried to engineer—is about to take place.

Fat Elvis is just entering a door that Fifties Elvis is trying to depart through, they can no longer avoid each other . . . and now I'll find out what they have to say for themselves. Will Fat Elvis be devastated at this reminder of who he was twenty years and two hundred pounds ago, of how he lost such innocence, insouciance, and art? Will Fifties Elvis be terrified at this look into his future, does he possess the insight to question what he's doing wrong *now* that leads to what he will become? And which one will apologize first? Can they both use the exact same apology: *I'm sorry what I did to you, man.*

Standing close by, I hold my breath as they stare at each other. Neither speaks until after the encounter, when one Elvis says of the other, "Who the hell was that?"

ABOUT THE AUTHOR

David Lozell Martin grew up on a farm, worked in steel mills, served in the military, wrote for magazines, and has had nine novels published, ranging from the classic love story *The Crying Heart Tattoo*, to the international best-selling thriller *Lie to Me*. Martin lived in the French Quarter while writing *Pelikan* and now lives in upstate New York with his wife, Arabel.